FALLING IN LOVE WITH A ROGUISH CAPTAIN . . .

Rob lifted her chin and kissed her gently on the lips. "You're a warm woman, Norah. A warm woman indeed." He smiled when he spoke, but his eyes burned to their very depths.

At his words, reality seeped back into Norah's mind with appalling clarity. How could common sense have deserted her so completely?

"You mustn't think . . ." Norah said, scrambling to think of some way to reclaim her dignity. "You mustn't think me . . ."

Rob's smile turned shrewd and knowing. "What I think is that you'd better leave before someone comes upon us and spreads the news all over the ship. Or before I'm tempted to make some more serious advances."

She backed away from him, wishing she could justify her behavior. But how could she justify to Rob what she couldn't explain to herself?

Turning, Norah hurried down the passageway to the main cabin.

Rob leaned against the pantry doorframe and watched her go. Well, well, he thought, Miss Norah Paige's calm waters certainly hid some turbulent seas. . . .

SEA OF DREAMS

ELIZABETH DE LANCEY

DIAMOND BOOKS, NEW YORK

SEA OF DREAMS

A Diamond Book / published by arrangement with
the author

PRINTING HISTORY
Diamond edition / April 1992

ISBN: 1-55773-681-2

Diamond Books are published by The Berkley Publishing Group,
200 Madison Avenue, New York, New York 10016.
The name "DIAMOND" and its logo are trademarks
belonging to Charter Communications, Inc.

PRINTED IN THE UNITED STATES OF AMERICA

10 9 8 7 6 5 4 3 2 1

For Jimmy
with love and thanks

Prologue

THE AROMA OF cinnamon, apples, and sweet dough filled the kitchen, mingling with the fragrance of fresh-baked bread. From his perch on a tall stool, Rob Mackenzie hungrily eyed the tarts and loaves cooling on the sideboard. The one thing he'd miss about his stay in Boston would be Annie Paige's victuals. Salt beef and ship biscuit were sorry substitutes for fish chowder, sausage pie, and hot apple tarts. Even a plate of duff soaked in molasses couldn't match the tasty dishes Annie made up in her kitchen.

The old yellow tomcat prowled toward the sideboard, sniffing the air. Rob nudged the cat with his boot. Tom sprang away, retreating to the hearthrug where he flicked his tail in annoyance.

"Be still, Robert. You're squirming," Annie said, laying a gentle hand on the boy's shoulder. "I don't want to clip your ear."

Rob's face went hot. He gave Annie's bright red curls a sideways glance and mumbled, "Yes'm."

The shears resumed their snapping, and more black hair fell into Rob's lap.

"My goodness, this hair of yours has a mind of its own," Annie said. "It stands right up wherever it pleases."

She laughed and touched his cheek. Rob cringed, but Annie didn't seem to notice; she went right on talking. "I'll have

Jody bring in the tub so you can have a good scrub before bed. And I want you to eat two helpings at dinner. You're too spindly by half."

Rob's face burned hotter. "Yes'm."

In his twelve years of life, Rob couldn't recall a woman once touching him, let alone fussing over him as Annie did. His mother, dead since before he could remember, was nothing but a disturbing emotion. And the factory women he'd known had been too careworn to bother with an orphan boy.

But Annie was relentless. Because of her, Rob was fatter and cleaner than when he'd arrived three weeks ago. And because of her, he now possessed two fine red-checked shirts. Even so, Rob couldn't wait for tomorrow when he and Jody would return to the *Rosa Sanchez* and their rigorous, manly life at sea. He'd had enough of this woman and her well-ordered house, and enough of the good manners that took up his time and taxed his patience. Most of all, he longed to escape Annie's behavior toward her husband. She bossed Jody around as if she owned him.

"There." Annie stepped back and took Rob's chin in her fingers, admiring him with bright blue eyes. "If you mind your language and stop gobbling your food, you'll pass for a proper young man."

A shout of laughter came from the doorway. "A proper young man! Why, bless me, Annie. To a seaman, being proper's not worth a bone button. I thought you knew that."

Jody's brawny frame seemed to fill the kitchen. His sleeves were pushed up to his elbows, revealing muscular forearms, wild with tattoos. In his ear he wore a small gold anchor, which he tugged whenever he needed to think.

Annie glanced at her husband and pursed her lips with displeasure. "It doesn't hurt the boy to learn a few manners. And he needn't hide a handsome face behind all that hair."

"That may be," Jody replied with a wink to Rob. "But I'd hate to see so fine a mongrel pup as Rob Mackenzie turned into a fancy Boston lad."

Rob grinned back at the man he revered above all others. With his nut-brown hair and smiling good looks, Jody made a splendid appearance. But it was his seaman's skill that filled Rob with fervent admiration. Every seafaring man from Bombay to Baltimore would have agreed that Jody Paige was the best deep-sea sailor to be found on an American ship.

"A mongrel pup!" Annie thrust her fists into her shapely waist and glared at Jody. "What a thing to say about one of God's own children."

Jody ambled over to his wife and gave her curls an affectionate toss. "I believe you're taken with that boy, Annie. Wouldn't surprise me one bit if you'll be wanting to adopt him."

"I'd adopt the both of you," Annie said tartly, "if you'd stay home long enough to get acquainted."

"Would you, now?" Jody looked at her in a teasing way that made Rob uneasy.

Annie's creamy skin turned pink with vexation, and her pretty eyes started to flash. "You made me a promise, Jody. But I suppose you intend to forget it."

Rob looked expectantly at Jody. Jody said if a man gave his word about something, he was bound to keep it. That was but one of many lessons Rob had learned during the past several weeks.

Annie turned to the sideboard and began banging the cooking tins. "You said when we had a baby, you'd stay home for good. Well, we now have a baby and I aim to hold you to your promise."

The blood froze in Rob's veins. Stay home for good? Jody? A sudden burst of panic nearly toppled him from the stool.

"Well?" Annie asked in her bossy tone.

Jody's grin faded. He started twisting the silver ring he wore on his middle finger. It was bent and worn from pulling at ropes. Without glancing up, he said quietly, "I think Annie and me had best be alone, lad."

Rob needed no further prodding. He jumped off the stool and dashed from the kitchen, trailing wisps of shorn hair across Annie's immaculate floor.

He paced the front room, bright with sunshine and wax. With a thumping heart, he listened to the murmur of voices from the kitchen. It didn't seem possible that a man like Jody would give up his life for a woman and a baby. But that's what he'd promised Annie, so that's what he meant to do.

Rob slumped into the worn wooden rocker and pushed off

with his toes. As the rocker creaked on the bare floor, he tried to remember his own mother, to capture the feeling of belonging to someone. As usual, memory eluded him. When he thought of his past, he recalled the factory and the brutal fourteen-hour shifts among cogs and spindles that roared a lad nearly to deafness. When he thought of home, he pictured a bleak, stinking room and his uncle dragging him from sleep to beat him with his merciless switch.

Rob wriggled his bony hips deeper into the chair. He hadn't come this far to be taken over by some woman, even if she was Jody's wife. He'd fled the factory to go to sea, and that's where he aimed to stay.

Rob thought back to the night he'd departed Manchester, hidden in a coal wagon. It had been a miserable ride that left him choking and covered with soot. He'd tumbled onto the flagged streets of Liverpool, clutching vague dreams of noble ships and the clean, endless ocean. Instead, he'd found hunger and fear and swarms of beggars. For days he survived on dirty, discarded hunks of bread and orange peels he found floating in the water. At night he laid himself out on a slab in a grave-yard and imagined being dead.

Then one bright crisp day Jody plucked him from a pack of beggars at the dock wall. The captain, Jody said, was looking for a ship's boy. Within the hour, Rob found himself aboard the *Rosa Sanchez*, bound for America.

At sea the work was hard and often dull, but there were spells of excitement, even danger. As for Jody, Rob did every-thing he could to please his new friend. He rushed to be first into the rigging. He strove to be the most daring on the bow-sprit while untangling the jib in a gale. When Jody found him worthy, Rob felt proud; when Jody disapproved, Rob redou-bled his efforts. By the time he sprang ashore in Boston, he'd decided to pattern himself after Jody, from the way he handled a serving mallet to his assortment of tattoos. He'd decided the seaman's lot was glorious for a man—vast, free, and compan-ionable. He would never give it up.

A distracting sound came from the basket that rested in a patch of sun on Annie's gleaming floor. Rob got out of the rocking chair and crouched beside the basket. He stared at the tiny creature that lay sleeping under the blanket. A little white cap covered her head. She had fat pink cheeks, silky, gold-tipped lashes, and a mouth shaped like a rosebud.

Rob poked a finger at one of the soft cheeks. "Your pa's got no business staying home with you. Hear that, baby?"

The baby's lashes moved. Big blue-gray eyes like Jody's stared up at Rob. Then she screwed up her tiny face and started kicking her feet beneath the blanket. She opened her toothless mouth and gurgled happily.

Rob shook his head in disgust. A baby! Of all things to hold a man, a baby made even less sense than a woman.

Rob tiptoed into the front hall and cocked his ear toward the kitchen. Not a sound could be heard. He knew what happened when Jody and Annie got quiet. It was downright embarrassing how they took to each other. Rob grabbed his cap and slipped out the front door.

He passed the rest of the day tramping the crooked streets of Boston. That night, instead of returning to Jody's house, he boarded the *Rosa Sanchez* and slept in the forecastle.

When he climbed out on deck the next morning, the crew was straggling up the gangway, looking sour after a final night of carousing. Rob hung over the rail, his throat tight with dread. He watched each man come aboard. Then he spotted Jody. His sailor's togs were freshly laundered, his earring was polished, and on his shoulders he bore a barrel of New England apples. Rob's anxiety was buried under a thunderous elation.

He followed Jody down into the forecastle.

"Annie missed saying good-bye," Jody said.

Rob wiped his nose with the back of his hand, relieved to discard his manners. "I ain't going back there," he said.

Jody chuckled. "Women aren't so bad, Rob. One day you'll discover they're mighty sweet."

Rob shrugged. It didn't matter anymore what Jody might think about women or about babies, either. He was back on the *Rosa* and they were putting out for Rio de Janeiro. Once again Rob had Jody all to himself.

Chapter One

BOSTON, MAY 1836

ON FINE SPRING afternoons Boston's fashionable citizens mounted their carriages and headed down Washington Street to the South Boston Bridge. After alighting at Dover Street, ladies and gentlemen took up their parasols and walking sticks and passed an hour or so strolling the bridge's wide wooden planks, exchanging discreet glances and appraising the latest efforts of Boston dressmakers to match the styles of Paris.

For Norah Paige, who cared little for Paris fashions and even less for exchanges with gentlemen, the primary attraction of the promenade was the view. Norah never tired of admiring her city, from the busy wharves that fringed the shore to the rosy brick houses of Beacon Hill, to the trim colonial steeples that thrust themselves into the sky. With an unassuming appearance and sound New England character much like her own, Boston was more than Norah's home; it was part of her very soul.

So it was with a vague disquiet that she surveyed the familiar sun-brightened landscape on a pleasant and breezy afternoon in May. In three weeks' time she would leave Boston for a voyage to London. Already Norah missed the tree-shaded elegance of Beacon Street and Washington Street's bustle of commerce. And she wondered how she would manage six months without breathing fresh New England sea air, without so much as a glimpse of the splendid State House dome.

Norah tried to scold away her apprehension. Any person in her right mind, she told herself, would jump at the chance to visit England. Certainly Boston wouldn't sink into the bay during her absence, nor would she lose her good sense and decide to marry a duke. When she returned home at Christmastime, Boston would be no different, save for the season, than it was right now. And she would be equally unchanged. The placid life she'd enjoyed would resume as if there had been no interruption at all.

A sudden gust of wind tugged at Norah's bright-bordered shawl, distracting her from her thoughts. She gathered the soft cashmere close about her and noticed gentlemen on the promenade clutching their tall hats. A lady's parasol cartwheeled off amid shrieks of dismay. Norah watched as the parasol flew over the railing and landed top down in the water. She looked down at the fragile craft of green silk sailing off on the current.

"The wind just launched a parasol, Alice," Norah said to the young woman at her side. "I daresay it won't survive the voyage to China. Oh, my, there it goes, swamped and sinking."

Alice Burnham made an impatient sound. "Norah, you haven't heard a word I've said! Sinking parasols indeed! We were talking about Rob Mackenzie."

Norah cast a mirthful glance over her shoulder at her companion's plump cheeks, glowing with annoyance. Alice's raven curls, peeking out from beneath her sturdy straw bonnet, stirred prettily in the breeze.

"You're the one talking about Captain Mackenzie," Norah said, feeling a twinge of guilt for ignoring Alice's chatter. "I have absolutely nothing to say on the subject. I'll be pleasant and civil this evening, but don't expect anything more." Norah returned her attention to the parasol, struggling gamely to stay afloat. The water shimmered like quicksilver in the breeze.

"But you said you fancied him!" Alice persisted. "Don't deny you said it. Even Mama heard you."

Norah grimaced. What had possessed her to disclose the secret childish infatuation she'd once entertained? Before all three Burnhams she'd commented that she used to think herself in love with Rob Mackenzie. Norah had meant the remark to be a joke, but instead of laughing, Mrs. Burnham and Alice had greeted her words as a confession. For days they had spoken of little else than the absolute perfection of a match between their Norah and Mr. Burnham's prize captain.

Norah's vehement protests had gone unheeded.

"My dear child, you're twenty years old," Mrs. Burnham had reminded her, "and you have to marry someone. Captain Mackenzie would be a marvelous challenge. Why, he's completely undomesticated—quite wild, really—yet so clever and attractive. And you, darling! You're the perfect girl to turn him into a proper Boston merchant. You've grown up into such a stable, sensible, beautiful young lady. He'll simply adore you."

Norah doubted that. Admittedly she was not the pudgy eyesore she'd been at fourteen, but she was no sugar-and-cream beauty. Her features were more handsome than pretty, and her figure fell far short of the demure ideal. Sighing, swooning females were in vogue at the moment, not tall, strong-limbed, healthy women who spoke their minds and were disinclined to lower their eyes and blush.

Norah followed the route of the parasol as it headed into Boston on the incoming tide. It was probably a blessing that she and Alice were soon to sail for England. Before the situation with Rob Mackenzie became too embarrassing, she would be gone and the Burnhams could have their captain all to themselves.

"Norah, listen to me," Alice said, moving so close that her bonnet brim bumped Norah's Tuscan straw. "This very afternoon Papa is offering Rob a partnership in the firm. If he accepts, he'll have to settle down and take a wife."

Norah made a sound of disgust. "Well, I wish him good luck." Settle down, she thought, studying the tall masts of brigs and schooners and fully rigged ships that crowded Boston's shoreline. What seaman ever settled down?

"What is that supposed to mean?" Alice demanded.

"It means there are plenty of girls in Boston for Captain Mackenzie to marry," Norah replied firmly. "And they're welcome to him. I want nothing to do with a sailor."

Alice cried out in exasperation. "Have you no womanly

feelings? If you did, you'd not speak so foolishly! Rob is handsome and rich and ever so kind. He only lacks breeding and refinement and familiarity with the ways of Boston. Any other girl would die to take on such a man."

"Alice, spare me," Norah pleaded with a sigh. Refinement! she thought. Womanly feelings! She would quite happily forsake her womanly feelings and remain a maiden lady to her dying day rather than attempt to domesticate a seaman. Rob Mackenzie's veins, like those of her own beloved papa, ran with salt water. At the first freshening breeze, he would pack his sea chest and sail away, leaving behind aching hearts and broken promises. If she ever married, Norah thought, the man who won her heart would have both feet planted firmly on dry ground.

Nevertheless, an image of Rob Mackenzie slipped through Norah's wall of stony indifference, an image of a tall man with tousled black hair, a splendid masculine figure, and the burned look of the outdoors. He'd been young when she'd last seen him, twenty-six to be exact, and Mr. Burnham's most trusted man in the Indies. As intriguing as his swaggering good looks had been his drawing room awkwardness. It turned out that the man who wrestled four-hundred-ton ships around the Cape of Good Hope and managed single-handedly the firm's Calcutta trade could barely hold a teacup properly. And his clothing was appallingly out of fashion. To Norah, however, his social deficiencies had mattered not at all. Captain Mackenzie told wonderful stories, laughed readily, and during the evening had inadvertently let slip a stunning "goddamn."

Perhaps he'd changed in six years, Norah thought. Perhaps by the age of thirty-two he'd acquired the polish that Mrs. Burnham said could only be bestowed by the girl he married. But that lack of polish had been part of his charm, she decided, remembering his reckless, unsettled way. A queer little shiver ran down Norah's spine, and she quickly focused her attention on the State House dome. She'd been a romantic child at fourteen. Now she was grown up and level-headed. And she had quite serious responsibilities.

Norah glanced at dark-eyed Alice standing patiently at her side. In her bright yellow gown and matching bonnet ribbons, Alice looked as pretty as a black-eyed daisy. If pressed, Norah would have had to admit that Alice was almost self-sufficient these days. Like a hardy wildflower, she could no doubt survive in the most unfavorable conditions. But to flourish, Alice needed a loving and undemanding caretaker. And that caretaker, regardless of what the Burnhams or Alice might say, was Norah herself. Alice had needed her for the past eight years and would continue to need her for the rest of her life.

Norah thought back to the day Mrs. Burnham had first brought her to live in the Summer Street mansion. Both she and Alice had been twelve years old. Norah could still recall her apprehension as she stepped into the cool elegance of the drawing room, so extravagant compared to her own mama's small, plain home. Alice had sat on the sofa, silent and sad, her shoulders drooping. When she lifted her head at the sound of her mother's voice, her dark eyes looked vague. For a moment Norah had thought her slow-witted. But Mrs. Burnham had said gently, "You mustn't be afraid, Norah. Alice is a girl no different from you, except that she is blind."

Norah slipped her arm through Alice's. There would be no wedding for her, she thought with calm satisfaction, while she continued to serve as Alice Burnham's companion.

"Let's go home," Norah said. "I have a new guidebook to Tewkesbury that you'll find interesting. Your papa says we'll be stopping there overnight on the way from Liverpool to London."

Alice looked suddenly pensive. "Norah, I have something to tell you, and I don't want you to be upset."

Norah smiled. "Have you been up to some mischief?"

Alice shook her head. "Oh, no, not me."

Norah watched her friend indulgently until she heard her say, "Last night Papa decided that Rob should command the ship taking us to England."

Norah's hand closed over Alice's arm, gripping hard. "But . . . but he wouldn't do that," she said, her voice soft with shock. "Why would a man like him . . . Why would he . . . ?" Her voice faltered, but her mind raced on, tumbling over reasons why such an arrangement made no sense. Rob Mackenzie spent his time outrunning pirates in the Indies' perilous straits. He commanded opium ships and organized cargoes from Calcutta. Carrying two young ladies safely across the Atlantic would seem silly and boring to him and utterly beneath his abilities. Why, he'd hate the assignment and absolutely refuse.

"Papa said only his finest captain should escort his girls across the sea," Alice continued. "Of course Mama agreed."

Something in Alice's face slowed Norah's thoughts, and with a clap of logic, she realized that her distress had nothing to do with Captain Mackenzie's preferences. Norah's burning cheeks and unsteady heart were a consequence of her own suddenly precarious position as a pawn in Mrs. Burnham's bold matrimonial scheme.

"This is part of your mother's plan," Norah said sternly. "Her plan to make a match between Captain Mackenzie and me."

Alice's mouth curved into a guilty but approving smile. "Perhaps," she admitted. "Mama says in the three weeks it takes to get to Liverpool, he and you will undoubtedly come to an understanding."

Norah would hear no more. She took Alice's elbow and set a brisk pace down the wooden planks of the promenade toward Washington Street and home. Mrs. Burnham's meddling would bring nothing but humiliation to her and to Captain Mackenzie. Somehow she had to put a stop to it. The only clear way to head off disaster would be through blunt honesty. Norah well knew that plain speaking was not an acceptable way for ladies to deal with gentlemen, but she had no other choice. She would confront Captain Mackenzie directly, explain Mrs. Burnham's ridiculous plan in the baldest possible terms, and tell him he must not pay it the least bit of attention.

By the time she and Alice turned into the gravel drive of the Summer Street mansion, Norah was formulating her strategy.

Rob tugged at the waistcoat that bound his broad chest and scowled at the feverish activity on India Street. The smells of land and humanity assaulted his nostrils; the scrape of iron-bound wheels on cobblestones offended his ears. Beneath his feet, the ground seemed to tremble from the rumbling carts and drays. Even the gulls, swooping and screaming amid the wharf's forest of masts, sounded impatient, not content as they did at sea.

Four months out of Canton, fresh off his brig, and headed for his first formal social engagement in years, Rob wished heartily for the tranquillity of the *Orion*'s deck. He hadn't set foot on American soil in six years, and he'd never felt partial to Boston.

Rob reached up to give his beard a reassuring tug and encountered instead clean-shaven cheeks. He swore softly. For the sake of polite society, he now had a face that was two distinct shades of brown. He'd grown accustomed to the beard, just as he'd grown accustomed to the feel of well-scrubbed deck boards beneath his bare feet and the sun beating down on his naked chest. In his going-ashore rig of tailcoat, waistcoat, and cravat, he felt trussed up like a Christmas goose.

Rob eyed the merchants and petty clerks who pushed past him, their pale, earnest faces furrowed in thought, their black broadcloth suits uniformly somber. So, Rob thought, Oliver Burnham expected him to become one of them, juggling numbers, shuffling papers, gossiping on the Exchange. Good God, the man must be going senile.

"Thirty thousand dollars, Captain," Burnham had said only a few hours earlier. He'd closed the door to his private room and motioned Rob to a large leather-covered armchair. "Thirty thousand for twenty percent of Burnham and Bradshaw. I think you'll agree that is a most generous offer."

For a moment Rob had thought his ears were failing him. "Are you offering me a partnership?"

Burnham smiled and pulled at his side-whiskers. "I presume you haven't done badly for yourself during your twelve years in my employ, Captain. I doubt thirty thousand would put a strain on your resources."

Rob ran a hand over his freshly shaved chin and tried to gather his wits. There was no denying he'd made a small fortune, both in the India trade and while commanding an opium receiving ship at Lintin Island near Canton. But he'd expected no more from his employer than a wage and the opportunity to invest in his voyages on his own account.

"I have the suspicion," Burnham said, settling his portly frame into his chair, "that you're thinking of going off on your own."

Rob glanced at the teakwood writing table on which lay a

sheaf of plans for a new Burnham ship and thought of the sweet-lined little clipper he'd considered buying in Canton, a ship that could outrun any pirate sail on the China coast. In six months he could have made another ten thousand running opium up to Nanking. But during negotiations for the twenty heavy guns he needed to arm the vessel, he'd changed his mind and decided to stick with Burnham for a while longer.

Rob twirled his cap on his knee. "I have no plans."

"Good!" Burnham exclaimed. "With the West prospering and new banks being chartered, the import business has never been better. Sails spread for fine weather, Captain. The firm could use a man of your talent."

Rob could more easily conceive of himself as a Bengali nawab than as a businessman growing soft in some dim India Wharf countinghouse, but he took care to express his sentiments politely. "I'm honored, sir, but I doubt the life of a sedentary merchant would suit me."

"I don't need a man in Boston, Captain. It's a traveling partner I have in mind, someone to study the European market and give discretionary orders to my agents. Milan, St. Petersburg, Paris. The British Isles, of course. You'd be tied down in Boston no more than a few months a year. I know you favor your independence, and I don't aim to hinder you."

Rob stirred uncomfortably. Burnham wasn't going to let him off easily. "I don't know a damned thing about the European markets, sir. I'm an East India man."

Burnham waved off Rob's protest. "At one time you knew nothing about the Calcutta trade, but in a season or two you were disposing of surplus India goods in the West Indies and Africa. A brilliant plan. I must say I enjoyed your correspondence during those years. Every one of your schemes turned a profit."

"I've been out of that trade for six years," Rob pointed out.

"You have a nose for business," Burnham said, an edge of impatience in his voice. "I don't want to lose you."

Rob held his ground. "What about your son, sir? Surely the partnership should go to him."

Burnham pressed the tips of his fingers together and sighed wearily. "Ollie has not improved in your absence, I'm sorry to say. He's larking about London at this moment, wasting his time and my money."

Rob stifled a smile, even as he felt pity for the older man. Some years ago Burnham had suggested his son interrupt his gaming and petticoat-chasing to ship out to Calcutta as Rob's supercargo. It was time, Burnham had said, for his heir to learn the firm's business. Ollie, however, had developed a sudden urge to acquire knowledge and had entered Harvard College. Now he appeared to have found his calling—perfecting a life of idleness.

"I'm losing my partner, Amos Bradshaw," Burnham continued somberly. "He turned seventy and moved to Brookline to cultivate roses. He has no children, not even a decent nephew. But even if he had an heir, or if Ollie somehow decided to apply himself, there's not a man I know who's better suited to this position than you are."

Rob's expression became thoughtful. He would pretend to consider Burnham's offer, but the idea that he could succeed as a partner in one of Boston's most prestigious importing firms was absurd. His home for the past six years had been a receiving ship crammed with opium, sacks of silver, and a crew of cutthroats. He'd worn a fighting iron on his wrist and slept with a pistol beneath his pillow. Figuring in his time sailing the Boston-London-Calcutta route, he'd probably spent a scant six months ashore in ten years. He'd lived so long in the company of rough men and strange cultures, it would take him weeks to regain even the few social graces he'd once possessed.

Still, it would be rude to refuse Burnham out of hand; Rob stalled. "I appreciate your confidence, sir. I'll give your offer every consideration."

Burnham nodded, apparently satisfied with Rob's response. "We're one of the soundest firms on the East Coast but we need new blood. Who knows, Captain? One day you might take over the whole operation."

When he left Burnham's office, Rob had agreed to no more than an invitation to dinner that evening at Burnham's Summer Street mansion.

He made a last swift appraisal of the traffic on India Street.

Drawing in a chest-tightening lungful of sea air, he squared his leather-billed cap, and stepped off the curb.

"Watch where yer goin', y'bloody sod!"

Rob jumped back from an overloaded dray that bore down on him, its driver bawling like a master-at-arms.

"Weigh off, lubber!" Rob raised his fist in a rude salute. "I'll see you on my foredeck and teach you some manners."

The dray rumbled by, drowning the rest of Rob's shouted comments in its wake.

"Goddamn insolence," Rob muttered to himself as he sprinted in three long strides to the safety of the shady sidewalk. Then he remembered that he would be in the company of ladies this evening. He'd better start minding his language.

At Bull's Wharf, Rob turned onto Summer Street. As his legs carried him deeper into the fashionable South End neighborhood, the noise of the waterfront faded into silence and the fragrance of the sea was replaced by the sweet scent of ripening gardens. Rob glanced at the stately homes of brick and granite and tried to put himself in a more agreeable frame of mind.

A young woman tripped by, her parasol tilted fetchingly over one shoulder. Rob lifted his cap and commented on the fine evening. The lady gave him a quick appraisal, her eyes lingering on his two-colored face, and hoisted her nose in the air. Rob turned to watch her skirts sway as she hurried on her way. It didn't say much for Boston womanhood, he thought with a shake of his head, when a fine, strapping fellow like himself, in the prime of life and worth near seventy thousand dollars, couldn't bring a smile to the lips of a local maiden.

Rob turned back to find himself before Burnham's gate. The handsome four-story mansion of red brick glowed in the early evening sunlight. Long-sashed windows framed by green slat shutters opened onto wrought-iron balconies. Beyond the wide courtyard stood the stables, sheds, and fruit rooms. Vast flower gardens extended well beyond Rob's view.

Rob gave his waistcoat a nervous tug. Burnham had said dinner would be *en famille*, which Rob took to mean that Burnham's wife, Julia, and daughter, Alice, would be present.

Alice was Burnham's treasure. She'd been a lively little thing before fever had left her blind. Rob had been afraid Alice would fade into misery after her illness. But when he'd last seen her, she was still a sparkling child. He remembered that she had a companion, a pretty dumpling of a girl with a round face and freckles.

Rob's boots crunched on the gravel drive. He heard a dog bark from inside the house. That would be Chance, the pup he'd given Alice when the doctors told her she'd never see again. Good Lord, Rob thought, the dog must be ten years old.

He mounted the wide stone step to the walnut door beneath the fanlight. Before he could lift the knocker, the door swung open and a butler with wispy gray hair and the bent look of age stood before him, beaming.

"Captain Mackenzie. Welcome back to Boston."

Startled by the sudden greeting, Rob mumbled, "Why, thank you, er . . ."

"Hoskins, sir."

"Ah, yes, Hoskins."

Rob stepped into the cool entry hall. The sweet scent of cut flowers filled the air. The carpet of subdued blues and browns felt soft beneath his feet. A carved teakwood hatstand stood like a sentry against the wall. It was a home—stable, permanent, and utterly foreign to Rob's experience.

He listened to the steady tick of the tall case clock and tried to recall when he'd last entered a real house. It was probably six years ago, when he'd last stood in this very spot. If he accepted Burnham's offer, this would be his future. A house, a wife, children. He would wear black broadcloth and meet with other merchants on the Exchange. On Sundays he'd hear Dr. Channing at the Federal Street Church and drive out with his horse and carriage. One of Boston's pampered belles would tame him into a likeness of her father and brothers and never understand that his first love would always be the sea and his freedom. Even three months of such a year would be unbearable.

Hoskins cleared his throat. Rob started from his thoughts and handed the butler his cap.

"This way, Captain." Hoskins offered one of his barely perceptible bows.

Rob followed the butler's curved back up the staircase. Sunlight poured through the window at the landing, illuminating woodwork that had been polished with beeswax to a dark, gleaming finish. In the upstairs hall Rob heard voices and laughter coming from the drawing room. Sweat prickled on his neck. Drawing rooms made him nervous. Too damned much silk and crystal and gossip.

Rob glanced at his hands. Preparing himself for this occasion had taken a good part of the afternoon. He had scrubbed himself raw, but he still couldn't get the tar out from under his fingernails. Willie, his Kanaka steward, had shined his buttons and boots, brushed his trousers and coat, and trimmed his hair. Rob had fought with his neckcloth for a good half hour, consigning it to hell and a few other places before he got it right. He hadn't worn a silk noose in years.

Hoskins preceded Rob through the drawing room doorway. "Captain Mackenzie, madam."

White walls and golden drapes bathed in evening sunlight dazzled Rob's eyes. He heard Julia Burnham's exclamations of welcome and her husband's rumbling voice as he struggled to his feet. Shimmering silks of plum and rose and vivid blue rustled toward him; bare shoulders gleamed. He smelled fragrant soap.

Rob bowed in the general direction of the commotion and hoped he wouldn't make a fool of himself.

Chapter Two

WHEN CAPTAIN MACKENZIE stepped into the drawing room, Norah's well-disciplined heart took a dismaying tumble. It was apparent that time had done nothing to diminish his appeal. If anything, his sun-browned features and striking masculine presence were more commanding than ever. His appearance was shabby, to be sure. Terribly shabby. Coarse black hair straggled untidily about his collar, and his blue wool coat, snug across his broad shoulders, appeared well chewed by moths. From the look of his carelessly tied neckcloth, she guessed that he'd spent little time dressing for the occasion. He probably hadn't been properly attired in months. Perhaps he'd barely been attired at all. That thought brought on an alarming sensation somewhere in Norah's midsection.

"Rob!" Alice cried.

The Burnhams were on their feet, rushing to greet their guest. Norah, blushing with sudden and unaccustomed shyness, reluctantly joined them.

Fortunately she didn't have to speak, for everyone else seemed to be talking at once, Mr. Burnham's voice booming out above the others. Then Norah heard Rob say, "Who is this? Alice?"

Alice laughed and moved toward him. She veered a few degrees off course and Rob reached out to guide her over by the shoulders. "Tell me what's become of my old friend Alice,"

Rob demanded, his voice deep with humor. "I expected to see a little girl."

"Little!" Alice exclaimed, waving her hands over her gown of rose silk. "I shall never be little again. See how plump I've become."

Mrs. Burnham, a trim, firm-featured woman, gave Rob a wry smile. "Pay Alice no attention, Captain. As usual she says exactly what comes to mind at the moment." Mrs. Burnham reached and pulled Norah firmly into the familial cluster. "Surely you remember our lovely and much more sensible Norah."

Rob gave Norah an appraising smile that sent a fresh wave of heat rushing all over her face. She avoided his curious eyes and focused instead on his wind-roughened cheeks, which appeared, rather oddly, to be two shades of brown neatly separated at the beard line.

"Norah," he said, as if to fix her name in his mind. "I see you have grown up as well."

Norah concentrated her gaze on his left cheekbone. "Beards . . . I mean, girls grow up all the time, Captain Mackenzie," she said and flushed hotter still at her slip of the tongue.

Rob's smile broadened. "So they do. Girls grow up into beautiful ladies. Beards, on the other hand . . ." He rubbed his chin with a rueful grin. "Beards are shaved off for the sake of fashionable society."

The Burnhams laughed, and Norah managed a faint smile. "It must have been a fine beard," she said.

An expression of lively interest came into Rob's eyes. "I'll begin another one immediately, if it would please you."

It suddenly dawned on Norah that he thought she was flirting. "Oh, no," she said hastily. "You mustn't undertake anything on my account."

"I can think of no better reason to undertake anything."

It was he who was flirting, Norah realized frantically, and he was looking her over most thoroughly. She was suddenly and intensely aware that her shoulders and a daring bit of bosom were utterly bare. Rob Mackenzie was taking in every exposed inch of her. Feeling herself flush from brow to toes, Norah glanced at Mrs. Burnham, begging to be rescued, but

Mrs. Burnham was too busy smirking at her husband to notice.

One agonizing moment passed before Mr. Burnham grasped Rob's shoulder. "The girls have grown into a fine pair, wouldn't you say? Twenty years old, both of them. Hard to believe how time flies. Do you think you could bear up under their company for a few months?"

Rob looked puzzled. "I beg your pardon?"

"I have in mind an arrangement that I hope will meet with your approval," Mr. Burnham said, as he showed Rob to his chair. "Mrs. Burnham's aunt, Lady Denmore, has invited my wife and the girls to be her guests in London for several months. They planned to sail on the Liverpool packet in a few weeks. As you know, Captain, the Atlantic is most agreeable this time of year."

Norah sat down beside Alice on the plush-covered settee by the fireplace and tried to pull herself together. The worst was over, she thought, clasping her icy fingers in her lap. A tiny bit of flirtation was harmless enough. Now she had to focus on discouraging Captain Mackenzie from entertaining any thoughts of partnerships or marriage. If she could accomplish that feat, the evening would be a success.

"Unfortunately," Mr. Burnham went on, "Mrs. Burnham's father is ailing and she must remain in Boston. I won't permit the girls to travel on the packet alone. But rather than disappoint them by canceling the trip, I thought we might get up a cargo for Liverpool and you could take them aboard the *Orion* as passengers."

Norah watched hopefully as Rob's expression changed from puzzlement to surprise. He ran a hand through his rumpled hair. "Take them on the *Orion*?" He cast Norah a quick glance. She arranged her face in a discouraging frown, but Rob seemed not to understand her glower. In fact, she actually saw the beginnings of a smile.

"I trust two ladies in the cabin would be no trouble, Captain," Mr. Burnham said.

"Why . . ." Rob paused and laughed. "No trouble at all, I'm sure."

"Perhaps you could sail at the end of the month," Mr. Burnham suggested.

With a shrug of his broad shoulders, Rob said, "There's nothing to hold me here."

Mrs. Burnham and Alice burst into exclamations of relief that the London holiday was not lost. Rob settled his large frame deeper into his chair and watched Norah with a faint, searching smile, no doubt wondering why she wasn't joining in the happy clamor.

For her part, Norah was counting up the weeks. If the weather held, there would be only three weeks aboard ship to Liverpool and another few days to London. It would be really quite manageable.

"Mighty good of you to take on the burden, Captain," Mr. Burnham said. "The girls would have been sorely disappointed to miss this holiday."

Conversation lapsed as Hoskins passed the sherry. Then Mrs. Burnham spoke. "My husband tells us you'll soon be joining the firm, Captain. We're ever so pleased."

Norah's heart quickened. Rob would surely decline this offer. He had to realize that he could never recast himself as a Boston merchant, with or without the help of a wife.

Rob looked taken aback at Mrs. Burnham's comment. "Actually, I—"

"Why, it will be like having you as one of the family," Mrs. Burnham interrupted. She smiled at him over the rim of her wineglass, and Norah saw Rob's face tense, as if he were suddenly on guard. Norah took a long, throat-searing gulp of sherry. If he didn't speak to the subject, she certainly would. She would speak up and remind him of the sort of man he was.

"I haven't yet come to a decision," Rob said. To Norah's ears, the hesitation in his voice did not sound sufficiently final.

"But surely you'll agree to the offer," Alice said, looking anxious.

Mr. Burnham chuckled. "Rob is entitled to take his time over so major a decision, my dear. But I've warned him I will not easily take no for an answer."

Rob stared at his sherry glass as if collecting his thoughts. He looked so vital and handsome that Norah momentarily forgot what she was about to say. Finally, good sense took over and she found herself speaking. "Surely, Captain, a man accustomed to your way of life would find it difficult to give up the sea."

Rob lifted his gaze to her. He twirled his wineglass by its slender stem and studied her soberly, as if considering her words. "Perhaps you're right," he said. "But then again, men leave the sea every day."

Norah grasped the arm of the sofa and leaned forward. "Some men leave the sea and never get over it," she said earnestly. "Either they pine away for the rest of their days or they stay ashore for a time and then simply abandon their responsibilities and go back to their beloved ships. They leave behind wives and children, broken hearts, broken promises . . ." Norah stopped, aware that she was speaking much too personally. "Once a seaman, always a seaman, Captain Mackenzie," she concluded firmly. "Quite frankly, I don't think you'd be at all satisfied with the sedentary life."

An awkward hush fell over the company. Norah couldn't be sure of Rob's reaction, since he'd ducked his head, but he appeared to be smiling.

Mrs. Burnham rustled her plum-colored silk. "Why, Norah, Captain Mackenzie is to be a partner with Burnham and Bradshaw. It's virtually settled."

Rob looked up again, fixing Norah with an expectant gaze. He appeared to be awaiting her next observation, which she hastily supplied.

"A partnership would keep you in Boston for months at a time, in a . . . a stuffy countinghouse on a noisy wharf. Why, you've traveled the world. Surely you're not prepared to sacrifice your command and your freedom for the prosaic life of a merchant."

Her remarks were followed by another silence. Alice drew in her breath and gave Norah a sharp jab in the ribs. Mr. Burnham looked dumbfounded. Norah chose not to view Mrs. Burnham's reaction, which she knew would be disapproving. Instead she focused on Rob and tried not to think of the dismaying consequences should he accept Mr. Burnham's offer and decide to settle in Boston.

Rob regarded her with a faint smile on his lips and a mirthful light in his eyes. "Thank you, Norah," he said. "I'm obliged that you're so concerned for my happiness."

Before anyone else had a chance to speak, Hoskins entered the room and announced dinner. Norah felt a wave of relief. It was finished. Rob would take her words to heart; surely he would forgo the partnership. No one could appreciate more than he the truth of what she said. After their brief sojourn in London, he could once again sail to the ends of the earth, happily uncivilized. Why, she would probably not have to mention Mrs. Burnham's matchmaking plan at all. She was silly to think he'd ever have gone along with it.

Mrs. Burnham rose from the sofa and began organizing the march to the dining room. "Now, Captain," she said, "if you'll kindly escort Norah, Mr. Burnham will see to his wife and daughter." She beamed at her husband and drew Alice to her side. To Norah, she directed a look that said, My dear, whatever in the world you are doing simply won't work. Then, before Rob could make his way across the gold and white Aubusson carpet, Mr. Burnham swept his wife and Alice through the doorway.

Startled, Norah stared after them. They had left her utterly alone with their guest—a gentleman guest at that. It was highly inappropriate, but obviously nothing was out of the question in Mrs. Burnham's scheme. Norah turned to Rob, wondering what to say next. He stood stock-still in his sizable boots of worn leather, his arms folded across his impressively broad chest, staring at her in what seemed to be baffled amusement.

"How do you know so much about a seaman's nature?"

His question caught Norah off guard. She hadn't expected to discuss herself. But of course, the intensity of her comments about seamen abandoning their wives and children had left her open for questions.

"I . . . Well, you see . . ." she began. But she didn't want to tell him about her papa's broken promises or discuss her conclusion that seamen were unreliable when it came to settling down. So she addressed the issue that seemed most obvious. "I don't believe, Captain Mackenzie, that you're the sort of man to fit in with the ways of Boston."

"Indeed," Rob said with a skeptical lift of his brows. "And why not? Is my attire so out of fashion, or is my hair not cut in the proper style?"

"Oh, no!" Norah cried. Heavens, she hadn't meant to insult him or even to allow that she'd noticed the dreadful state of his clothing. "I mean nothing of the sort. I was speaking of your temperament and experience, not your appearance."

"My dear Norah," he said, leaning a bit closer, "I don't particularly care for people making judgments about my temperament and experience or, for that matter, telling me where I do or do not fit in. Most especially when they cannot possibly know about either."

Norah cringed. She couldn't tell if Rob was annoyed or simply teasing her. But she was so mortified at even the possibility of giving offense that she felt compelled to tell him the truth. She gathered her courage and plunged ahead.

"You must forgive me, Captain Mackenzie," she said. "I'm behaving very badly. I truly believe you would not be content as a merchant in this city, but I never would have presumed to express myself on the subject were it not for something that might embarrass us both." Norah lowered her voice. "I should say nothing on the matter, but in light of the circumstances, I must explain. You see, the Burnhams want to make a match of us."

Rob drew back in surprise. "A match?"

Norah nodded gravely. "Should you accept the partnership, you would, they feel, need a wife. Mrs. Burnham and Alice are taken with the idea of our suitability. In fact, I suspect Mrs. Burnham contrived for Alice and me to travel on your ship for the purpose of furthering our acquaintance."

A smile spread across Rob's face, a smile he quickly checked. "And since you don't favor the match, you thought my refusal of the partnership would spare you the ordeal of marrying me."

Norah adopted a tone of gracious apology. "I enjoy my life as it is, Captain. You are most likely equally satisfied with your own. Are you not?" She looked directly into his dark, pensive eyes.

"Oh, of course," Rob said solemnly. "Of course I am."

"I'm glad we understand each other," Norah said, relieved that he had taken her confession in stride. "I daresay if you choose to marry, you will have your pick of Boston's eligible young ladies. You have wonderful prospects."

"I'm afraid I have few prospects at the moment," Rob said, looking amused. "And no plans to marry. No plans at all."

He held her gaze and smiled. Norah looked back at him, feeling a heightened awareness of something that left her oddly breathless.

Suddenly Mrs. Burnham bustled into the room. "Gracious sakes! You're supposed to be escorting Norah to dinner, Captain Mackenzie, not entertaining her alone in the drawing room. What's a person to think?" She rapped Rob lightly on the arm with her fan. "But never mind. No harm done." She glanced up at him with a cunning smile. "I can't blame you. Our Norah is a delightful girl."

Rob gave Norah a conspiratorial glance and a wink. "Quite so, Mrs. Burnham," he said. "A delightful girl indeed."

For dinner Mrs. Burnham served mulligatawny soup, roast lamb, new potatoes, and baby peas. Rob took care to eat slowly and with some semblance of grace, while listening to the discussion of Alice's teaching duties at the Boston Institution for the Blind. With imprudent frequency, his attention wandered across the dining table's polished silver and china to Norah, who chattered brightly and tried now and again to include him in the conversation.

Rob didn't quite know what to make of this lovely, guileless girl who claimed to have no interest in him. She wasn't his sort of woman, that was certain, serious and virginal as she was, and loaded down with New England propriety. Yet her earnest manner and admiring gaze amused him. And her handwringing confession about Mrs. Burnham's match had stirred him in a way he couldn't quite fathom.

Rob speared a steaming potato and glanced at Norah again. She was unlike the common run of sheltered girls with their simpering vanity and plaster perfection. Her cheeks were a healthy pink, and her thick, straight brows gave her a look of staunch resolve. She was as pretty as a peach, he thought, especially when he'd teased her. Rob smiled to himself. He'd enjoyed trimming her sails; he would like to do it some more. His eyes lingered on Norah's bare shoulders, the rosy softness above her bodice. Taut and tidy, every inch of her. He'd had no experience with well-bred young ladies; he'd never wanted any. But Norah was damned appealing. And she liked him well enough. It showed in her eyes, clear as a moonbeam.

"Perhaps you could arrange for Captain Mackenzie to spend a few weeks in London, Oliver," Mrs. Burnham said, interrupting Rob's thoughts. "I know the girls would be delighted if he looked in on them at Berkeley Square."

Rob glanced down the table at Mr. Burnham. "A splendid idea!" Mr. Burnham said as he sawed at a slab of roast. "I'll send along a letter to Sprague, our London agent. Wouldn't hurt for you to look in on the English operations while you're there, Captain."

"Oh, Rob, will you?" Alice asked. "Will you really visit us in London?"

Rob's gaze drifted back to Norah. Her light brown hair had a golden cast to it that made it seem laced with sunshine. "I'm at your command, ladies."

"Then I command you to call on us every day," Alice said. "Norah and I will study our guidebook and decide what sights you will take us to visit. Won't we, Norah?"

Rob gave Norah a questioning look. "You'll visit the sights?"

"Alice's blindness never keeps her from enjoying excursions," Norah explained. "But you needn't trouble yourself on our account. Alice's brother, Ollie, will see to our entertainment, and Lady Denmore has a grandson who I'm sure won't object to squiring us about."

"Oh, don't pay her a scrap of attention," Alice said. "I think Norah would be content to remain here with Miss Peabody and never see an inch of the world outside Boston."

"Alice, that's not true," Norah protested. But she knew if the trip was canceled, she wouldn't be unduly disappointed. She enjoyed her predictable life, her steady routines, and she'd never felt a great urge to travel.

"And who is Miss Peabody?" Rob asked.

"Miss Lydia Peabody is the proprietress of a ladies' bookshop at number twelve Bromfield Street," Mrs. Burnham said. "Norah assists in the shop in the afternoon."

"You're employed?" Rob asked Norah in astonishment.

"Not for a wage," Mrs. Burnham said quickly. "We

wouldn't allow such a thing. It's just a little activity to keep her occupied."

"Sitting about in the company of book-reading old spinsters does Norah no harm," Mr. Burnham said, giving Norah an affectionate glance.

Norah sighed. "They're not old spinsters, Mr. B." She had long ago given up trying to convince the Burnhams that her duties at the bookshop involved anything more taxing than reading and gossiping. But it was probably best they didn't know the extent to which Miss Peabody depended on her to operate the business.

To Rob, Norah explained, "Miss Peabody's clientele is made up of ladies with an interest in literature and current affairs. She sponsors lectures on the second Wednesday of each month."

Rob gave her one of his disconcerting smiles. "I've been known to turn a page or two myself. Perhaps you'd care to visit a few of the London booksellers."

"I really don't know what our schedule will be," Norah began doubtfully.

"Then it's decided. We'll have an outing."

"Yes," Alice said emphatically. "Just the two of you."

Norah flushed. The Burnhams were being much too obvious about their matchmaking efforts. Thank heavens she'd mentioned the situation to Rob and cleared up any possible misunderstanding. "I'm afraid, Captain," she said, "you'll find I'm rather dull company."

A mischievous light kindled in Rob's eyes. "You seem lively enough to me."

The family fell into an amused and knowing silence. Norah ducked her head and felt a little stab of distress. Despite their understanding, Rob apparently intended to continue his flirtation. Norah supposed it was to be expected, since women no doubt spoiled him terribly. Surely he collected hearts like pearls on a string. As for her own, she would keep it carefully guarded, reminding herself every day that Rob Mackenzie was a seaman. He might be master of his world, but that world was a woman's most bitter rival. She intended to have no part of it.

* * *

The dishes had been cleared, the brandy poured, and the ladies had retired to the drawing room. Oliver Burnham leaned back in his chair and loosened the bottom button of his waistcoat. "This talk of panic is a lot of damned nonsense, if you ask me," he said. "Prices are high, credit is favorable, and demand continues to expand. There's no end to prosperity in sight. You've seen the activity on the waterfront, Captain. Does it look to you as if hard times are coming?"

Rob moved his snifter of brandy about on the white linen tablecloth, leaving a pattern of circular indentations. "Can't say that it does, but then, I've been out of touch."

"Stop by the Exchange tomorrow and hear what's being said. When you get to London, I want you to make your decisions based on the facts as they are, not on rumors started up by a bunch of doomsayers."

Burnham had talked Rob into spending the summer and early fall in England filling the firm's orders for the spring season. Rob didn't object to this assignment. He'd see a bit of the country and look up a few old acquaintances who'd retired from the Indies. He might enjoy keeping his feet dry for a spell.

"Cornelius Sprague is our man in London," Burnham said, folding his hands over his well-rounded belly. "He'll bring you up to date on the state of the European markets. Jonathan Wildes at Baring Brothers is the man to see for credit, and Simon Williams in Liverpool has a specialized knowledge of trade in the United States."

Rob nodded, feeling a mild disquiet. He was accustomed to making up his own mind about things; in Europe, it seemed, he'd be taking everyone else's advice.

"The final decisions, I gather, would be up to me."

"By all means, Captain," Burnham said. "I wouldn't entrust this responsibility to you if I didn't have faith in your judgment and ability."

Burnham reached for a cigar and fired it up, his bushy gray eyebrows working like pistons. Once smoke was flowing, he glanced at Rob. "D'you think you could manage another voyage out east, Captain?"

"Calcutta?" Rob asked in surprise. "I thought the firm was finished with the India trade."

"We were. Haven't had a man or a ship out there since you took over the Canton opium station. But if you should stumble across a cargo of Turkish opium in London and the market's right, you could turn a tidy profit in Batavia or Canton. Bring back a cargo of East India goods, and whatever I don't dispose of at auction, I'll send down to the West Indies."

Rob grinned. Burnham knew that after a few months of civilization, his captain would start to yearn for the Indies. "If I stumble across a cargo of Turkish, I just might do that," he said.

"No more business tonight, Captain; there are more interesting things to discuss. I don't mean to interfere, but you seem quite taken with our Norah."

Rob laughed. "Are you trying to marry me off?"

Burnham looked mildly embarrassed. "She's a splendid girl, Captain."

"I can see that."

"Got a fine mind, too, but once it's set, it ain't always easy to change."

"I can see that, too."

"Think she's pretty, Captain?"

Rob thought of Norah's blue-gray eyes, thickly fringed with gold, her straight sensible nose, lightly dusted with freckles. "I think she's beautiful."

Burnham slapped his knee. "Damn it, Rob, that pleases me. You and she would suit each other fine."

Rob stretched out his legs and folded his hands behind his head. The evening light had faded from the sky. Candles burned brightly in the chandelier, sending flickering shadows across the ceiling. "I'm not in the market for a wife," he said, "but tell me about her anyway."

Burnham sucked loudly on his cigar. "Her people are from Salem. Seafaring folks. Her mother operated a small boardinghouse for seamen, but she wasn't well and couldn't keep it up. She brought Norah to Boston when the girl was about ten. Did seamstress work. The mother died in an accident, a dreadful business—run down on Broad Street by a wagon loaded with bricks. Norah was attending Mrs. Burnham's charity sewing school at the time. The girl was twelve years old, a serious little thing, mature beyond her years." Burnham puffed thoughtfully. "Norah has worked miracles with Alice. Sometimes even I forget Alice is blind, just as I forget Norah isn't my own daughter."

"You adopted her, then."

Burnham shook his head. "No, she preferred not. Her name's Paige. Norah Paige."

He stared at Burnham. "Paige?"

"Hmm," Burnham said puffing again.

"Spelled with an *i*?"

"That's right, with an *i*."

Rob lifted his glass and took a long swallow of brandy. "Is that a common name around these parts?"

Burnham shrugged. "Common enough. Why do you ask?"

"No reason." Suddenly Rob's head was pounding. "What of her father?"

"Dead. An undependable sort, it seems. Couldn't get hold of him when the mother died. Later we heard he'd been lost at sea. Norah took it all damned hard. To this day she doesn't speak of her parents."

"Did he . . . Does the family have any connection with Boston?"

Burnham removed the cigar from his mouth and studied Rob. "None I know of. As I say, they're Salem folks. Is there a problem, Captain?"

"No," Rob said quickly. "No problem at all." He picked up an unlit cigar and held it tight in his fist. He thought of her hair, those eyes. It was too farfetched to consider.

"I'm prepared to settle a few thousand on her."

"I've got no interest in marriage, Burnham," Rob said absently. To himself, he thought, There's no point in dragging up the past. Rob had put Jody's family out of his mind years ago. He wondered if they had any idea what had happened to him.

"Suit yourself," Burnham said cheerfully. "But I won't be surprised if you change your mind about the partnership and the bride as well."

Burnham was offering her like a bonus, Rob thought, an incentive to sweeten the deal. He recalled Norah's blushing smile, the shining approval in her eyes. For three weeks they would be together on the *Orion*. Three weeks at sea, with her shy glances, her pretty figure, and no chaperon save Alice. Rob felt a stirring of masculine impatience.

Burnham cleared his throat. "Captain, I needn't remind you that Norah has been brought up a lady. I assume I can count on your honor as a gentleman during these next few months."

Rob felt his face go hot with embarrassment. "Of course," he replied smoothly. Good God, he thought, had he sunk so low as to consider seducing his employer's ward, a girl entrusted to his care? Rob gave himself a hard mental kick. He'd been too long at sea with no one for company but a crew of rough men and an ocean full of fishes. A spell in civilized London would do him good. If he put his mind to it, he might even retrieve those few shreds of moral character he once possessed.

Chapter Three

NORAH BENT OVER the worn cherrywood counter of Miss Lydia Peabody's Ladies' Bookshop, hard at work on her new system of cataloging. She dipped her pen and wrote on a card, "Cicero. *Selected Orations*," followed by "1237." She set the card aside and took up another. "*Selected Orations*. Cicero, 1237," she wrote. Then she enfolded the volume in brown paper and carefully wrote the number on the spine.

Miss Peabody's old method of keeping track of her stock had been haphazard, to say the least. She entered a new book in the ledger sometimes by author, sometimes by title, never by both. To call her numbering system erratic, Norah thought, was being charitable. A fifty-five-volume set of Goethe might be assigned only one number, while Schlegel's four volumes of Shakespeare bore a separate number for each volume.

Under Norah's new system, each book received its own number and two little cards, one for the author's name and the other for the title. Norah thought the card file was convenient and flexible, since the cards could be kept in alphabetical order.

"Rousseau, J. J. *Confessions*, 1238," she wrote.

The little bell over the door rang, announcing the arrival of a customer. Norah didn't look up. When she heard footsteps proceed to the parlor across the hall, she decided the customer had come to socialize. Dr. Everett's lecture on Greek antiquities had just concluded, and several ladies lingered, sipping tea with Miss Peabody.

Norah dipped her pen to prepare Rousseau's title card. Suddenly she heard a familiar masculine voice ask for her. Norah straightened up and listened. No, it couldn't be, she thought. Not here!

She felt a flutter of excitement as she slipped off her stool and removed the spectacles she needed for close work. It had been nearly two weeks since the dinner party at the Burnhams'. During that time Norah had seen neither hide nor hair of Rob. It was a relief that he had not come around pestering her, but at the same time she'd lain awake at night wondering if he'd found her lacking.

Norah adjusted the shoulders of the fichu of white embroidered muslin she wore over her red plaid wool, smoothed a few wayward strands of hair behind her ears, and rushed for the door. Before she was halfway across the room, she heard Miss Peabody in her most scolding voice informing the visitor that indeed he might *not* speak to Miss Paige.

Norah ran across the entryway into the parlor. Miss Peabody, tall and stout, wisps of gray hair flying, was drawn up to her indignant best. Facing her, looking decidedly wary, stood Rob Mackenzie.

For a moment, Norah didn't recognize him. His black broadcloth suit fit his tall, muscular frame to perfection. His neckcloth was snowy white and tied masterfully, and his hair was cropped to his ears. Norah stared in astonishment. Why, he looked thoroughly respectable.

Rob glanced at Norah. "I came to speak to you."

"My dear sir," Miss Peabody interrupted in her most imperious voice, "I do not tolerate gentlemen entering these premises to accost my ladies. Mr. Burnham would be quite distressed should Miss Paige be subjected to the attentions of whoever of the male sex might choose to walk in off the street and engage her in conversation."

"Miss Peabody," Norah said, dismayed at the scene.

"Let me assure you, madam," Rob said with admirable politeness, "that I have Mr. Burnham's fullest confidence. I mean to speak to Miss Paige in a civil manner. I have no plans to imperil her in any way."

At the tea table, Miss Peabody's ladies rustled with interest. Norah heard a discreet cough, a less discreet giggle, and much rattling of chinaware. She glanced at the ladies, mortified to be the cause of a scene.

"Captain Mackenzie is an associate of Mr. Burnham, Miss Peabody," Norah said. "I'm sure the purpose of his visit is to purchase a book." She glanced meaningfully at Rob. "Isn't that so, Captain?"

"A book," Rob repeated, glancing first at the ladies and then at Norah. She saw a smile lurking about his mouth. "Ah, yes, a book."

Miss Peabody's small blue eyes narrowed as she surveyed Rob from head to foot. No doubt such a large and handsome man had never before crossed her path, let alone the threshold of her establishment.

"Very well," Miss Peabody said, continuing to wither Rob with her glare. "But please inform the captain that this shop is for ladies only. Ask him in the future kindly to call on one of the Washington Street booksellers who cater to gentlemen."

"I'll tell him," Norah said. "Come along, Captain."

She hurried back across the hallway into the book room. Rob followed her, his boots pounding the floorboards that normally whispered with the gentle brush of slippers.

"I believe you said your interest was travel in the Indies," Norah said in a voice loud enough for Miss Peabody to hear. Her heart was beating fast. She didn't know if her agitation resulted from the confrontation with Miss Peabody or from Rob himself, who seemed much taller and broader in the shoulders than he had two weeks ago.

"Did I say that?" Rob asked, bemusement in his voice.

Norah stepped behind the counter to consult her card file. She put on her spectacles and took a deep, calming breath. Her hands were freezing, while the rest of her had broken out in a most unladylike sweat. "We have just received Mr. Hall's account, which you'll find most informative." She closed the file. With a glance that ordered Rob to follow, she hastened to the east corner shelf and number 1225, Hall's *Voyage to Java, China and Loo Choo*.

"Actually," Rob said, "I'm looking for Parker's *New Semaphoric Signal Book*."

Norah opened Mr. Hall's account to an engraving. "This is a ladies' shop," she said, adopting her crisp, official bookshop tone of voice. She refused to fall into the casual banter that Rob apparently favored. "For a book on semaphores, you must inquire at Hilliard and Gray or down at Central Wharf." Norah glanced up and caught the teasing look in Rob's dark eyes. An annoying blush crept over her cheeks as she realized what he was up to. "You're joking," she said reprovingly.

Rob rested a black-clad arm against the bookshelf over Norah's head. "Does Miss Peabody allow such a thing in her shop?" He smiled down at her, a slow, searching smile that extended deep into his eyes. He looked so attractive and engaging that Norah couldn't help but smile back. And as she did, she thought there was something different about him, something . . . "Why, look at your chin," she said. "It finally matches the rest of your face."

Rob rubbed it thoughtfully. "And I promised you a beard."

"Oh, no," Norah protested without thinking. "I like you much better this way."

Rob's smile broadened. "Are you quite certain?"

Oh, dear, Norah thought. Here she was, falling into unacceptable familiarity. She took a step backward, away from the close proximity of his arm. "You mustn't tease me," she said, trying to sound stern. "Miss Peabody will think you're flirting."

The mischievous expression left Rob's face, and he scowled. "I don't give a damn what Miss Peabody thinks. I walked in here, polite as a parson, and she jumped all over me."

"Hush!" Norah said in a loud whisper. "If she hears you swearing, she'll have Constable Reed here in no time."

Rob pushed himself away from the shelf and shook his head in exasperation. "All right, Miss Norah. Wrap up that book before I change my mind."

Norah hurried behind the counter, relieved to turn once again to business. She wrote up the receipt and recorded the transaction in the ledger. Rob handed her two dollars.

"Those spectacles make you look distinguished," he said.

Norah returned his change and busied herself wrapping the book. "I might say the same about your new suit of clothes."

"It's kind of you to notice. You must have thought me rather ragged the other night."

Norah snipped off a length of string. When she tried to tie the package, she found she was all thumbs. She wished Rob would stop staring at her. "Not ragged exactly," she said, "but not exactly à la mode."

Rob laughed. "I've never been à la mode in my life."

Norah stopped her tying and pressed the back of her hand to her mouth, pretending to cough. Rob seemed to have a knack for making her want to laugh for no apparent reason.

"Since you're the judge of what's fashionable," he said, "tell me what you think of my haircut."

Norah glanced up as Rob ran a hand through his thick black hair. It was tidy and shining clean, with no trace of pomade. His fingers left the slender plume of a cowlick.

Norah studied him thoughtfully. "It's most flattering. Most flattering indeed."

His eyes sparkled. "Think I could pass for a Boston merchant?"

Norah pressed her lips together to thwart another smile. "You know very well you could." She handed him the package.

"What time do you finish here?" Rob asked.

Norah removed her spectacles. "Six o'clock."

Rob planted his palms on the counter and leaned toward her. "Join me for tea."

The air in the room grew oddly still. Norah looked into Rob's searching eyes and was seized by another rush of warmth. It flowed up to her cheeks and down to her toes. It curled and crested. She felt lost in a gentle, radiant haze. She swallowed hard and stumbled over her refusal. "Th-thank you, but no, I . . . I really can't."

Rob continued to lean on the counter, watching her with thoughtful intensity. Norah stared back at him, not daring to breathe. At last he straightened and dropped his gaze. When he spoke, his tone was all business. "I want to talk to you about Alice."

"Alice?" Norah asked faintly. She let out her breath gradually so it wouldn't sound like a sigh.

"We have to discuss Alice's safety on the *Orion*. I can't set restrictions without your advice, Norah. You know her capabilities better than I."

"Oh." Norah's fingers played nervously with the top button of her dress. She looked at Rob warily. He appeared perfectly sincere. There was nothing in his face that could be construed as teasing or speculation, no further threats to her composure.

"I'll pick you up at six and have you home by seven," he said. "I've already told Burnham."

Mr. Burnham, Norah thought sourly. Of course Mr. Burnham would give his permission. He'd have the two of them married within a fortnight. Still, Rob was right. They needed to discuss Alice before the voyage. "All right," she said. "But don't let Miss Peabody see you waiting for me."

"What? And risk arrest?" Rob picked up his package and gave her a wink. "Six o'clock," he said. "At the corner."

At six o'clock Norah closed the door of the shop and stepped out into Bromfield Street. The air was unusually cold for May. She gathered her shawl of Indian cashmere close about her and glanced down the street. Rob was pacing the corner of Washington Street. When he saw her, his face brightened and he waved. Norah brushed away the red bonnet ribbons that blew in her face and walked quickly toward him, feeling inexplicably happy.

He took her arm without a word, and they rounded the corner of School Street where Mrs. Abner Havens kept her coffee shop. Mrs. Havens showed them into the large, dim back room. The room, half filled with customers, was lined with black high-backed horsehair sofas. Before each sofa stood a round marble-topped table framed with mahogany. Norah seated herself on a sofa and slipped off her shawl. Rob pulled up a chair. He ordered boiled coffee and an assortment of delicacies that Norah knew would spoil her supper. Against her better judgment, she removed her bonnet and allowed herself to feel quite festive.

Once Mrs. Havens had departed, Rob leaned his forearms on the table, clasped his huge callused hands, and said, "Tell me what you do for Miss Peabody."

Norah was glad to see that he was in a serious frame of mind. Concentrating on subjects such as the bookshop and Alice would discourage jokes and teasing that might lead to misunderstandings.

She began speaking of the bookshop cautiously, prepared to stop once Rob's attention flagged. She decided to spare him the details of her cataloging system, describing it in the briefest possible terms. Then she went on to the business aspects of the book trade—auctions and jobbers, subscriptions and discounts. She figured a businessman like him would find those topics more interesting than her methods of keeping track of the books.

Rob appeared so absorbed in her discourse that Norah added an account of Boston's annual trade sale and the prospects for growth among American publishers. By the time she had finished expounding on the relative popularity of American and English authors, Rob was staring at her in amazement.

"You certainly know the book business," he said.

Norah flushed with pleasure. It was so very satisfying to discuss her work with someone who understood, and Rob did seem genuinely interested. "Most ladies find business dull, and most gentlemen don't care to hear a lady's views on the subject," she said, feeling a bit apologetic for chattering on for so long. Rob's admiring gaze inspired her to add, "Miss Peabody says I could probably run the entire shop myself."

Rob smiled. "Does she indeed?"

Norah glanced at the other patrons, hoping no one had heard. She leaned toward Rob and said confidentially, "You mustn't tell the Burnhams. They would be scandalized if I should even *think* of operating my own shop."

Rob nodded solemnly. "Your secret is safe with me." Then his eyes grew thoughtful. "I suppose once you marry, you'll give it up?"

The conversation, Norah realized, had suddenly veered onto a dangerous path. She also discovered that her head was bent much too close to Rob's. She straightened up and folded her gloves across her lap. "Forgive me for rattling on," she said. "I usually don't talk so much."

Rob watched her attentively. "You don't talk so much."

"Oh, I'm afraid I do," Norah said ruefully, wishing she felt more composed.

He smiled again. "You haven't answered my question. When you marry, will you give up the shop?"

Norah kept her face carefully expressionless. "I have no interest in marriage. As I told you before, I'm content with my life as it is."

The coffee arrived, along with plates of lemon pie, Brighton biscuits, and plump cream cakes. Norah took a thick slab of pie, and Rob poured the coffee. He drank some and ran a hand through his new haircut. Norah jabbed at her pie, aware of his eyes on her, wondering what he was thinking. The silence seemed oppressively intimate. Norah gazed miserably at her plate, wishing Rob would stop daydreaming and speak.

After a moment she said brightly, "We're supposed to be discussing Alice."

"Ah," Rob said, sitting back in his chair, his forehead creasing with interest. "So we are. Tell me how clever she is."

The topic reverted to Alice, and Norah regained her appetite. Between bites of pie she explained that Alice had learned to read with her fingers at the Institution for the Blind, and to do housework as well. She could make beds, dust, sweep, and set a table. In fact, Norah said, Alice knew more about housework than her pampered friends.

"It doesn't sound as if she needs you very much," Rob said.

Norah agreed. "She's remarkably self-sufficient. Once I help her memorize the layout of a strange place, she manages very well, as long as the things she needs are left in their proper place. Even her clothing is marked so she knows what bonnet goes with which dress. All I do is read to her and accompany her on walks."

Rob drummed his fingers thoughtfully on the marble table. "I'm afraid she'll be more restricted on the *Orion*. I don't mind her being left alone below as long as the sea is calm, but I want you to be with her every moment on deck."

"Alice doesn't like restrictions," Norah said. "Sometimes she slips out of the house and explores the neighborhood alone. She counts her steps to measure the distance."

Rob winced. "There'll be none of that on the *Orion*."

Norah helped herself to a shiny Brighton biscuit. Rob refilled her cup. The coffee was hot and exhilarating. It was said that Mrs. Havens flavored it with a good dose of brandy, a rumor the proprietress vigorously denied. Brandy or no, Norah was feeling remarkably pleasant and relaxed. She noticed several women in the shop directing frequent glances at her table. Norah couldn't help but feel flattered that her escort was the object of their admiration.

She had her eye on a cream cake when Rob, who had not eaten a bite, said, "I'd like you to come with me to the theater tomorrow evening."

Norah barely suppressed a cry of exasperation. An invitation to the theater! Oh, what a nuisance. The cursed man purposely engaged her in interesting conversation and then as soon as she let down her guard he caught her in another trap. How could she possibly get out of this one?

"Tomorrow?" she asked, stalling for time.

"Tomorrow," Rob said, adding with a smile, "if you're free."

Norah looked down at her plate and thought fast. She could say she was engaged tomorrow, but that would be a lie, and he would simply ask her for another night. If only she had behaved with more care! She had flaunted her business knowledge as if she were a man and then bragged that Miss Peabody thought she could run the bookshop. Worst of all, she had asked Rob to keep a secret from the Burnhams. Norah's spirits, so buoyant just moments ago, plummeted. There was no way to deny it; she had led him on.

Rallying her courage, she looked Rob directly in the eye and said, "Thank you kindly, but the answer is no."

Rob inclined his head politely. "May I ask why?"

Norah could think of no reason she felt capable of expressing. She settled for "A lady needn't explain herself."

Rob chuckled. "Come, Norah, I'm not proposing marriage. We settled that question two weeks ago. I'm merely asking you to the theater."

Norah flushed. "Your persistence is annoying, Captain Mackenzie."

He ignored her reproof. Leaning on the table, he said with a tease in his voice, "I wish you'd call me Rob. If you continue to address me as 'Captain,' I'll think you're one of my crew."

Norah stared at her plate, stifling yet another smile. She really had to escape this man who seemed to breach her defenses at will. Norah peeked at the little gold watch pinned over her right breast. "It's time I went home."

Rob made no move to leave, nor did he take his smiling eyes from her face. Norah glanced around the room, struggling to maintain a dignified expression.

At last Rob spoke. "Will you change your mind about the theater if I invite Alice to join us?"

Norah looked back at him, prepared to decline. Then she hesitated. Alice adored the theater. If the three of them went together, it wouldn't be quite so awkward.

"Think about it for a moment." Rob stood up, looking vastly amused. He took some coins from his pocket and tossed them on the table.

The most sensible thing, Norah thought as she reached for her bonnet and shawl, would be to refuse his invitation, to put a stop once and for all to his attempts to deepen their friendship.

Rob held out his hand to her. "Well?"

"I think," Norah said as he helped her to her feet, "that if Alice goes with us, your invitation would be acceptable."

Rob smiled gravely and bowed. "Miss Paige, I am deeply honored."

Norah pulled the last pins from her coil of hair and watched it tumble down over her shoulders. She sat still for a moment, staring at herself in the mirror, then picked up her silver brush and attacked the golden brown waves that lay across her breast. After a dozen good strokes, she stopped brushing and reached across the little table to turn down the lamp. Behind her, the cozy blue and white bedchamber dimmed into shadows. Norah stared at her reflection, gone mysterious and quite lovely in the faint light. She laid her brush down and lifted her hair from her shoulders, fanning it out over her arms. She let it go and watched it pour down over the white lace of her bedgown. Norah turned her head slightly to one side. Her freckles vanished. Her lashes threw shadows on her cheeks. She caught her lower lip in her teeth.

Suddenly she opened her mouth in a long, shuddering yawn. Good heavens, she could barely keep her eyes open. They had eaten oysters and drunk champagne at the Tremont

House after the performance. Rob had filled her glass at least three times; no wonder she was sleepy. She turned up the lamp and resumed her vigorous brushing.

"It's nearly midnight, Alice," she said wearily. "We should both be asleep."

Alice sat curled on the window seat, dressed in a pale blue silk wrapper. Her long dark braid lay over her shoulder. In her arms, she held Chance, her little black and white spotted dog.

"I have something to tell you," Alice said.

Norah rested her chin on her palm and stared into the mirror, smiling dreamily. Rob had laughed so heartily at the theater that people had turned to stare. She'd never seen anyone so enjoy himself. And of course as soon as Rob laughed, she'd laughed, and then Alice had joined in. Oh, they'd been a merry trio. Afterward at the Tremont House, Rob had kept her and Alice giggling all through their champagne supper.

"Norah, are you listening?"

"Hmm?"

"Norah, I've decided to marry."

Norah swung around on her chair. "Marry! Alice, what on earth are you talking about?"

"It's very simple," Alice said, toying with Chance's ear. "I'm going to marry in London."

"Marry in London! But who . . . ?" Norah fixed her face sternly. "Alice Burnham, you've had too much champagne."

Alice smiled, all innocence. "I'm perfectly serious."

Norah stood up and crossed to the window seat. Hands on hips, she said, "You're being ridiculous. You know very well marriage for you is out of the question. Why, the reason your mama is bothering with this ridiculous match between Rob and me is because of you." Norah had earlier voiced her conclusion that since Alice couldn't marry, Mrs. Burnham was devoting her matrimonial enthusiasms to her.

Alice's dark eyes gleamed in the lamplight. "Why should marriage be out of the question for me?"

With growing alarm, Norah realized Alice was serious. She sat down on the window seat. "Because it's never been discussed," she said, gesturing widely. "Because your parents would forbid it. Because we've never even considered it."

"Well, *I've* considered it," Alice said, her voice mild but firm.

Norah stared at her, dumbfounded. "You're *blind*, Alice."

Alice's cheeks flushed. "Surely you're not telling me there's something I can't do because I'm blind," she said. "Ever since we were twelve years old, you've been telling me I can do *anything*. Anything at all."

"But that doesn't mean—"

Alice's voice rose. "You forced me to learn my way around this house, Norah. You insisted I continue when I was tired and frustrated and wanted to stop. You pushed and pushed until I was no longer afraid. You taught me to hold my head up and turn toward people who spoke to me. And now you think I can't do something as ordinary as marry?" Alice's eyes glistened with sudden tears. "I thought you were my champion."

"But, Alice," Norah cried in dismay. She felt caught in a crosscurrent of loyalties—to her friend on the one hand and to the Burnhams on the other. The Burnhams would never allow Alice to live apart from them. Gaining their approval of the trip to London had been a battle, and only because of their implicit trust in Norah's good judgment had they finally given their consent. If Alice became involved with a gentleman, Norah would have failed in her duty. She couldn't bear to hurt the people who, since her mother's death, had treated her like a daughter.

"I surely can do whatever a husband wants of me," Alice said. "Please say you'll help me."

Norah sat stunned, trying to imagine Alice with a husband, children, a home of her own. Why, it was inconceivable. Impossible. Impractical. She imagined a man in love with Alice, a man entranced by her dimpled chin, her plump figure, her pretty manner. But what would he think when he looked into the dark depths of her eyes? Would he see a charming wife, a loving mother for his children, or a tragic and burdensome blind girl?

"How could I go against your parents' wishes after all they've done for me?" Norah asked softly.

Alice felt for Norah's hand and gave it a squeeze. "Once they see I'm happy, they'll be happy, too."

But Alice's certainty couldn't assuage the guilt that nipped at the edges of Norah's thoughts. Her complicity in such a plan would hurt the Burnhams terribly. Of course the entire scheme was most likely futile. Alice's blindness all but doomed her hopes for a husband. For a moment that reality comforted Norah. She could placate Alice by agreeing to the plan, even while making sure it never came to fruition. But then she looked at Alice's hopeful face and knew she could never practice such a deception. Alice was entitled to her happiness. And she was indeed capable of caring for a home and a husband.

Norah sighed. "It won't be easy."

"I know that," Alice said. "It might be too silly even to consider. Still, I want a man for myself, Norah, and children." She smiled mischievously. "Besides, when you marry Rob and start having babies, you'll be too busy for me."

"Marry Rob!" Norah jumped to her feet. "Alice, I've told you a thousand times—"

"Oh, posh! I know what you've told me, and I don't believe a word of it," Alice said as she nuzzled Chance's neck. "He's probably half in love with you already, just as we predicted."

"Alice, you're as drunk as a sailor." Norah sat down again before the mirror and attacked her hair with renewed fury. After a moment she turned around to glare at Alice once again. "If you're so interested in becoming a wife, why don't *you* marry him?"

Alice laughed. "Rob Mackenzie would be a handful for any woman. I couldn't possibly manage him. But you, Norah. You're so capable and resourceful. Why, you'll make him as sweet and tame as my little Chance."

Norah turned back to the mirror. "You're a wicked girl, Alice Burnham," she said. "I pity the poor man who takes you for a wife. Your blindness will be the least of his problems."

Chapter Four

NORAH STOOD AT the quarterdeck rail, her bonnet ribbons flying in the breeze, and watched Rob climb the ratlines. He appeared more the common seaman than the *Orion*'s captain, laden as he was with a strap and block, a marlinespike, and a coil of rope; his well-worn shirt and shapeless dark trousers did nothing to alter that impression.

Shipmasters, Norah knew, normally didn't work in the rigging. Her papa used to say a tar-stained skipper was as rare as a three-legged mule. But Rob seemed personally acquainted with every timber, spar, and strand of hemp on his brig. When he wasn't climbing the towering masts, making endless adjustments to wires and lines, he was bellowing aloft to his men to lay ahold here or hoist away there. Norah wondered if he ever went below, other than to eat, even at night.

In the three days since they'd left Boston, Rob had been so absorbed in his sea duties that even their dinner conversations centered on the *Orion*. He went to tedious lengths to explain the crew's activities on deck. A ship, he said, was usually in poor order when she sailed from port. Decks and sides were dirty from taking on cargo, the rigging was slack, the masts in need of staying. Once the vessel was under sail, it seemed, the entire apparatus needed overhauling.

Rob's duties took all his attention; he had no time for flirtations. Norah told herself she should be relieved, but in truth she missed his smiling banter.

Clutching at her ribbons, she followed Rob's progress aloft. He passed aft of the mainsail, fattened by the wind. The breeze grabbed him, rocking him on the lines, and Norah's heart gave a jump of fear. She hastily reminded herself that for men like Rob and her own papa, a climb in the rigging was no more eventful than a stroll down Washington Street. But she let out a breath of relief when Rob grabbed a line and pulled himself onto the platform at the head of the lower mast.

Having seen Rob safely onto the mast, Norah turned her attention down the length of the busy ship where crewmen scrubbed the deck to a flaxen white. On the lee side of the deck, the winch hummed out a long line of rope. Mr. Crawford, the wiry chief mate, paced the planks, shouting orders into the web of lines and yards where men perched like so many birds in a tree. Norah placed her hand on the crown of her bonnet and tilted her head back so she could see the very top of the foremast. It was ever so high, even higher, it seemed, than the steeple of the Old South Church. Her papa had once said that when he worked on the fore-royal yard in the blue sky among puffs of clouds, he felt he could touch heaven.

"Begging your pardon, miss."

Norah glanced down at the main deck, searching for the source of the interruption, and found Mr. Crawford's tough, wrinkled face squinting up at her. The quick lowering of her sight brought on a slight dizzy spell, and Norah clutched at the quarterdeck rail.

"Yes, Mr. Crawford?"

"You might find it more comfortable standing aft, miss. The men ain't used to ladies watching them work."

Norah noticed then that deck activity had slowed. A half-dozen pairs of eyes rested on her. She felt a spurt of annoyance that she would have to forgo the pleasure of watching the interesting bustle of seamen's chores just because the men found her a distraction. Rob had laid down only two rules for his passengers' use of the deck: Alice was never to be left there alone, and both of them were to remain below until eight o'clock in the morning. The rest of the time, Norah figured, she could wander where she chose and watch whomever she fancied.

She looked back at the chief mate. Mr. Crawford didn't seem to care for ladies aboard ship, and Norah certainly didn't care much for him. During Rob's introductions, Mr. Crawford had stared at her in a curious, prying way that made Norah uncomfortable. Since then, he'd said virtually nothing to either Alice or her.

"Of course, Mr. Crawford," Norah said, deciding not to challenge the mate's authority in front of the men. "Please excuse me."

She turned back to the poop and crossed the unsteady deck toward the taffrail. Rob had rigged a tarpaulin so that she and Alice could sit shaded from the sun. Alice reclined there in her deck chair, her book of Gospels, printed with embossed letters for blind readers, open on her lap. She was fast asleep, her fingers still, her eyes closed. The sea air made the normally animated Alice so relaxed she could barely drag herself around the deck for their twice-daily walk, while Norah, who considered herself more complacent, often felt restless, even a bit bored.

Norah loosened the ribbons on her straw bonnet and let it flop down her back. Leaning on the taffrail, she stared at the *Orion*'s wake. The little curls of foam that covered the sea seemed to match the sunny clouds perched just above the horizon. The breeze felt invigorating, the sun deliciously warm. Despite an occasionally uncertain stomach, Norah found the ship's motion tolerable.

"Begging your pardon again, miss."

Norah jumped. The mate had come up beside her, catching her unaware. "Oh, Mr. Crawford," she said, "you surprised me."

The mate stood no taller than Norah, but he was compact and muscular. He looked at her, his blue-eyed squint deepening, and shifted a chaw of tobacco in his cheek. "I hope the sea ain't too rough for you."

"Not rough at all," Norah replied, concealing beneath a cheerful manner her displeasure at this further interruption. "Both Miss Burnham and I are quite comfortable, thank you."

Norah turned her gaze back to the horizon and wished heartily for Mr. Crawford to go away.

"I don't suppose you had a pa who practiced the seaman's trade."

Norah swallowed so abruptly, she almost choked. She turned back to Mr. Crawford. "My . . . my father?"

Mr. Crawford chomped steadily on his tobacco. "He wouldn't have been a sailor, now, would he?"

Norah felt a sudden shiver of apprehension. She had no interest in discussing her papa with a stranger; merely thinking of him was trying enough. She answered evasively. "My . . . my father has been dead for many years."

Mr. Crawford's eyes tightened in a further squint. "Might he have been Jody Paige?"

Norah stared blankly at Mr. Crawford. In nearly eight years she hadn't mentioned her papa's name, nor had she met a soul who'd known him. After coming to live with the Burnhams, she'd tried to put both her parents permanently out of her mind. The past was over and done with, the pain finished. But now, on this ship, observing with her own eyes the life her father had loved, she was besieged by memories of the past. He was once again a vivid and disturbing presence. And with him came thoughts of her beautiful mother, whose lively spirits had faded into sorrow.

"How did you know he was my father?" Norah asked softly.

Crawford shifted his gaze away from her. "I saw you one time at Fortune's when you were a small lass. You came to fetch him. 'Twas just before we shipped out for Smyrna in February of 'twenty-seven, as I recall."

Norah grasped the rail tightly, her heart thudding in her ears. "You . . . you have a remarkable memory, Mr. Crawford. My father fell from a masthead in the South China Sea and drowned years ago. After that, I . . ." Sudden tears flooded Norah's eyes. "I quite put him out of my mind."

Mr. Crawford was silent for moment. Then he said gently, "Begging your pardon, miss. I didn't mean to interfere, only to figure if you was his girl."

"Well, I am his girl." Norah's voice rose with her attempt to control its tremor. "I mean, I was. . . ."

Despite her desperate blinking, Nora felt tears coming hard. "If you'll excuse me," she managed through jumpy breaths, "I must see to Miss Burnham."

Turning abruptly, she strode toward the tarpaulin, pressing her hand against her mouth to still its trembling. Alice's sleeping form blurred before her eyes, and Norah felt uncontrollable sobs gaining fast. Oh, she was being quite childish! But during these past days aboard the *Orion*, Papa and Mama had been so much on her mind.

A moment alone was all she needed to compose herself. Norah changed course and headed for the companionway. Gulping hard, she felt her way down the stairs, dark after the bright sunlight of the deck. The main cabin was deserted. Norah sat down at the round table bolted to the timbered floor and drew in deep shuddering breaths. How could she have permitted herself this appalling collapse? She was easily given to tears, but to burst out like a blubbering child! Not only had she embarrassed herself, but she'd surely frightened Mr. Crawford half to death.

Norah dabbed at her eyes with a handkerchief. She had to stop thinking about the old days. It was being at sea that crowded her mind with memories. The sea had been her father's life and the ruin of her mother. Norah wiped her hot cheeks. Each night since leaving Boston, she'd dampened her pillow with tears. It was time to get control of herself and stop this morbid wallowing in the past.

But to think Mr. Crawford had been there that night at Fortune's! Oh, it was not easy to snuff out the burning memory of the last time she'd seen her papa. Norah felt her throat close up. Her eyes filled again, and she pressed her fist hard against her lips.

She remembered waking to the murmur of grown-up voices rising from the kitchen. Mama had spoken through sobs, soft and terrible. When Papa answered, his voice was so low she could barely hear him.

"Maybe you're right, Annie. Maybe it's better I don't come back at all."

In the thick feather bed, Norah's body had turned to ice. He was joking; he had to be. Norah waited for him to tell Mama he would quit the sea, this time for good. She waited for him to take Mama in his arms and bring her up to bed. Instead, Norah heard him close the kitchen door. She lay still, paralyzed with disbelief. When Mama came upstairs alone, she was weeping.

Norah slipped out of bed, dressed, and ran down the stairs. She ran all the way to Water Street without a wrap, freezing in the frigid February air. The tavern, crowded with loud men, smelled of damp wool and ale. She found Papa standing at the bar with his mates, laughing and handsome, his long fingers wrapped around a foaming mug. When he caught sight of her, he drew her into his arms.

"What's my girl up to now?" he asked and gave her a hearty squeeze.

He didn't scold her; he never did. Norah burrowed against him, shivering with cold and fear, desperately inhaling his smoky scent as if to preserve it for all time. Papa put his coat around her and held her till she got warm. She drank some sweet cider before they set off for home.

On the street she told him what she had heard, tears freezing on her cheeks. She blurted out all her terrors in breaths that were cold puffs of white. Papa stopped beneath a street lamp. He crouched beside her and wiped her cheeks, his rough hands warm on her tingling face. Then he took off his silver ring, bent and dull from years of hard work, and folded it into her palm. "Keep it safe, sweet girl, and I promise you'll see me again. Let's see a smile. Cheerily, now."

He had ruffled her hair, tickled her until she laughed, and whistled as if nothing were wrong as he led her home. Later that night he'd packed his sea chest and left. She'd never seen him again.

Norah blinked up at the brass lamp that swung with the creaking rhythm of the brig. Beyond the overhead beams she heard the muffled footfalls of sailors going about their duties on deck. Dim light fell through the skylight. She wiped her eyes and gave her nose a vigorous blow. No more sad thoughts, she told herself. It served no purpose to grieve for memories best forgotten.

Suddenly she heard footsteps pounding down the companionway, and Rob's voice bellowed, "What the devil are you doing down here?"

Norah tucked her handkerchief into her sleeve and jumped to her feet. Rob pulled off his cap and threw it on the table. His wind-tossed hair lay in a coarse tangle.

"Alice is wandering around the deck by herself, and you're sitting down here in the dark." Rob's brows drew together in a hard scowl. "Good God, Norah, I thought you had more sense."

Oh, dear heaven, Norah thought. She'd gone off and left Alice! She hurried toward the stairs. "I'm sorry," she said as briskly as she could manage. "Alice was sleeping, and I came down for only a moment."

Rob seized her arm. "What's the matter with you?"

Norah averted her face from the light that brightened the companionway. She blinked hard at the annoyingly persistent tears that continued to burn behind her eyes.

"What's happened?" Rob demanded. "Why are you crying?"

"I'm not crying." Norah twisted away, trying to free her arm. "You'd better let me go before Alice falls into the sea."

"One of the men is looking after her." Rob's voice was no longer abrupt. He grasped Norah's other arm and turned her to face him. "Are you homesick? Did one of the men insult you?"

"Of course not," Norah whispered. She hung her head so Rob couldn't see her red nose and swollen eyes. "I'm perfectly fine." But her lips trembled and the heavy weight of sadness still lay on her chest.

Rob led her back to the table and pushed her firmly into the chair. He untied the bonnet hanging down her back and placed it on the table beside his cap. He bent over, hands on his knees, and peered at her lowered face. "Tell me what's wrong."

Norah focused on the embroidered flowers on her dress. They blurred and cleared as she blinked. Embarrassment at her infantile behavior was overwhelmed by a sudden need to confide in someone. "Sometimes," she said, her throat tight, her voice little more than a squeak, "sometimes I can't help thinking about the times when I was small . . . with my father and mother . . . I miss them so."

Norah covered her eyes and sobbed. She heard Rob's feet

shuffle, and he cleared his throat. When he spoke, his tone was gruff. "Then don't think about it," he said sternly. "Don't think about anything that makes you sad. I don't want you crying, do you understand?"

He spoke as if he could command her happiness as easily as he could order a man up the mast. Norah raised her head and looked at him. He was half crouched before her, his rough wool jacket crusted with seawater, his hair standing damply on end, his face dark with concern. For some reason, his expression and his words struck Norah funny. An odd sound— half sob, half laugh—came from her throat and she discovered she was smiling.

"Is that an order?" she asked, wiping her cheek with the heel of her hand. In his presence, she felt suddenly comforted, almost happy.

An answering smile spread slowly across Rob's face. He straightened, picked up his cap, and tugged it back on his head. Then he reached for Norah's hands and drew her to her feet. "Yes, damn it, that's an order. Now go wash your face. It's nearly time for dinner."

At dinner Mr. Crawford, fuzzy wisps of reddish hair covering his head, sat on Norah's left. She dreaded some comment from him about her father, but the mate appeared to have no interest in discussing Jody or anything else. After a perfunctory exchange with Rob about knots and currents and wind directions, he fell to eating his stew, scooping it noisily into his mouth.

Willie, Rob's Kanaka steward, limped around the table barefoot, carrying the stew pot and frowning at Alice's plate. As part of her campaign to find a husband in London, Alice had decided to follow the regimen of vegetables and water prescribed by Dr. Graham in his *System of Living*. A slimmer figure, Alice thought, would increase her chances for matrimony. She subsisted on carrots and potatoes and fresh vegetables from the garden Rob kept in a longboat.

"Missy no eat meat, Missy get sick," Willie complained.

The steward was a small, handsome man with smooth reddish brown skin and straight black hair. A bright red shirt hung out of oversize white trousers. He limped—a result, Rob had said, of a fall from a yard during a Pacific storm.

"Why, Willie, that's utterly absurd," Alice said, adjusting the little sandbag that kept her plate from sliding around. "I've heard that your people in the Sandwich Islands eat only fruits and vegetables and they are perfectly healthy."

Rob caught Norah's eye and smiled across the table. He'd been watching her throughout the meal, and Norah was making an effort to appear cheerful. By tomorrow her memories would be tucked away, her equilibrium restored.

"Missy not Kanaka. Missy white man," Willie said. "Kanaka like meat. Kanaka like dog best."

Alice gave a little shriek. "Dog!" Her fingers flew to her lips. "You eat dog?"

"Dog very good," Willie said. "Very sweet."

"But that's horrid! It's no better than cannibalism! Norah, have you ever heard of such a thing?"

Norah had no chance to respond, for Willie, apparently pleased to have provoked such dismay, was explaining the various methods of baking and boiling the delicacy, which only brought on more cries from Alice and shouts of laughter from Rob.

"Kanakas are also fond of dogs as pets," Rob said. "They only serve up disagreeable dogs for dinner. Isn't that right, Willie?"

"Captain right." Willie beamed at Norah, who smiled wanly and pushed away her bowl with its great hunks of meat. Her appetite had suddenly vanished.

"Meat is meat," Rob said, "whether it's lamb or dog or kangaroo, for that matter. Eating only vegetables is a pretty strange custom itself."

Alice remained implacable, her arms folded. "If you had a little dog at home, as I do," she said irritably, "you'd think it dreadful, too, and not the least bit funny."

But Alice could never resist laughter for long, and when Rob started recounting some of the bizarre customs he had encountered in his travels, the dimples started popping on her round cheeks. As the two of them laughed merrily, Norah glanced at the silent Mr. Crawford. He was staring at her with a hard, haunted expression that made her shiver. Then his face darkened, and he muttered something about a task on deck. Pushing away his bowl, he got to his feet and hurried off.

Norah tossed restlessly on the walnut sleep sofa that served as her bed. It was well past eleven, but she was too hungry to sleep. As a result of her encounter with Mr. Crawford and the dog discussion, she'd barely eaten a bite at dinner. Now her stomach felt achingly empty.

She threw back the covers and fumbled in the dark for her shift and dress. She had to find something to eat or she'd lie awake till dawn. After dressing hastily, she opened her door and slipped quietly into the main cabin. It was empty. Willie had apparently gone to bed, and Rob was most likely on deck. The lamp above the round dining table was turned low, and the compass swung lazily from the skylight. The wood paneling groaned in earnest, one of the many ceaseless noises that were part of life under sail.

Norah glanced around, wondering where she might find some food. The cabin contained only the table and chairs, a massive sideboard, and two battered chests. Rob kept his desk and logbook in his stern cabin, which, like the one Norah shared with Alice, opened off the main cabin.

Norah looked through the sideboard, but could find nothing edible among the cigar boxes and blankets. Then she remembered the pantry and padded barefoot down the passageway, past the officers' quarters. She opened the pantry door to the powerful smell of coffee and spices, but she could see nothing in the darkness. Trotting back to the main cabin for a lamp, she stopped short when she saw Rob at the sideboard pouring himself a glass of brandy from the decanter.

He glanced at her, surprised. "Well, well. You're prowling about at a late hour."

His hair was wind-tossed, and a brush of whiskers shadowed his cheeks. His shirt hung open halfway down his broad, dark chest. Norah's heart gave an imprudent thump. Rob caught her stare and grinned as he hastily buttoned the shirt up to his throat.

"You look far more beautiful in your disarray than I do in mine," he said, glancing at Norah's bare feet and ankles.

Norah curled her toes in embarrassment. She had never appeared before a man in such a state. Her hair hung down about her shoulders, and she wore no stockings, stays, or petticoats. Worse, she hadn't fastened her dress all the way up the back, a chore that Alice normally performed for her.

"I'm foraging," she explained, realizing as she spoke that her appetite had abruptly disappeared, leaving her stomach full of butterflies.

Rob leaned back against the sideboard and took a swallow of brandy. "Felt too sorry to eat much today, did you?"

"I'm fine now," Norah said cheerfully, hoping to cover her sudden case of nerves.

"Sit down and I'll find you something to eat."

Norah glanced at her cabin door and wondered how she could sidle past Rob without his seeing her dress gaping open down her back. "I think I should go to bed."

"If you're hungry, you must eat."

"Really, you needn't bother."

"Sit," he commanded.

Norah seated herself at the table. As an afterthought, she tucked her bare feet over the rungs of the chair, well out of his sight.

"What sounds good from the larder?" Rob asked.

Norah thought. She recalled Alice's appetizing plate of fresh vegetables. "I've never eaten a tomato," she said.

"A tomato." Rob smiled. He secured his glass in the magogany holder on the sideboard. "I'll see if I can find one for you."

He took the companionway two steps at a time. As soon as he disappeared, Norah tiptoed into her cabin. She pulled on her stockings, draped a shawl over her shoulders, and wondered why she suddenly felt so bashful. Except for this morning's tears, she had maintained a cordial but dignified manner with Rob, which she intended to continue. But the dim, shadowy cabin late at night seemed dangerously intimate. Perhaps, Norah thought, it would be best just to climb back into bed and forget Rob and the tomato. No, she decided, that would be rude. Clutching slippers and shawl, Norah glanced at Alice, fast asleep on her own sleep sofa, and hurried back to the main cabin.

She was stuffing her feet into her slippers when Rob returned. He carried two fat red tomatoes beaded with water, an enormous green pepper, and a bunch of slick green onions that looked as sweet as sugarcane.

"You're very clever to plant a garden in the longboat," Norah said.

Rob looked pleased. "Let's hope it doesn't get washed away in a storm."

He assembled a plate, silverware, and a wooden-handled knife. Seating himself across the table from her, he pushed up his sleeves. Amid the black hair on his forearms, Norah glimpsed an array of tattoos, which brought on a quick sting of memory. As a girl, she'd loved sitting on her papa's lap, poking at the pictures on his arms. Norah scolded away her thoughts, telling herself she'd recalled too much for one day.

Resting her elbows on the table, she watched Rob's fingers, scrubbed clean, yet stained with tar and work, slice a tomato into precise wedges. The knife made little clicking sounds on the plate.

"You seem to be no stranger to kitchen work," she said.

Rob didn't look up from his chopping. "A sailor has to be expert in just about everything. At Lintin, the cook taught me to fry vegetables in the Chinese style."

"Chinese style?" Norah asked.

"You stir up the vegetables with garlic over high heat, then serve the whole mixture over rice. We carried a sparse crew on opium runs up the coast, so the mate and I had to take turns cooking." He glanced up at Norah. "I'll do it for you sometime, if you like."

His offer was so unexpected and so improbable that Norah had to scramble to find an appropriate response. "Why, that's very kind," she said, wondering what Mrs. Burnham would say if she learned that the undomesticated Rob Mackenzie had offered to cook her dinner.

They sat in silence as Rob sliced the pepper into thin strips. Norah noticed that he was very tidy about how he cut vegetables. Papa always said the best sailors were the most precise; carelessness on a ship, he said, could result in disaster.

Norah's gaze drifted back to Rob's thick, muscular forearms. She counted seven tattoos. Amid an assortment of anchors and eagles, she saw two names: Rosa Sanchez and Harriet.

"Where is Lintin?" she asked abruptly, feeling a twinge of annoyance that Rob should wear the names of his women so boldly.

"It's an island downriver from Canton where British and American receiving ships anchor. The ships take on opium that traders bring from Bengal and Turkey. They store the stuff for a price, then it's sold directly to the Chinese merchants or delivered by clipper up the coast to Namoa or Foochow. That's what I've been doing for the past few years, commanding the firm's receiving ship at Lintin."

"Opium." Norah made a face. She had heard a lecture at Miss Peabody's about the evils of the trade, which brought huge profits to nearly every commercial house from Boston to Baltimore. Perfectly respectable men dealt in opium, men like Mr. Burnham, who only laughed when Norah preached to him about the wickedness of making a profit from the misery of the Chinese.

"I think the opium trade is disgraceful."

Rob shrugged. "It's not up to the merchants to correct the Chinese people's vices. As long as there's a demand for the stuff, men will gladly supply it."

"But it's immoral," Norah protested, feeling the stirrings of indignation.

Rob looked up at her, his face dark with annoyance. "Immoral compared to what? Whiskey? Gunpowder? Liquor makes men drunk. Guns kill people. How about razors? One day while a man's shaving he might decide to cut his neighbor's throat. Or his own."

"But men sacrifice every decent instinct for opium," Norah argued, trying to recall some of the gruesome details she'd heard. "Their bodies, their souls, their families—"

"The Chinese have been buying and smoking opium for more than a hundred years," Rob interrupted sharply. "We don't force it on them." There was a dogged look about his mouth, and his eyes were hard and bitter. Norah decided to hold her tongue.

Rob went back to his chopping. Norah watched him work,

her heart suddenly heavy. She realized how much she'd admired him until this moment. With his knowledge of ships and the sea and his head for business, Rob Mackenzie was the most capable man she could imagine. And he seemed to have a kind heart. This morning, he'd all but dried her tears with his own hands, and he was endlessly patient with Alice. But what was there to admire in a man who trafficked in opium and then spoke so callously about its consequences?

As if he'd read her thoughts, Rob pushed away the plate of vegetables and sighed. "Try to understand, Norah. It all comes down to business. Opium is the currency for trade in the Indies. The Chinese will accept only silver specie in exchange for their tea and porcelain and silks. Specie is scarce in the Far East. Selling opium is the only means for Western traders to get hold of it."

Norah was unmoved. "Selling opium is illegal in China," she said stubbornly. "You're breaking their laws."

"The Chinese authorities outlawed the trade not for moral reasons but to keep silver from leaving the country. And Western traders don't sell it in China; the Chinese traders do."

"I still think it's wrong."

Rob smiled sourly. "I'm afraid, Norah, that for a businessman, right and wrong is measured by profit and loss, nothing more."

He looked away from her and into the distance. There was a melancholy expression on his face that Norah hadn't seen before, and a new sternness to his jawline. He seemed to be remembering something, something that made him doubtful, that made him less certain of his views.

"You don't mean that," she said.

Rob glanced back at her. He sat forward and sprinkled oil and vinegar on the salad. "A plate of vegetables doesn't seem like enough to fill up a bird," he said, pushing the food toward her.

Norah ignored his comment. "I don't think you believe half the things you just told me."

Rob started up out of his chair. "Eat your supper." His voice was sharp, his face scowling.

The atmosphere in the cabin suddenly became tense. Rob

went to the sideboard and took up the decanter of brandy. He poured a long slug of it down his throat and refilled his glass.

Brandy, Norah thought, picking at her salad. Opium. Lewd women. Men's vices were brought on by despair, by loneliness and guilt. It was hard to imagine the swaggering Captain Mackenzie carrying the burden of sorrow in his soul or feeling lonely or guilty about anything. But some part of him was in pain; she was sure of it.

Rob came back to the table and sat, avoiding her eyes. "I'll tell you what I believe . . . what I *believed*. I believed that the Chinese smoked opium the way Western men smoke tobacco. I also believed it was an Eastern custom, that Western men would never take it up. But I was wrong. Any man can become a slave to it, just as a drunkard takes to spirits."

Norah set aside her plate and leaned forward, hope leaping in her breast. He was redeemable. She could see it in his face; she could hear it in his tentative confession. Her mind tumbled backward, trying to match ideas she'd read in books with this flesh-and-blood man. It was said that remorse was the first step to redemption.

"You mustn't trade opium any longer," she said.

Rob smiled sadly. "It's not that easy, Norah."

"Of course it is," Norah said and immediately thought she was moving too hastily. Perhaps she should just listen and encourage, not offer advice. It would take time to lead Rob back to the righteous course. If she tried to force him, he'd surely rebel.

"Perhaps you could encourage me," Rob said.

Norah leaned farther across the table toward him. "Yes," she said, not bothering to temper her enthusiasm. "Oh, yes, I shall."

The lamplight chased shadows across the paneled walls and over Rob's face. He watched her, a thoughtful line deepening between his brows. Norah felt a quickening beneath her ribs. She thought of her success in transforming Alice. Under her tutelage, Alice had gone from a frightened and hesitant child to a clever, ebullient young woman. Certainly Rob could be changed as well. All that was needed was her womanly patience.

It crossed her mind that once he was saved from opium trafficking, he might even be tamed into some semblance of a normal man, one who would be content to live in Boston.

Rob leaned toward her, covering Norah's clasped hands with his own. "You can't know," he said softly, "what it does to a man."

The gentle appeal in his eyes made Norah go all soft inside. She gazed at Rob's rough, warm hand covering hers, and her heart brimmed with affection, doubled, tripled, by his need for her moral ministrations.

She lifted her eyes to his. Abruptly her cheeks went hot. Something had changed in his face. Gone was the sorrowful expression. In its place was a devilish smile, a knowing gleam. Rob's hand tightened on her own. "Come on deck with me, sweetheart. You should see the night sky."

Sweetheart! Norah pulled back, her face burning with confusion and dismay. He was teasing her. He'd been teasing her all along with his hangdog expression, his words of regret. Why, he didn't mean to be reformed at all! Norah's eyes stung with hurt tears. "We were talking about—about opium," she said, stammering with mortification. "About *you*."

"Dreary subjects. Both of them." Rob got to his feet. He smoothed down his hair and tugged on his cap. "Come up top with me. The moon's near full."

Norah saw no trace of remorse on Rob's face, only unrepentant amusement and some sort of intention, as if he wanted to add her to his list of worldly sins.

"No," she said faintly. She could hardly bear the crush of disappointment. She'd thought he was sincere.

"Suit yourself."

He bent down and looked straight into her face. There was a darkness to his expression, although his mouth was smiling. Norah gazed back at him, her eyes hot and full, threatening to spill over. "You were teasing me," she said in a soft, catching voice. "I think you're dreadful."

Rob leaned closer. "I'm afraid I'm far worse than that."

Before Norah knew what was happening, his mouth met hers. His lips felt warm and gentle, with only the briefest pressure.

He pulled away. "Good night, sweetheart."

Norah sat very still beneath the swinging lamp, listening to his footsteps on the companionway. Then she touched her fingers to her lips and thought he really was the worst sort of man imaginable.

Chapter Five

IT WAS PAST midnight when the topsails were finally set. Rob sent his second officer below and stood the midwatch himself. He often took the deck in the dead of night. Even in the best of circumstances, sleep didn't come readily to him. Tonight he felt wound tight as spun yarn.

Stepping to the binnacle, Rob studied the compass and ordered the helmsman to drop off two points to larboard. Then he bent to light his cigar on the lamp. The temperature had dropped ten degrees in the past hour, and a low cover of clouds hid the moon and stars. Rob yanked up his jacket collar against the cool wet air and crossed the deck. Except for the glow of the lamp on the foreyard and the water washing by the hull, the night was as black and still as a grave.

Leaning his forearms on the rail slick with dew, Rob stared out into his dark domain. It was just as well Norah had gone to bed. If he'd brought her on deck tonight, he'd have kissed her and put his hands on her breasts, and God knew what else. Strange, how she attracted him, a girl who was innocent, who knew nothing of pleasing a man, a girl firmly anchored in a life he knew nothing about. In Norah's world, young women wept for dead parents and cared for afflicted friends, virginity was sacred, and right and wrong were simple judgments.

Rob smiled grimly as he thought of the intention he'd seen in her face tonight. Norah wanted to make him part of her world. He'd seen it plain as day. She wanted to save him from a life about which she had only the haziest notion. He would let her do it, Rob thought, if it meant the past would disappear, if it meant his private hell of guilt and sorrow would vanish. If Norah could give him peace, he would let her gather him up and close the circle about them both.

But he knew too much about desperation and loss and the sickening waste of human life to change himself. Tonight, watching Norah's lovely eyes, so solemn and curious, he'd wanted to tell her what really happened out there on the China coast. He'd felt an uncanny urge to confess to a past that continued to follow him like a guilty shadow.

Rob sent his cigar spinning over the rail into the black watery void. It was just as well he'd said nothing. Norah would never have understood. She might have tried, but a girl like her could never understand the true meaning of betrayal.

Norah threw back the covers and swung her feet onto the Turkish carpet that covered the cabin floor. She caressed the swirling blue pattern with her bare toes and stared out the window at the gray light of dawn. All night she'd had restless dreams, vague dreams of Rob. She'd been awakened by a strange, exquisite shiver that made her cheeks burn just thinking of it. Norah told herself it was only a dream, a brief nocturnal trick of the imagination. But it was distinctly carnal, and she couldn't help feeling ashamed.

Norah locked her hands behind her head and arched her back in a long stretch. If she was awake for the day, she might as well do something useful. A bit of tidying, she decided, would divert her mind from wanton thoughts. Alice's book of Gospels lay open on the floor beside her bed. Her knitting was strewn on the carpet. Her rose-colored dressing gown was draped over the tea table like a silken cover. Humming softly, Norah set to work.

Once she had the cabin shipshape, she took from the bookshelf volume two of Mrs. Child's *History of the Condition of Women in All Ages* and sat down on the window seat. But as her eyes scanned the pages, the words blurred, reality faded into the pleasurable haze of imagination. Norah thought of Rob looking at her last evening, the feel of his hands enfolding hers, the way he'd kissed her. She saw his broad shoulders, clad in rough wool, his sun-browned cheeks bristling with black whiskers. She thought of his tangled hair, his dark, knowing eyes. And then his lips against hers. Just like that. A thrilling flush rose on Norah's cheeks.

She dug her nails into her palm and hauled herself back to her senses. A brief, silly kiss had brought on a mild fever of admiration. She could not allow it to develop into anything more serious. Rob Mackenzie was a seaman who trafficked in opium and wore the names of past loves stamped on his arms. He had no interest in reforming himself; he'd made that plain enough. She, on the other hand, led a perfectly happy life in Boston with the Burnhams and Miss Peabody.

Setting aside Mrs. Child, Norah looked out at the sea, rosy from the rising sun. Patches of fine mist rode lazily on the waves. The eastern sky would be brilliant, the deck lovely and quiet before the normal routines of the day began. What she needed to exorcise her foolish thoughts, Norah decided, was a good lungful of sea air.

Willie wouldn't bring warm water until half past seven, so Norah washed and brushed her teeth in water from last night's pitcher. She dressed quickly, making sure all her buttons were fastened. As she pinned up her hair, she glanced anxiously out the window at the brightening sky. She didn't want to be too late to see the sunrise. After scuffing into her slippers, she snatched up her shawl and tiptoed from the cabin.

As she ran lightly up the companionway, Norah could smell the fresh air and hear familiar deck sounds. The chickens were clucking on the poop. Mr. Crawford shouted an order. At the top of the stairs she blinked at the sudden light and gasped with pleasure. The entire eastern sky was ablaze. A breeze carried the *Orion* along at about five knots, brisk enough to keep her from rolling. Norah stepped out onto the deck.

She heard a splash and a shout and turned to see Willie standing on the larboard poop holding an empty bucket whose contents he had just spilled over his captain. Norah froze. Too late she remembered Rob's order: "I don't want you ladies on deck before eight bells."

He stood dripping wet and stark naked. His dark body gleamed with water that ran over him from slick-soaked hair

to heels planted firmly apart. On torso and limbs, muscles stood out, ribbed and hard, every line sharply defined. A mat of black hair covered his chest, tapered down to his flat belly, then widened below.

Norah stared, transfixed.

"Blast you, Willie! That's cold!" Rob dug his fingers into his face and threw back his dripping head. "Have some mercy, man."

Then Willie saw her. His eyes widened, his jaw went slack. "Captain!" he cried, gesturing wildly. "Missy come!"

Rob shook the water from his face and gaped at Norah. Their eyes met and held. For a moment neither moved. Then Rob's muscles tensed, his burly shoulders seemed to draw in, and he let out a roar loud enough to alert the *Orion*'s entire crew and that of any ship passing within a mile.

The sound of Rob's anger jarred Norah from her trance. In stumbling confusion, she turned and hurried toward the companionway. Tripping and panting, she made her way down into the main cabin. All her instincts told her to hide. She heard Rob shouting and swearing, the pounding of feet. Dear Lord, what had she done? What should she do? If she went to her cabin, he would come after her, waking Alice and making a dreadful scene. Norah frantically sought a hiding place. Suddenly she remembered the pantry.

She could hear Rob's feet on the stairs as she slipped through the pantry door and softly closed it behind her. She bumped against a crate in the darkness, then worked her way into a corner against a bank of shelves behind the door. He would never find her here, surely he wouldn't. Norah laid a hand on her pounding heart and waited.

She heard Rob storming around the main cabin, opening and closing doors. She thought of his look of astonishment, his swift bellow of outrage. What would he do to her? What would he say? Norah had never before laid eyes on a naked man. Sweet heaven, he was magnificent, every bit of him, like a plate from Miss Beard's *Greek Statuary*. Norah pressed back against the shelves and told her heart to be still. She had embarrassed him and herself as well. Her unforgivable blunder should fill her with shame. Instead, she felt an odd, mounting exhilaration that made her whimper with dismay.

Rob's footsteps grew louder, then silence. Norah relaxed. Thank heaven. He'd given up.

Suddenly the door flew open, smashing against her. Norah let out a yelp of surprise. The pantry filled with lamplight and Rob was there, glaring down at her. Without a word, he hung the lamp on the hook driven into the overhead beam and slammed the door with a long bare foot. He faced her, a great looming oak of a man, all broad chest and muscled arms, naked to his narrow hips where a pair of trousers hung precariously low.

"What do you have to say for yourself?" His eyes shot sparks. Beads of water glittered on the crisp dark hair on his chest.

Norah reached up to pull her shawl close, but she had lost it in her scramble, and her hair was falling down as well. Somehow she managed to speak. "I . . . I wanted to see the sunrise."

Rob took a step toward her, his eyes flickering over her from brow to toes. "You disobeyed an order. I told you not to come on deck before the end of the morning watch. Until then the deck belongs to the men. It's an order to protect our privacy and your reputation."

Norah lowered her eyes, then lifted them quickly as a rush of heat surged to her hairline. The damp fabric of his trousers clung to him indecently. She avoided looking at Rob's face and his naked body by focusing on his neck and the pulse beating there, strong and steady. Her own heart danced wildly in her throat.

"I'm sorry."

"I'm afraid, Norah, that being sorry is not enough."

Rob's voice was low with heart-swelling danger. Norah cowered deeper into her corner and looked up at his face. The anger in his eyes had faded to a knowing gleam. Drops trickled from his wet black hair and glistened on his forehead. He wiped them away with the back of his hand and moved closer.

"I'll have to punish you for your disobedience."

He spread his legs and braced his hands on the shelf behind her, pinning her between his muscular sun-browned arms. Norah could smell the salt air on him, the soap. In his face, so man-handsome, so close to hers, she could see every line, every stray bristle of beard. She saw in his eyes the anticipation of some sweet revenge, and she felt her insides go soft.

"Punishment?" she heard herself whisper, "What sort of punishment?"

He smiled lazily. "Flogging," he murmured, bending toward her. "Irons . . ."

His lips brushed hers once and then again, as if to decide whether or not she was worth a proper kiss. Norah's heart lost its rhythm. She leaned back hard against the shelves, trying to maintain at least an appearance of reluctance.

"You mustn't do that." She wondered how she could speak with her breath so completely taken away.

Rob lifted his head and looked at her. Even in the shadows, his eyes glowed like coals on a hearth. "You spied on me without my britches. I'm entitled to take a few liberties with you."

He stood so close she could feel the heat and dampness radiating from his body. Norah reached back to steady herself against the shelves. Her own body pounded with energy. She had never felt so alive.

"You're being terribly silly," she said, floundering about for some gesture of resistance. "Mr. Burnham would quite disapprove."

"Hang Burnham." Rob's voice dropped to a growl, and he bent once more to find her mouth.

His lips were warm and sure and brazenly parted. They moved on hers languidly, taking slow, succulent bites, depleting her strength. When he took her about the waist, Norah moved into his arms, unthinking, as if it were the most natural thing in the world. His pungent saltwater scent, his rough male skin, saturated her senses. His hands moved on her back, pressing her close. When his tongue slid lightly across her parted lips, Norah sagged against him, feeling dizzy and compliant and quite wonderfully depraved. Softly, willingly, she kissed him back.

"Put your arms around me."

It was an urgent whisper. For an instant Norah didn't know where her arms were. Then she realized they lay crushed against his chest. She reached up to circle his neck, and Rob pulled her hard against him. His kiss swept her like fire. His tongue touched her lips and moved inside her mouth. Instead of struggling against his powerful grasp, his daring kisses, Norah clasped him tighter and answered his kisses with her own.

Too soon Rob pulled away. "That's enough, sweetheart." His words, barely a whisper, brushed her cheek. Norah felt his heart pounding against her chest. "You'd better let me go before we get into trouble."

Reluctantly Norah relaxed her grip, but she continued to rest against him, scarcely able to breathe for the crush of longing on her chest. Her lips burned from his kisses; her body throbbed with his warmth. Dazed, she brushed the hair from her forehead.

Rob lifted her chin and kissed her gently on the lips before setting her away from him. "You're a warm woman, Norah. A warm woman indeed." He smiled when he spoke, but his eyes burned to their very depths.

At his words, reality seeped back into Norah's mind with appalling clarity. She had compromised herself. How could her common sense have deserted her so completely? Suddenly the little pantry was stifling, and her mind felt thick with confusion.

"You mustn't think . . ." Norah said, scrambling to think of some way to reclaim her dignity. "You mustn't think me . . ." To her dismay, she could think of nothing to say. She fell utterly and disconcertingly mute.

A faint smile played on Rob's lips. "Mustn't think what?"

She had to make him understand that it was all a dreadful mistake, that she didn't do this sort of thing as a habit, that before last evening she'd never actually kissed a man at all. But she could think of no adequate way to clear up the misunderstanding, so she maintained her miserable silence.

Rob's smile turned shrewd and knowing. "What I think is that you'd better leave before Willie comes upon us and spreads the news all over the ship. Or before I'm tempted to make some more serious advances."

Rob reached behind her and opened the pantry door. With a gentle shove, he pushed Norah into the passageway. She backed away from him, wishing she could justify her behavior. But how could she justify to Rob what she couldn't explain to herself?

Turning, Norah hurried down the passageway to the main cabin.

Rob leaned against the pantry doorframe and watched her go. Well, well, he thought, Miss Norah Paige's calm waters certainly hid some turbulent seas. In bed with her, he'd be driving his ship in a whole gale.

Then he remembered who Norah was—a respectable young lady, Burnham's ward. He was supposed to be looking out for her welfare, not taking advantage of her tender feelings. Rob ran a hand over his bare chest and tried to feel ashamed. But all he could think of was how sweet she'd been, how truly eager.

"A word with you, Captain."

Rob glanced at Crawford, who had come out of his mate's quarters across from the pantry. "What is it, mister?"

The mate glanced about nervously. "In private, if you don't mind."

Rob saw tension in Crawford's grizzled face. His pale blue eyes were squinted nearly shut.

Puzzled, Rob nodded toward his cabin door. "Come along, then."

Once inside, Rob went to the cabinet and took out a clean shirt. He pulled it on and watched Crawford curiously. "What's on your mind, George?"

The mate shifted his feet. "She's Jody's girl, Captain," he said in a low mumble. "I thought you better know."

Rob's hands froze. A shock quivered through him right down to the soles of his feet. He stared at Crawford. "No," he said in a voice so low he could barely hear himself. "I don't believe it."

But even as he spoke, Rob knew it was true. In a horrible flash, he felt he'd known all along; in some corner of his mind he'd recognized the truth and chosen to ignore it.

"She told me," Crawford said.

Rob wiped a hand over his face to clear away his bewilderment. "She told you?"

Crawford jerked his head toward the partition. "She'll hear you, Captain."

Rob realized he was shouting. "She told you?" he repeated stupidly, this time in a loud whisper.

Crawford nodded. "I suspected it. I saw her once when she was a small thing. Came to a tavern after Jody. He'd had a go-round with his wife, and the girl was worried he'd leave and never come back." Crawford frowned. "She's grieving for him, Captain. I didn't mean to start her crying yesterday, but that's how it happened."

"My God." Rob turned away from the mate and laid his palms flat on the ceiling beam. Shock cut him so deeply he could barely breathe. "Burnham said she was from Salem," he said. "Jody's wife lived in Boston." As if that could make a difference, he thought, as if that small inconsistency could change this absurd joke of Providence, this bizarre twist of fate.

"Her mother's people are from Salem, Captain," Crawford said. "She took the girl back soon after she was born."

"Jesus."

Crawford nervously cleared his throat. "You going to tell her, Captain?"

Tell her? Rob tightened his fist until the knuckles showed white. Tell Norah? What could he tell her? That her father didn't die all those years ago, although he might as well have? Or should he tell her how Jody looked last time they'd met—wasted to a shadow, teeth gone, skin the color of lead? How would she feel to learn that her father preferred destroying himself to seeing her again?

Rob leaned his forehead against the beam. Every nerve in his body stung with guilt. "I concocted the lie she cries over, George," he said softly. "When I sent word back to Boston, I thought that would be the end of it."

Crawford made an impatient sound. "Stow it, Captain. It ain't your fault."

Platitudes offered Rob no comfort. In the space of a few seconds the past had swamped him like the rushing tide, and Norah had been snatched from him forever. As far as he was concerned, she might as well have been struck dead. But it was just as well. Hadn't he already decided he had no business getting involved with her?

"I won't tell her anything," he said to Crawford. "I'll de-liver her to London and forget her. She's better off without any of us." He took a long deep breath and expelled it in a rush. "She thinks he's dead. Maybe by now he is."

Crawford made no response. Rob watched the patches of sunlight on the floor move with the motion of the ship. He forgot the mate was in the cabin until Crawford said gently, "You all right, Captain?"

Rob nodded. "Fine, George. You'd better go."

When the door closed, Rob fell into his chair and ground his palms against his burning eyes. Damn you, Jody! he shouted in silent anguish. Look what you've done to me. Look what you've done to us all!

Nora pushed her spectacles up higher on her nose and busied herself with her embroidery. She'd started work on a length of Irish linen that would serve as a replacement for the cabin's dreary green baize table cover. But this project, like the others she'd begun on the voyage, seemed incapable of holding her interest. Now her mind was distracted by angry shouts coming from the foredeck where Rob was berating the crew for some transgression.

Alice, seated beside Norah in a cane-backed deck chair, cocked her head to one side and listened. "Good heavens. I can't imagine such swearing this side of hell. I wish I knew what was happening."

A chilly breeze rattled the tarpaulin shielding them from the sun. Despite the weather, Norah's face burned hot. She yanked her thread tight, poked the needle through the linen, and pricked her finger. "Damnation!" She sucked away the sting, studied the little puncture, and said curtly, "What happens between the officers and crew is none of our affair."

Alice laughed. "Oh, Norah. Aren't you curious?"

"Not a bit," Norah replied coldly. She had no need to be curious. She knew the reason for Rob's foul mood: it was entirely her fault. She had come upon him in his bath and embarrassed him before his men. Rob had taken his revenge on her, first by reducing her to harlotry in the pantry and then by virtually ignoring her at dinner. To reclaim his authority with the crew, he had to employ even more brutal measures.

Norah punched her needle hard through the linen. How she

wished she could shout and swear like a man! Instead, she had to wait with ladylike patience for her turmoil to abate.

"My, my," Alice commented with a wry smile that flashed her dimples and brightened her dark eyes. "You seem to be in as bad a temper as he is."

Norah removed her spectacles and glared at her friend. How could Alice, who had surely never entertained an unchaste thought in her life, possibly understand her own terrible jumble of emotions? Norah was furious at Rob, and yet she was half sick with disgraceful urges. Above all, she was thoroughly embarrassed. Last night's delicate peck on the lips had been seared from her memory by this morning's thorough, bone-crushing kisses. When Norah thought of what Rob had done to her—and what she'd done back to him—she nearly swooned with shame. Worst of all, she couldn't shake her yearning for more.

Norah threw down her embroidery and picked up her sketch pad. "If you'll excuse me," she said to Alice, not bothering to conceal her annoyance, "I'm going to the rail to do some sketching."

"Of course," Alice said merrily. "Don't let me keep you."

Norah's sketch of the *Orion* looking toward the bow was proceeding about as badly as everything else on this voyage, but sketching absorbed her interest more than embroidery. She leaned on the rail and peered forward into the breeze to capture the line of chicken coops at the break of the deck. She noticed that Rob's tirade was apparently finished. The men had drifted off to their various duties. The captain was nowhere to be seen.

Norah scratched her pencil angrily across the pad. Opium, she thought. He was an opium smuggler who wore lewd women's names on his arms. Dear heaven, what had happened to her good sense? Everything in Boston had been so easy, so clear-cut. Now frightening things were happening to her, things she could barely control. She'd meant to reform Rob . . . oh, she still would, if he was willing. But it seemed that he was pulling her down into depravity rather than allowing himself to be lifted from it. Norah snuffled miserably and, as further proof of her decline, wiped her nose on her sleeve.

"Sail ho!"

The cry floated down from the foremast top. Looking ahead, Norah saw all hands rushing to the bow. She squinted hard, barely making out a speck on the horizon. How very curious, she thought, wiping at her damp eyes, to meet a ship in the middle of the ocean.

She closed her sketch pad and prepared to rush forward with everyone else. Then she saw Rob on the quarterdeck with his spyglass and felt a renewed rush of misery and shame. Better she stay on the afterdeck with Alice, she thought, and watch from the rail.

At midafternoon, Norah heard Rob shout to Mr. Crawford that the vessel was the *Rajah* flying under English colors, most likely bound from Calcutta to Liverpool or London by way of the West Indies.

"I'll be hanged if Marsh isn't commanding her," Rob called to the mate. "Damned if I don't think we can catch her."

Norah, tired of straining her eyes at the rail, returned to Alice under the tarpaulin. She had just picked up her embroidery again when a young blue-eyed sailor named Janner appeared, cap in hand, his pale yellow hair flying in the breeze. Jan was bright and agreeable, and Rob had assigned him to look after Alice on those occasions when Norah was indisposed.

"Captain wants you midships," Jan said to Norah.

"Me?" Norah asked, suddenly seized with tension.

"If the captain bids, Norah, you must go along," Alice said. Then she said to Jan, "I don't suppose, Mr. Janner, you would care to sit with a lady."

"Those are my orders," Jan said with a grin. "He's a driver, the captain, forcing such unpleasant duty on a sailor."

Norah wondered why on earth Rob would suddenly request her presence. Probably he had some new plan to humiliate her. She set aside her embroidery, nervously straightened her bonnet, and hastened forward, determined to treat him with chilly restraint.

Rob stood at the break of the deck, his spyglass trained on the *Rajah*. His cap was pulled down over his forehead. The breeze whipped wayward dark curls about his ears.

Rob lowered the spyglass and motioned for Norah to come closer. "A ship under full sail is as rare a sight as you'll ever see," he said, thrusting the spyglass into her hands. "Do you know how to work one of these?"

Norah nodded. One of her most treasured gifts from her papa had been her own little spyglass. She'd used it constantly, scanning Salem Harbor, imagining every ship to be his.

"You won't see a ship with that much sail on her going into or out of port," Rob said, excitement in his voice, "and you certainly can't see it on your own vessel."

Norah watched him warily. He didn't seem to be teasing her. To her dismay, she felt a familiar tender stirring in her breast. Hurriedly she put the glass to her eye, focused, and managed to keep it still in her trembling hands, despite the hard, pounding thrusts of her heart.

The *Rajah* was a glorious sight. The ship rose out of the water, a great pyramid of white, reaching the clouds, dwarfing the hull. The sails curved full before the wind, holding so still they could have been carved from marble.

Norah held the glass until her arms tired. She handed it back to Rob with what she hoped was a formal smile. "Thank you," she said. "I'm glad I had the chance to see her."

As he took the spyglass, Rob's glance brushed Norah's face. Then he met her eyes directly. He regarded her for no more than an instant, but Norah glimpsed a barely checked frustration that nearly made her heart stop. She tried to see deeper, to find in his expression even the merest reflection of her own feelings, but the moment had passed. Rob lowered his eyes and again looked out to sea.

Norah glanced back at the *Rajah*, her throat tight and pounding. "You'll speak to her?" she asked faintly.

"Of course." Rob fastened the glass to his eye, all business. "I'd wager Elias Marsh is pacing his quarterdeck at this moment, fuming because he can't outrun our little brig."

He resumed his vigil, once again oblivious of her. Norah lingered a moment longer and then headed dejectedly aft.

Early that evening the *Rajah* ranged alongside the *Orion*, blocking the sun and casting the smaller vessel in shadow. The great ship was at least eight hundred tons, Rob said, more than twice the size of the brig. Norah led Alice to the rail and described the majesty of the massive Indiaman. The *Rajah*—with her teak and mahogany hull, her towering sails, the intricate gingerbread carving on the squared-off stern galleries—overwhelmed the *Orion*.

Rob sat on the taffrail with his speaking trumpet. "Ahoy, the *Rajah*!" he called. "Captain Marsh!"

"Who asks for him, sir! And for what purpose?" The *Rajah*'s captain did not sound pleased to be so hailed.

"Captain Mackenzie of the *Orion* out of Boston, bound for Liverpool and then Calcutta. Come along, Marsh, I've been chasing you all afternoon. I'm not about to let you get away now!"

"Rob Mackenzie, you sogering fool, why didn't you say so! Crowded your sails to beat us, eh? Well, heave to and lay aboard here. I've got a bottle of brandy that's been waiting two years for you."

Both vessels trimmed their sails and fell off the wind. The *Orion* lowered the jolly boat, and two hands sprang in to ferry the captain to his social call. Knowing that Rob might be hours at his brandy and cigars, Norah took Alice belowdecks, out of sight of the sunburned men in wide hats who stared silently down from the *Rajah*'s deck.

Chapter Six

ELIAS MARSH, A short, round, bearded man of fifty, motioned Rob to a seat in his spacious, well-appointed cabin.

"Living in the lap of luxury, I see, Marsh," Rob said as he settled into a deep leather chair and glanced around at the heavy mahogany furnishings and gleaming brass appointments.

The *Rajah*'s captain smiled as he poured a glass of brandy and slid it across the table to his guest. "I'd prefer the simplicity of your command, Captain. A little brig that can tack in a pint of water. You can keep these old tea wagons as far as I'm concerned." Marsh took a swallow of brandy and leaned back in his chair. "What's your cargo, Mackenzie?"

Rob explained that the *Orion* was loaded with raw cotton and lumber. After leaving the cargo in Liverpool, the brig would return to Boston under the command of the mate while Rob spent a few months in London. In October he would meet the *Orion* in Liverpool for a run to the Indies with ice and luxury goods to be dropped at Batavia and Calcutta.

"Ice!" Marsh exclaimed and laughed. "I never cease to be amazed at the ingenuity of you Americans. You've got all the Anglo-Indians buying iceboxes, icing their drinks, buttering their toast."

Rob smiled. "This time out I'll try to sell to the Dutch in Batavia. We'll be carrying close to a hundred tons of the stuff.

I'll even consign some cheeses to help persuade the Hollanders to take my cargo. You may laugh, Elias, but ice has saved Boston's East India commerce. What with all the factories in New England, the American market for Indian cotton is ruined."

"I'm not laughing," Marsh replied good-naturedly. "I never laugh when a man turns a profit." He snipped off the tip of his Dos Amygos, went through the ritual of sniffing it and studying it, then applied a taper and drew contentedly.

As the two men smoked in silence, Rob thought how quiet and private was the world of an East Indiaman's skipper. In a way he envied Marsh his comforts. But the Englishman was remote from his men and would have been out of form joining the crew. Rob decided the intimacy of the *Orion* suited him.

"You're finished with opium?" Marsh asked.

Rob glanced at the *Rajah*'s captain, who watched him with small, keen eyes. Rob had first met Marsh when the English captain transported a cargo of opium from Calcutta to Rob's receiving ship at Lintin Island. After engaging him in a heated argument about storage charges and the broker's commission, Rob found he liked the man enormously.

"I'll see what the price of Turkish is in London," Rob replied. "The harvest should be coming in August, so by September I'll have a good idea if it's worth the investment."

"The opium market's changing fast, Captain," Marsh said. "Since the British started carrying Turkish, some of the smaller American houses are withdrawing from commerce with China altogether."

Rob shrugged. "It'll be a few years before the American trade in opium diminishes significantly. By that time my firm will be out of the Indies altogether."

Marsh raised his brows in surprise. "Out of the Indies? Well, that's a surprise. What are your plans then?"

Rob stared soberly at the glowing end of his cigar and shrugged. He thought of Burnham's offer. A partnership. Traveling in Europe. A sweet wife at home.

"Settling with a wife, I'd wager," Marsh concluded with a smile. "One of those pretty young things I saw on your deck? What sad news for the ladies of Calcutta."

Rob said nothing for a moment. He drew on his cigar and

watched the smoke curl toward the beams. "No, Marsh. I've no plans to marry."

"Then you may find this bit of news of interest. Sir Anthony Downing died in Barrackpore. His wife is now a widow, a rather wealthy one at that. You were quite well acquainted with her as I recall, Mackenzie."

Rob avoided the captain's shrewd glance. "I was acquainted with both Sir Anthony and Lady Downing. I'm sorry to hear of his death. I'll write a letter of condolence at once."

"Of course, Captain." Marsh inclined his head but continued to grin. "No offense intended."

"None taken, sir," Rob replied.

Amanda, he thought, and couldn't help but smile. She'd thrived in Calcutta like a tropical flower, scandalizing the Anglo-Indian community with her appetite for younger men, while the rest of Britain's fair sex withered and turned yellow with fever. Their brief affair had been finished for a decade, but Rob would always consider Amanda a friend.

"I've seen your mate, Jody Paige," Marsh said.

Rob took a great gulp of brandy, held the burning liquid in his mouth, then swallowed, searing his throat. He shoved his glass at Marsh, who promptly refilled it.

"Word is, he's shipping on the opium clippers that ply their trade up the coast of China. Dangerous business. Those vessels return from their trading loaded with specie. They're sitting ducks for pirates."

"Can't say as I care," Rob said. He fought the urge to crush the glass in his hand.

Marsh watched Rob closely. "The man's a slave to opium. Not a pretty sight. He takes his pay and disappears into the filthy dens for days at a time. It's a pity, a good man like that gone to waste. He seemed exceptional. Intelligent, witty. Why did he never try for his master's papers?"

Rob stared into the amber liquid in his tumbler. He felt the prickle of sweat start all over his body. "Jody was a sailor," he said quietly. "The best sort of seaman. He loved his work."

"Well, now he seems bound to kill himself," Marsh said.

"He chose his hell." Rob took another gulp of brandy. A pleasant numbness settled over his limbs and brain, keeping his rising anguish at bay.

Marsh smiled. "All right, Captain, no more hard news. Now tell me why a rogue like you should be blessed with a cargo of two pretty ladies, while all I have aboard is a hold full of cotton and some foul-smelling lascars."

Rob was drunk when he returned to the *Orion*. He managed to get the vessel under way before stumbling down the companionway to his bunk. The brandy was wearing off, leaving a foul taste in his mouth and a sickening ache in his head. But worse, it had unleashed all the desire and desolation he'd been struggling so hard to master since he'd learned that Norah was Jody's daughter. Unbidden thoughts of her swam through his mind. He remembered the feel of her in his arms, the taste of her mouth, the glow in her eyes. He thought of her bustling primly about Miss Peabody's bookstore, he thought of her earnest attempt to reform him. What would it be like, he wondered, to share her life? What would it be like to have a home, to father children, to be loved by one woman for a lifetime?

A home? A man like him? Rob stared bitterly into the darkness. What did he know of homes and families? He'd been weaned on the brutality of the factory and his uncle's cruel beatings. He'd been raised to manhood by Jody Paige, who trained him in the ways of the sea, who taught him that the happiest man was the man with no claims on him.

Rob thought of Jody, ruined by opium, barely alive in Calcutta, abandoned by the two people who had loved him best. What happiness had Jody found, for all his free-souled principles?

Jody. Rob closed his eyes and threw an arm over his face. He wanted to hide behind closed lids and feel nothing. But he couldn't shut out memory and despair, loneliness and guilt. They throbbed and burned in his soul, raw as a wound. He thought of Norah, of being honest with her. But she would never understand, nor would she forgive. The truth would crush her, and she would surely despise him.

At last Rob slept. He dreamed dreams with no images, and in his dreams, a familiar, haunting presence came to him. He woke with a start, sweating, his heart pounding. His mother. He'd dreamed of her again. Not an image, but an emotion, a vivid longing for something lost. In all these years, he had not

outgrown her, that sense of some place back in time, a safe
and happy place, beyond memory.

Rob sat up, feeling groggy and disoriented, and rubbed his
eyes. *A factory whore.* That's what his uncle had told him.
Mary Cuthpert, a worthless woman who coupled with all
manner of men, spawned a bastard, and died young. "She
cared nothing for you," his uncle had said. "She tried to rid
herself of you before you were born."

Rob had believed his uncle's words. He'd accepted his state
as a child of shame. But then he would hear certain sounds—
the swish of cloth, the tapping of heels on the floor, a woman's
voice raised in song—and a sharp sense of the past would
steal over him, bringing with it a flush of long-vanished happiness.

Happiness. A child's wishful thinking, Rob told himself. A
child's fantasy that continued to haunt the man.

Rob got up from his bunk and staggered on deck. He'd
missed the setting of the midwatch, and it was now almost two
in the morning. Crawford took a look at him and told him to
go below, but Rob stayed at the taffrail, letting the fresh sea air
clear his head and wash the stink of cigar smoke from his
clothes.

He wondered how Crawford would react to Marsh's news.
George and Jody's relationship had always puzzled Rob. It
seemed to be a comradeship gone wrong. The two men had
sailed together for years, but rarely spoke, as if held by a bond
of silent hostility. Rob would never have dreamed of asking
the reticent Crawford a personal question, but once he'd asked
Jody about his friendship with George.

Jody had shrugged and replied tersely, "Crawford's a
strange bird, Rob."

Rob found the mate returning from the lookout at the bow.
"Marsh saw Jody before he departed Sands Head." Rob
kicked at the brass banding on the quarterdeck steps. His chest
felt tight and panicky. "He's running mud up the coast."

Crawford spat and wiped his mouth. For a moment the two
men stood silent.

"Christ, George," Rob said softly. "Why didn't he die?"

In the darkness he could feel Crawford's eyes on him, cool
and appraising. "If you figure he's dead, then he's dead, Cap-

tain. You'd best put him out of your mind, and that girl of his, too."

Rob folded himself onto the step and ground his fist into his palm. "She means nothing to me." He clenched his jaw hard, willing his words to be true.

"Not from what I see," Crawford said. "Begging the captain's pardon, you've got the itch like I ain't never seen it in you. Now, there's two things you can do: forget you ever seen that girl, or if you want her so bad, tell her the truth and marry her. It ain't your style to use a girl like her for sport."

Rob dropped his aching head into his hands. "I can't tell her, George."

"Then get control of yourself." Impatience crept into Crawford's voice. "You'd think you was the first man who wanted a woman he couldn't have."

The mate turned and tramped forward again, disappearing from view beyond the dark shape of the boat.

Norah woke with a start to a violently pitching cabin. She lay still for a moment, uncertain where she was. Not until she sat up did she realize she'd fallen out of bed and was lying on the cabin floor. She got to her feet and looked out the stern window. The sea was gray and furious. Mean white-topped waves churned in all directions.

Willie knocked on the door and struggled into the cabin with a big tin pitcher of water. He grinned cheerfully. "Big blow. Captain say big blow coming."

Alice was sitting up, looking ill and frightened. "Well, I hope it blows away," she said, clinging to the side of the bed. "My stomach feels as if it's ready to part company with the rest of me."

Alice elected to remain in her bed. Norah dressed and breakfasted alone on sea biscuit and cold tea that sloshed about in her cup.

Rob came down, his oilskins wet from spray. "It's too rough for you and Alice on deck," he said.

"Is it a hurricane?" Norah asked. The lamp over the table swung vigorously. The groaning timbers and thumping sea forced her to shout.

Rob shook his head. "Not quite, but she's a handful. We've

got a foretopsail about to split and a tricky sea. I'll send a couple of men below to put up your deadlights. You'll have a tedious day in a dark cabin, but under no circumstance are you to light a lamp." He started back up the companionway. "Make sure things are secure in your cabin. Then climb back into bed. That's the safest place for you and Alice."

In the cabin, Alice was moaning with each yaw of the ship. Norah packed away hairbrushes and shoes, secured the washbasin and ewer, and locked their scattered books into the caged bookcase. Mr. Brisker, a wiry and wrinkled old salt, and Mr. Denny, a young, freckle-faced seaman, arrived to put up the deadlights. The shutters kept the heavy seas from washing in through the windows. Except for a few cracks of light, they left the cabin in darkness.

Norah took a last anxious look out the window at the wild sea before the deadlights were secured. Mr. Brisker caught her eye. "Seen worse 'n this, that's sure," he said, banging the shutter into place. "After ten year on a spouter out of New Bedford, I seen some real weather. Naw, this ain't nothin', miss. Nothin' at all."

Mr. Denny grinned. "That's right, miss. Just a little breeze to give you ladies a chance to stay tucked up for a day. Hope them fancy beds is bolted to the floor. Myself, I'd feel safer in a hammock."

Norah imagined the sleep sofas, the table and chair, and the little writing table flying about the cabin. "All bolted fast, Mr. Denny."

After the sailors left, Norah felt her way to her sea chest. She peeled off her clothes while balancing herself against the vessel's motion, and put on a warm nightdress and her cashmere shawl. Then she lay down on her bunk to wait out the storm. The violence of the brig's motion increased. Someone banged on their door and hollered that the captain ordered them to keep to their bunks. Norah was sure the big blow was turning into something worse, but when she yelled the question through the door, she heard no answer.

Norah clung to her bed as the bucking vessel strained and strove to throw her to the floor. Listening to the heaving groans of the *Orion*'s timbers and the pounding and shouting on the deck above, Norah wondered how the men could keep from being pitched into the sea. Her papa used to say that at times like these, a good sailing master earned his pay. She felt an urge to mount the deck and see how Rob was handling the emergency, but her curiosity was snuffed out by an earsplitting crash.

Alice let out a frightened yelp.

"The men have seen worse than this," Norah shouted, remembering Mr. Brisker's assurance, but she closed her eyes and offered a long, fervent prayer for the safety of the men above. Then she offered a special prayer for Rob. She promised God that if he was spared, she would not forsake him. She would renew her efforts to show him the error of his ways, no matter what the sacrifice to herself.

The storm seemed to grow worse by the hour, tossing the brig about like a cork in a waterfall. The *Orion* struggled up one side of a wave, then paused and shuddered before descending into the trough, leaving Norah's stomach spinning with sickness and fear. She hated lying still, helpless and useless, monitoring every leap and tremor of the ship, hoping the motion was easing, but being forced to admit it was not.

She and Alice didn't speak, but used all their energy to hang on to their beds. Suddenly Alice cried out, "Norah! I'm wet!"

Shivering, Norah stumbled toward Alice and fell in a frightened heap on her bed. Water was coming through the seams in the deadlights. She reached out to feel the window seat. It was drenched. She pulled Alice close, for comfort and warmth.

"Come over on my bed," she shouted. "I'll get some more blankets!"

"Rob said not to leave our bunks!" Alice cried.

"I know exactly where to find blankets—in the cupboard in the main cabin."

"Oh, Norah! Be careful!"

Norah staggered to the door. The main cabin was pitch black. No light came from the skylight overhead, and it occurred to Norah that it must be covered, just as the windows were secured. For a moment she thought of searching for Willie, but with all hands called, the steward as well as the cook would be working on deck.

The ship climbed up a wave, and Norah braced herself

against the wall. Water spilled down the companionway through the closed hatch. It rushed over her bare feet, numbing them. For a terrifying moment, Norah thought of being sealed up below. The freezing water would rise higher and higher until she and Alice drowned. Norah scolded the thought from her mind and grasped the edge of the sideboard. Her hand knocked against the crystal decanter and glasses, secure in their holder. She had just bent down to feel for the cupboard where the extra blankets were stored when the ship gave a violent twisting lurch. Norah clung tight to the sideboard as the cabin pitched and rolled dizzily. She heard a crash overhead and looked up. She saw a faint light. The next yaw of the vessel brought water pouring down through the shattered skylight.

Dear Lord, the entire sea was coming in!

Norah groped toward the safety of her cabin, the blankets forgotten. Footing was treacherous on the heaving floor, slippery and ankle-deep in seawater. Norah spread her legs and bent her knees, trying vainly to maintain her balance. Darkness and panic closed in on her. She no longer knew in which direction her door lay.

Suddenly the cabin floor bucked like an angry bull and the wall disappeared from beneath Norah's hands. She teetered for a moment, then felt herself falling. She groped wildly, futilely, for a support. The next lunge of the floor sent her flying. She screamed. For a sickening eternity, she seemed to travel through the air until the floor crashed against her. Pain exploded in her shoulder and cheek, and the hard, biting edges of what felt like glass scraped her chest and stomach. Powerless, she began to slide. The tilt of the vessel and the water on the floor carried her along like the tide driving her onto a beach. Water filled her mouth. She tried to reach out and break the inevitable collision, but her arms were pinned beneath her. For an instant she saw a great burst of light and then only darkness.

"Need any help, Brisker?" Rob shouted at the helmsman wrestling with the wheel, his face obscured by his oilskin hat.

"Nah, sir, I got 'er, but if you could ring six bells, sir. I can't spare a hand."

The shrieking wind grabbed at Rob as he made his way to the binnacle and stared at the compass. They were five points off their course in a feeding gale. The wind was close to fifty knots and working its way around to the north. The *Orion* was drifting rapidly south and west. Rob knew if the storm kept up, they'd be halfway back to Boston by the time she blew herself out.

He'd been trying to maintain his course by keeping the brig under close-reefed main topsail and reefed foresail. Now, seeing the *Orion* losing her battle, he decided to hold his latitude and keep the vessel riding safely by lying to under storm staysails. Better to shorten sail and make no headway than risk broaching to in the trough of a running sea. He'd order Denny back on the helm with Brisker. The big fellow was strong enough to lay the course in a hurricane.

Grasping the rail, Rob pushed forward over the slippery deck, his shoulders hunched against the wind's fury. The rain drove itself into his face like fine needles. He found Crawford and relayed his orders. The men swarmed aloft to take in sail. Glimpsing Willie's slight form, swathed in oilskins, Rob reached out and grasped him by the shoulder. The steward looked up and grinned.

Rob leaned close. "Go below and see about the missies."

Willie had just struggled off toward the companionway when the wind blasted the brig with the fury of a full hurricane, heeling her down, sending the crashing sea completely over her. The men on deck grabbed at any safe hold. Aloft, the masts tilted almost parallel to the sea. Rob clung to the mainmast and watched the galley's tin roof fly off toward the scuppers. He cursed himself for his delay in giving his orders.

He grabbed at Crawford. "Denny!" he yelled. "To the helm!"

Crawford mouthed words to the effect that Denny was already aft, and Rob fought his way back to the helm where he found Brisker and Denny struggling to master the wheel. Sea after sea crashed over the brig, which staggered valiantly out of each burial. Rob wiped the rain and spray from his face and trained his eyes aloft. The men hung on the yards, fighting the wind to haul in canvas. He remembered the first time he'd rid-den a yard in a storm, his fingers numb, nails torn away by the furious sails. He'd been determined to be brave for Jody.

Once the changes aloft were accomplished, Rob ordered Denny to lay a hold. The helm came down, and the *Orion* swung nearer the wind.

Rob went forward to assess the damage. He had hardly gained the quarterdeck when someone tugged urgently at his sleeve. He turned to see Willie, hat gone, water coursing down his hair and face. His mouth was going, jabbering nonsense. A hard, choking fear climbed from Rob's gut to his throat. He grabbed Willie's shoulder and shook him.

"Speak some sense, damn you!" he hollered against the tumult.

"The missy!" Willie cried. "Missy Norah dead!"

Chapter Seven

THE LIGHT DREW Norah close to consciousness, but she didn't open her eyes. The pain in her head and shoulder ebbed and flowed in rhythm with the freezing water that swept back and forth over her body. As she drifted toward wakefulness, the pain no longer receded, but gathered and swelled to a constant, excruciating agony. Norah fought to sink once again into oblivion, but the light and the noise and the prickling of her half-numbed body forced her farther out of her blessed, painless cocoon.

"Norah!"

She opened her eyes to protest the intrusion. Rob bent over her, water from his oilskin hat dripping on her face. He wiped the water from her eyes. His hand came away red with blood.

"Put your arm around me," he commanded.

Whimpering, Norah clutched at his slippery wet sleeve, then slowly slid her arm up to his neck. Rob worked his hands beneath her and swung her out of the water. He carried her into his cabin, staggering to keep his balance as the ship heaved beneath his feet. Every jolt shot pain through Norah's shoulder. She began to sob and shiver from fear and cold and the relentless pain.

Willie, his eyes wide, his wet hair plastered to his head, held a lantern, which swung crazily with the movements of the ship. Rob laid Norah gently on the floor, kept dry by the bulwark that separated the compartment from the main cabin. He placed his hand firmly on her middle to keep her from sliding with the motion of the brig.

"Don't touch me," Norah cried as Rob pulled her soaking nightdress open and ran his fingers over her left shoulder, the source of her agony. "Please. It hurts so much."

Rob didn't respond, and Norah realized she was thinking the words, not speaking them. She tried again, but the persistent racket of the storm drowned out her plea. Rob took a cup from Willie. Planting his knee on Norah's stomach to hold her still, he raised her head and held the cup to her lips.

"Swallow," he said. His face was drawn, his dark eyes pitiless and intent.

Norah took the draft and gagged on its bitter taste. Rob laid her head down and sat back on his heels. Then, leaning close, he said, "I can't wait any longer. I've got to set this shoulder before it swells."

Norah was feeling mercifully groggy when Rob tore her nightdress down the front and away from her arm, leaving her naked to the waist. She tried to speak but had no strength. Willie knelt on her legs and pinned her right shoulder and wrist firmly to the floor. Norah couldn't understand why she was being restrained. Then Rob wedged his knee into her armpit, laid hold of her left arm, and began to pull. The realization of what was happening crashed down on Norah with a sudden fury. As Rob's steady strength tore her arm from her body, she heard the grinding of bones, felt the blinding agony. Her cries of protest became screams. And then, blessedly, she swirled again into darkness.

Norah awoke to the pungent odor of ointment and a cold wet cloth across her throbbing forehead. Her shoulder beat with a dull pain. She lay warm beneath a blanket, her soaking nightdress gone. The hard floor rocked from side to side, but at least it was dry. Suddenly someone pulled the blanket back and Norah realized with a start that she was completely naked.

Her eyes fluttered open. "No," she whispered weakly and reached out to reclaim the blanket's protection.

Rob grasped her wrist. He had discarded his oilskin hat, and his hair stood on end like a clump of weeds. His face was lined with fatigue and worry.

"You fell on glass, Norah. Now, let me do my work."

Norah squeezed her eyes shut, trying to hide her nakedness in the darkness of her mind. But a hot flush seemed to follow Rob's fingers as they worked their way from her chest to her knees, picking out glass, rubbing stinging salve into raw skin. Norah tried to hold her breath to still the rise and fall of her breasts. She moved her hand to her thighs, hoping to cover herself, but Rob brushed it aside. Biting her lips, Norah willed herself to become invisible.

Rob talked to her while he worked. He reported that Alice had been badly frightened, but was holding up bravely. He told Norah she must stay in his bunk until the storm ended, and he would look in on her whenever he could get away from the deck.

Norah kept her lips and eyes closed tight and tried to ignore his touch. Despite her efforts, she became even more aware of his fingers. She floated in and out of wakefulness, listening to the rhythm of his voice. Even in her groggy state, she realized his hands upon her felt pleasantly soothing.

When he was finished with the salve, Rob laid her arm across her chest and bound it tight to her body, immobilizing her shoulder. He pulled the blanket into place, and Norah opened her eyes. Willie grinned down at her. Norah cringed anew, until she remembered that in Willie's island society, naked women were nothing out of the ordinary.

Rob lifted her into his arms and laid her on his bunk. "I haven't got time to bind your shoulder properly, so you must lie perfectly still. I gave you a small dose of laudanum. It will ease the pain and help you sleep."

Norah nodded, her eyelids again growing heavy.

"I'm going to strap you onto the bunk so you don't roll off. I'll be down to check on you later. And, Norah"—his hand rested for a moment on her cheek—"promise me you won't try to get up."

"Promise," Norah whispered. As she drifted off to sleep, she thought she felt his lips on hers, but when she opened her eyes, the cabin was dark and he was gone.

She dozed, continually aware of her throbbing shoulder and

the unceasing motion of the *Orion*. Rob came and went through the endless night. At each visit, he appeared more exhausted—eyes red-rimmed, voice hoarse from shouting and fatigue, beard sprouting in earnest—and still the storm didn't wane.

Rob put her into a clean nightdress, which he fetched from her cabin, and helped her with the chamber pot. To Norah's relief, his exhaustion apparently left him oblivious of her body and its functions. His mind seemed to remain on deck, or asleep, and Norah sometimes had to shout a question twice to get his attention. It was obvious he was dead on his feet. He'd told her that all of the men had snatched a few hours below, so when he stumbled through the door after what surely had been more than two days of wakefulness, Norah insisted he close his eyes.

"You're of no use to anyone in such a state," she said. "Why, *I'm* more alert than you are. Surely Mr. Crawford can see to things."

"Insubordination," Rob said hoarsely as he cast off his oil-skins and knelt beside her. "Usurping command by giving orders to the captain." He tried to smile, but succeeded in producing only a tired grimace. As he bent over her shoulder, Norah brushed her fingers across his cheek, rough with whiskers. Rob didn't seem to notice.

He inspected her bound shoulder and the gash on her forehead. He swabbed the wound with a burning liquid and covered it with adhesive plaster and a bandage.

"How is Alice?" Norah asked.

"Bored and complaining," Rob replied in his hoarse whisper. He tightened the straps that held her. "But determined to survive."

Norah saw his eyes close for a moment, then snap open. She touched his shoulder. "Lay your head down. A few moments of rest will sharpen your judgment."

Rob looked at her, closed his eyes, and was asleep before his head reached the pillow. His knees remained on the floor, his arm thrown across Norah's hips. He was so silent he might have been dead, except for the rise and fall of his back as he breathed. Norah moved her hand cautiously from his back to his neck, damp with sweat and warm with fatigue. She rubbed the tight cords between his collar and curls, taking a guilty pleasure in her daring caress. He didn't stir. Emboldened, she ran her fingers through his thick, springy hair. His scalp felt moist and hot, like a baby's. Turning her head, Norah touched his forehead with her lips.

She felt a quiet delight, holding him. Perhaps it was the dose of laudanum or the bump on her head, but for the moment Rob's shortcomings seemed to fade into insignificance. Norah could only think of how brave he was, how capable. He had set her shoulder and tended her cuts. He had saved her life. He had stripped her bare and rubbed her all over with salve.

Norah imagined his eyes appraising her with desire. With a delicious shiver, she recalled their dalliance in the pantry, the raw power of his embrace, the hungry kisses. She thought of his hardness pressing against her body. At the time she'd chosen not to think of that part of their encounter. Only in the vaguest way did Norah understand the nature of a man's desire, and the idea of it had always been rather frightening. But now, lying on his bunk and holding Rob in her arms, the thought of what he had wanted made Norah's insides feel soft and yielding.

"Dearest Rob," she whispered, and kissed his forehead again.

Suddenly the cabin door flew open and banged hard against the wall. Mr. Crawford, holding a lantern, his oilskins glistening, stood in the doorway, staring at the scene before him.

Norah's arm tightened protectively about Rob. "Is there an emergency on deck, Mr. Crawford?" she asked as the mate drew closer.

Mr. Crawford shook his head. "Storm's dying down a bit, that's all. Wondered where he'd got to." He paused. "You feeling well, miss?"

"Much better, thank you."

Crawford braced himself on the overhead beam and looked embarrassed. "Let me take the captain to the mate's quarters, miss. It don't look right him lying there like that."

"No," Norah said firmly. "He's fine right here."

Crawford scratched his whiskery chin and shifted his feet, obviously discomfited at speaking to a woman in bed while his captain lay sprawled across her. Norah stared back defiantly. Rob was her charge now. She would not be hampered by silly social conventions.

"Captain Mackenzie is exhausted," she said. "He must get some rest. Undisturbed."

Crawford looked skeptical. "Guess I'll go along, then," he said. "Mind if I douse the light? Dangerous to have it lit belowdecks in such a blow."

The cabin faded into darkness. Norah rested her cheek against Rob's hair and closed her eyes, feeling a precious contentment. Drowsy with carnal thoughts, she waited for sleep to take her.

When Norah awoke, the sun was shining, the deadlights were down, and the *Orion* was rolling gently like a huge wooden cradle. Except for the ache in her shoulder, the endless night might have been no more than a bad dream. She glanced around the cabin. On Rob's desk, his sextant rested like a great paperweight. The brass chronometer gleamed on its gimballed stand. Rob's books lay in tumbled disarray on the shelves behind the cage.

The door latch lifted and hinges squeaked. Norah looked at the door, hoping to see Rob. But it was Willie who stuck his head in and grinned. "Missy awake? Missy hungry?"

Norah shifted in the bunk, wincing as she moved her sore shoulder. "Yes, Willie, I'm very hungry." Indeed, she was starving. She couldn't remember when she had last eaten.

"I get food," Willie said. "First you wash."

He limped into the cabin with a pitcher of water. He filled the basin and helped Norah sit up, piling pillows behind her back. She managed to splash her cheeks and eyes using one hand. After brushing her teeth, she leaned back and asked for Alice.

"Missy in her cabin. Captain say no see now. You rest. Tomorrow maybe." He hurried to the door. "I get food."

Willie returned bearing a tray of coffee, pancakes, ham, and a rather shriveled orange. He set the tray on the desk and bustled to the bunk. He smoothed the linen and blanket and straightened the cloth that bound Norah's head. She tolerated his fussing, even when he arranged the collar of her night-dress.

"What are you doing, Willie?" Norah asked, puzzled by his attentions.

"Captain come," he explained, grinning, and slipped away.

Rob ducked through the doorway, his handsome face shaved and reasonably rested. Norah's heart quickened with happiness.

"I'm going to stand over you while you eat," he said, taking the tray from the desk and placing it on her lap. He drew up a chair next to the bunk. "Dislocated shoulders and banged heads require plenty of food."

Norah reached up to smooth her hair, hoping she looked presentable, and touched the bandage on her head. "Tell me how long it's been since I fell. And tell me how things are on deck."

"It's been three nights. You've slept nearly around the clock. We're still under reefed topsails, but the decks are squared off, and each man has had a watch below and an extra tot of rum. They're looking lively again."

"I might say the same about you," Norah said, and then blushed. "How much damage was done?" she asked quickly.

Rob smiled wanly. "Aside from a few pinched fingers, the mainmast, the fore-topsail, and the galley roof, you're our only casualty." He shifted his broad shoulders and glanced down at his fingers, laced together between his knees. "Willie found you in nearly half a foot of water. He thought you were dead." Rob's voice was still husky, and for a moment he looked exhausted again. "Why you didn't drown, I don't know."

"Well, I'm fine now," Norah said, feeling herself growing pink again. He cared for her; she could tell from the worried look of him. And the nervous tension she'd once felt in Rob's company had magically disappeared. She felt something different now, something bolder and deeper and quite wonderfully compelling. The thoughts she'd entertained while he slept against her during the storm came back to her with breathtaking clarity.

Norah happily turned her attention to her breakfast. While she ate, Rob told her about the storm. He said the *Orion* had been blown so far south and west that they'd added at least four days' sailing time to Liverpool. The news didn't bother Norah. She discovered she was no longer in a hurry to end this voyage.

Rob stood up. "When you finish eating, I'll get rid of that jury rig I put on you the other night and bind you up properly. I'll take Alice on deck for a stroll now and get her settled with Janner. He'll look after her until you're well enough to go up top."

"And when will that be?"

"A few days. Don't hurry things, Norah. And don't try to get out of bed alone." Rob paused. "Above all, don't let Willie try any of his potions on you. He'll concoct all sorts of brews and pastes that he'll swear will have you hale in no time. Leave the doctoring to me, understand?"

Norah smiled. "Yes, Captain."

After Rob left, Norah tried to clean her plate, but her stomach quickly felt full. Setting aside the tray, she threw back the covers and swung her feet to the floor. She cried out from the effort. Her entire body felt stiff and sore. Gingerly she eased herself upright and worked her way unsteadily across the cabin toward the mirror affixed to the teakwood paneling.

Norah lifted her free arm to arrange her hair around the bandage, but as she stepped before the mirror, her hand froze over her head. For a moment she felt faint, not from her injuries, but from the sight that confronted her in the glass. Her skin was as pale as paste, and her hair had snarled into impossible knots. A scratch carved a red line across her left cheek, and a large brown scab had crusted along the length of her nose. But none of that mattered compared to the unsightly greenish purple bruises that surrounded her eyes. They made her look like a raccoon, or worse, a corpse.

Norah gaped at her reflection, unable to look away, powerless to repair the damage. One-handed, she couldn't even brush her tangled hair. She opened her nightdress, took one look at her body, and groaned. She was covered with scrapes and bruises, as if she'd taken the worst of a grogshop brawl.

By the time she crawled back into bed, Norah's good spirits had vanished. No amount of scolding about the wickedness of vanity could console her for her dreadful appearance.

When Rob returned with his strips of binding cloth, she greeted him quietly, her face averted. He removed the tray of half-eaten breakfast and sat down on the bunk. Taking her chin in his fingers, he turned her face. "Did you get out of bed?" he demanded.

Norah kept her eyes lowered, wishing she could twist her battered face away from his sight.

Taking her silence as an admission of guilt, Rob exploded. "Jesus, woman! Won't you listen to me? If you'd stayed in your bed during the storm as I told you, none of this would have happened. My orders are for your safety, not for my own amusement."

"I look awful!" Norah wailed.

"For God's sake, you're alive! Isn't that enough? You're banged up, but not seriously hurt. Now stop behaving like a child."

Norah sat in quiet misery as Rob pulled her nightdress down over her shoulders and unfastened the silk neckcloth he had used to bind her. Glancing at her shoulder, yellow and swollen, Norah shuddered. She arranged her injured arm across her bosom, not so much to preserve her modesty as to conceal the ugly bruises from Rob's gaze. For good measure, she crossed her good right arm on top of her left.

Rob gently pulled her arms away and spoke in a kinder voice. "Pretend I'm Alice's doctor. What's his name?"

"Dr. Shattuck," Norah said dismally.

"That's it. Pretend I'm Dr. Shattuck. I'm sure he's examined you once or twice."

"Dr. Shattuck has never . . ." Norah began. "I mean, he only . . . I was never undressed."

Rob laughed. "If Shattuck examines ladies without removing their clothing, then perhaps I'm better acquainted with the female form than he is."

A shaft of jealousy thrust itself into Norah's heart. "I suppose you are," she said, her mood suddenly precarious. "Harriet's and Rosa's forms in particular."

Rob laid her injured arm across her ribs and began winding strips of wet cloth from her shoulder to her right side. Norah kept her eyes away from his face. She didn't want to see his expression as he studied her bare breasts with their hideous display of bruises. He probably found her repulsive. Her head was throbbing again, and the ache in her shoulder was worse.

"Who the devil are Harriet and Rosa?"

"Your women," Norah snapped. "The ones tattooed on your arm."

Rob suspended his winding and looked down at his arms, bared to the elbow. "These girls?" He pointed to his tattoos.

"Yes, them." To Norah's dismay, her lips began to tremble.

Rob gave a shout of laughter. "My God, you're jealous."

"I'm not!" Norah retorted. "I don't care in the least!"

But she did care. Never in her life had Norah experienced such a sting of jealousy. All she could think of was his other women, women who would never permit him to see them with bruised eyes or a battered body or hair like a rat's nest. Rob removed their nightdresses for purposes other than binding an ugly yellow shoulder. Norah blinked away tears of frustration and longed for her stable life in Boston, where her ups and downs were mild and easily managed.

Rob resumed his wrapping, an annoying grin on his face. After a minute he said, "They're ships, Norah, not women."

Norah stared at him. "Ships?"

Rob nodded. "The *Rosa Sanchez* was the first ship I sailed on. The *Harriet B.* was my first command."

Norah's face grew hot. "Oh," she said.

"Feel better?"

Norah didn't feel better. She felt foolish, which only added to her misery.

Rob finished trussing her until she was discreetly covered with yards of cotton, which he said must be kept wet to reduce the swelling. He pulled a fresh nightdress over her head and worked her right arm through the sleeve. Norah squirmed and struggled under the covers to pull the gown down over her hips and thighs.

"Here, put your arm around my neck," Rob said.

She clung to him, stifling a cry of pain as he grasped her waist and lifted her. With his free hand, he reached beneath the blanket to pull the gown down to her knees. He held her snugly against his chest and repositioned the pillows behind her back. His shoulder felt hard and warm under the coarse cloth of his shirt. Norah released him reluctantly and he eased her back on the pillows.

"I think those bruises become you, Miss Norah," Rob said, scrutinizing her face. "And that scratch brightens up a rather pale complexion. To tell the truth, I find you quite lovely."

Norah gave him a sheepish smile. "I'm sorry I'm causing you so much trouble."

A thoughtful expression replaced Rob's grin. He leaned forward and kissed the tip of her nose. "Thank God you were so slightly injured," he said softly, "and so easily repaired."

He stood, put his cap on, and in two strides was gone from the cabin.

Chapter Eight

THAT NIGHT NORAH was exhausted and restless. Her shoulder ached too much to sleep, and the wet binding didn't add to her comfort. Rob refused to give her more laudanum, but he poured her some brandy. Norah succumbed gratefully to its warm glow. In the shadowy light of the cabin, she lay against her mound of pillows, clutching her tumbler, and watched Rob examine some business papers at his desk.

Norah had all but forgotten that in addition to his duties as captain and chaperon to herself and Alice, Rob was in charge of filling Burnham and Bradshaw's orders for the spring season. Now, watching him at work, she recalled Mr. Burnham mentioning that Rob seemed troubled by American merchants' huge demand for imported goods. Mr. Burnham dismissed such concerns as wrongheaded. He'd said that America always offered a favorable market for English products, and while profits varied with the season, they were generally high.

While Norah thought Mr. Burnham an astute businessman, she wondered if perhaps in this matter he was mistaken. She had read some articles in the *Transcript* that seemed to support Rob's more cautious view.

When Rob looked up from his work, she brought up the subject. "I understand that you and Mr. Burnham differ on the subject of imports."

Rob set his papers aside and folded his hands on top of his head. "Ah, the businesswoman again."

"I'm perfectly serious," Norah said in a way that let Rob know she didn't appreciate his patronizing tone.

Rob smiled. "I know you are, Norah. Forgive me." He rubbed his hair thoughtfully. "To be truthful, I don't believe half the English goods Burnham is requesting can sell to a profit. I may have to cut orders. Drastically."

"Cut orders?" Norah's eyes widened. "Oh, my. Mr. Burnham surely wouldn't approve of that."

"No," Rob agreed. "He wouldn't approve at all."

Norah watched him expectantly. "But you'll cut orders anyway?"

Rob sat forward and drummed his fingers on the desk. "What would you suggest I do?"

Feeling pleasantly bleary and emboldened by the brandy, Norah was more than willing to offer her views. She considered his question for a moment before speaking. "I think you should see what the British bankers have to say. Their credit rates will give you an idea of which way the winds are blowing."

Rob studied her for a long moment, a look of admiration in his eyes. "That's just what I'd planned to do, Norah," he said. "Just what I'd planned."

Norah flushed at Rob's approving comment and drained her glass in one long gulp. She felt drunk and drowsy and quite pleased with herself. She was even more pleased when Rob got up and came over to her. He sat on the edge of the bunk and ran his hand over her bound shoulder, testing the binding to see that it was tight. Norah thought of the night of the storm when he'd slept in her arms and wished she weren't so tired. She stifled a yawn.

"Get some sleep now," Rob said.

"Oh, I'm not sleepy," Norah said. In truth, she was struggling to stay awake. It was so enjoyable, sitting with Rob, discussing serious topics. He was, as Alice had said that day on the South Boston Bridge, clever and handsome and very kind.

Boston, Norah thought with a start of surprise. Why, she rarely thought of Boston any longer, let alone miss the place. The farther the *Orion* carried her from American shores, the more Boston faded into the past, and along with it the judgments and strictures that had guided her life. Norah thought of her earlier objections to Rob. In light of recent events, they seemed rather harsh and unfair.

Norah blinked hard one last time, sighed contentedly, and closed her eyes. Just as she drifted off, she felt Rob's callused fingers slip around her own. She gave his hand a firm squeeze.

When she was fast asleep, Rob untangled their fingers and laid Norah's hand on her stomach. As he watched the slow rise and fall of her chest, he thought of her limp form the night of the storm, the wet, clinging nightdress spotted with blood. When he'd knelt beside her in the water, he'd uttered his first prayer in memory. Now, seeing her safe and mending, he felt overwhelmed by gratitude and tenderness. But beneath his relief lay a burning frustration. This bruised and tangled beauty, with her quick mind and earnest heart, could never be his. He had saved her only to give her up once more.

Rob yawned and rubbed his tired face. He'd been toying with the idea of accepting Burnham's partnership offer. After all, he had no other plans. But there seemed to be no point in exchanging his freedom for the monotonous life of a landlocked businessman. Especially when the lovely bonus that came with the partnership was beyond his reach.

Rob got up and turned down the lamp. As darkness fell upon the cabin, Norah stirred in her sleep and made a soft sound of pain. Rob reached down to straighten her covers. Then he pulled a chair close to the bunk, sat down beside her, and dozed there till dawn.

The next day a stiff breeze came up, roughening the sea. Norah begged to go on deck, but the planks were wet and slippery. Rob ordered her to remain in bed and sent Alice to entertain her. By nightfall the weather had calmed. After giving Norah another dose of brandy for her pain, Rob wrapped her in her shawl and took her on deck.

A thick sparkle of stars encrusted the sky. The fragment of moon hung down, close and brilliant. Above, the sails swayed like ghosts. Norah sat down gingerly in her deck chair. Her body still felt sore and her shoulder ached, but getting out in the fresh air greatly improved her spirits.

She expected Rob to take Alice's chair, but he declined. "A skipper keeps to his feet on deck," he said. "You rest. I'll have a look forward."

"I'll come with you," Norah said, heaving herself back to her feet.

When Rob objected, she argued that she'd barely moved a muscle in five days. "If I don't begin to use them, they'll forget how to work."

"Very well," Rob said, taking her arm. "One turn, and then you sit down."

They made their way slowly around the deck, quiet save for the soft thunder of the sails and the slapping of waves against the hull. Norah felt a drowsy contentment. The deep feelings she'd developed for Rob had not faded. She glanced up at his dim profile and thought how very little she knew about him.

"Tell me about yourself," she said.

"Myself?" Rob seemed taken aback.

"Yes, yourself," Norah said, giving him an encouraging smile. "Your past."

"Well, there's not much to tell." Rob grasped the bill of his cap and gave it a tug. "I went to sea at twelve, became a second officer at eighteen, a chief mate at twenty, and took my own command at twenty-two. I've been working for Burnham ever since."

"But where did you grow up?" Norah persisted. "What of your family? Surely you had a life before you went to sea."

Rob shrugged, avoiding her curious stare. "That was a long time ago," he said lamely. "I guess I've forgotten it."

Norah watched him with a faint, disbelieving smile. Rob was thankful that she asked no more. He knew if he started telling her the truth, he might never stop.

When they completed their walk, Norah didn't want to go below, but she agreed to rest in her chair. She promptly fell asleep. When Rob tucked her shawl around her, she stirred and sighed.

"Rob," she murmured. It was the first time she'd spoken his given name.

For a long time afterward, Rob stood at the rail, staring at the silver path of the waxing moon. He wondered if it really mattered that Norah was Jody's daughter. If he kept his secret to himself, she'd be none the wiser. Maybe he could settle down with her. Forget Jody. Learn the ways of Boston. Travel for Burnham.

Rob groaned inwardly at his reckless speculations. The fact that he even considered living such a lie proved how dangerously he was entangled. Crawford was right; he'd best make up his mind to forget her. Norah was consigned to London. Once he delivered her to Berkeley Square, he'd give her no more thought than he would to the load of lumber stacked in the *Orion*'s hold.

When Norah was finally released from bed rest, Alice helped her bathe, applied fresh salve to her cuts, and dampened the bandage that bound her shoulder. Norah's hopelessly snarled hair, however, could not be repaired. After several attempts by Alice to brush out the tangles, Norah acknowledged she had no choice but to cut it off.

Rob agreed to perform the operation. As she waited for him at the appointed time, Norah paced restlessly about his cabin. She was heartily sick of her invalid state. Her arm was still strapped to her body and she could wear nothing but a flowing nightdress. She could do no handwork, so she occupied herself reading and making forays about Rob's cabin. She'd inspected his silver brushes and his small functional wardrobe; she'd studied his angular handwriting in the logbook and on scattered papers. On his bookshelf she'd found a well-thumbed copy of Mr. Cooper's *Red Rover,* along with accounts of voyages and ship disasters, and *The Planter's and Mariner's Medical Companion,* which described the treatment for injuries far more gruesome than her own. Norah dared not rummage through his drawers or boxes, although she was sorely tempted.

After a jaunty knock on the door, Rob entered the cabin, followed by Alice, who had been walking on deck with Jan.

Rob flourished a formidable pair of shears. He snapped them at Norah menacingly. "Are you ready?"

"I'll never be ready for this," she answered mournfully.

Alice, bright-cheeked from the sun and prettily attired in a mauve and white frock, settled herself on Rob's bunk. "Short hair will be ever so easy to care for," she said.

"I comfort myself with thoughts of Miss Wright," Norah said, thinking of the English reformer who had dared take to the public platform and argue that women were equal to men.

Alice burst into laughter. "Frances Wright, of course. Oh, she has a lovely mop of curls."

"She's planning another lecture tour in America," Norah said, seating herself in the chair. "I wish they'd allow her to come to Boston. Miss Peabody's fondest dream is for Miss Wright to speak at one of her Wednesday afternoons at the bookshop."

"Frances Wright?" Rob asked as he draped a cloth about Norah's neck. "Not the one they call the red harlot of something or other?"

"Oh, yes," Alice said. "The very one."

Norah gave Rob a disapproving look. She thought it bad form to succumb to the easy condemnation of a woman who spoke out so bravely against slavery and the oppression of women. "Alice and I read Miss Wright's *Course of Popular Lectures* and found her ideas quite sensible," she informed Rob. "You mustn't judge a person until you understand what she stands for."

"I understand exactly what she stands for," Rob said. "Free love and promiscuity."

"Oh, my," Alice said and burst into giggles.

Norah set her lips in a firm, unsmiling line. She found nothing amusing in Rob's misguided statement. "Miss Wright favors a free union rather than a legal contract between a man and a woman," she said. "I would hardly call such an arrangement free love and promiscuity."

"Oh, you wouldn't, would you?" Rob said with a smile. "What would you call it, then?"

Norah felt a rising irritation. At Miss Peabody's bookshop, she had participated in many discussions of controversial issues, from organized religion to Negro slavery to birth control to the institution of marriage itself. She'd found the discussions both stimulating and enlightening. From Rob's teasing manner she inferred that he thought her incapable of entertaining advanced ideas.

"I'd call such an arrangement good sense," she retorted.

She meant to return Rob's gaze defiantly, but the thoughtful look that came to his eyes brought on a profuse blush. Norah realized that while she entertained advanced ideas all the time, only recently had she thought of applying them to herself.

"We're very progressive in our reading," Alice said, coming to the rescue. "It's important to be acquainted with a variety of views. These days ladies need not be ignorant of anything at all."

Rob began cutting. Norah could feel the great clumps of hair falling to the floor as he sawed away at the tangled mess.

"What does Mrs. Burnham think of your reading matter?" Rob asked.

"Oh, Mama doesn't pay any attention to what we read," Alice replied. "But if she did, she'd certainly disapprove of Miss Wright."

"Mrs. Burnham is not progressive in her thinking," Norah said, wishing Alice wouldn't giggle so much. "Not like Alice and me. And Miss Peabody."

Rob gave Norah's head a smart turn to the right. "I suppose Miss Peabody carries that sort of bilge water in her shop."

"It's not bilge water," Norah answered impatiently. "They're books containing perfectly reasonable ideas. How can a book cause anyone harm?"

"A book can do a great deal of harm, Miss Norah, if it gives a lady too many wild notions."

Norah decided to let the matter rest. Rob's teasing manner was most disheartening. Obviously he didn't take her seriously, as a social philosopher, a woman, or anything else. Maybe he'd only been teasing her that day in the pantry. Maybe he hadn't wanted her at all. That conclusion brought to Norah's stomach a feeling of hollow disappointment.

Rob finished cutting in silence. He bent Norah's head over the china basin and poured warm water through her hair. He scrubbed her scalp with Castile soap and massaged her neck with strong hands. With a towel he rubbed her dry. Then he ran his fingers through her hair, trying to arrange it in some manner.

"Want to take a look?"

Norah declined. She doubted she'd ever again glance in a mirror, what with her ghastly face and body, and now her hair shorn like that of a martyred saint. It was no wonder Rob found her entirely resistible. He'd changed her bandages that morning and seemed no more moved by the sight of her breasts than a pillar of stone. In fact, he'd hardly looked at them at all. She, on the other hand, had felt a wanton longing for him to touch her. Brushed by his gaze, her nipples had tightened sweet and hard, and she could barely swallow for the ache in her throat.

It tortured Norah's pride and her heart to realize that Rob felt no urge to take advantage of her.

After her haircut, Norah moved back into her own cabin with Alice. Once settled, she found the courage to examine herself thoroughly. Her reflection in the mirror wasn't as terrible as she'd expected. Her cropped hair sprang away from her head in thick, shining waves, not beautiful by any means, but in a curious way attractive. Once her bruises cleared up, she decided she might look rather interesting. But when she appeared on deck, wearing over her skirt a shirt of Rob's that hung to her knees, the crew broke into wide grins, and Norah knew with renewed disgust that she must look ridiculous.

As the days passed, her bruises began to fade, but her shoulder continued to ache. When it woke her at night, she went on deck. More often than not, Rob joined her at the rail. Sometimes they talked until she grew sleepy. At other times they stood quietly, watching the stars wink above the churning blackness of the sea. Norah wondered why Rob didn't sleep. When she asked, he shrugged and said he didn't seem to feel the need.

In truth, Rob was exhausted, kept awake night after night by thoughts of Norah. So thoroughly had she enchanted him that he barely recognized his feelings as lust. But it was lust, this burning need to have her, the need that tormented him without mercy. He would close his eyes only to see her rosy curves, the way she blushed when he changed her bandages, the shy excitement in her eyes. He'd see it all and imagine her lying in his arms. Norah would permit him to take any liberties; Rob knew that. But her willing embrace would be the end of him. Once would lead to twice, and next he knew, she would have a ring and his name, and he'd be caught in a lie that would destroy them both.

To keep from touching Norah, Rob talked to her. On deck in the evening, he told her of exotic cities in the Far East and described the perilous coasts of Africa. He talked of pirates and banians, shipwrecks and tiger hunts. He took care to evade her questions about himself. But as time went by, her curiosity and warm concern made him reckless, and he talked about the Manchester factory and his uncle's beatings and how he ran away to sea.

One night Rob discovered to his horror that she had dragged out of him the deepest secret of his soul. Even when he spoke, Rob couldn't believe he was actually telling someone about the mother of his fantasies, a mother who was less a memory than a feeling and, worst of all, that he thought of her now and then when he needed comfort.

Rob stopped abruptly, mute with embarrassment and self-reproach. He endured a moment of excruciating silence, bracing himself for Norah's response.

When she spoke, her voice was soft with concern. "Surely there's a way of finding out what became of her."

"No," Rob said harshly. "No there isn't."

"Of course there is. There are records in Manchester that can provide the facts of your birth."

The tenderness in her tone was unbearable. Something broke in Rob then. Some tenuous hold he had on his temper, frayed from frustration and lack of sleep, gave way. Suddenly he wondered if Norah was making him crazy. Suddenly he knew he could hardly wait to be rid of her.

"Forget the whole goddam thing," he snapped. "Forget it! It's nothing but a child's wishful thinking." He clamped down on his cigar, biting it nearly in two.

Norah spoke again, sounding bewildered. "It's your mother, Rob. Your own past—"

"I'm sick to death of the past," Rob said savagely. "Your past and mine. If you ever bring this up again, Norah, I swear I'll never forgive you."

Norah looked at his agonized face and said nothing. All Rob's barriers were in place, his shoulders were set high and tight. He drew hard on his cigar, then sent it spinning into the blackness below.

"Go to bed," he said roughly. "I waste too much time gossiping with you."

He pushed off from the rail, leaving Norah speechless with astonishment. She stared after him, not hurt so much as confused. The pain in his voice and the misery in his face spoke of something beyond annoyance with her. No, she thought, he couldn't possibly be angry with her. He was irritated with the crew or concerned about filling Mr. Burnham's orders. It was a phase that would pass, nothing more. And in that moment, Norah realized how much she would miss Rob if he turned away from her, how desolate and dreary her life would become. He meant that much to her. Oh, he meant everything to her. With mounting dismay, Norah realized she might have made the terrible error of falling in love.

The days passed in pleasant sunshine and warm breezes. Aside from a few welcome downpours that replenished their water supply, the *Orion* had encountered no spell of bad weather since the storm. Rob had predicted landfall during the middle of their fourth week at sea. On a perfectly delightful afternoon the cry of "Land, ho!" sent everyone rushing to the railing.

"Irish coast," Rob told Norah, handing her the spyglass.

The strip of land, Norah's first glimpse of foreign soil, was a faint purple cloud on the horizon. Alice peered out to sea with the rest of the company, eager for a description. She was disappointed when Norah explained that Ireland from that distance offered nothing worth relating.

Long after everyone else had lost interest, Norah continued to stare at the faint line between sea and sky. The notion of land had somehow lost its meaning after so many days in her watery environment, but viewing Ireland meant that England was only days away. Soon there would be time for nothing but good-byes. Norah knew she would not see Rob in London. He had retreated from her abruptly the night he'd spoken of his mother. He left her alone on deck at night, and in his free time he immersed himself in the navigation lessons he was giving Jan. Even after the lessons were finished, Rob continued to play around with star shots as if the charts and numbers and the demands of logic could ease the pain that showed so plainly on his tired face. When Alice pressed him about excursions and visits in London, Rob responded vaguely, saying he'd be out of the city for weeks at a time. Norah made no comment. But she knew with a profound sorrow that even if Rob did come to call at Berkeley Square, the closeness they'd shared would be no more than a memory.

And just as well, a rational voice told her. He's not the man for you, with his restless charm and his wandering ways.

But Norah's heart and body had long ceased listening to her reasoning self. She stared at Rob openly, memorizing his little mannerisms. He had a way of rubbing his palms on his thighs, leaving his trousers streaked with tar, and when he puzzled over his nautical calculations, he tugged at his hair and scowled. Whenever he came on deck, his quick eyes sought her out, as if by instinct, and she never failed to answer his glance with a smile.

One morning when Rob was bandaging her, his fingers inadvertently brushed her breast. He snatched his hand away as if her skin were red hot, but the sensation of his touch lingered for hours. Norah imagined what would have happened if he'd caressed her. Her carnal thoughts brought on such an agony of yearning, she thought she must be deranged.

On the afternoon they sighted land, Rob told Norah to have Alice help her remove the binding for the last time. If she'd had two hands available, Norah would have clapped for joy. At last she could get out of Rob's big shirts and reclaim her left shoulder and arm. At last she could once again wear dresses and look pretty.

Willie brought the hip bath into her cabin, and Norah spent an hour splashing happily and scrubbing herself with lemon soap. Alice helped her wash her hair, then brushed it till it shone with red and gold lights. The waves fluffed prettily about her face, which was nearly healed and tinted a healthy brown from the sun. Norah selected a white muslin dress embroidered with tiny pink rosebuds. Once she was laced snugly into her stays, with the score of buttons fastened up her back, she felt properly attired for the first time in three weeks. Norah pulled Alice up the companionway, certain that Rob would be stunned by her appearance. But he gave her only a perfunctory nod and told her he'd fashion her a sling later.

After supper, the sea fell almost calm. Norah paced the deck nervously. Rob spent what seemed like hours tacking to and fro into a head wind while looking for a pilot boat. Not until dark did he tell the impatient Norah to come down to his cabin.

"And bring Alice," he ordered.

When Norah stepped into his cabin, eager and pretty and quite alone, Rob looked tired and annoyed. Norah noticed his hands had worried his hair into a fine tangle.

"Where's Alice?" he demanded.

"She's . . . resting," Norah answered, quite untruthfully.

Alice in fact, was reading the Gospels. She'd declined to accompany Norah. "It's a good sign if Rob figures he needs a chaperon after all the doctoring he's done for you," she said with a grin. "You must have frightened him with that talk of free love."

But it was obvious from Rob's manner that love of any sort was the farthest thing from his mind. "Go get her," he said.

"But . . . but I can't," Norah said, despising the need to lie. "She's . . . I mean, she's probably asleep."

Rob seemed to forget about Alice. He turned his attention to Norah's dress, which he eyed critically. "Why did you get into that rig when you knew I had to look at your shoulder?"

Norah gulped and stared at the floor, suddenly deflated by his angry words and hard look. She had tried to look pretty for him. She wanted desperately to please him, to have him smile and joke again and make her feel special. "It's only a few buttons," she said, and her chin trembled ominously.

Without a word, Rob began unfastening her dress. His hands were clumsy on the tiny buttons and Norah heard him swear under his breath. She stood very still, her heart beating with hopeless despair. After all they had shared, Rob no longer considered her a friend, let alone a lover.

"Come here by the lamp."

Norah followed obediently, her dress hanging off her shoulders. She thought of allowing it to drop to her waist, but knew if she did, Rob would most likely shout at her.

She said nothing as Rob pulled aside her shift. He inspected her shoulder to see if it was tender. His fingers, gentle as a caress, sent a wave of heat through her body that burned her cheeks.

"You seem well healed," he said.

"It feels stiff," Norah said, forcing a cheerful, hopeful tone.

"When you're not wearing the sling, move your elbow, but keep the shoulder still."

Rob's voice continued gruff and impersonal. Norah wondered if he felt anything when he touched her. She allowed her bodice to slip lower and glanced at Rob from the corner of her eye. He didn't seem to notice.

"You needn't sleep in the sling," he said, "but make sure you wear it when you're up and about."

"All right." If only he would look at her, Norah thought mournfully. If only he would smile.

Rob stood close to her, so close that if he bent down and Norah stood on her toes, she could reach his mouth. She leaned upward. Rob stepped aside and began rearranging her clothing.

Norah thought frantically. Their encounter was just about over, and she'd accomplished nothing. She had to make a move, and quickly. "Rob?" she said, sounding as desperate as she felt.

He grunted.

"Do I still look so terrible?"

He began fastening her up the back. "You look fine."

"But—"

"I said you're *fine*," he said harshly. "You're healthy. There's nothing more to say."

Rob tucked her arm into the sling and tied it around her neck. The ache in Norah's heart was more than flesh and blood could bear. Suddenly words were tumbling out of her mouth, headlong, imprudent words that no self-respecting woman would dare to utter. "That day in the pantry, did you . . . didn't you like it? I mean, didn't you like kissing me?" Her voice sounded forlorn and pleading. Norah cringed as she waited for his response.

Rob did not meet Norah's distraught gaze. He said tersely, "I behaved inexcusably."

"Oh, but you didn't," Norah burst out. "I don't think you behaved badly at all."

Rob's face appeared immobile, carved from stone. "I can't help what you think. Now leave me, Norah. I have things to do."

Norah stared at him, trembling at her own audacity and his unfeeling reaction. She burned with shame from brow to toes. "I—"

Rob turned his back to her and said tightly, "Please go, Norah."

She fled.

Back in the cabin, Alice slept, snoring softly. Norah paced from the tea table to the window seat and back again, pressing her fists to her temples, reliving every agonizing instant of her humiliating rejection. Oh, how could she have spoken so boldly, and why did Rob hate her so? She could come up with no answer. There was no reason for his cruelty, no memory of having caused him offense.

Suddenly the tiny cabin was unbearably small and oppressive. Norah could barely breathe in such close quarters. One more moment and she would surely suffocate. She snatched her shawl from its hook and ran up on deck.

The evening watch was set and all was quiet. The breeze carried the *Orion* along with hardly a rattle of canvas or rigging. Transparent clouds raced across the stars, and the moon hung brilliant above the horizon. Norah sat in her chair and hugged herself in her shawl, not bothering to wipe her streaming eyes. The breeze curled seductively about her, aggravating the searing hurt that cut too deep to be healed by reason.

Hearing a step beside her, she pulled deeper into her shawl.

"Norah."

Norah covered her tear-soaked face. "Leave me *alone*!"

Rob crouched beside her chair. When he spoke, his voice was low and unbearably kind. "Remember what you said that night at the Burnhams'?" he asked. " 'Men leave the sea and regret it,' you said. You were right, Norah. Men like me come and go like shadows on a cloudy day. Who knows what I'll be doing in a year, two years? I may go with Burnham, I may sell out and go back to the Indies. I may not take his offer at all."

Norah emerged snuffling from behind her hands, but she

didn't turn to look at Rob. She lifted her arm in its sling and wiped her cheeks.

"And if I do stick with Burnham," he went on, "I'll be traveling in Europe most of the year. I can offer you nothing that you deserve—permanence, fidelity, a real home." He reached out and stroked her hair, a gesture that warmed Norah to her hopeless core. "You don't want a man who can't stay in one place."

Norah turned to him. In the moonlight, beneath the bill of his cap, his angular features seemed softer, the rough edges blurred. His lips curved into a tired smile, but his eyes remained solemn and anxious.

Norah knew that everything he said was true, but mere words and logical explanations couldn't fill her need or soothe the pain. "No," she whispered. "I guess I don't want that at all." Reason spoke; her heart didn't believe any of it.

"And don't forget the opium. If you think about it, sweetheart, I'm really the worst sort of man."

One final sob broke through. "You're not the worst sort. I th-think you're wonderful."

She whimpered like a baby into her sling. Rob stayed utterly still, his hand resting on her hair. Then slowly he rose to his feet. "Go to bed, Norah," he said wearily. "One more day and we'll be on English soil. You want to be rested for London."

Chapter Nine

No sooner had Norah returned to her cabin than she realized she was imprisoned in her clothing. A score of tiny buttons securely fastened the back of her dress, and her stays were snugly laced. She considered waking Alice to help her, but decided against it. Alice would ask sympathetic questions, and Norah couldn't bear the thought of explaining what had transpired in Rob's cabin. Norah sank onto the window seat. Drained of tears and pride, she wanted nothing so much as to fall into a deep, obliterating sleep. She would just have to make do with sleeping in her clothes.

Norah removed her slippers and lay down on her sleep sofa. She closed her eyes, folded her hands on her chest, and tried to make her mind a blank. After only a few seconds, thoughts of Rob intruded. "I can offer you nothing you deserve," he had said. Norah's eyes began to sting. Of course, he was right, she told herself. She had known from the beginning that she and Rob were entirely unsuited to each other. A hot tear slid down her temple and into her hair. Oh, what a nuisance, she thought, and rubbed her damp nose. Couldn't she put him out of her mind for even a moment?

Her stays seemed to be growing tighter. Her belly began to itch, and then her back. The high collar of her dress was choking her. Norah wriggled and squirmed. Maybe Rob would assist her, she thought. She hated to go crawling back to him;

surely he thought her a terrible pest. Her eyes pooled with hot, spilling tears. Oh, he'd hurt her so! But unbuttoning her dress would only take a moment. She might ask for a brandy to help her sleep.

Before she could reconsider her plan, Norah was on her way to the main cabin.

She came to an abrupt halt when she saw Rob. He sat at the table, slumped over a glass of whiskey. As she stood watching him, he picked up the tumbler, drained it, and banged it down on the table. Keeling forward, he rested his forehead on his palms and emitted a soft groan.

Gracious, Norah thought, the decanter was empty. The last time she'd looked, it had been nearly full. She hadn't seen Rob take a drink since the night they'd argued about opium. Now here he was, badly in need of a shave and decidedly drunk.

Rob pushed himself into a sitting position and reached again for the glass. It was empty. He swore and groped for the decanter.

"Rob?"

The back of his neck prickled. He shook his head to clear his vision and found Norah before him. In the wavering lamplight, her eyes looked swollen. He remembered she'd been crying. Crying over him. Rob frowned and felt a sting of remorse. He tried to recall exactly what he'd said to upset her, but before he could think of it, her dress caught his attention. It was a pretty frock with little rosebuds dancing on white cloth, little pink buds like the tips of her breasts. He stared at the curve of her bodice and decided her nipples were more like berries.

"Strawberries."

"I beg your pardon?" Norah asked.

Rob smiled. "Nothing," he said. "Nothing at all."

"I'm sorry to bother you, but I need you to unfasten me."

Rob captured her face in his bleary gaze. Ah, she was lovely, even looking so forlorn. He thought of her awkward attempt to seduce him and felt a stir of warmth. "Unfasten you?"

"My dress," she said sorrowfully. "You see, I can't reach the buttons, and Alice is asleep, and I'm all laced up."

A pink ribbon held her shining hair away from her brow and ears. A narrow streak of downy skin lay along her hairline, a pale contrast to the brown of her sun-kissed face. She looked as fresh and succulent as new-ripe fruit. Rob stood up unsteadily. He didn't feel drunk so much as floating in a strange timeless state, somewhere between the past and the future, but blessedly free from the present.

Norah glanced at the decanter and his empty glass. "You've had a lot to drink," she said. He heard in her voice a trace of disapproval.

"I'm not drunk," Rob announced. He drew himself up to his full, imposing height, forgetting he was too tall for below-decks. He heard his skull crack on the beam. "Jesus Christ!" He grabbed his head. "Goddam beams," he said, rubbing the bump.

Norah took a step backward, shaking her head doubtfully. "I think I'd better wake Alice—"

"Wait!"

"Or I can sleep in my dress."

Rob had a mental flash of her naked image. "Come here, Norah."

Norah clasped her hands and hesitated. She could see that the whiskey had washed away Rob's earlier constraints. But he wasn't himself; he was drunk. Norah couldn't tell if he wanted to kiss *her* or if he just wanted a woman, any woman. Oh, it was ever so confusing with a man, not knowing from one moment to the next what he was feeling.

"I don't think you're really in any condition—"

"Come here, goddammit!"

There was no tenderness in his eyes, only a blaze of dark, impatient passion. With alarm, Norah realized that Rob had no intention of satisfying himself with a kiss. He appeared to be set on having her in a most thorough manner. The act that Norah had imagined as hazy and exciting, perhaps even uplifting, was now graphic and complicated. She suddenly felt afraid.

"As I say, I don't think—"

Rob reached for her.

Norah leaped aside and collided with the mahogany paneling. Before she could scramble away, Rob was upon her.

Rough fingers slipped around the back of her neck. His palms cupped her jaw, forcing it upward. Norah tried to wriggle free, but he straddled her with his legs, pressing her back with the hard length of his body. His mouth, hot and open, assaulted hers, choking off her breath. Norah twisted away, but he only pushed her head back, kissing her avidly, hurting her lips. Her anger flared against him, and she struck out with her fists. Pain wrenched her tender shoulder. He would have his way, she thought wildly, no matter what she did! And she no longer wanted him!

"Stop!" she managed to cry out. "You're hurting me!"

Rob's mouth abruptly left hers. The pressure of his body eased. He stared down at her, his face drawn with shock, blinking as if he'd just awakened from a dream.

Norah sagged against the wall, gasping for breath. "You hurt my shoulder."

Rob reached out to touch her, then seemed to think better of it. His hand hovered in midair. "Christ, Norah. I'm sorry." The little lines around his eyes furrowed with remorse. "Are you all right?"

"I . . . I guess so." Norah's pulse slowed, and the cloud of anger was lifting. "You shouldn't have done that, you know."

Rob ran a hand over his face. He looked exhausted, his eyes blurry and baffled, his jacket collar twisted. With his tousled black hair and his jaw shaded with whiskers, he looked like a dark repentant devil. "I don't know what got into me."

Norah looked at him warily and rubbed her shoulder. "Too much whiskey?"

"Seems so. I just . . . You were so damned pretty, Norah, standing there. I wanted to . . ." He looked embarrassed. "I guess I'll go on deck. Clear my head."

"That's a good idea," Norah said, feeling less angry than sorry. "You should get some fresh air." She looked at Rob's rumpled frown, at the expanse of hairy chest visible beneath his opened shirt, and wished things had developed differently. If only he hadn't jumped on her. If he had spoken a few tender words and kissed her gently, she would have responded in quite a different fashion. Why, she would have let him do anything he wanted. Norah looked at Rob's strong neck, his husky shoulders, and wondered if he would mind her going on deck with him.

But he made no move to leave. Instead, he moved closer, leaning an arm on the wall beside her. "Norah." He looked down at her with an expression both stark and wistful. "What I wanted . . . What I want . . ."

In one quivering moment, Norah felt something pass between them, something fresh and sharp and almost visible. She looked at Rob's face, etched with misery and longing; she looked in his eyes with their curious, unsteady brightness, and her knees went weak. Their encounter was not over; the night was ripe with possibility.

"You want?" she prompted softly.

"You." Rob leaned down. His lips hovered close to her own. "I have such a need for you, Norah. Such a need."

Norah felt herself dissolving into liquid happiness. He wanted her. He thought of her as a woman and he wanted her. She laid her palm on Rob's bristly cheek. At her touch, his eyes closed tight. "I can't help myself." His voice was no more than a wisp of breath; he sounded as if he were telling her a secret. "Can't help it."

His lips touched hers. "So lovely . . . so beautiful." The tip of his tongue licked at the corner of her mouth, making Norah shiver with excitement. His hand closed on her breast with a gentle pressure. Norah dared not move; she felt dizzy, full of heat. He stroked her in a way that was unbelievably stirring, that made her insides leap with delight.

"Stay with me tonight," he murmured. "Let me love you."

Norah's limbs grew heavy, her insides yielding. She pressed her lips against Rob's; she kissed him until she heard him groan. Then, with a soft, hungry sigh, she breathed, "Yes."

A door latch clicked behind her, and strong arms enfolded her. In one smooth movement, they were inside his cabin.

Darkness filled the stern window. The low-burning lamp threw mysterious shadows across the walls and flared against the brass chronometer. Rob pulled off his jacket, threw it in the direction of the chair, and drew Norah back into his arms. He kissed her with hard, sweet lips, with beguiling tongue. Norah clung to him, washed in a drowsy languor, while deft fingers moved up her back. Buttons and loops that had confused him an hour ago now fell open at his touch. With a sailor's skill, he unwove corset lacing and knots. He pulled up her skirts, running his hand over her flank, burning through sheer linen, leaving her shaken beyond reason or imaginings. Norah felt the tug of ribbons and strings. Petticoats and pantalets fell at his command.

She was naked. Her skin tingled beneath his hungry appraisal. She twined her arms before her.

"Don't be shy," Rob urged, easing her back on the bunk. "Don't hide. You're so beautiful."

He bent over her, a dark and gentle presence. Knowing hands stroked the curves and indentations of her body, leaving a rippling pattern of warm sensations. His lips whispered on her skin and nipped at her breasts. He sucked deeply, stroking with his tongue, bringing on a wildness in her, an urge for something strong and primitive and forceful.

Then he was touching buried places she'd never dared explore.

"No, no, you mustn't," Norah panted, shaken and alarmed. She hadn't imagined this. She had not imagined half of it.

"Hush," he said, "it's all right."

"Oh, it's not," she protested, breathless with the sensation of it. "It's so . . . Oh, you mustn't. Oh, dear . . . it's so . . ." She dug her fingers into his hair and said no more, because it felt so wonderfully good, and because she didn't want him to stop.

"It's what, sweetheart? Tell me what you feel."

But Norah couldn't answer. Her mind hazed. She clung to him with desperate kisses. Their breath rushed and mingled in the deep quiet of the cabin. She heard nothing of the sea, no groan of timbers, only the sound of their lips and her own sighs as he stroked her and her body melted into honeyed compliance.

She made no more protests. Each thing he did was lovelier than the last. With his mouth, he took her into dimensions she'd never imagined. She lay stilled with pleasure, trembling at the unspeakable intimacy of his kisses, the delicate enticement of his tongue. All her being seemed squeezed to a tight point that curled and pulsed and quivered on the edge of some enormous excitement. She hovered there, past breathing, fighting to keep her silence lest Rob think he was hurting her. Then she felt a shiver that grew and grew until her whole body lit up with a bright burst of ecstasy. The cries she'd kept locked in her throat tore out of her, and she could no longer lie still.

Rob's lips came down hotly on her own. Then he was gone—gone from her! Norah reached out wildly with a small, anxious cry.

"I'm here, sweetheart. I have to undress." He sounded short of breath.

Then he came to her, hard and naked and invincible, her beautiful lover, her tender conqueror. Norah, in her daze, opened her limbs. Rob moved over her, direct and impatient. She tried to accommodate his urgency, but before she could adjust to his rough kisses, his hands gone clumsy and grasping, he pushed hard at her. Norah bit her lip. Oh, dear, it would never be accomplished, she thought desperately. There was no place for him to fit. And, oh, he was hurting her. . . .

The pain was sharp and swift and blessedly brief. Norah lay limp and bewildered beneath Rob's heavy weight. It was finished, she thought, it was done. She told herself to relax; there was nothing to do but trust him, wait it out. Then he was kissing her, moving deeper inside her, mumbling her name. His hand, then his mouth, touched her breast. Norah closed her eyes. Her legs slackened, and she realized she'd been holding herself very rigid, anticipating more pain. She touched Rob's hair, his back, feeling his tension, all those hard, dense muscles lashed tight to his bones.

Rob moved slowly, teasing her with kisses, and Norah felt a rising restlessness. Her breath came quicker, she sighed and stirred, feeling his unyielding presence, no longer painful but full and pleasing. His hands curved under her hips, lifting her, fitting himself deeper still. Norah took his face in her hands and drew him closer, licking his lips, kissing him. His mouth opened, and she advanced boldly, exploring, searching. A rough sound came from his throat and he moved hard. Norah felt a throb of pleasure. She wrapped her arms around his neck and whispered his name.

He said, "Norah, I love you."

Her eyes filled with happy tears. "Oh, Rob, I love you, too."

The tension in her limbs had vanished. Her arms and legs felt soft and pliant. She shifted her hips, enjoying his kindly weight upon her, his hardness inside. With a sense of heady wonder, Norah thought how inextricably they were bound together, how lovingly entwined.

"I'm so happy," she whispered.

Rob's head dropped against her shoulder and he choked out her name. It was as if the spring that held him had snapped. He rose and fell against her, enjoying her with a sort of exquisite agony that intoxicated all Norah's senses, that carried her off on a tide of extraordinary emotions. She clasped him, delirious with his loving words, his hard, headlong drives. She hadn't expected to feel the wildness again, the same throbbing ache as before, but there it was, sudden and frantic. She told him. She grasped him and tried to tell him what was happening. But he was beyond her reach. He thrust hard, and then again. He strained against her. For one long, shuddering pulse, for one deep savage cry of love, Rob crushed her to him and then lay still.

Norah felt his heart knocking against her chest, heard his labored breath. He mumbled something she couldn't hear and then mumbled it again. He rolled away, covered his eyes with his arm, and groaned. "Oh, God, Norah." Then he drew her close and murmured against her hair, "Stay with me, sweetheart. We'll do it again."

Norah rested against his warmth, her body quivering and tingling. She felt all opened up from him, almost as if he were still inside her. She listened to his breathing fade almost to nothing. Against the hull, the sea bumped in a regular rhythm. Above, Norah could hear the groan of the wheel, and in the distance the sound of two bells. One o'clock.

She rose up on one elbow and looked at Rob. Despite his words, he didn't appear to be in any condition to do anything again, let alone what he'd just finished. He lay sprawled on his back, fast asleep, his lips slightly parted. Norah's fingers drifted over him, from shoulders and arms packed with muscles, to waist and hips whittled to nothing, to his legs, long and hard as oak. She touched his male parts, quiescent now, and quite curiously made. Leaning over, she brushed her lips along the trail of hair that descended from his navel. Dearest Rob. He'd surrendered his body and his heart. He belonged to her forever.

Norah tenderly pulled the blanket up over his chest. His delight in her had been astonishing. And what he'd done to her . . . Well, never in her wildest imaginings . . . Norah flushed. Carefully, so as not to wake him, she slipped from the bunk and doused the lamp. Smiling to herself, she gathered up her clothes and stole quietly from the cabin.

The cabin window was still dark when Rob rose, naked and stumbling, to face the day. He'd slept deeply, and yet his head throbbed from whiskey and fatigue. Lighting a lamp, he stared at the battlefield that was his bunk and remembered. *Norah.* He grabbed his aching head with both hands and cursed softly, summoning every epithet he could conjure up, but no words were bitter enough to express his opinion of himself.

Turning to the dressing stand, he filled the basin with water and lathered his face. With each stroke of the razor, he recalled more details of his night of drink and seduction. He'd done to Norah what no decent man would ever practice on an innocent girl. It was unbelievable what he'd done to her. It staggered his mind. As for the rest, it had been mindless lust with no thought to anything but himself, little better than rape.

He'd made no accommodation for her innocence. He'd kept it in the back of his mind, but then at the critical moment, he'd gotten so desperate with wanting her that he'd just plunged ahead. Rob threw down his razor, mopped the soap off his face, and turned from his reflection in disgust. The thought of his stupidity, his heedless passion, set his teeth on edge. If any other man had so misused Norah, he would have killed the bastard.

Rob pulled on his trousers, shirt, and boots, dreading the moment when he would face her. Gathering up his jacket and cap, he slammed out of the cabin. He mounted to the dark, misty deck and stood in the fog, berating himself. If only he'd been sober, if he hadn't had the whiskey, he would have re-membered and been more careful. If he'd been sober . . . Then he remembered that if he'd been sober, none of it would have happened at all.

The pilot came aboard soon after dawn. He ordered the crew about with an arrogance that was normal for a man of his profession, but that aggravated Rob's already foul mood. Rob remained on deck for an hour. When he could tolerate no more of the pilot's manners, he went below to put his gear in order and set his mind toward Liverpool. He decided that once the *Orion* was in her berth and the custom officials satisfied, he would settle Alice and Norah at the Royal Hotel and seek out Burnham's Liverpool agent. The prospect of a good cigar, a deep leather chair, and masculine talk of cargoes and discount rates cheered Rob considerably.

He was tossing papers into a case when Willie's head popped in the door, his forehead puckered with concern. "Missies on deck, Cap'n. Pilot swear very bad. No good missies hear."

Rob pushed aside the clutter on his desk. He had to face her sooner or later, he thought. It might as well be now. "I'll see to them, Willie." He grabbed his cap and headed reluctantly up the companionway.

Norah stood at the rail with Alice, studying the bleak, foggy Lancashire coast. Rob narrowed his eyes at her lovely profile, the curve of her throat. Her straw bonnet was tipped back, and beads of dew sparkled on her hair. Beneath her open shawl, the bodice of her dark blue dress was firm and full. Looking at her, Rob felt a prickle of sweat and the hard stir of desire. Last night came back to him in a blur of tastes and scents and shattering sensations.

He cleared his throat and said loudly, "Norah."

She turned. A slow, radiant smile lit her face, her cheeks glowed with shy delight. Rob met her eyes, brimming with happiness, and his heart began to pound. No, he cautioned himself, no more of that. He had to get her out of his life. He had to tell her that last night was a mistake, that they could never be together again.

As he crossed the deck, Rob maintained a casual air that belied the turmoil within. "I'm sorry, ladies. You'll have to stay below so the pilot can do his work."

A veil of disappointment fell over Norah's face. "But we want to see Liverpool."

Rob waved at the mist. "There's nothing to see. There won't be anything to see for hours."

He glanced at Alice and wondered what she knew of last night. Her face betrayed no secrets.

Alice said, "If it's the pilot's language you're concerned about, we've heard all those words before from the crew. From the captain himself, on occasion," she added dryly.

Rob didn't feel like arguing. He met Norah's happy, expectant gaze. "Take Alice below. Then come to my cabin." He turned and retraced his steps to the companionway.

When Norah entered the cabin, Rob sat at his desk before untidy piles of papers. As he rose to greet her, Norah thought he looked younger and less controlled than usual. His chin was freshly shaved and his hair neatly brushed, but there was a trace of melancholy about his eyes and his expression was distinctly wary.

Norah wasn't surprised. When she'd awakened this morning in a stupor of happiness, it had occurred to her that Rob would probably withdraw from her again. Even though he'd told her he loved her, even though his passion had stripped him of all reserve and restraint, she expected he would deny his feelings. Looking at him now, she knew her instincts had been correct.

"I hope you slept well," Rob said, sounding absurdly formal.

"I had an excellent sleep," Norah answered cheerfully. "And you?"

"Very good, thank you."

A distinct flush darkened Rob's cheeks. There was a weariness about him that had nothing to do with lack of sleep; it rather suggested that he was carrying a burden that was slowly wearing him down.

Norah ran a hand over her hair, dampened by the fog, and waited for his declaration of regret.

She didn't have to wait long.

"I'm sorry for what happened last night." Rob crossed his arms, tucking his wrists under them.

Norah joined her hands together and gazed at them for a moment. She listened to the pulsing silence in the cabin and told herself to be calm. With time, she would figure out what drove Rob so mercilessly away from her, even as he wanted her with such palpable emotion. For now, she would bear his remoteness with patience.

She looked up at his face. "I'm not sorry," she said firmly. "No matter what you say, I'll never be sorry for what we did."

He turned to stare desolately out the window. His great shoulders drooped, his arms hung at his sides. "I should never have touched you," he said in a voice that sounded rusty and hoarse. "It can't happen again."

"Don't I have anything to say on the matter?" Norah asked.

Rob shook his head. "I've told you, Norah, I can offer you nothing—no marriage, no love affair, nothing. I'm not a man to be tied down."

Norah moved next to him and slipped her arm through his. She was pleased that he didn't draw away from her. "I won't tie you down," she assured him. "Whenever you want me, you can have me. It will be a free union with no obligations."

Rob looked down at her. His eyes were sad, but she saw a smile touch his mouth. "Miss Frances Wright again, is it? No, Norah, no matter what nonsense you read, you're a woman made for a husband and children, not a lover."

"I think I'm the best judge of what's best for me," Norah replied. She felt astonishingly mature after last night, really quite transformed.

A tremor of emotion, fleet as a shadow, passed over Rob's face. He disengaged his arm from hers and moved to his desk. "If you need me in London, I'm staying at this address off Gray's Inn Road." He scribbled something on a paper and handed it to her.

Norah glanced questioningly at the paper and back to Rob.

He shrugged and looked embarrassed. "If there's a . . . any reason. I'm not talking about a liaison, Norah, but an emergency."

Norah studied the paper that bore Rob's familiar angular scrawl and glanced back at his face. The bleakness she saw there filled her heart. A most satisfied smile came to her lips.

"Of course," she said. "An emergency."

Norah tucked the paper into her sleeve. She wondered how long it would take for him to come to her in London. It was plain as day that Rob Mackenzie was far from finished with her.

Chapter Ten

LIVERPOOL WAS A city of heartless buildings, chilly mists, and horrifying poverty. A pathetic array of beggars huddled against the dock walls in the mournful drizzle. As Rob hurried Norah and Alice into the waiting cab, thin, ragged boys clustered about them, shouting and pushing. Rob put Alice and Norah into the cab, then distributed money. When they finally drove off, the boys ran shouting after the cab. A few stones bounced off the roof. Norah watched Rob's face, expressionless and remote, and trembled to think of his own dreadful past, scrambling to survive in this very same place. The idea of it was so depressing that when they departed for London the next morning, Norah announced she would never set foot in the wretched city again.

As the London stage carried them out into the Lancashire countryside, the sun burned through the mist, the air filled with sweetness, and England at last appeared as Norah had imagined it. She described for Alice the picturesque cottages, their dooryards bright with flowers. She spoke of the cows and sheep grazing beneath magnificent oaks, the thick hedges trailing up the hills, the arching bridges, the charming little streams.

When Norah wasn't talking to Alice, she listened to Rob's conversation with the only other passenger, a bald gentleman in the insurance business on his way to London. From what

Norah could gather, London banking houses were losing confidence in American merchants. According to the gentleman, whose name was Mr. Partridge, Americans were borrowing heavily to finance their cargoes. There was talk that speculative expansion in the United States and overly generous credit on the part of London banks would result in a panic.

As Norah listened to Mr. Partridge's dire predictions, it became clear that Rob would soon be making crucial decisions about the future of Burnham and Bradshaw. Perhaps, she thought hopefully, he might once again ask for her advice.

They spent the night in Tewkesbury and reached London late the next afternoon. Compared to this vast metropolis, Boston was a village, Liverpool a sordid dream. London's streets were clogged with rumbling, clattering vehicles, all trying the squeeze between sooty walls of mortar and brick. It was impossible to describe to Alice the confusion of carriages and cabs, coaches and carts, the press of hurrying gentlemen, the shouts of boys sweeping muck from the street, the street sellers crying their wares into the echoing clatter. The tumult assaulted all the senses. If Norah hadn't seen it with her own eyes, she would never have believed so much commotion.

Alice needed no eyes to see the turmoil. "Please, Norah, don't even try to explain. It sounds dreadful and I'd prefer to hear what I'm missing in the comfort of Denmore House after a bath."

The coach stopped at the General Post Office, a huge stone structure that covered an entire block. While Rob set off to locate the Denmore carriage, Mr. Partridge attended to Norah and Alice. Soon a shiny black landau drew up, its well-oiled hood folded back. A footman in gray tights and a blue coat with silver buttons accomplished the transfer of baggage. When he handed Norah through the door emblazoned with a coronet, she felt like a princess.

They left the City and headed toward Mayfair. Norah sat forward on the black morocco seat and exclaimed over the busy streets and the grand mansions, the profusion of splendid carriages and their crews of outriders and footmen.

"Is she always such a chatterbox?" Rob asked Alice, giving Norah a wry smile.

Alice sighed. "I declare, I hardly know her. Norah was once

a girl of few words and good sense. Now I fear she's gone quite out of control."

At Alice's statement, Rob lowered his gaze, suddenly and obviously uncomfortable. Norah smiled to herself. Rob looked very handsome in his high-collared, double-breasted frock coat, white plain-bow stock, and tall hat. A person meeting him for the first time would have assumed he was perfectly at ease leaping from the deck of a ship into the heart of fashionable London. But Norah knew that beneath the fine tailoring and the bold headstrong manner there breathed a man who didn't know where he fit into the world's grand scheme.

She had thought a great deal about her reluctant lover during the past few days, and she'd come to some conclusions about his state of mind. Despite his vague memory of a loving mother, Rob believed she was a factory whore. It was this uncertainty about his origins, Norah decided, that explained why he was torn between the life of an opium profiteer and that of a respectable merchant. His unfamiliarity with family life also explained why an honorable commitment to a woman was utterly beyond him.

Unfortunately, Rob's view of himself as some sort of outlaw would keep him running for the rest of his life. Norah had no idea what it would take for him to settle in one place. Perhaps learning that he was not a child of shame would transform him. Perhaps his love for her would tame him. But of one thing Norah was certain: she wanted this man for her own. How that could be accomplished without breaking her heart or his spirit left her at a loss. Her cleverest move, Norah decided, would be to do nothing. Declarations of love or hints at domestic bliss would send him flying. But she knew for sure that he loved her. He had said so. Norah told herself she would simply have to wait patiently.

The carriage turned off Oxford Street into a quiet residential neighborhood. The town houses of brick and stone, with their lovely doorways and wrought-iron balconies, reminded Norah of a very grand Boston. The air had turned cool and fresh, the lowering sun cast long shadows over the streets. Norah smelled the faint scent of the country. Except for the clatter of hooves on the cobblestones and the cheerful chirping of birds, the street was silent.

The driver stopped before a stone house of four stories with boxed flowers on the first-floor balcony. The front steps curved gracefully inward, leading to an entrance door of dark polished wood topped with an elegant fanlight.

Norah glanced at the impeccable facade and felt a current of apprehension. During the voyage, Denmore House had seemed far away. Since landing in Liverpool, thoughts of Rob had kept her mind too occupied to worry. But now Norah realized she had little idea of what to expect from the elderly Countess of Denmore and her artistic grandson, Alice's cousin Guy. Alice, who had visited the family at age seven, recalled being frightened by the grim old countess. Norah hoped Alice's fear had been no more than a child's unfounded wariness of someone old and unfamiliar.

A liveried servant ushered them through a square, high-ceilinged entry hall to a small sitting room with pale green walls decorated with carved white moldings. Upon close examination, the moldings proved to be nymphs riding on sea horses. Norah was so busy staring at the naked figures that she barely heard the butler explain that her ladyship had not expected her guests quite so soon and had only just risen from her rest.

"Perhaps after a refreshment the young ladies would care to see their room," the butler suggested. "And if Captain Mackenzie would be so kind, her ladyship would look forward to greeting him shortly in the upstairs drawing room."

Norah nodded her acquiescence to all the butler's suggestions. She communicated with Alice, who seemed awed into silence, with small, reassuring squeezes to her elbow.

A cool drink was served, and then a young woman dressed in a plain black frock and white apron entered to claim Alice and Norah. As she led them away, Rob gave Norah a reassuring wink.

They entered a great circular hallway that opened the entire height of the house. The light that came from a shallow dome of glass in the roof reflected off pink marble walls, turning the air a soft, enchanting hue. Norah dared not say a word as they proceeded up the staircase. The Burnhams' Boston mansion was larger than Denmore House, but it was cozy and familiar. Norah hoped the cold elegance of the London town house did not reflect the humor of its inhabitants.

She and Alice followed the maid down the first-floor hallway to a service stair that led to their second-floor bedroom. Norah was pleased to see that the room was snug and bright. The wallpaper pattern of rose and white swirls was copied in the fitted carpet, and the gilt-framed mirror over the fireplace reflected light from windows hung with deep rose brocade. The stout old-fashioned furniture was made of superb English oak, mellowed to a rich, dark finish.

Mavis, as the maid introduced herself, brought hot water and towels and helped wash away the dust of the journey. By the time she and Alice descended the stairway to greet their hostess, Norah was feeling a good deal braver than when she'd arrived.

The first-floor drawing room was painted pale blue and lavishly hung with paintings and mirrors. Couches and drapes of deep cinnamon velvet were complemented to stunning effect by blue silk chair coverings.

Rob was seated on the couch talking loudly to an old woman dressed in gray silk. When Norah and Alice entered, he stopped speaking and got to his feet. Norah stood for a moment, gazing about her. At the sound of a loud thump, she jumped.

"Come in, young lady! Bring my great-niece here so I can look at her."

Straight and slender with a hawklike face and smooth pale skin, Lady Denmore appeared vigorous despite her eighty years. A muslin cap rested on her hair, gray as iron but thick and heavy as a girl's. Her ornately carved walnut chair amid the more delicate rosewood furnishings suited both her severe expression and the thick staff on which she rested her hands. If her ladyship hadn't been so intimidating, Norah would have found her quite admirable.

The countess again thumped the staff, and Norah, feeling as if she were being presented at court, quickly led Alice across the blue and brown patterned carpet to stand before her.

"Kiss me, my dear girl," Lady Denmore said, her voice softening as she addressed Alice. "You seem to have grown to a healthy young lady despite your affliction."

Alice bent to kiss the offered cheek. She missed the mark and brushed her lips against the old countess's cap. "I am delighted to find you well, Aunt Isabel," Alice said.

"Speak up, girl! I'm a touch deaf!"

"I said," Alice repeated more loudly, "I'm glad to find you are well."

Lady Denmore nodded. "I regret I was unable to greet you when you arrived, but I nap from five until six in the evening. I trust you were well taken care of by Wiggins and Mavis?"

"Yes, Aunt," Alice replied. "Mama sends her regrets that she was unable to accompany me, but Grandpapa is quite ill."

"Poof!" Lady Denmore waved a hand in annoyance. "I'm not surprised. It's just like Giles to have a stroke and prevent my niece from paying me a long-overdue visit. My insufferable prig of a brother would sacrifice his life if it meant depriving me of something I wanted." She turned her piercing blue eyes on Norah and snapped, "What are you standing there for, young lady, gaping at me so? Take my great-niece to the couch!"

Stung by Lady Denmore's rudeness, Norah hastily guided Alice to one of two couches that faced each other before the fireplace. She looked at Rob, seated across from her, and found him frowning at his hands.

"I'm afraid London will be quite tedious without your mother to look after you," Lady Denmore said to Alice. "She knows best what a girl in your situation enjoys, taking walks, being read to, that sort of thing. I have quite retired from society and lead a very quiet life. Even if you were capable of attending balls and other such amusements, you would find this household a great disappointment."

"Oh, I'm really perfectly normal, Aunt," Alice said brightly. "Norah and I go about freely in Boston, and she explains what she sees. I do remember what the world looks like." She added hopefully, "I'm quite able to dance."

Lady Denmore turned her attention to Norah and regarded her with a fierce stare that traveled from her cropped hair to the toes of her shiny black slippers.

"Miss Paige, is it not?"

Norah squirmed under her inspection. "Yes'm," she answered. At a nudge from Alice, she corrected herself. "My lady."

Norah thought she saw a tug at the corner of the old woman's mouth, but a second glance showed a decidedly stern expression. "Miss Paige," the countess said, "kindly explain to me what has happened to your hair."

A self-conscious flush crept from Norah's neck to her cheeks. She glanced at Rob, who seemed to be trying to hide a smile, and wondered how she would explain the phenomenon of her short hair. "I . . . I had an accident," she said.

The countess stared at Norah with narrowed eyes, her mouth set in a tiny disapproving pucker. "Pray, what sort of accident?"

Norah didn't know where to begin. There was the storm and the fall and her shoulder and the matted hair. The old lady's severe expression was not conducive to lengthy explanations that involved Rob's removing her clothing. To simplify matters and to hurry the conclusion of the countess's examination, Norah said simply, "Captain Mackenzie cut it off."

Norah heard a sound from Rob that fell halfway between a sneeze and a cough. When she looked at him, he was studying his boot toe.

The countess's attention swung to Rob. "Captain Mackenzie, you are a most interesting man and I have enjoyed your views on the subject of India this afternoon, but I am a bit in the dark as to why you should go about cutting off a young lady's hair."

Before Rob could respond, a voice came from the doorway. "Indeed, Captain, do enlighten us."

Norah looked up to find a thin, rather stooped man entering the room. He appeared to be in his late twenties and had sandy hair, a long chin, and blue eyes that were small but kind. His coat and trousers were baggy and spotted with paint.

"It's about time you put in an appearance," the countess grumbled. "Alice, my dear, I don't suppose you remember your cousin Guy."

"Of course I do," Alice said with a tone of impatience that Norah attributed to the countess's rudeness. "I have lost my sight, not my memory."

Norah drew in a breath at Alice's impudent remark. She waited for an explosion. But the countess, apparently finding Alice's disrespect amusing, gave a surprising shout of laughter. "Well said, my girl. Guy, the child has spirit."

Guy cast a smile at Alice, whose cheeks had turned a charming pink. "And beauty as well," he said.

Guy approached Rob, who had risen at his entrance. "You're fortunate indeed, Captain, to have escorted these two lovely ladies across the ocean. As for Miss Paige's hair"—he glanced at Norah—"a most expert job of barbering, I'd say. Far better than I could do."

Rob shook Guy's hand. "I can assure you, Miss Paige won't allow it to happen again."

Norah gave Alice a nudge to signal her approval of Cousin Guy. His clothes might be ill-fitting and paint-spattered, but he had turned the entire disconcerting episode with his grandmother into a joke.

The countess, however, was not yet finished with her appraisal of Norah. "My grandson is an artist and as such has rather peculiar tastes," she said. "Now, Captain Mackenzie, I'm awaiting your explanation of your assault on Miss Paige's hair."

Rob gave a blessedly abbreviated summary of the mishap and its aftermath. When he finished the account, he rose and announced his departure.

The countess regarded him with an expression of shrewd amusement. "It's all very well that you leave us for now, Captain, but I request your company at dinner this evening. We dine at nine o'clock. I shall expect you at half past eight."

Norah thought suddenly how very fortunate it was that the countess seemed to approve of Rob. The old lady would most likely encourage him to call; she might even invite him frequently to dine.

Rob bowed politely. "It would be a pleasure, my lady."

"My grand-nephew Oliver will be joining us as well," the countess said.

"Oh, Aunt Isabel!" Alice cried happily. "I'm so looking forward to seeing Ollie."

"He's a dandy and a rascal," the countess grumbled. "But I suppose we should be honored that he has agreed to forsake his evening of riotous pleasure to greet his sister."

Lady Denmore launched into a lengthy criticism of Ollie, which brought a grin from Guy and a look of dismay to Alice. Seeing Alice's distress, Guy gently admonished his grandmother, reminding her that many young men of Ollie's age and station never rose before noon and thought of nothing but cards and drink and pretty girls.

In their room as they prepared for dinner, Alice exclaimed over Guy. She thought he was much changed since her last visit. She recalled him as a freckled and awkward boy, so bashful he could barely speak. He'd only recently lost his parents in a coach accident and had wept frequent and profuse tears. Now he was the most agreeable cousin that one could wish for. His kind, humorous voice made him sound very handsome as well.

Norah confessed that Guy was still freckled and awkward, but his appearance was pleasant, and he certainly knew how to manage his grandmother.

As Mavis brushed and dressed Alice's hair, she responded to questions about Guy and the countess. She revealed that Guy kept much to his artist's studio and rarely socialized. Her ladyship, Mavis said, was strict but not unkind.

"Have you met Mr. Guy's brother, Charles, the earl?" Alice asked.

The maid shook her head. "No, miss. I've been with her ladyship but two years. His lordship has been gone to India for much longer." She added hesitantly, "I heard he was coming home to be married."

"Married!" Alice and Norah cried together.

Mavis flushed. She was a homely girl with bony cheeks and prominent teeth. Her dark eyes, however, were soft and prettily fringed with thick lashes. "I shouldn't say nothing."

"Cousin Charles had a wife who died years ago," Alice said.

"I know nothing of that," the maid responded and would relay no more Denmore gossip.

* * *

When Norah descended the stairway that evening, she thought both she and Alice looked equal to any woman in London. Norah wore a gown of rose-colored silk with a close-fitting décolleté bodice. Satin ribbons of a darker rose tied her full sleeves. Alice looked demure in sage-green silk, and in her hair she wore silk flowers that matched her dress. Norah wanted no decoration to draw attention to her own coiffure, so Mavis had given her hair a vigorous brushing and fluffed out the waves to frame her face.

At the door of the drawing room, ablaze with candlelight, Norah halted. She put a cautioning hand on Alice's arm. "Three silent men have gathered at the fireplace," she murmured. "Your cousin, your brother, and Rob. My goodness, they look uncomfortable."

Each man was quite unlike the other. Ollie, outrageously attired in scarlet waistcoat, tight purple trousers, and white lace ruffles, had the stamp of the dandy on him from his padded chest and nipped-in waistline to his shiny pointed slippers. Beside his absurd sophistication, Guy appeared amiable and unpretentious. Rob, severely handsome in formal black, loomed over them both. His unfashionably sun-browned face was tense, and when his eyes met Norah's, she saw an expression close to desperation. Her heart went out to him. Surely he hated such occasions; he probably wanted nothing so much as to flee back to the *Orion*. Norah acknowledged his distress with a quick knowing smile; then, linking her arm through Alice's, she entered the room.

Ollie looked up. "Sissy!" He set down his glass and strode across the room to Alice.

With a happy cry, Alice threw her arms around her brother's neck, clinging hard. Ollie freed himself, laughing, and smoothed his ruffles and flowing neckcloth. His lean elegance and thick golden hair were unchanged from his Harvard days.

"I say, gentlemen," Ollie said, turning toward Guy, "I left a little girl in Boston four years ago, and here appears this lovely creature who claims to be my sister. It leaves a man quite at a loss."

"Nonsense!" Alice blushed prettily and touched the dark curls that framed her face. "I'm no different than when you last saw me, except a bit slimmer, thanks to Rob's vegetables and Norah's encouragement."

Ollie glanced across Alice's shoulder and met Norah's eyes. His long, fine-featured face was even more handsome than she remembered. "Can it be?" he said in a hushed tone, his gaze sweeping over her. "Our little Norah?"

"Hello, Ollie." Norah returned his smile, but she felt a tingle of apprehension. She'd never quite known how to respond to Ollie's overbearing charm.

He took her hand and bowed with dramatic flair. From beneath gilded lashes, his gaze made a slow and daring journey down her bodice to the satin sash at her waist. It was a practiced glance that made Norah feel more annoyed than embarrassed. She caught the distinct aroma of whiskey. Ollie's habits had apparently not improved during his years abroad.

When he straightened, he frowned thoughtfully. "Now, what have you done to your hair? Ah, you're copying the style of the scandalous and lamentably late Lady Caroline Lamb."

Norah was growing tired of explaining her odd appearance. "I'm not copying anyone," she said.

"Might be taken for a viscountess, eh, cousin?" Ollie said to Guy.

"I'm afraid Miss Paige is too much a democrat to aspire to nobility," Guy replied. "But she and your sister quite outshine any viscountess I've ever met."

"Gallantly said, cousin," Ollie responded. He gathered Alice and Norah into the circle of his velvet-clad arms. His eyes sparkled down at Norah. "This is what I've been missing all these years in London. There's nothing lovelier than an American woman."

Norah extricated herself from his embrace. "You turn a pretty compliment, Ollie, but your sister is entitled to both your arms. As an acquaintance from the past, I don't deserve such an honor."

"The deuce you don't," he said in a tone that warmed her face. "You're far more than an acquaintance, Norah, and you're quite welcome to as much of me as you wish."

"Enough, Burnham," Rob said. His voice was low and full of warning. "You're speaking to a lady."

Ollie's eyes, gleaming with cold satisfaction, didn't leave

Norah's face. "You misunderstand, Mackenzie. Norah is as much my little sister as Alice. She's been a member of our family since the age of . . ." He looked helplessly at Norah and shrugged.

"Twelve," Alice put in. Her rosy cheeks had paled, and Norah felt a growing dismay at Ollie's graceless conduct.

"Twelve." Ollie smiled brilliantly.

Norah stood frozen with embarrassment. She didn't enjoy being the center of attention, and now suddenly she had become the center of controversy. Ollie was goading Rob, who was furious, and it all had to do with her. It was obvious the two men despised each other. Norah looked from one to the other, wondering what to do.

"And what a charming twelve she was," Ollie went on. "The most tantalizing little girl I ever laid eyes on—"

"I said enough!" Rob's eyes held a kind of madness, barely checked and threatening to explode. Norah tried desperately to think of something diverting to say, but before she could open her mouth, Rob added, "If you weren't as drunk as a musketeer, Burnham, I'd bust your stripes."

Rob's appalling breach of manners made Norah's head spin. She steadied herself against the rosewood card table and took an unladylike gulp of sherry.

Ollie, a blur of scarlet and purple, whirled to face Rob. "I'm cheered to see that Norah has such an ardent defender, Mackenzie," he sneered. "I'd been led to understand that ladies were unsafe in your company."

Rob's face turned gray with anger. "By God, I don't tolerate insults, Burnham. And I settle accounts with my fists, not with your fancy pistols."

Ollie made a careless gesture with his glass, spilling amber liquid onto his sleeve. "Is that a challenge?" he asked with a mocking laugh. "If so, you're quite out of form, *Captain*."

An icy shiver ran down Norah's spine. "Be quiet, both of you!" she said hotly. She glanced at Alice, who looked positively ill.

Guy, apparently surprised into silence by the exchange, finally found his tongue. "It's always a pleasure entertaining Americans," he said with forced levity. "You're so plain-spoken and humorous. Come, Alice, let me tell you about these special goldfish."

He took Alice's arm and led her away to a long table on which rested a profusion of flowers and ferns interspersed with large glass vases containing goldfish.

Norah turned on Ollie and Rob, the one sullen, the other livid. "You should be ashamed of yourselves! Not only have you upset Alice, but you've monstrously insulted your host."

Before she could continue her scolding, Ollie glanced at the doorway and burst into one of his simpering smiles. "My *dearest* lady!" he cried, sweeping into a precariously low bow. "I am honored by your presence."

Lady Denmore, swathed in lavender silk and lace, entered the room, leaning heavily on her staff. A countess's coronet of diamonds hung from a pearl necklace about her neck.

"Fiddle," she said, brushing away Ollie's arm. "You put me in mind of my brother Algernon who was full of nonsense and never worked a day in his life."

Ollie laughed and followed her to her carved throne. "Why, that's a compliment, Aunt Iz. Algernon was your favorite brother."

"That doesn't mean he was worth a farthing to anyone but himself and his tailor," the old lady sniffed. "Spent so much time before the mirror, he took his meals standing up."

Rob muttered under his breath, "How his father came to sire that paper skull is beyond my comprehension."

"And how you could behave so rudely is beyond mine," Norah retorted, furious that he had so frightened Alice. "You're no longer on your opium ship, but in a proper drawing room, an *earl's* drawing room."

Anger flared in Rob's eyes. "Oh, I beg your pardon, my lady," he snapped. "I didn't realize that an *earl's* drawing room was so sacred to you. Being insulted by that good-for-nothing fop is evidently not offensive in an *earl's* drawing room."

"It was you who offered the insult with your threats," Norah whispered fiercely. "While you're in London, you'd be well advised to hold your vulgarity in check."

Rob stared at her in disbelief. "My vulgarity!" His face twisted into a bitter smile. "My vulgarity should be no surprise to you, my dear Norah. You know it well from intimate experience."

The hurt in his eyes brought to Norah the hot sting of guilt, swiftly followed by annoyance that he should so misinterpret her words. She opened her mouth to respond, but the butler chose that moment to announce dinner.

Ollie appeared before Norah to claim her as his partner. He turned on Rob an infuriating smile. "You've had this lovely creature to yourself these past four weeks, Mackenzie. I hope we shan't vie too vigorously for her attentions."

Rob answered with a sour grimace. "Be my guest. She's had enough of my company."

Norah tried to meet Rob's gaze and offer a silent apology for her hasty words, but his eyes were focused elsewhere.

The trip to the dining room was unbearable. Ollie chattered on and on, expecting some sort of response, but all Norah could think of was Rob's wounded expression. Perhaps he'd behaved abominably, but he'd only been responding to Ollie's mischief. And he'd spoken in defense of her honor. In an agony of self-reproach, Norah despaired of ever setting things right. She had struck Rob's most tender core; he now thought she scorned both his manners and his morals, which to him meant she scorned his breeding.

The dining room gleamed with polished silver and crisp white napery. Overhead, two crystal chandeliers glistened like icicles, turning the damask draperies to liquid gold. Servants stepped softly, carrying dishes of scalloped oysters, ham, and pheasant pie.

Norah felt so miserable that she hardly noticed the beauty of the room. Nor did she pay much attention when Ollie leaned close and murmured, "I look forward to renewing our acquaintance, my dear little sister."

During the interminable dinner, Ollie droned on about clubs and card games and riding in Hyde Park. The kind but inelegant Guy seemed to sense Norah's distress. When Ollie left off chattering to take a gulp of wine, Guy mentioned entertainments that she and Alice would enjoy. But Norah's attention centered on the far end of the table. She stared at Rob with a frozen heart. He was entertaining the countess with gusto, but he took no notice of her. Not a glance, not a smile, not a flicker of an eye.

After dinner the company adjourned to the music room. Alice played the piano, while Ollie, Guy, and Norah took turns singing popular ballads. There was no occasion to speak, no chance to resolve a stupid misunderstanding.

Rob took his leave quietly. He gave Norah an unsmiling nod and bent to speak to the countess, half asleep in a red velvet chair. The others, arguing at the piano over various musical arrangements, didn't notice his departure. Norah watched in piercing misery as Rob crossed the shiny parquet floor. He'd said he loved her. Now, because of one slip of the tongue, everything they had shared was spoiled. As Rob disappeared through the door, Norah could only believe he was walking right out of her life.

Chapter Eleven

LADY DENMORE INSISTED that Alice become as comfortable in her new surroundings as she had been in her own home. To that end, the old countess summoned the household staff, apprised them of her great-niece's needs and capabilities, and instructed them to offer any assistance that might be required. Then Lady Denmore left her young guests to their own devices. She demanded a progress report each day at dinner, but observed Alice's accomplishments for herself only when invited.

Alice spent each morning with Norah, counting steps and doorways and acquainting herself with every possible impediment, from the harp in the music room to the globe in the library. After a week Norah was satisfied that Alice could manage on her own, and Alice herself said she felt right at home.

Guy passed the morning hours in his third-floor studio. He emerged at noon to offer Alice and Norah his company for the rest of the day. If the weather permitted, he drove them in the phaeton to various London sights, while his grandmother spent the afternoon gossiping and playing cards in the second-floor card room with a group of dowagers who had been her friends since girlhood.

Guy made every outing a delight. His artist's eye for detail and his witty asides painted verbal pictures that far outstripped Norah's ability. She gratefully relinquished to him the role of Alice's "eyes." Guy took them to the Zoological Gardens and for a stroll along the prettily sheltered Birdcage Walk in St. James's Park. Alice purchased French silk flowers at the Burlington Arcade, and Norah visited the booksellers on Oxford Street. At Week's Mechanical Exhibition, Norah and Alice giggled helplessly as Guy described the tarantula that wiggled its horns and claws. The white mouse, formed of Oriental pearls, ran about the table looking so tempting, he said, that a cat might find it tasty.

Norah was so busy sight-seeing and helping Alice that only late in the evening did she have time to write to Miss Peabody the long detailed letters she had promised. London, she wrote, was more thrilling than she had ever imagined. That very afternoon she had sat among the evergreens of Kensington Gardens and listened to the music of the Life Guards' band. And on the Promenade at Vauxhall Gardens, Guy had pointed out Lord Melbourne and Lady Robert Lorton, leader of the *ton* and sister-in-law of the rich and powerful duke of Lisborough. Norah had never heard of Lady Lorton or the duke, but she was impressed by their credentials and was certain Miss Peabody would be as well.

Ollie dropped by the Berkeley Square house almost daily. He rode in Hyde Park late each afternoon and encouraged Norah to join him. She had a gorgeous habit of purple velvet and a pert little hat, but she was a poor rider and felt ashamed to appear on the same path with the expert horsewomen who dazzled passersby with their roguish style.

It was Alice who finally convinced Norah that she must ride on Rotten Row at least once while she was in London. "No one in London could possibly care about how you sit on a horse," she argued. "Besides, Ollie is a good teacher and an expert gossip. He'll entertain you with tidbits about the other ladies and gentlemen on the riding paths, and then you can report it all back to me."

So during her second week in London, Norah agreed to accompany Ollie to Hyde Park. Lady Denmore's stableman arranged to hire a gentle mare from the proprietor of a nearby livery stable, and Ollie came to collect Norah shortly after noon. He looked as if he'd been driven into his top boots and breeches, so perfect was the fit. His brown riding jacket, its velvet collar brushed smooth as a mink's pelt, fit snugly over his broad shoulders and tapered down his slender torso. Whatever his faults, Norah decided, Ollie was certainly a good-looking man. And he'd become surprisingly agreeable during the past week. After Norah told him bluntly that she found his flirtatious manner tiresome, he had shown himself to be quite manageable and diverting. Heaven knew, she needed constant diversion. At the most unexpected moments she was swept by a sense of loss that threatened her composure and spoiled her fun.

As they entered the park's vast expanse of green, Ollie filled Norah in on the latest gossip about Mrs. Caroline Norton. Mrs. Norton's trial in June on charges of adultery with Lord Melbourne had been a sensation. Everyone in London seemed to have an opinion on the subject. While Norah was as curious as the next person, she found the publicity disturbing.

"I think the newspaper accounts are horrid and spiteful," she said. "Lady Denmore says that in her day the friendship between Lord Melbourne and Mrs. Norton wouldn't have signified a straw."

Ollie laughed. He looked golden and handsome in the sparkling afternoon sun. "My dear New England Norah, how charming you are, defending the libertine woman."

Norah thought of her own carnal appetites and felt a brief pang, not of guilt but of longing. She hurriedly protested, "But the public examination of a matter so private is disgraceful, not to mention hypocritical. Why, Lady Denmore says Melbourne's own sister is the lover of Lord Palmerston, and Melbourne's late wife, Lady Caroline Lamb, had an affair with Lord Byron. Lord Melbourne himself carried on with both Lady Stanhope *and* Lady Branden."

Ollie shouted with laughter. "I can't believe my great-aunt is filling virginal minds with such scandalous gossip! And you, Norah! To speak so freely of infidelity! Has your Boston upbringing completely deserted you? My mother would succumb to the vapors if she heard such talk."

Norah ignored Ollie's patronizing grin and impatiently shrugged. "It seems to be an accepted topic of conversation in the drawing rooms of Lady Denmore's friends."

Ollie shook his handsome head and chuckled. "Those old hags should be ashamed of themselves. It's highly improper to speak so to unmarried girls."

They entered the riding path, blessedly free of the crowd that would later throng the park. A morning shower had cooled the air but left the paths thick with mud. As they plodded along, Norah wondered if her interest in the amorous transgressions of other women was brought on by her own passion for Rob. Had Mrs. Norton and the other noble ladies felt as compelled toward their men as she felt toward him? The familiar thump of her heart reminded Norah that today was the eleventh day since he had left her. She missed him desperately. On every outing with Guy and Alice, she wished Rob were beside her. She would have loved to show him the bear pit at the Zoological Garden and the diorama at Regents Park. At night in bed she reviewed the day as if she were telling him each detail, and she never failed to hold him in her thoughts as she fell asleep.

"Since you find Mrs. Norton so worthy of defense," Ollie said, distracting Norah's spirits from their downward spiral, "you'll be pleased to learn that she has been rehabilitated in society. After the trial, the Duchess of Sutherland invited her to sit by her side for a drive in Hyde Park. Within the hour the fallen woman was once more acceptable."

Norah no longer felt like discussing Mrs. Norton. She nudged her mare with her boot heel, and the beast jounced into a trot, tossing Norah about with unpleasant vigor. At Ollie's urging, they broke into a canter and raced along the muddy path until Norah was jostled to breathlessness.

"You're not a bad rider," Ollie said, as he wheeled his mount. "Just remember to keep your hands down and loosen up a bit on the reins. With a bit more practice, you'll be a pretty picture on Rotten Row."

Norah was panting for breath. "Oh, Ollie, I'm hopeless on a horse. I can see that when I compare myself to the other ladies."

Ollie's face went suddenly serious. He drew up beside Norah, so close that his knee bumped hers. "My dear Norah, if I tell you how beautiful and enchanting you are, and how greatly you underestimate yourself, you must promise me you'll never change. It takes all my restraint not to speak hastily and spoil all I have planned for you."

Norah stared at him in wonder. Surely she hadn't heard him correctly. The very last thing she wanted was for Ollie to begin his teasing again.

"I'll court you properly," he said solemnly. "I do remember my Boston manners."

With a jolt of astonishment, Norah realized he wasn't teasing. The Ollie who sat so easily on his mount, regarding her with cool wintry eyes, was no longer the flirtatious Ollie who could be reined in with an irritable scolding, but an ardent, determined man.

Norah found enough of her voice to protest. "But I don't want to be courted, Ollie. I don't want a husband."

His blue eyes turned suddenly frigid. He looked at her in a bold and knowing way that seemed to strip away her maidenly facade and reveal the shameless, yielding woman beneath. "Then perhaps you'd consider a lover," he said. "You speak so freely of the affairs of others, a man might wonder."

Heat leaped to Norah's face. "How dare you!" she cried, appalled that their conversation had inspired him to suggest such a thing. "What a dreadful thing to say. You have no right—"

"What does Mackenzie mean to you?" Ollie demanded.

Blood throbbed in Norah's cheeks. She gaped at Ollie, her wits too confused by the truthful implication of his words to consider a response.

"Come, come, I'm not blind," Ollie said sourly. "I see your blush. You're in love with him."

Norah pulled hard at her mare's mouth and looked about frantically for the best direction to run. She had no idea how to deal with Ollie; all she wanted to do was escape the humiliation of this situation. The thought of anyone discovering the truth about her and Rob was more than she could bear.

Norah urged her sluggish mount forward, but Ollie grasped her bridle, holding her back. "Your captain is a dangerous man, my little dove. I'm afraid you've gotten in a bit over your head. He uses and discards women like yesterday's newspaper."

"It's not true!" Norah cried, risking her seat to knock

Ollie's hand away. Terrible pulses beat in her throat, her head, even her eyes. "I forbid you to speak so rudely!"

"Then where is he, Norah? From what I hear, he's yet to darken your doorstep. You've been used, sweetings, used and tossed aside."

Norah kicked the mare. Ollie's shouts were lost in the sound of hoofbeats as she pounded down the path.

"Captain Mackenzie." Jonathan Wildes rose from behind his gleaming mahogany desk and held out a large hand in greeting. "Welcome to London. I understand from your agent that you're about to set off to the north country."

Rob took quick measure of the impeccably dressed merchant banker whose firm acted as the chief source of credit in England for Burnham and Bradshaw. It was said that Wildes had an instinctive understanding of when, to whom, and for how long it was wise to extend credit. He was greatly trusted in the business world, and Rob was prepared to listen to his advice.

"I'll be off to Manchester, Leeds, and Glasgow in a few days," Rob said, taking a seat. "But in light of financial conditions, I thought it wise to discuss credit before bargaining for woolens."

"And well you might, sir," Wildes said, returning to his desk, which was as tidy as his person. "The Bank of England has just raised the discount rate to four and a half percent. The outflow of gold to America has caused considerable alarm."

"Yet other major English banking firms engaged in the American trade are encouraging increased exports from Europe," Rob said. "And in Boston just about any businessman on the Exchange will tell you the American boom bodes most favorably for the investor."

Wildes watched Rob thoughtfully. "I know what is being said in some quarters, Captain, but I also know that a panic is brewing in the money market as far as American paper is concerned. Remittances from the United States are slow, and American merchants are renewing their credit by borrowing to pay on past engagements, hardly a healthy practice."

He paused and looked at Rob sharply. "You are a sea captain, and a brilliant one from what I hear. For that you have my compliments. But you are inexperienced in finance. This is no time for amateurs, sir, no time for apprenticeships or for waiting ten to twelve weeks for instructions from Boston. What authority have you been given over the affairs of Burnham and Bradshaw at this critical time?"

Rob had expected the question. Cornelius Sprague, Burnham's London agent, had warned Rob that Wildes was skeptical of his qualifications to carry out the firm's transactions. Rob responded to Wildes with a question of his own. "Have you any knowledge of the business aspects of the Calcutta trade?"

Wildes nodded. "A complex system, I understand. No end of difficulties converting commercial paper into rupees."

"And that's only the beginning," Rob said. "There are no large local merchants or manufacturers. The weavers are so poor that money must be advanced to them during the period of manufacture. And the middlemen will do what gives them the least trouble, not the lowest price." He smiled. "More than once I've considered buying a loom and making the cloth myself."

Wildes laughed. "Your point is well taken. I suppose India makes doing business in England a child's game."

"At least the rules here are understood. As for my authority"—Rob reached inside his coat, removed a letter, and dropped it on the desk—"you will find Mr. Burnham trusts my judgment."

Wildes picked up the letter and scanned it quickly. "He appears to have the greatest confidence in you, sir." Then his eyebrows rose. "Burnham asks for fifteen thousand pounds to continue until December. I'm afraid our firm must now insist on reimbursement at four months. And I cannot permit redrawing to extend the time of payment on your past engagements."

"Perhaps six thousand would be more agreeable at three months," Rob said, warming to the debate. "And another three thousand at six months for assembling a cargo for Calcutta."

Wildes looked up in surprise. "Well, that is independent thinking, Captain. Do you propose cutting the orders your firm requests for the Boston market?"

"My instincts, like yours, Mr. Wildes, tell me there's a gale coming. Now that I hear of your concerns, I feel even more strongly that buying heavily in such an advancing market would be a mistake. Better to keep stocks low, get our business snug, and ride out the storm."

"And you will survive the consequences when the merchants on the Boston Exchange make a fortune in the American boom?" Wildes asked.

Rob knew his course of action would probably infuriate Oliver Burnham, but he had to take that chance. "Perhaps my firm will have the last laugh."

Wildes sat in a thoughtful silence. "Very well, Captain Mackenzie," he said at last, "I shall do as you ask. And I must retract my initial doubts as to your competence. I had no idea you had spent time in the Calcutta trade, which is enough to try the patience of the shrewdest businessman. Tell me, what sort of profits do you turn on your investments in that part of the world?"

"The norm for a successful voyage is twenty percent," Rob answered, "with a few highly exceptional ones near one hundred percent."

"I see. And your share in the profits, Captain, if I may ask?"

"With the cargo space allotted to me for my own ventures, as well as a percentage of the invoice value of the cargo and the percentage I own in the vessel, approximately twelve percent of the total profit."

Mr. Wildes rubbed his chin. "Had you considered borrowing on your own account for this voyage?"

Rob had Wildes exactly where he wanted him. "That would have been my next request, sir."

Wildes chuckled. "Your terms, Captain, and your cargo?"

"Five thousand at six months on a cargo of opium for Canton and luxury goods for the Anglo-Indians in Calcutta. I've heard there's little opium on the Canton market and the price has nearly doubled. The Turkey crop will be harvested in August and arrive in London warehouses in September. I sail from Liverpool in October."

The banker tapped his fingers on his gleaming mahogany desk. "You have experience in the opium trade?"

"I commanded an opium receiving station off Lintin Island. And I've sailed opium lighters up the coast of China."

Wildes's eyes lit up with interest. "Dangerous work, Captain. From what I understand, Chinese authorities would not hesitate to kill anyone violating their prohibition against trading in opium."

Rob laughed. "The authorities are the last to disrupt the opium trade. A bribe, paid with all due attention to ceremony, satisfies the officials of the Celestial Kingdom. The danger comes not from them, but from the pirates who plague the coast. They're the ones who slaughter the crews and plunder the cargoes. A vessel returning from a northern province loaded with silver must be swift and heavily armed. I've come across plenty of wrecks adrift, their crews' throats slit and hanging open to the sun."

Mr. Wildes stirred uncomfortably. "I see."

"So you see, sir, the international money market doesn't frighten me a bit."

Wildes continued to look thoughtful. "Such dangerous work could have made you a wealthy man, Captain, had you kept it up."

"I am a wealthy man, Mr. Wildes," Rob said as he rose and extended his hand. "I'll call by when I return from the north. Perhaps we can further our business acquaintance."

After leaving Moorgate, Rob pushed his way through the congestion of the City's business district to a chophouse off Fleet Street. He found Cornelius Sprague seated at a small table behind a partition.

A beefy, red-faced man and a Bostonian by birth, Sprague had begun his career in England looking after the affairs of his father-in-law's Boston firm. Finding London to his liking, Sprague connected with a British merchant to form Crafts and Sprague, commission agents who represented several Boston houses.

"Success?" Sprague asked.

Rob sat down and took in the vastly busy room. The place was insufferably hot and noisy, the smoky air thick with the smell of cooking meat. Beyond the diners' roar and clatter rose the shouts of waiters and the banging of the cooks' pans and knives. Rob glanced at the slab of greasy beef hanging off Sprague's plate. It didn't look appetizing.

"I'm cutting orders for the spring season, Con."

Sprague slammed his glass of ale on the wooden table. "Cutting orders! Good God, Mackenzie, are you mad? You're listening to Wildes's talk of panic when conditions in the States couldn't be better! Listen, my good man, you're new at this game, so let me give you some advice."

Rob signaled the waiter for a glass of ale. "Advice?" he asked Sprague, grinning. "By all means, Con, I'm all ears."

"This spring was the best season in memory. Look at the situation in the States: new banks being chartered, wholesale firms springing up all over, the West booming. Why, importers can't keep up with demand."

Rob shook his head. "When a man like Wildes warns that credit's too generous, prices are too high, and he's reminded of the bad times of 'sixteen and 'eighteen, I'd pay attention."

Sprague tugged at the puffs of whiskers that framed his cheeks. "Aw, Rob, you're throwing it all away."

"Throwing what away?"

Sprague leaned close. His chin above his tucked linen gleamed with grease. "The firm!" he exclaimed in a hushed voice. "Look, man, Bradshaw is senile and out of the business, and Oliver Burnham is getting tired and lazy. You've got brains and youth and money enough to buy out the both of them."

"How do you know about my money?" Rob asked sharply.

Sprague sat back with a laugh. "Burnham has ways of knowing his number one captain has salted away a fortune over the years. What is it, Rob, fifty thousand? A hundred?"

Rob scowled at his ale. Sprague was good company, but Rob resented any man's intrusion into his personal affairs.

"Oliver Burnham's had his eye on you for years," Sprague went on. "He knows Ollie won't amount to a thing and Alice will never marry. He has no one but you. All you have to do is continue to please the old man, get some experience in the European markets, and one day B and B will fall right in your lap."

"My business isn't to take over the firm," Rob said irritably. "It's to place orders for the spring season and ensure that

Burnham and Bradshaw can meet its obligations. Reducing the stock in Burnham's warehouses is the only way to do it."

Sprague shook his head sorrowfully. "The old man ain't going to like it, Rob, and neither do I. Every reduction in your cargo reduces my commission. I hate to see that."

"We're not in business to keep *you* in business, Sprague."

Sprague took a long swallow of ale and wiped his mouth. "Enough of this. Come to dinner tonight. The girls like you, and I need a man's company now and again."

Rob eyed Sprague warily. Sprague's wife and twin daughters had recently joined him in London. Boston gossip reported that Sprague had been enjoying his bachelor status with unseemly abandon, openly squiring his mistress to the theater and the opera. Since his wife and the girls arrived, he was behaving discreetly, but Rob doubted he was forgoing his pleasures altogether.

"I hope you're not shopping for a son-in-law," Rob said.

Sprague replied with a grimace. "I would not wish either of my daughters on you, Captain. Empty-headed fools, both of them. Filled with gossip and fashions and all sorts of ways to spend my money. Come along, Rob. One evening won't compromise you."

Sprague looked so insistent that Rob agreed to the visit. "I tire easily," he warned, "especially of marriageable misses who find me fascinating."

Sprague stared thoughtfully at his glass. "Sometimes I wish they'd been boys," he said. "But then again, a son can disappoint more than a daughter. Look at Burnham's son, a fancypants good-for-nothing if I ever saw one. But a daughter, now. A father need not expect much from a daughter. If she has looks and a smattering of sense, some young fellow will take her off his hands."

Rob shook his head. "For myself, it's a daughter I'd worry about."

"And how's that, Mackenzie?" Sprague said with a laugh. "Don't trust the likes of you? A handsome bachelor aiming to do her no good?"

Rob frowned, feeling suddenly melancholy. "Perhaps." He tossed some coins on the table and prepared to get up.

"Speaking of girls," Sprague said in a low voice. "I know a

place in Belgravia where they serve up young ones. No older than fourteen. Young Burnham fancies that sort of thing, and I must admit it's quite an experience."

Rob winced. "Not to my taste, Con."

Sprague chuckled. "I thought you seamen had a superior and practical knowledge of all modes of vice."

"No more, evidently, than do commission merchants and young dandies with time on their hands," Rob said, picking up his hat. "I'll come by this evening at seven."

Rob left the chophouse and headed down the Strand toward Charing Cross. He fancied a stroll down Pall Mall to Hyde Park to watch the pretty equestriennes riding in Rotten Row. It was a fine day for a walk. The normal gloom of London was suspended for the day; instead of gray dampness, the air sparkled after a morning shower. Even the grimy stone buildings had a more cheerful aspect.

Rob glanced up at the flat soot-blackened Georgian-paned windows that looked out upon the bustle of London business. He thought of a future traveling about Europe from city to city, visiting factories and dull, cloistered offices, making do with inconvenient accommodations and the companionship of merchants and bankers and paid-for women. He thought of Sprague's prediction that Burnham was grooming him to take over the firm. Was that what he wanted? An importing company? Burnham and Mackenzie . . . It didn't sound right. Mackenzie and . . . Sons? Rob put that thought out of his mind; the very idea raised painful feelings best left unexamined. What was the alternative? To command vessels for the rest of his life? To retire into idleness?

To tell the truth, Rob didn't much care what he did. Risking his capital as a dry goods merchant or risking his own skin off the coast of China seemed equally unappealing. Lately his life seemed like a burden to be borne, a number of years to get through. He had little to be proud of. Jody was too far gone to be recovered. The fortune he'd made in opium was undeniably immoral. He'd seduced a girl entrusted to him and then lied to her by not telling her the secret that would break her heart.

Rob kicked at a pile of refuse in his path. Norah had called him vulgar. She hadn't meant to hurt him, but she was right.

He'd tried damned hard with his new suits and rusty manners, but it all came down to breeding, and he surely didn't have that. He'd better accept the fact he had come from nothing and he'd leave nothing behind.

Rob paused at Charing Cross long enough to glance at the jumble of traffic before venturing out into its midst. A barouche passed by with a crest on the door and a liveried footman standing at the rear. A woman in a richly plumed hat the color of deep wine rested against the plush cushions, her parasol opened against the sun. Green eyes met his and Rob felt a jolt of recognition. Then she was gone, disappearing behind an omnibus. Rob jumped quickly out of the way of an onrushing cab. Once he was safely across the street, he searched for the carriage, but it had been swallowed up in traffic. Frowning, he continued on his way. He must have been mistaken; it couldn't possibly have been she.

In Hyde Park, Rob leaned on the railing of the riding path and watched a young woman in a snug green habit canter toward him on a sleek bay, clods of mud flying off behind the horse's hooves. From beneath the little veil that dipped provocatively over her eyes, the woman gave him a bold glance. Rob touched the brim of his hat. The flirtatious mistress of some old lord, he thought, a woman skilled in the ways of love and adept at easing a man's murderous loneliness.

Loneliness. It was a sign of age, Rob decided. When he was young, he hadn't given a thought to his purpose or his future. He hadn't felt anything but invincible. He'd simply followed his ambition, loving and hating with careless gusto, taking risks and making money for the satisfaction it gave him. Life had been easy because he hadn't given it a thought. Now he couldn't stop thinking, and his thoughts brought him no peace.

A couple approached, deep in conversation, their mounts walking slowly. The woman was dressed in purple, a small hat set rakishly on her light brown hair. She was holding the reins much too high and her seat was unsteady. Rob leaned on his walking stick and watched, amused by her awkwardness. There was something about her . . . With a sudden chill, he recognized Norah, then Ollie Burnham. Rob stepped back into the shade of a great oak tree. He told himself to walk away, but he couldn't take his eyes off Norah. The purple velvet of her habit was stretched tight across her full young breasts. Her waist looked tiny above voluminous skirts; her broad shoulders were straight with unjustified confidence. She was perched so precariously high that Rob suddenly tasted panic. What if she fell? What if the mare should kick off and throw her? Rob fought the urge to run onto the path, grasp the bridle, and command her to dismount.

He forced himself to turn away from the riding path. With sickening certainty, he knew how irrevocably he had fallen in love and how impossible it would be to erase Norah from his heart. Avoiding her, ignoring her, sailing off to China, none of it would free him. He now understood his loneliness. Every moment aboard the *Orion*, he had felt alive with pleasure or desire or anger, even misery, and all because of Norah. Removing her from his life had left him empty and uncaring.

Rob found a bench and sank down on it. So this was love: a sick feeling in the pit of one's stomach. No joy, no satisfaction, only emptiness and disappointment.

He heard a rustle of skirts, smelled the vaguely familiar scent of frangipani, and glanced up. A woman sat down next to him, her green eyes studying him with the smug look of accomplishment. The woman in the barouche.

"Amanda!" Rob said in astonishment, a smile breaking over his face. "I don't believe it."

"So I found you, Rob Mackenzie." Her voice was light and full of laughter. "I thought I recognized you at Charing Cross, and here I've finally caught up with you. Now, what on earth are you doing sitting on a bench in Hyde Park, looking so incredibly glum?"

Chapter Twelve

NORAH JOUNCED DOWN the riding path, gripping the mare's coarse mane, while she slid all over the saddle. She kicked futilely, searching for a stirrup, and groped for the reins she'd lost in her haste to flee Ollie. *Bother!* She could barely keep to the mare's back. Suddenly Norah lost her tenuous hold. She grasped at air and felt herself sliding from the saddle. Her feet struck the muddy path, her legs crumpling beneath her as she pitched forward, face first, into the soft mud.

Norah lay stunned, more surprised than frightened, her face in the muck, her rear in the air, aware only of the unpleasant wetness seeping through her habit and the mortification of having created a scene. After pulling her head out of the mud, she wiped at her eyes and struggled to her feet. Her legs got tangled up in the heavy folds of her skirt, and she fell back. Hell and damnation! she thought. How clumsy can one be?

Suddenly she felt herself being scooped into strong arms.

"I'm not hurt," Norah protested, dismayed that she needed assistance. How embarrassing to have a stranger soil his clothing on her account! She blinked away drops of muddy water and gasped. "Rob!" she cried and felt a burst of happiness.

He carried her out of harm's way, set her down on the grass, and crouched beside her. "You don't know a damned thing about staying on the back of a horse," he said, giving her a furious look. "Where the devil is Ollie?"

Norah couldn't take her eyes off his face, so dear to her, so sorely missed. "He . . . he's teaching me," she said.

"Well, he's doing a damned poor job of it." Rob took out his handkerchief and wiped her face and hands. "A fall like that could injure your shoulder again."

Norah reached up to straighten her stylish little hat, but found it gone. Muddy water dripped from her hair. "I must look terrible!" she exclaimed. If only Rob had seen her well seated in her fashionable riding habit.

"Terrible indeed," Rob said more kindly. Tossing aside his handkerchief, he sat back on his heel, draped one arm over his bent knee, and looked at her radiant mud-streaked face, her luminous blue-gray eyes. "I don't suppose you purposely created this disturbance to get my attention."

Norah's shoulders lifted in a bashful shrug. "As you well know, I'll stop at nothing," she said and blushed.

Rob cleared his throat and glanced away. Dear God, she was lovely. And she hadn't lost her affection for him. For that he felt a vast but futile gratitude. "How's Alice?" he asked.

"Very happy. Guy takes us to see the most remarkable things. Yesterday we visited the Pavilion of the Gigantic Whale on St. Martin's Lane. Last week we heard Signor Paganini play his violin, and tonight Henriette Sontag is appearing in *The Magic Flute* at Covent Garden."

Norah drew her mud-covered knees to her chin and hugged her legs with contentment. Rob's cravat and coat were spattered with mud, he'd lost his hat, and his hair was rumpled, but he had never looked more wonderfully handsome than he did now, as he crouched beside her, his dark eyes drinking her in.

"I wish you'd call on us," she said.

Rob shifted his gaze. "I'm leaving for Manchester in a day or two," he said quickly. "I'll be out of town for a few weeks."

So, Norah thought, he was going to Manchester. She glanced up at the sunbeams winking through the leaves and took a breath to summon her courage. "You should look up your parents in the Manchester city records."

Rob's face fell into a scowl. "My parents! What the devil—"

A petulant voice interrupted, "I'll see to her, Mackenzie."

Ollie walked up the little rise of grass toward the grove of trees where they sat. He carried Norah's veiled hat out to one side so it wouldn't drip on his jacket. Of all the times for him to claim her, Norah thought hopelessly, just when she was in the midst of this critical discussion with Rob. Well, Ollie would just have to wait. She mustered her most authoritative tone. "Leave us for a moment, Ollie."

Ollie hesitated, looking surprised and annoyed.

"I'd best go, Norah," Rob said hastily and prepared to get up.

Norah seized his arm. "Not yet. I have something to say to you." She gave Ollie a fierce look. "I want to speak to Captain Mackenzie in private, Ollie. Be so kind as to leave us."

A look of disgust twisted Ollie's handsome features. Norah could see the fury in his eyes. "You're too bold by far, Norah," he said and stomped off.

Rob turned to her. "What's this cursed business about?"

The tight impatience of his lips and the restless flicker of his eyes told Norah she had best not tarry in coming to her point. "It's about your mother."

Rob uttered a short, ugly word that was unfamiliar to Norah but nonetheless shocking. "Christ, are we back to that again?" he muttered.

"What was your mother's name?" she asked.

Rob's voice was soft with warning. "Don't do this, Norah."

Norah gazed resolutely into his angry face. "Tell me her name."

Rob viciously pulled a clump of grass from the ground. "I told you her name," he said through clenched teeth. "Mary Cuthpert."

Rob's tiny gesture of cooperation gave Norah a trace of hope. "And your father?"

Rob sifted the grass through his blunt, stained fingers and maintained a scowling silence. Norah waited. After a moment she prodded him. "Rob?"

"Who the hell knows?" he snapped. "He didn't leave a calling card."

Norah smiled patiently. "Why, his name was Mackenzie, you foolish man. Where do you think you got *your* name?" She paused to give him a moment to consider her words before she continued. "If your mother had been unmarried, your name would be Cuthpert, not Mackenzie. Now, go to Manchester and do some investigating. You might find a different story from what you think."

"What I'll find is a promiscuous factory woman who named her bastard for a passing encounter."

"Maybe you will, and then again, maybe you won't."

Rob stared off in the distance. "Is it so important to you that my people be respectable, Norah? Is a bastard too *vulgar* for your tastes?"

Norah had prepared herself for that question and disposed of it easily. "Where you came from matters not at all to me, Rob Mackenzie," she told him. "But I know it matters to you."

Rob looked at her with the cold, tight expression that portended an explosion. But when he spoke his voice was grimly calm. "Stop interfering where you have no business, Norah. My life is no concern of yours."

"Oh, yes, it is," Norah responded softly. "Everything about you is my concern. Ever since the night we were together on the *Orion*."

Color bloomed on her cheeks, and Rob felt something warm sweep over him. An ache started up in his chest, and some sort of lump seemed to swell in his throat. Norah smiled, a gentle smile full of promises, and for a blinding instant every intimacy they had shared ran through Rob's mind and flooded his body. He tasted her lips and felt her softness; he knew again the secrets of her body. Before he could stop himself, his fingers were on her cheeks and he was bending to kiss her willing mouth.

Ollie's voice broke the spell. "Look here, Mackenzie, I don't favor standing around minding the horses while you do your courting."

To his own surprise, Rob laughed. Norah's sweet face was shining up at him, and her hand rested lightly on his knee. She made him feel reckless and light-headed and unexpectedly happy. He glanced at Ollie, who was rigid with annoyance. "Why, Ollie, I thought you would understand. A courting man doesn't like to be rushed." He helped Norah to her feet. Taking the hat from Ollie's hand, he gave it a shake and placed it on her head. "In the future, Burnham, take better care of her. She's precious cargo."

Rob touched Norah's cheek and gave her a wink. Then he turned and strolled away, down the grassy rise, across the riding path, and through the fence. Norah looked after him, blissfully happy. Rob hadn't forgotten her. Far from it.

Then she saw the woman. Despite the distance that blurred her features, Norah could see that she was beautiful. Tall and full-figured, she wore a shimmering wine-colored gown with a matching hat. A large plume swept across her forehead. As Rob approached, she laughed up at him as if responding to something he was saying. Rob took the woman's arm without a backward glance, but the woman with the feather turned and looked over her shoulder at Norah, the smile still on her lips. Norah stared back, her heart twisting in her chest, her hands suddenly cold and shaking.

Ollie gave a short laugh. "Mackenzie's doxy. Very nice. He has excellent taste."

Norah felt the blood drain from her face. "Doxy." She choked on the word, knowing perfectly well what it meant. Rob had a mistress. A mistress who claimed him with her smiles while Norah stood covered with mud, her hat trampled, looking like a fool. A mistress who held Rob in her arms as Norah had held him on the *Orion*. A mistress who was mature and experienced and who knew far more about men than a twenty-year-old girl from Boston.

Ollie took Norah's elbow. "A man long at sea often finds it convenient to have one in each port of call."

Dazed, Norah allowed Ollie to lead her to the horses. He boosted her onto her mare. Norah sat still, feeling the iciness of winter settle over her. A mistress. A woman he loved in that most intimate way.

"Perhaps she's simply a friend," she said faintly.

"Friend!" Ollie snorted as he swung himself into the saddle. "Use your head, Norah, and put Mackenzie out of your mind. Believe me, I speak out of friendship and concern for your reputation. Now come along. I'm taking you home."

Amanda Downing swept off her hat and turned so Rob could admire her finely chiseled nose, the firm chin, her smooth throat. She was as lovely as the day he'd first laid eyes on her at a Calcutta levee ten years ago. The auburn hair had lost some of its luster, and Rob detected a few lines around her eyes and mouth, but Amanda remained a stunning woman.

She smiled at him over her shoulder. "Do I look like an old lady, *chéri*? I'm thirty-eight, you know."

Rob lay back against the couch pillows and folded his hands behind his head, his stocking feet resting on the brocade ottoman. Amanda's footman had claimed his boots to clean off the mud. "You'll never age, Amanda."

Amanda gave him a grateful smile and sighed. "Time goes by too quickly. Before I know it, I'll be a grandmama."

"A scandalous one, no doubt," Rob said with a grin.

Amanda frowned prettily. "I'll have you know, *mon petit,* I'm as chaste as a nun these days. I had no trouble resisting a quite handsome young officer on the ship coming back from Calcutta."

Rob chuckled. "I admire your fortitude. Now, tell me why you've returned to London. With Sir Anthony gone, you could surely have found another husband to keep you in India."

A footman entered with a tray and set it before Amanda. After he left, she set out the cups and poured the tea, a smile curving her lips.

"What's the secret?" Rob asked. "Come on, Amanda, you're bursting to tell me."

"I am now a countess," Amanda said, handing him a cup and saucer.

Rob sat up, genuinely surprised. "A countess!"

"I can tell you no more. My husband will not arrive in London for another week or two, and I promised not to discuss our marriage with anyone until he has spoken with the dowager countess." She gave Rob a sharp look. "You, *chéri,* are to be trusted, *n'est-ce pas?*"

Rob suppressed a smile. Amanda's habit of punctuating her conversation with poorly accented French had always amused him. Before he could reply with his promise, she continued her story. "Charles wanted me to wait and sail with him, but I came back early to see my precious sons. They're off to Paris until August."

"A countess," Rob mused. "I must congratulate you. First a baronet and now an earl. Quite a leap."

Amanda formed her lovely mouth into a severe line. "You can forgo the sarcasm, *mon enfant*. I really do love this man."

"You'd have no trouble loving any man," Rob said, teasing, "as long as he came with a coronet."

Amanda put down her cup and looked at him solemnly. "I'm perfectly serious, Rob. Charles has loved me for years. After Sir Anthony's death, he was wonderful to me, a real comfort."

"No doubt."

"I'm going to be cross with you in a moment, Captain Mackenzie," Amanda scolded. "My husband and I were not intimate until our marriage. Charles is quite ridiculously old-fashioned. I finally had to insist on marrying in India and not waiting to return to London." Amanda blushed and lowered her eyes. "I confided my entire past to him, and he was willing to take me on if I vowed to be a faithful wife. And I did just that. I'm now a respectable and virtuous woman, a contessa, and I won't be teased."

"Contessa?" Rob asked, feeling the rumblings of a great guffaw.

Amanda lifted her lashes, and Rob was surprised to see tears glistening in her emerald eyes. In the past the two of them had bantered ruthlessly, trading insults and gossip with hilarious abandon. Now she appeared to have lost her taste for that game. In truth, he had as well.

"Forgive me, Amanda," Rob said. "I'm not accustomed to your truly being in love."

Amanda busied herself with the tea things. "And you?"

Rob looked up questioningly.

Amanda smiled, a knowing gleam in her eye. "Who is she, *chéri,* your lovely young girl covered with mud?"

Rob flushed. Amanda had earlier tried to elicit a response as to Norah's identity, but he had neatly evaded the question. Now he tried lamely to explain again. "I went to the assistance of a fallen rider, Amanda. I don't know why you have to assume anything more."

Amanda's brows rose. She looked thoroughly and annoyingly amused. "My dear man, your face turned ashen when she fell. And to wallow in all that mud when it was perfectly obvious the girl was unhurt and already escorted. Why, you all but made love to her on the grass. Now, who is she? I demand to know."

Rob had never spoken to anyone about his feelings for Norah. But here was Amanda, curious, her claws drawn in, and Rob felt the need for a confessor. He began to talk.

Amanda listened with quiet attention. When he was finished, she tapped her fingers thoughtfully on the sofa arm. "Who was the boy with her? Not another suitor, I hope?"

"Burnham's son," Rob said. "Two weeks ago I could have strangled him for looking at her. Now, I know he means nothing."

Amanda nodded with satisfaction. "I hope you realize you must tell her the truth about her father."

Rob's teacup clattered into its saucer. "Damn it, Amanda, I can't do that! If she knew the truth, she'd be devastated. What's more, she'd blame me for what happened to him. She's better off thinking him dead."

"Now, you listen to me, Rob Mackenzie," Amanda said sternly. "If Miss Norah Paige has any sense at all, she is wondering why on earth you haven't declared yourself. You're certainly transparent enough."

"You don't understand," Rob said with growing exasperation. "Jody abandoned her for the opium pipe. If she knew that, it would break her heart."

Amanda snatched up her fan and cast her eyes to the ceiling. *"Mon Dieu!"* she cried. "I've never heard such drivel! The girl is no longer a child in love with her father, but a grown woman in love with an extraordinary man."

Rob groaned. He should never have opened his mouth. Now he had Amanda's meddling advice to add to his burdens. "Norah thinks opium is the greatest curse since the plague, and I'm up to my ears in it."

Amanda snapped open her fan. "Bull feathers! You must take her in hand. Tell her the truth about her father. Then tell her you want her more than anything in the world, that for her you'll dump all your opium into the sea. Tell her you must have her, that you insist upon it, that you will never let her go. That's all a woman needs to hear."

Rob ground his fist into his palm. "No, goddammit."

Amanda snapped her fan shut. "*Diable!* I used to think you were the bravest, most daring man I'd ever met. Now I discover this slip of a girl has you cowed and trembling. It's not the father who worries you. You're frightened to death of love and marriage, of being hurt, of the truth. Oh, *mon petit,* if you do not take this girl, you will keep your heart closed forever!"

"Enough!" Rob roared. His head was throbbing. God save him from Amanda when she started acting. She'd been off the stage for twelve years, but she would never abandon her taste for dramatic diatribes. Rob got to his feet and headed for the door, stopping only when he realized he was in his stocking feet.

Amanda sailed after him with all the majesty of a three-master. "Oh, my stubborn *ami,*" she cried. "Do forgive me for going on so. But I do understand how you suffer. And I do know about women. Until now you've only played at love. Now you've found the woman who fills what is unfilled, who completes what you never knew to be incomplete. To win her you must take risks, you must make promises."

Rob clutched his aching head. "Goddammit, Amanda, leave off those speeches or I'll be headed for Bedlam. Now where in hell are my boots?"

Norah had never had much use for the Sprague twins. Alice had grown up with the daughters of Mr. Burnham's London agent, and Norah had encountered them during her years with the Burnhams. She'd heard that during the first several months of Alice's blindness, Daphne and Maybelle Sprague hadn't once called on their friend. Not until Alice was being praised for her accomplishments did the twins revive the friendship. Even then they treated Alice as a curiosity, demanding that she perform for them on the piano and parade about the drawing room while they clapped and exclaimed over her cleverness. Norah thought the twins ignorant and insulting. Alice had little fondness for them, either. But their mothers were friends, so little could be done to avoid them.

Each Tuesday afternoon, Norah and Alice called at the Sprague house on Baker Street near Portman Square. On Fridays the twins and their mother returned the call at Denmore

House. For Norah, the precious London hours wasted with the twittering Spragues were an exercise in tedium. She was sickened by the relish with which they gossiped about people they had never met and never expected to meet. Like everyone else in London, they salivated most profusely over poor Mrs. Norton, whose liaison with Lord Melbourne had cost her her marriage, her home, her possessions, and even her children. By some terribly unjust law, Mrs. Norton's husband had been able to strip her of everything, even her books. Norah imagined the Honorable George Norton to be the most hateful man alive. She declared her feelings to the Sprague ladies.

"Why, Norah, I'm surprised at you," Mrs. Sprague said with a condescending frown. "Mrs. Norton is a libertine. Lady Robert Lorton says a woman is a victim only of her own weakness and wickedness."

"Lady Lorton told you that?" Norah asked, thinking how ridiculous Mrs. Sprague was, quoting a leader of the *ton* as if she were an intimate.

"I find that remark quite impertinent," Mrs. Sprague snapped. Her flush of rage was immeasurably satisfying to Norah, who had recently discovered herself leaping to the defense of any woman accused of immoral behavior.

"Since Mrs. Norton's misbehavior wasn't proved in court," Norah said, "I'd say she is entitled to her innocence."

"But the appearance of sin is equal in importance to actual sinning," Daphne offered. Daphne's blond hair was brushed to a sleek finish on her small head. Her little nose stuck up in the air, pulling her upper lip away from the lower and giving her an expectant look.

"Norah knows nothing of London society," said Maybelle, a plumper, less animated version of her twin.

"Norah will learn in time," Mrs. Sprague said, her voice still trembling with anger. She looked at the maid who stood timidly by the door. "Gwyneth, don't just stand there," she snapped. "Pass the cake."

Perhaps it was the weather—it seemed to rain each time they visited—but the Spragues' drawing room was dreary, the colors of the walls and furnishings drab. Even the draperies, a glum olive shade, drooped lifelessly. Norah took a piece of quince cake and glanced at Alice, who seemed uncharacteristically remote. Alice didn't look tired, but she wore a peculiar smile as if her thoughts were a thousand miles away.

Daphne broke the leaden silence. "It has been *so* dull since Captain Mackenzie went north. He calls here ever so often. Why, just two weeks ago he dined with us three times!"

Norah choked on her tea. Her coughing and sputtering went on for so long that she was obliged to set down her cup and saucer and dab at her eyes with her handkerchief. Through her tears, she stared at the pink and white confection seated on the sofa across from her. Surely, she thought, Rob would have no interest in a thimble brain like Daphne Sprague!

"He's the handsomest man in London," Daphne went on as Alice thumped Norah's back, "but Mama says he's entirely unsuitable. He has no family at all."

"No family?" Norah gasped through her chokes. Could Rob possibly have confided his secret about his mother to Daphne?

"Of course, he has family somewhere," Daphne said impatiently. "I mean he has no family of *consequence*."

"Oh, I see," Norah mumbled with relief. She reclaimed her cup and took a gulp of tea to clear her throat.

Then she noticed that Daphne was looking at her with sudden interest. "He tells terribly amusing stories about India," Daphne said. "Don't you find him amusing, Norah?"

"Quite amusing," Norah replied. Actually, she thought miserably, Rob had not amused her for some time. All he'd succeeded in doing was breaking her heart.

"It would be too awfully easy to grow fond of a man like him," Daphne went on, her eyes hard, suspicious little beads. She turned to her mother, who was bent over her embroidery, yanking her thread with tense, bony fingers. "I think he fancies one of us, don't you, Mama?"

Mrs. Sprague's prim mouth tightened with disapproval. "It's best you not try your flirtations on Captain Mackenzie, my dear. He's an experienced man who has seen too much of the world for your innocent mind."

"But that's what makes him exciting, Mama," Daphne cried, turning back to Norah. "He must call on you often, Norah, since he carried you on his ship all the way from Boston. Why, he quite saved your life. You must be ever so grateful to him."

Norah clung to her teacup and stared at her cake plate. She felt weak as water. First Ollie and now Daphne seemed to have discovered the secret of her heart. Dear heaven, she thought, did something show in her face that indicated her feelings for Captain Rob Mackenzie?

"Surely he must call," Daphne persisted.

Norah looked up and gritted her teeth. "No," she replied tersely. "No, he doesn't call."

Daphne looked smug. Her little mouth quivered into an unpleasant smirk. "Well, surely he will when he has time," she said. "Papa says he's *ever* so busy."

Chapter Thirteen

NOTHING ADVANCED NORAH'S contentment at Berkeley Square as much as Alice's cousin, Guy Massingham. Everything about him she found endearing—his perpetual look of amusement, his quick, trenchant observations, his kindness to her and Alice, and his endless patience with his grandmother.

It was evident that Alice had fallen in love with him. She had spells of preoccupation during which she failed to answer when addressed, but when Guy entered a room, she became all attention. Even if he made no sound, Alice seemed to sense his presence, turning toward him with a smile of such radiance that Norah felt her own heart quiver. The possibility of a match delighted Norah. She watched anxiously to see if Guy noticed Alice's feelings, but he gave no indication that he saw anything out of the ordinary. The old countess, however, was shrewd enough to recognize love when she saw it. With growing frequency, her eyes met Norah's with a meaningful arch of a brow.

Guy finally spoke one afternoon while he and Norah were viewing an exhibition of watercolors on Pall Mall. Guy was perusing a delicate seascape, hands behind his back, shoulders hunched in his customary dreadful posture. Without taking his eyes off the painting, he said, "Do you think Alice would sit for me?"

Norah turned to him in surprise. "For a portrait?"

Guy nodded, staring at the seascape.

"Oh, she would love to, I'm sure!" Norah exclaimed.

Guy continued to look thoughtfully at the painting. "She's an extraordinary young woman, my cousin. Not only is she beautiful and accomplished, but she sees with her soul what others cannot see even with their eyes."

Norah tried to quell her excitement. She warned herself not to speak rashly, but as soon as she opened her mouth, she forgot all caution. "It's a pity her blindness eliminates her from gentlemen's consideration," she blurted, and immediately wished she could snatch the words back.

Guy didn't react for a moment. Then his eyes left the painting, and he looked at Norah. "Eliminate her?" A slow smile spread across his long, thin face. "I can hardly imagine Alice being eliminated from anything. Unless, in your judgment— and you know her best, Norah—you think certain things are beyond her capabilities."

Guy looked her straight in the eye, and Norah flushed. She responded carefully. "I find it wiser to assume too much of Alice rather than too little."

Guy moved on to the next painting, an exquisite little landscape. Norah hardly glanced at the picture; instead she couldn't take her eyes off Guy. He was so wonderfully homely, a gentle Ichabod Crane, all lanky and stooped. She noticed a streak of sky blue on his right jaw. Each day she discovered paint somewhere on his person or clothing.

Norah continued cautiously. "But I'm afraid . . ."

Guy looked at her quickly, brushing a lock of limp sandy hair from his eyes. "Afraid of what?"

"Her parents are very protective of Alice," Norah explained. "They think she is not like other girls, that she cannot endure the demands that . . . that ladies"—perspiration sprang onto Norah's gloved palms and she struggled onward—"that are placed upon married ladies," she concluded lamely.

Guy's eyes narrowed. "That's what I am trying to ask you, Norah," he said, as close to impatience as Norah had ever seen him. "I want to know if Alice is a strong girl. Does she understand life? Does she want happiness with a man?"

Guy's frankness made Norah light-headed. She took a deep breath to steady herself. "I think . . . I *know* that Alice understands such things. She is strong and curious. I know she wants very much to be happy." Norah blushed, even as thoughts of Alice and Guy brought happy tears to her eyes.

Guy smiled and moved to the next painting. He seemed well satisfied with her response. "I think we should return home now," he said with a playful sideways glance at Norah. "I am about to begin painting Alice."

Guy suggested red silk. Norah reminded him that red was not an appropriate shade for a young unmarried lady. Guy laughed and said if Alice had no red gown in her wardrobe, that deficiency must be remedied, for red was certainly her color. So Alice, Norah, Guy, and the countess paid a visit to a draper's shop on Regent Street and selected a length of true crimson silk. A seamstress was summoned to the house, and Guy gave her a sketch of the neckline he wanted. The seamstress measured Alice and departed, eyebrows raised, muttering about the propriety of a gentleman requesting such a daring design for a young lady who was not his wife.

Four days later Guy's sketches were complete, and the gown was delivered. In the bright airy studio on the top floor of Denmore House, Guy seated Alice before the easel. He arranged her dark curls on her forehead and over one naked shoulder. He adjusted the crimson silk so her plump bosom was almost totally exposed. With her luminous black eyes and her lips and cheeks enhanced by the red gown, Alice looked ravishing.

Guy glanced at Norah, a faint smile on his lips. It was obvious that he was painting Alice not as a demure maiden but as a woman of passion, all crimson and black and creamy white. This kind, awkward man had depths Norah had never imagined. Goodness, she thought, what have I done? What would the Burnhams say?

A few mornings later, as Norah browsed through a portfolio of watercolors Guy had painted while traveling in Italy, Alice said, "You must tell Norah about Brightsgate, Cousin Guy."

Alice sat beneath the skylight. The day was overcast, but the studio admitted the morning light to good advantage. Guy glanced at Norah with the sideways look he gave a person before saying something amusing. "It's a house full of foreboding and the ghosts of my many ancestors."

"Guy!" Alice cried. "There are no ghosts. Tell Norah the story of the magic panel, the secret room where you hid as a boy."

Guy studied his canvas. "Norah would perhaps be more interested in the paths and lanes through the orchards. Do you enjoy walking in the country as much as in London?" He began to apply paint to the canvas with short, steady strokes.

Norah stood up. "I think I'll step outside for some fresh air," she said. "I'll bring back some warm buns and order up some tea." With a pat to Alice's shoulder and a teasing frown to Guy, she left the studio.

Norah and Guy had worked out a signal. When he and Alice wished to be by themselves, Guy mentioned taking a walk and Norah, grateful to be alone, slipped away. She rarely had time for herself. When she wasn't with Alice, Lady Denmore requested her company for backgammon and reading aloud. Only when the countess was napping, when the dowagers were in attendance, and when Guy managed to whisk her off on an excursion was Norah free of Lady Denmore's demands.

Norah's favorite walk took her down Piccadilly to Regent Street, then back along Pall Mall to Green Park. But she eventually found herself returning to the spot in Hyde Park where Rob had picked her off the muddy riding path. He had nearly kissed her there on the small grassy rise. She had nearly won him back, right under his mistress's very nose. Norah imagined encountering him in the park one romantic afternoon. She imagined him taking her off to a secluded wood where he would explain away his hurtful behavior and then finish the kiss he'd never quite begun.

Norah's sensible self found such fantasies ridiculous and pathetic, a sure sign she'd quite lost her mind. How could she hope to find, let alone kiss him, among the press of people in the park? And if he wanted to see her, why didn't he simply call at Denmore House? Besides, he most likely was not even in London. He would probably remain in Manchester for another week. And above all, why did she persist in ignoring the fact that he was entirely unsuitable?

Yes, Norah told herself firmly, unsuitable. Rob straddled

two worlds, one honorable, the other disreputable, and there was no denying that his foot rested more firmly in the latter— the world of opium, mistresses, and a seaman's reckless and uncouth ways. Norah's rational self could make no sense of her longing for him. No sense at all. Except that he struck sparks in her heart. Except that he challenged her mind and delighted her body. Except that she loved him with a passion of tenderness and desire that transcended his shortcomings. When she considered her feelings, Norah could only conclude that the great good sense she'd been born with, the good sense that had guided her for twenty years, was in eclipse. By loving an unsuitable man, she had somehow suspended the essential logic of her life. What the consequences would be she dared not consider.

After leaving Guy's studio, Norah stopped in her room to fetch her bonnet and shawl, then stealthily descended the staircase. When she reached the ground floor, she was waylaid by Wiggins.

"Excuse me, miss," the butler said. "Her ladyship wishes to see you in her sitting room."

Norah groaned. Was there no time of the day she could call her own? She mounted the stairs again and found Lady Denmore, spectacles perched on her nose, seated at a small desk. The blue and white room matched the countess's eyes and hair. Like her ladyship, it smelled of lavender and licorice drops.

"There you are," Lady Denmore said irritably, removing her spectacles and motioning to a chair with a shallow-buttoned seat. "I suppose you've heard of the row I had with my elder grandson, Charles?"

Norah was taken aback at the abrupt question. Uncertain how to answer, she took her time seating herself. Indeed, she had heard of the row; it was the talk of the household. And although she'd never met the earl, his predicament was causing Norah great distress.

Charles Soames Massingham, Fourth Earl of Denmore, just arrived from India, had called at Denmore House the previous afternoon. No one had been at home but his grandmother. Not until they returned from their outing with Guy did Norah and Alice learn from Mavis what had transpired.

The maid had only glimpsed him, but she reported that the earl was a large man with thinning ginger-colored hair and a great mustache. Lady Denmore had received him in her room. Voices were raised. The entire second-floor staff heard her ladyship berate her grandson not only for marrying hastily in India but for marrying a most unacceptable woman. His lordship responded by bellowing that he didn't give a tuppence what anyone, including his grandmother, thought of his wife. His Amanda was a warm and generous woman, kinder and infinitely more beautiful than the lot of gossips who would no doubt be feasting on her past for years to come.

Lady Denmore retorted that her grandson had no more sense than that old fool Sir Anthony Downing, by whom she herself had been courted almost sixty years ago. By marrying the notorious Amanda Jessup, the countess ranted on, Sir Anthony had made himself a laughingstock and a cuckold, for no one would ever believe he had sired those two boys. Now her grandson had been duped by the very same woman and had made her a countess.

About that time Wiggins chased away the curious maids and footmen, and Mavis went downstairs to learn more gossip about the new Countess of Denmore. Later Norah and Alice had sat open-mounted as Mavis reported that Lady Amanda Downing, widow of a British East India Company official, had once been a stage actress. She was also a fortune hunter who had behaved scandalously during her marriage and would no doubt bring shame upon his lordship as well.

Norah was dismayed to learn that Lord Denmore had selected an unsuitable wife. From all accounts, his lordship was a hearty, congenial man who enjoyed hunting at Brightsgate, his country estate in Hertfordshire, and fraternizing in London at the Oriental Club and at his regimental mess. According to Guy, he was solid and manly and hadn't a frivolous bone in his body. Ten years ago, grief over the death of his wife and infant son had driven him to sell his commission in the Tenth Royal Hussars and request a posting to India. The army and blood sports became his life.

Now he had married a woman who was not only too old to give him an heir but was also tainted with scandal. His lordship's bride carried with her a past that made Mrs. Norton seem as pure as a dove with folded wings. Norah wondered if she would ever feel inspired to defend Lady Amanda Downing.

Facing the current dowager countess, Norah was uncertain how to respond.

"Speak up, girl!" the old countess snapped. "I want to know what gossip goes on in my house."

"From what I hear," Norah said uncomfortably, "you don't approve of the new . . . of his wife."

"Humph," the old woman said, confirming Norah's observation. "Nevertheless, it is done and I must make the best of it. It would be unseemly not to have an occasion to celebrate the marriage of the Earl of Denmore, so I'm planning an assembly in two weeks' time. It need not be grand, since the season will have ended and almost everyone will be out of town. Be that as it may, I need your assistance."

"My assistance?" Norah asked in surprise. "But, Lady Denmore, I know nothing of balls."

"Before you say more," the countess said curtly, "kindly permit me to state my request. I want you to address the invitations."

"Oh," Norah said, relieved at the simple nature of her task.

"I have seen the letters you send back to America," Lady Denmore said, "and you have a pretty hand. We shall begin this afternoon after my rest."

"Yes, my lady."

With no more instructions forthcoming, Norah prepared to leave. But the countess was not yet finished. "Sit down," Lady Denmore commanded. "I have something more to say to you." She offered Norah a licorice and popped one into her own mouth. After savoring it for a few moments, she said, "My great-nephew, Ollie, is a scamp. He has his eye on you, but I don't think I have to tell you he's all fuss and froth without a sensible thought in his head."

Norah smiled. "I have no interest in Ollie, my lady."

A shrewd look crossed Lady Denmore's face. "But Captain Mackenzie is quite another pair of shoes, is he not?"

Norah jumped on guard, her heart thundering.

"I expected him to call around," the countess said, "but he has rather disappeared."

"He's . . . he's gone north on business," Norah said haltingly and thought, good heavens, another person had read her feelings!

The countess made an impatient sound. "He returned four days ago."

"Four days ago!" Norah cried, her spirits collapsing. Four days back in London and he hadn't called on her! "But how do you know?"

"I have ways of learning such things," Lady Denmore replied, watching Norah closely. "I admire your captain. He's a fine figure of a man. In my day, when gentlemen wore clothes that showed a woman something, he'd have given us all quite a turn with those legs." She fixed Norah with a stern look and said, "Now, you listen to me, young lady. If you've done something to discourage that man, you're a foolish girl. The afternoon you arrived, he was looking hound's eyes at you, and you were as pink as a morning sky. Don't think I didn't see what was going on."

Norah stared at her hands. Her cheeks and eyes burned, and her throat was suddenly achingly tight. All the ups and downs of the past weeks, all her hopes and hurts, all the fantasies and sorry realities of loving Rob, bubbled up through her chest and burst out of her mouth in a little sob. She was thankful that the countess didn't seem to notice.

"How old are you?" Lady Denmore demanded.

"Twenty," Norah whispered. She concentrated on taking slow, regular breaths, furiously trying to stem her tears and avoid a scene before the stern old lady.

"At the height of your beauty," Lady Denmore observed. "Let me tell you, it won't last forever. Captain Mackenzie makes a decent living, he's of your station in society—if that means anything in America—and he's no doubt had enough practice to know how to please a woman. Whatever quarrel you've had is of no consequence. I intend to send him an invitation to the ball."

Norah looked up at the countess and felt the full crushing weight of her sorrow. "Oh, my lady," she said with a little choke of despair, "he . . . he has a mistress." There was no longer any hope of holding back her tears. They spilled out of her eyes and rolled down her cheeks.

The countess stared at Norah as if she'd said something particularly inane. Then she cried, "Of course he has a mistress! All men have mistresses. But they don't marry them, you silly girl. When they marry, they choose a bride who's fresh and pretty and unused."

Norah wiped her cheeks. Lady Denmore's words were small comfort, since Rob seemed to have more interest in the unused Daphne Sprague than in her. "He calls on the Sprague girls," Norah said, her words coming out in small hiccups. "He might offer for one of them."

The countess snorted. "Fiddlesticks! A man like your captain would sooner cut his throat than marry one of those ninnies. We'll send him an invitation to our ball, and one to the Sprague chits as well. Then we'll see where his interests lie. Now go along and wash your face. And if you're going on one of your secret excursions, have Mavis accompany you. There is nothing more common than a woman walking alone in the park."

The next morning at breakfast, the footman delivered to Norah an envelope on a silver salver. While the countess looked on, Norah tore it open and glanced at the message. Her hearty morning appetite vanished.

"My dear Norah," it said. "May I call on you this morning at eleven? R. Mackenzie."

"What is it?" Lady Denmore demanded.

Wordlessly, Norah passed the note across the table. The countess glanced at it, nodded, and addressed the waiting footman. "Albert, tell the messenger we shall receive Captain Mackenzie at the hour he wishes."

"Very good, m'lady."

After the door closed, Norah turned to Lady Denmore, prepared to accuse her of contriving some sort of plot. But before she could speak, the countess began giving orders. "I had nothing to do with this! Go upstairs and put on your prettiest dress. Send Mavis to the studio in your stead. My grandson is a decent man, but I don't want his appreciation of beauty getting the best of him during one of his mornings with Alice. Now stop gaping at me as if I were a witch on the heath and make yourself presentable!"

Two hours later Rob was bending over Lady Denmore's hand. Norah, attired in a morning dress of blue-green silk with a draped bodice, sat stiffly on the sofa trying to calm her pounding heart. Rob seemed to fill the room with his splendid height, his comfortable nonchalance. Smiling, he turned to her. "It's a pleasure to see you looking so well, Norah."

The countess grunted. "You are evidently not a man who indulges his pleasures. She looks well every day and you've not called in nearly a month."

"You must forgive me," Rob said. "Business called me to Manchester and Leeds."

"Manchester!" The countess snorted. "Brummel resigned his commission because of a posting to Manchester. He said he was not prepared to go on foreign service."

Rob laughed. "Last week it seemed none the worse for all its soot and racket. In fact," he remarked with a subtle humor that made Norah smile, "it reminded me a bit of England."

"You and my grandson Charles are of a kind," the countess said, struggling to her feet. "Forsaking civilization for the outposts of Christendom. But I suppose someone must tame the heathen, whether in Lancashire or in Bengal."

Rob leaped to her side and took her arm, but Lady Denmore pushed his hand away. "I'm not as decrepit as I look, Captain," she said.

Rob backed away. "I hope you're not leaving us, Countess."

Lady Denmore gave him a withering stare that swept from his well-brushed hair to the toes of his polished boots. "My dear Captain Mackenzie, don't insult my intelligence by pretending you prefer the tedious conversation of an old woman to the solitary company of a pretty young girl."

"Countess, please," Rob protested, but he was smiling.

"I'm leaving you alone because I trust you're a man who knows how to mind his manners. I shall look in on you in a half hour's time." Leaning heavily on her staff, Lady Denmore marched out of the room, her head high.

Rob turned to Norah. "She's a clever old bird." He sat beside her and draped an arm along the back of the sofa.

"I've grown rather fond of her myself," Norah replied, surprised at how naturally her words came out. She was feeling both resentful and wretchedly confused. Why had he come to her with such cheerful ease, as if he owed her no explanations, as if he had no idea of the misery he'd caused her with his neglect and his other women?

Rob crossed his long legs before him. "I want to tell you a story, Norah."

Norah was relieved she wasn't expected to speak. The only subjects of interest to her at this moment were his auburn-haired mistress and his intentions toward Daphne Sprague.

"It's a story about what happened one summer evening almost thirty years ago in a draper's shop in Manchester."

Norah suddenly understood why Rob had come. Catching his excitement, she sat forward, her previous concerns overwhelmed by curiosity. "Your parents!"

Rob smiled and waved her quiet. Norah listened intently while he spoke.

"Two men knocked at the shop door about midnight while the proprietors, one Matthew Mackenzie and his wife, were enjoying a glass of ale and a mess of oysters. The men were admitted, an argument ensued, and in a matter of minutes Matthew lay dead, a knife in his ribs. His wife, Mary, ran to her husband's aid, but was knocked down, striking her head on the counter with such force that she lay unconscious for three days before she died. The ruckus brought the neighbors, and the night watch was summoned. Two men were seen fleeing the scene and were quickly apprehended. Inside the shop, a boy of four was found in a bin filled with scraps of fabric. His mother had evidently snatched him from his bed when she sensed danger and had hidden him."

Norah's fingers flew to her lips. "You!" she breathed.

Rob smiled. "The very same."

"But how—"

Rob raised a cautioning hand. "Let me finish. It seems my mother's brother had argued with my father over some money my uncle owed. My uncle sent two toughs to threaten Matthew, and things got out of hand. The murderers were hanged, but my uncle, while implicated, remained a free man."

"And you?"

"My uncle was my only known relative. I was sent to live with him. He was a carter by trade until his remorse drove him to drink and he lost everything. He sent me to the factory to support us both. You know the rest."

"Is he—"

"Dead," Rob said. "If he lived today, I'd take care of him with my bare hands, but he's been gone for nearly twenty years."

Pride, excitement, and anger flickered across Rob's face, one emotion hard upon the next. Norah felt so overcome she didn't know whether to weep or laugh, whether to feel happy that Rob had learned the truth of his birth, or to console him for the loss of his family.

"I hired a solicitor and told him what little I knew of myself," Rob said. "Once he found out who my parents were, he recalled the case, which was closely followed in the newspapers. It caused a sensation for several months, but soon died down and was forgotten." He looked at Norah, his smile fading into wistfulness. "See what you've done by forcing me to search for my past, Norah? You've made me a new man."

Norah's eyes were damp with the same weepy happiness she'd felt when Guy declared his intentions toward Alice. "I rather liked the old one," she said softly, but Rob was talking again and didn't hear her.

". . . and I've gained an extra year of life. I find I've yet to reach my thirty-second birthday. I was born in 1804. August tenth. It's less than a fortnight away." He looked thoroughly pleased. "I suppose one must celebrate one's first birthday."

"You never knew your birth date?" Norah asked, blinking back her apparently endless supply of tears.

Rob shook his head. "Had no idea."

"Then you must come here. We'll have a fine celebration for you."

"Ah, Norah," Rob said, his face suddenly guarded. "I didn't mean to—"

"But I insist!" Norah said warmly. "The countess would love to have you, and so would Alice and Guy, and . . . and so would I," she added gently, unable to contain what she felt for him.

Rob fell silent. He folded his large brown hands and contemplated them as if they were recent appendages he had just discovered attached to his arms. With a sinking heart, Norah knew that learning the truth of his parentage had not yet had the desired effect; something continued to hold him away from her. In desperation, she blurted out one of the many worries that burdened her mind. "Oh, Rob, you're not courting Daphne Sprague, are you?"

He looked up, incredulous. "Daphne? Courting her? Good God, Norah, have you taken leave of your senses?"

Rob looked so horrified, so utterly dumbfounded, that Norah felt immeasurably warmed. Relief curled through her, overwhelming the humiliation she felt at the need to ask such a question. "Daphne and Maybelle both implied that you had serious intentions," she said, then added reproachfully, "You call on them often enough."

Rob wore a faint, unreadable smile. "I call on their father, who is a friend and business associate. But Daphne? Come, Norah, Daphne Sprague is hardly to my taste."

He glanced away from her, and Norah strained to see if he might be hiding a tender emotion. For a few moments they sat in silence. When he turned to her again, Norah hoped for some intimate words. But Rob only said, "Why don't we call for Alice. I'm impatient to see her."

After leaving Denmore House, Rob headed for Amanda's. He needed to distract himself from thoughts of Norah, thoughts that brought on a deep and restless yearning, a feeling more dangerous than simple desire. Each time he was with her, Norah offered what he could never accept: passion, tenderness, understanding. With her eyes, with her smile, with her small jealousies, she offered her heart, unsullied by bitterness and care.

But he could never accept what she offered and what he so desperately desired—not without telling her the truth. And he would never inflict that on her, the truth about Jody's downfall and his own complicity. The most searing truths, Rob decided, must be kept from the person one loves best. In two months' time he would be gone. Until then he would rally his strength and discipline and honor. He would be civil and kind to Norah. But he would be nothing more to her, nothing that would raise her hopes.

As Rob approached Amanda's house on Great Cumberland

Place, he thought of what Norah had given him—a family, a worthy past, a fresh vision of himself. Because of her, he could stand prouder, he could feel decent. Norah's gentle prodding to search for his parents had given him more than he could ever repay. For that alone he would always love her.

At Amanda's town house, Hayes, the butler, answered the door. Rob brushed past him, tossing his hat and a cheerful greeting on his way toward the drawing room. He hadn't seen Amanda in more than a fortnight. He needed a frivolous evening at the theater with a beautiful woman.

Hayes was two steps behind him. "Captain Mackenzie, sir. Her ladyship is not alone."

Rob stopped. "I see. Well, perhaps you would announce me, and if she is otherwise engaged, I'll call back later."

"Very good, sir." Hayes mounted the stairs while Rob went to the footman's bench and picked up the *Times*. He scanned the headlines and frowned. Financial conditions seemed to worsen each day. Oliver Burnham was a fool if he thought he could fill all his orders on nothing but paper credit.

Hayes reappeared. "Her ladyship will see you now, Captain."

"Thank you, Hayes. I'll see myself up." As the butler retreated, Rob raced up the stairs, spurred by the euphoria that had burned in him since Manchester and had flared brighter still in Norah's company. Norah had given him a past; if only he could figure out a way to give her a future.

"Rob!" Amanda, stately in smoke-colored silk, came toward him, hands outstretched, her cheeks flushed like a girl's.

As Rob entered, a large, muscular man of about forty with fair sparse hair and a sweeping mustache got to his feet. Her husband, Rob thought immediately, checking his smile. A formidable-looking man.

Amanda beamed as she took Rob by the arm and pulled him toward the gentleman whose small blue eyes under heavy brows appraised him narrowly. "May I present my husband, Colonel Charles Massingham, Earl of Denmore."

Denmore! Rob stared in astonishment. Amanda's husband was none other than Charles Massingham? For a moment Rob wondered if Amanda was playing one of her jokes, but the stern look on the man's face made it clear that he was not one given to frivolous tricks.

Rob's mind galloped over Denmore's accomplishments. His distinguished service with the Sixteenth Lancers in Burma was well known, and Rob had heard that he was now a member of the Ministers of Council, advisers on military and civil matters to India's governor general. By God, Rob thought, Amanda had snagged a real prize.

Recovering himself, Rob held out his hand. "You'll be surprised to learn, Colonel, that I have only just come from calling on your grandmother."

Amanda spent the next few minutes exclaiming over the remarkable coincidence, while Rob and Lord Denmore made appropriate comments and eyed each other warily. Rob could understand the colonel's misgivings at facing a stranger who had called upon his wife, expecting to find her alone. Although he topped the powerfully built earl by a good four inches, Rob was anxious to lay any suspicions to rest.

"I know very little of my Boston relations, Captain," Denmore said stiffly, resuming his seat. "I recall hearing that my cousin Alice, whom I met once as a child, is now blind. A pity."

After Rob assured him that Alice was remarkably able and charming despite her handicap, Denmore regarded him coolly. "And what is your business, Captain, apart from delivering my cousin into my grandmother's care?"

Before Rob could reply, Amanda broke in with an explanation. "Captain Mackenzie represents the Burnham firm in Europe and the Indies, Charles. We met years ago in Calcutta, but I had no idea he was here in London until I stumbled upon him in Hyde Park." She gave Rob a warm smile. "He's been ever so kind to me. Twice he's accompanied me to the theater."

Rob glanced anxiously at Denmore. The earl allowed a tight smile, not taking his eyes off Rob as he addressed his wife. "It is indeed fortunate, my dear, to have such an agreeable escort. So you are an India man yourself, Captain."

"I've spent a good many years in the Calcutta trade," Rob said. "Over the years your cousin's firm imported some of the finest Indian cottons and silks in New England. I'll be taking out one last cargo in October. Burnham and Bradshaw will then sever its connection with India."

"Yes," Denmore said thoughtfully. "The trade is no longer advantageous for Americans now that the East India Company has relinquished its monopoly." He paused. "And how do you find India, Captain? Most Europeans find it tedious, filthy, and quite beyond comprehension."

Rob felt he was under close scrutiny for correct answers, but he had no compunction about expressing his views. "I take it as it is, Colonel—barbaric and beautiful, fascinating even in its wretchedness. Best to leave it that way."

"Do I understand you to say," Denmore asked, his voice an impressive growl, "that you don't think India is worth civilizing? Surely it would do the natives no harm to emulate our superior moral life."

Rob smiled. "I often wonder if your country's interest in civilizing India isn't merely an excuse for expanding English power."

The colonel's bristling brows slammed together, and Rob awaited an explosion. Instead, Denmore chuckled. "A courageous opinion to offer a man whose life is devoted to expanding British rule in India. But surely, Captain, you realize that we are obliged to act as the police force for the native rulers. Otherwise they would be constantly at war, making government and trade impossible. The sooner all parts of the subcontinent are brought under British authority, the better for us, and the better for men like you who are engaged in commerce."

"I must agree that the trade situation in India ranks with widow burning as one of that country's most barbaric customs," Rob said.

Denmore's guffaw seemed to rattle the windows. "You have a sense of humor, Captain Mackenzie. Yes, indeed."

Amanda frowned. "I see nothing humorous about it. Suttee is hardly amusing." She rose. "Now, if you gentlemen will excuse me, I will see to the tea."

Amanda departed, and the men seated themselves again. Denmore cleared his throat and fixed Rob with a hard gaze that was no less intimidating than his grandmother's. "Captain Mackenzie, I am grateful for your recent attentions to my wife, but now that I have returned to England, I will relieve you of the burden of attending to her. I love her dearly. We have been acquainted for many years, and I am aware of her, shall we say, past weaknesses. She is now, however, a countess; but more than that, she is my wife and shall remain my wife in every sense of the word. I trust you take my meaning."

Rob considered denying in an obscure manner that he and Amanda had been anything more than friends all along, but Lord Denmore, he suspected, was not one to be hoodwinked. "That goes without saying, sir," Rob replied, maintaining an impassive expression. "May I congratulate you. You are a most fortunate man." And the perfect man to keep Amanda Downing in line, he thought to himself with a smile. She will be as faithful as a hound.

"Your thoughts, Captain?" Denmore hadn't missed the smile.

"Only, sir," Rob replied, "that Lady Amanda is an equally fortunate lady, I'm sure."

Chapter Fourteen

NORAH STEPPED IN front of the gilt-framed mirror that hung over the mantel. She studied herself, frowned, and shed the peach-colored gown, adding yet another heap to the floor, which was already littered with bright silks and satins. Most of the gowns she hadn't worn even once, and here she was discarding them as if they were unsatisfactory rags. Norah sank onto the chaise longue, her shoulders drooping with the weight of decision. Tomorrow night was the party for Lord Denmore and his bride. The drawing room would be filled with spectacular ladies. Norah was determined that Rob would have eyes only for her.

Mavis entered and bobbed a small curtsy. "Her ladyship asks that you come down, miss," she said. "His lordship and the new countess have arrived."

Norah jumped to her feet. "Oh, gracious! I forgot all about tea! Can it be four o'clock already? Do fasten me into something presentable, Mavis. And don't bother with the gowns. I'll put them away later."

"It'll be no trouble, miss." Mavis scooped up an armload of dresses. "It's not your place to pick up after yourself."

Not my place to pick up after myself! Norah thought. She tugged a simple blue muslin over her head and told herself she should be ashamed, making all that work for Mavis, as if she were a grand lady.

"I'm so sorry for the mess," Norah said. She stood on one foot, then the other as Mavis fastened her dress. "You must think I'm terribly spoiled."

"Not at all, miss," Mavis answered with a sigh. "Not so spoiled as some."

Norah stopped at the mirror to swipe at her hair and pinch her cheeks. She stuffed her feet into leather slippers and ran out into the hall and down the stairs. She could hear the murmur of voices, the clink of china. Alice's clear laugh rang out, followed by Guy's low rumble. Tea had been served. After pausing in the hallway for a calming breath, Norah stepped through the drawing room doorway and stopped dead in her tracks. She stared with open mouth and astonished eyes, certain that some monstrous error had been made. *It couldn't be!* Seated on the sofa, daintily holding a cup and saucer and attired in a brilliant green satin gown, the modest neckline of which only drew attention to her remarkably ample bosom, was Rob's mistress.

The woman raised her lovely eyes. A smile of recognition flashed from their bright green depths to a mouth both voluptuous and amused. She was without a doubt the most beautiful woman Norah had ever seen. Struggling to recover her composure, realizing even as she gaped that she was causing a scene, Norah heard the woman speak. Her voice was low and so provocative it seemed to resonate against Norah's own insides.

"So this is Miss Paige, about whom I have heard so much. Come here, *chérie*. I have so looked forward to meeting you."

Guy's familiar voice said, "Norah, may I present my brother, Charles, Lord Denmore, and his wife, Lady Denmore."

Tearing her gaze from the green-eyed beauty, Norah found Lord Denmore before her. He expressed his delight at making her acquaintance and brushed his great mustache against her hand. Norah stared dumbly into his small blue eyes, so like Guy's and his grandmother's. Then her glance stumbled once again upon the new countess, who continued to smile at her.

"Captain Mackenzie has told me so much about you," she said. "I'm sure we shall be the best of friends."

Captain Mackenzie has told me . . . Norah could scarcely

believe her ears! The woman had the temerity to mention the name of her lover in the very same room with her new husband! Norah groped her way to a chair. She felt as if her jaw were hanging halfway to the floor. It was impossible even to force a smile of acknowledgment, let alone murmur a few polite words. She accepted a teacup and a plate of cakes and barely listened as the conversation buzzed on. Every voice was overlaid with the gay laughter and warm chatter of the beauteous new countess. Norah choked down her cakes and tea, tasting nothing.

Then, out of the blue, the bride said, "Your coiffure is most becoming, Miss Paige. You put me in mind of . . . Oh, dear, who is that *scandaleuse* woman who pursued General Lafayette from Paris to America?"

"Frances Wright!" Alice cried, while Norah reeled at the countess's atrocious French.

"Ah, oui," the new Lady Denmore said, beaming. "Her writings are radical, but ever so sensible. Tell me, Miss Paige, had you Miss Wright in mind when you cut your hair?"

Norah's mouth was too clogged with dry unswallowable crumbs to respond, but it was no matter, since Alice took upon herself the burden of answering.

"Captain Mackenzie cut her hair," Alice announced.

The countess looked momentarily surprised; then she threw back her lovely head and laughed so charmingly that her husband soon let out a guffaw and even his grandmother smirked.

"Formidable!" the young countess cried, wiping her eyes. "Cutting a girl's hair indeed! Do tell me the circumstances."

Everyone turned to Norah with smiling expectation. After casting a nervous glance at Lord Denmore's bride, Norah washed down her mouthful of crumbs with a long gulp of tea, rallied all her wit and good manners, and related the entire story of the storm and Rob's heroic efforts to save her life. Through it all, the young countess's attention didn't once waver. Norah wished she had the courage to allude to the romantic conclusion to the tale. But the longer she observed Rob's mistress, the more certain Norah became that she could never dislodge this rival for Rob's affections. Nor would the beautiful countess be moved to jealousy. More likely, she would find Rob's trifling with such a callow child as she nothing short of hilarious. By the time she concluded her story, to exclamations of wonder and admiration, Norah's spirits were thoroughly and quite hopelessly dampened.

The evening of the party was pleasantly mild after a week of heat. The moon shone high, and by ten o'clock when the carriages discharged their guests in front of number 10 Berkeley Square, the colorful dresses of the ladies were shown to bright advantage.

Norah watched the scene from the window of her room while Mavis fussed over Alice's hair, clustering the dark curls behind her ears.

"Amanda is so brave," Alice said with a sigh. "Imagine living in India all those years."

Norah turned from the window with a scowl. Since yesterday's tea, Alice hadn't shut her mouth for a moment about the new countess's charm, intelligence, and good humor. And at dinner that evening, Amanda had seemed equally enchanted with Alice. The two of them chattered so amiably, one would have thought they'd been dearest friends for years. Then it occurred to Norah that one day they might be sisters-in-law. Contemplating that eventuality made Norah feel quite childishly left out.

She diverted herself by stepping before the mirror that hung over the mantel. Her reflection somewhat boosted her spirits. She had selected a gown of ice-blue silk trimmed with the same material plaited and arranged in a fan-shaped bodice. The sleeves were tight to the elbow, then flared below before gathering again at the wrists. The neckline spread into a wide oval that left her shoulders bare but revealed little of her bosom. Norah had decided that entering a bosom competition with Amanda was hopeless. She'd selected her gown for its simplicity and its color, which flattered her rosy brown skin tone. There was more than one way to win a gentleman's notice, she decided.

"Norah," Alice said impatiently. "I asked you a question. Don't you find Amanda charming?"

Norah narrowed her eyes at her reflection in the glass. "Whatever she is, she's not a lady. She murders the French language, and she hasn't an ounce of modesty. You should see what little there is to her gown. It leaves her virtually naked to the waist."

Alice giggled. "Why, I'm surprised at you, Norah. First you defend Mrs. Norton, who clearly deserved the gossip, and then you judge so harshly a woman who appears completely devoted to her husband."

Norah turned back to the window, pursing her lips. Poor Alice! So naive! So easily taken in.

"I believe you're jealous," Alice said innocently. "But I can't fathom the reason why. Surely it can't have anything to do with Amanda's friendship with Rob?"

Norah clenched her fists. "Don't be absurd," she snapped.

To herself, she thought how dearly she would love to spill the truth. How Alice's admiring smile would fade once she knew that Amanda was betraying her new husband. How Mavis's pure Evangelical sensibilities would recoil in horror when she learned the countess was flaunting her lover in his lordship's very face.

But Norah said nothing. She took Alice's place at the dressing table and allowed Mavis to fasten a bunch of blue silk flowers in her shining golden brown waves. Jealous! she thought. What nonsense! It wasn't jealousy she felt, but justified indignation that Lord Denmore should be so shabbily deceived.

As she and Alice descended to the party, Norah knew she would not utter a word about the sorry situation. The truth about Amanda would only bring sorrow to the Denmores, of whom Norah had grown most fond, and it would also expose Rob to the gravest danger. Lord Denmore was not a man to settle insults with his fists. Surely he possessed a fine set of dueling pistols that he kept cleaned and oiled and in the best working order. And when he faced his wife's lover, his pistol would no doubt be most carefully aimed.

Sounds of a violin, harp, and piano drifted through the house. In the drawing room, blazing candlelight glowed and sparkled off rosewood and silver, ladies' jewels, and rich fabrics. Above the sideboard, dominating all, hung the massive Rubens Scripture painting that outshone even the most brightly bejeweled guest.

The splendor of the evening almost drove Norah's distress from her mind. Then she caught sight of Amanda, laden with diamonds and sapphires, her star-bright shoulders and breasts shimmering, and she lapsed again into unhappiness. It was all so tiresome and debilitating, Norah thought glumly. Perhaps she did envy the young countess. But the cause of her envy was not Amanda's beauty or her adventurous nature; it was simply her possession of Rob. Norah glanced hopefully about the room, looking for him. Instead, she found a flush-faced Ollie, resplendent in mustard-colored trousers and a coat of bittersweet red, making his way toward her and Alice, a glass of punch in his hand.

After their quarrel in the park, Ollie had been a font of apology. He'd protested that Norah's charms had blinded him to all manner of decency. If she could only forgive him, he would swear on his honor to comport himself in a sterling manner. Norah decided he was really quite harmless, and she knew Alice would be hurt if she excluded her brother in any way. So Norah had accepted his apology and provisionally returned Ollie to her good graces.

"You ladies will set hearts pounding tonight," Ollie said, giving Norah a long, approving appraisal. He did the same to Alice, who looked charming in apricot silk trimmed with blond lace. "Sissy, here comes our cousin Guy to claim you for the evening."

Guy looked very smart. Carefully brushed, groomed, and free of paint, he took Alice's arm and led her off to meet some friends.

After they departed, Ollie said, "I am privy to a secret, Norah, that you would find most interesting."

"Oh?" Norah replied absently. She watched the door with impatience. The Spragues were announced. Daphne and Maybelle, all pink flounces and lace, fluttered into the room.

"God help us," Ollie said, turning his back. "The dreadful Daphne." He grasped Norah's elbow and pulled her in the direction of the refreshment table. Gleaming plates filled with beautifully arranged sweet cakes and cookies rested between bowls of negus and rum punch.

"You will protect me, Norah," Ollie said, helping himself to a fresh cup of punch. "Daphne won't bother me if you're nearby."

"And why is that?" Norah looked beyond the Spragues to the door. She wondered why Rob hadn't arrived. He'd accepted the invitation, so surely he would appear.

"You must realize that Daphne dislikes you."

"How kind you are to enlighten me," Norah said wryly. Now that Daphne was no longer a threat, Norah felt a bit sorry for her.

"I daresay the revelation doesn't break your heart," Ollie said. "Norah, are you paying the least bit of attention to me? Here I am with the prettiest girl at my side, and I can't even get her to listen."

Norah watched Amanda greet her guests and felt a resurgence of irritation. "You come too easily to flattery, Ollie. You made rather a fool of yourself at dinner, gushing over the new Countess of Denmore."

Ollied grinned and gulped down his third cup of punch. "Ah, the glorious Amanda. Can you imagine my shock to discover that my own cousin had married Mackenzie's mistress? But by God, she's a beauty. I envy both men. What a constitution that woman must have."

Norah responded with a steely glare and a thunderous silence.

"Hmmm," Ollie said. "The green-eyed monster."

"I'm not jealous!"

Ollie sighed. "Would it were I who aroused your possessive spirit."

At that moment Albert called out the name of Captain Mackenzie, and Norah turned anxiously to the door. Her eyes drifted past a tall, elegantly attired gentleman and then abruptly reversed direction. Heat rushed to her face. Oh, dear heaven, it was Rob! She scarcely recognized him. The cut of his deep claret dress coat broadened his marvelous shoulders, and tight nankeen evening trousers clung to his long, muscular legs. Above his white satin waistcoat a white cravat was tied in a dignified bow, leaving his shirtfront uncovered.

Even as Norah admired Rob's impeccable costume and his scrupulously clipped hair, she felt a pang of longing. It wasn't this fashion plate she wanted, but the more disheveled man with tar-stained trousers and broad bare chest, the man who had aroused her affection and respect and then had shown her what it meant to love.

Ollie nudged her. "Your keeper has arrived. Now you can breathe freely. No danger will befall you."

Norah forced herself to watch as Amanda turned on Rob a glittering smile. Rob took her hands in his and bent to kiss her cheek. He said some words, no doubt of an intimate nature, and Amanda's charming laugh rang out. For what seemed like the next eternity, the two beautiful and worldly lovers gazed happily into each others' eyes.

Norah turned away, her cheeks burning, her courage sinking to her toes. She'd had a vague notion of mounting a spectacular coup this evening, of dazzling Amanda right out of Rob's mind and heart. Now, comparing herself to the new countess, Norah felt foolish and graceless and overwhelmed with ignorance. She knew nothing of wooing a man with flattering blushes and witty asides, not to mention more brazen seductions. She'd tumbled into Rob's bunk completely by chance. Quite simply, he'd been drunk and she'd been willing. At their subsequent meetings, she'd insulted him by calling him vulgar, she'd forced him to face a past he preferred to forget, and at their last encounter she'd quizzed him like a jealous harridan about his intentions toward Daphne Sprague.

This evening she'd intended to bring up the subject of the recent actions by the Bank of England with regard to interest rates. He must think her an utter bore; it was better she not speak with him at all.

Ollie's grating sarcasm only added to her misery. "He scans the room, looking for a special person. Ah! He has found his charge." Ollie gave a stiff bow in Rob's direction as Norah kept her eyes averted. "Miss Norah Paige is now carefully under his watch."

"Don't, Ollie," Norah begged. She moved toward the windows that overlooked the gardens. As she watched the lanterns winking through the foliage, she thought how futile it was, wanting Rob. He had loved her once, but he also loved Amanda. Just as he would never be tied to one place, so he would never be fettered to one woman, not even by the silken threads of passion.

"Now Daphne has set down her glass and is stalking him," Ollie said in disgust. "Is there no woman in this room who hasn't fallen victim to that arrogant bastard?"

"Oh, hush, Ollie, don't be so angry," Norah said impatiently.

"Why the bloody hell not?" Ollie drained yet another glass of punch and was beginning to look undeniably bleary. "Mackenzie is an opportunist and a rakehell. I'll be damned if I'll be civil to him."

Norah sighed. Thanks to the efforts of Rob and Ollie, she'd been subject to more swearing than any young lady of her age and station deserved. To divert Ollie, and herself as well, Norah asked, "What was the secret you promised to tell me?"

Ollie looked puzzled for a moment. Then he broke into a drunken grin. "The Honorable Guy Massingham has spoken to me about my sister."

Norah drew in a sharp breath. "To marry her?"

"Nothing else but," Ollie said absently. He turned to face the room and leaned heavily against the wall. "Nice for Sissy to be flattered with a proposal."

"How wonderful!" Norah cried. She searched the room for Alice and found her laughing and talking with a group of strangers. Guy stood at her side, his hand touching her waist. Suddenly Norah's own troubles were buried under an avalanche of joy. "I *knew* he would ask!" she exclaimed. "Guy is such a fine man, and Alice loves him so. Oh, Ollie, aren't you just thrilled? To think of how miserable she was just ten years ago, and now to be—"

"I told Guy he was kind to ask, but not to raise Sissy's hopes by proposing."

Norah gasped. "You *what*?"

Ollie stared vaguely at Norah as if trying to get her in focus. "You know she can't marry," he said. "We all know that."

"You told Guy that?" Norah cried, aghast. "You told him not to propose to her? Oh, Ollie, how *could* you?"

The puzzled look on Ollie's face turned hard. "The eternal romantic, aren't you?" he said. "Well, it will comfort you to know that Cousin Guy thinks he can persuade my parents to give up their precious girl. He said he's bound to have her, fool that he is." Pushing himself away from the wall, Ollie walked unsteadily toward the punch bowl.

Norah remained where she was, gazing across the room at Alice and Guy. They *will* marry, she thought fiercely. She would permit nothing to disrupt their happiness, neither Ollie nor the Burnhams nor anything so trifling as Alice's blindness. Yes, Norah promised herself, Alice and Guy will marry. She would see to that.

Rob lit his cigar and stepped off the rear portico onto the wide terraced lawn that led down to the stable block. Festive lanterns hung in the trees, illuminating the night with soft colors. The distant voice of the buxom soprano engaged for the evening's entertainment was blessedly muted, yet still annoying to a man who preferred the gentler sounds of nature to the music of those who called themselves artists. Rob settled himself on a garden seat and clamped his cigar between his teeth. He gave it a few hearty puffs. Clouds of smoke swirled away into the colored light.

It was a relief to get away from the stifling crowd. Rob felt like a fool, decked out like some exquisite amid this herd of strangers. There wasn't a seaman in the whole bloody bunch, unless he was an admiral in disguise. And aside from Cornelius Sprague, there wasn't a man in trade.

Daphne had stalked Rob mercilessly, annoying him with her chatter until her father gave her a sharp reprimand and sent her pouting back to her mother. Plenty of other women had looked him over, but Rob had no desire for an assignation. It was Norah he wanted. Fortunately, Ollie's hovering presence and her own cool demeanor had kept their exchanges formal and brief.

Rob heard a sound and glanced up to see Ollie making his way unsteadily across the terrace.

"So here you are, Mackenzie, hiding out in the garden while the ladies upstairs glance about, lamenting your absence." Ollie seated himself on an adjoining garden bench, glass in hand. "I gather Mozart and Rossini are not to your taste?"

"I'm afraid not." Rob stared up at the trees. He would try

his best to be pleasant. He hadn't the stomach to be baited into
an argument.

"Sprague says you've cut orders for the spring season."

"The credit situation requires conservative measures,
Ollie."

"My father won't like it."

"I daresay you're right about that."

"Look here, Mackenzie," Ollie said, sitting forward in a
belligerent posture. "If you think you'll be getting the firm,
you're wrong. That's not the way business is done in Boston.
Merchants don't take partners unrelated by blood or marriage. You're an outsider. You always will be. I admit, you've
ingratiated yourself quite cleverly, and now you think you can
make decisions in defiance of my father's wishes. But he
won't stand for this."

Rob watched a flying insect circle a golden lantern and kept
silent.

"I'm surprised you don't offer for Alice," Ollie continued,
slurring his words in drunken haste. "That way you'd have
your future locked up and me locked out. That's the route to
take, Mackenzie. You're the only man my father would give
her to, but I guess you wouldn't take on a blind girl, even if it
meant the firm."

"Don't underestimate your sister's appeal," Rob said quietly. "She doesn't need a dowry to interest a man."

Ollie drained his glass and threw it across the lawn, where it
rolled harmlessly under a bush. "When my father hears what
you've done, he'll throw you out. And when I'm ready, I'll return to Boston and take what's mine."

"I think not, Ollie," Rob said. "You had your chance to
learn the business any number of times, including taking
charge of a cargo to Calcutta."

Ollie sneered as he adjusted his elegant cuffs. "And travel
on one of your sorry little brigs? You must be joking."

Rob managed to control his mounting anger. "I run a sound
ship, Ollie. I would have taught you well. Lord knows, your
father and I discussed it often enough, but you hated me too
much for us to be anything but enemies."

Ollie laughed bitterly. "Yes, I hated you, a mongrel from

nowhere, turning my father away from his own flesh and blood."

A mongrel from nowhere. Not long ago, such words would have made Rob see red. Now they were empty of meaning. "Enough, Ollie," Rob said wearily. "You're embarrassing yourself."

He rose from the bench and ambled toward the portico, leaving Ollie alone to stumble among the bushes.

The recital concluded to polite applause, and Norah glanced around the music room. Half the men, it seemed, had disappeared. There was no sign of Ollie or Rob. Lord Denmore had long ago been lost in a cluster of crimson coats belonging to men from his old regiment. Aside from the women, only Guy, seated between her and Alice, and several sleepy-eyed older gentlemen had attended the recital. Norah thought the selections were lovely and the soprano beautiful. She said so to Alice and Guy as they strolled to the drawing room for more refreshments.

They were soon joined by Amanda, floating in a scent of frangipani, her jewels and bare flesh gleaming. "I do hope you enjoyed the recital," she said. "Signora Grisi is one of the world's most talented sopranos."

"Oh, the music was glorious, my lady!" Alice gushed. "The entire evening has been a delight."

Amanda smiled. "Alice, my dear, we are now cousins. There is no need for formality. I will answer only to Amanda."

Then, to Norah's surprise, the new countess turned to her and asked to have a word. Norah followed her back into the music room. It was empty save for the accompanist and a cluster of well-wishers around the signora.

"Captain Mackenzie wishes to speak to you privately, Norah," Amanda said. She raised her perfectly arched brows and added with a smile, "May I call you Norah?" Norah acquiesced, wondering what alternative she had, and the countess continued, "He's waiting for you downstairs in the library."

Norah tried to achieve a frigid smile, but quickly realized she didn't know how. So she merely produced her normal smile and said, "Thank you, my lady."

"Amanda," the countess corrected gently.

As she descended the staircase, Norah tried to formulate a plan of action. Regardless of what Rob had to say to her, she felt she must address his part in this unfortunate business with Amanda. Rob was as much to blame for bringing dishonor to Lord Denmore as was the new countess. But Norah knew it was imperative that she maintain a cool tone and an uncaring posture while discussing the unpleasantness. Above all, she mustn't appear jealous. Nevertheless, she would let Rob know in no uncertain terms that she was disappointed in his lapse of propriety. The countess was married to a good and trusting man, and Rob had no business trifling with her.

Outside the library, Norah stood for a moment, gathering courage. Then she opened the door.

The lamps, turned low, threw a subtle glow over the dark paneling and the walls of books. Rob stood at the window, looking out. He turned and smiled when she entered.

"Hello, Norah."

In the flickering light, every line and scar showed on his weathered face. He no longer looked elegant. He was her Rob again, rugged and manly and very handsome. Norah felt her stern frame of mind begin to crumble.

"Are you enjoying the party?" Rob asked.

Norah nodded and wove her fingers together in a tight, steadying grip. "The recital was lovely. You missed it."

"Is that why you summoned me here? To scold me for missing the concert?"

Norah stared at him. "Summoned you here? Amanda said *you* wanted to see *me*!"

Rob looked surprised. Then he laughed. "Oh, did she? Well, well. I think we've been tricked."

"Tricked?" Norah asked, bewildered. "What do you mean? Did she purposely arrange for us . . . ? But why would she do that?"

Rob looked vastly amused. "Amanda thinks we would make a fine match—a common assumption, it seems."

"But . . . but Amanda is your mistress!"

Rob felt a momentary start, and then everything became clear. So that was the reason for the averted eyes, the uncertain smile, the reluctance to leave Ollie's side. That was why

Amanda said she detected the scent of jealousy. Norah thought Amanda was his lover, and she felt betrayed.

Rob gazed at his lovely Norah, ravishingly demure in ice-blue silk, and mastered the urge to cross the few steps that separated them and take her in his arms.

"Don't be ridiculous, Norah. Lord Denmore would run me through with a broadsword—or, more likely, a cannon ball—if I directed my attentions to his wife."

"But . . . but you knew her before," Norah said lamely, beginning to feel very foolish.

"Amanda and I knew each other years ago in Calcutta. Now we're the best of friends."

Norah gulped. It was Rosa and Harriet all over again, the tattoos that had turned out to be ships. Oh, how ill equipped she was to manage these obstacles to love.

"Amanda is a good-hearted woman, Norah," Rob said. "The gossips say she married above her station. They'd like nothing better than to humiliate her. I know you're too fair-minded to make such judgments."

Norah felt lost in shame. How very wrong she had been to accept Ollie's word without a shred of evidence. She had believed Rob guilty of a dreadful treachery. As for Amanda . . . well, it might take a bit more time for her to be redeemed.

"I wouldn't say anything against her," Norah said glumly. "I was just . . . envious. She's so beautiful and clever."

"You have nothing to be envious about, sweetheart. You are equally beautiful and clever."

Norah met Rob's tender gaze and felt her color rise. He still cared. Norah's parched hopes began to sprout, weaving their tendrils about her heart.

Rob turned to the window. "Come look at the lanterns hanging in the trees. It's a pretty sight."

Norah moved closer. The lanterns swayed gently in the breeze. Pastel lights played with the shadows in the dark foliage. All was silent, except for the music from above, the muffled laughter. Norah felt a lovely contentment, standing with Rob in the dim privacy of the library, listening to the distant cheerful sounds.

Then she glimpsed a golden-haired man proceeding unsteadily through the shadows. Ollie. Norah's mood turned grim.

Ollie deserved a good scolding for his mischief; he'd made her appear to be a gullible fool.

"Ollie wanted me to believe you and Amanda were lovers," Norah said. "He's so very jealous of you, Rob."

Rob rested an elbow on the window frame and stared thoughtfully out at the lanterns. "Ollie and I had a set-to a short while ago. He heard I'd cut the spring orders. Claims his father will toss me out when he learns about it and turn to him."

"But in light of the rise in the discount rate, surely Mr. Burnham will agree with your decision," Norah said earnestly. "It's the most sensible course to take."

Rob smiled at her bright, eager face. Hearing Norah talk about financial matters made the blood warm in his veins. He thought how tempting she looked standing beside him, how much he wanted to slip his arm about her waist and pull her close. "Plenty of men say the bank's policy is unwarranted, Norah," he said. "There's talk it might be reversed."

"Oh, I certainly doubt that," Norah exclaimed. "The *Times* predicts the rate will soon advance to five percent."

Rob shook his head. "If they're mistaken, Burnham and Bradshaw will lose thousands of dollars."

"You'll be proved right," Norah said firmly. "I know you will."

Rob couldn't help but laugh. "You'd wish for a panic just so I might be proved right?"

Norah frowned. "Oh, dear, that sounds very wicked, doesn't it?"

"It certainly does. But then, you're rather a wicked woman, as I recall."

Rob knew immediately he shouldn't have spoken the words. Norah's face went pale and still. The silence ran with currents of memory. Rob could see the longing in her eyes; he could feel it throbbing through his body.

"Oh, Rob," she whispered.

In an instant the heat of desire melted all reason and resolve. Rob reached out, and Norah moved into his arms. Her lips were soft against his, tentative at first, then pliant and eager as his kisses deepened. She clung to him hard, stopping time with her sweet mouth. She made a soft, desperate sound against his lips, inflaming him, taking him beyond desire. She moved her hips, pressing against him, and Rob felt an agony of need that threatened to vanquish him.

"Well, that's a pretty sight."

Rob jerked his head up and saw Ollie in the doorway. Norah stiffened and tried to pull away, but Rob held her fast.

"Get out of here, Burnham." Rob felt a rage so dangerous that he dared not remove his arms from Norah for fear of what he might do.

Ollie leaned on the doorframe and laughed drunkenly. "In respectable circles, such a compromising situation would force a marriage. I suspect you have no such honorable intentions, Captain."

Rob released Norah from his embrace. "Go upstairs," he said to her, his voice tight with fury.

Norah grasped his sleeve. "Don't fight him. Not in this house, not tonight. It will cause such a—"

"I said *go!*"

"Rob! Promise me!"

Rob tried to shake her off, but Norah persisted. She clung to his arm, begging, demanding, until he regained some control. "All right! I won't fight him. Now, damn it, go!"

Norah gave Ollie a ferocious look as she swept past him. "You quite astonish me, Ollie Burnham." With a rustle of luminous silk, she was gone.

Ollie stepped into the room and slammed the door. "Do you plan to ask for her hand?"

Rob pressed his knuckles hard on the windowsill. "None of your goddam business."

"I know about you and my cousin's wife. You and Amanda suit each other. You're a nobody, a man in trade. She's equally common."

"You wasted no time bringing the news to Norah," Rob said.

"She was the first to know." Ollie fumbled in his pocket and took out a snuffbox. "I'm going to marry her." He took a pinch and held it to his nose. "She fancied me once. She will again."

"Oh?" Rob folded his arms to control his fists. Norah was

right; for Amanda's sake, there must be no violence. Not tonight. He would maintain his temper by sheer force of will.

"It's just as well you don't want her, Mackenzie." Ollie in-
haled deeply and sneezed, then found his handkerchief and
wiped his nose. "She's no longer a virgin. I took her innocence. There's not a trace left for you."

Rob lunged. Grabbing Ollie by the neckcloth, he threw him
back against the door. "You lying bastard. She was as pure as
the day she was born."

Ollie's choking laugh mocked him. "You've tipped your
hand, Mackenzie. I hope you enjoyed yourself, clearing the
way for the next man."

"Christ, you're despicable. Sprague told me all about you.
A man who finds pleasure in young girls . . ." A sudden fierce
apprehension seized Rob. He tightened his grip on Ollie's
neck and with a rough shake thumped his head against the
door. "Did you ever touch her?"

Ollie's eyes widened as he gasped for breath. "There's no
need—"

Rob pushed his face close, the terrible rage inside him
growing anew. "Did you ever touch Norah when she was a
girl?"

Ollie flushed, his face fearful. "Good God—"

"Answer me!"

"No," Ollie rasped. Rob twisted the neck cloth tighter.
"I . . . I never touched her. Jesus, Mackenzie," Ollie whispered desperately. "I swear it."

Rob released him. Ollie collapsed on the floor, struggling
for breath. Rob looked down at him in fury and disgust. "If
you ever hurt Norah in any way," he said, "if she sheds one
tear over you, you miserable fop, I swear I'll kill you."

Chapter Fifteen

THE DINNER PARTY in honor of Rob's birthday was scheduled for the second Wednesday in August, just days before Guy, Alice, Norah, and the dowager countess were to depart for Brightsgate, the Denmore estate in Hertfordshire. Norah looked forward to the evening with great anticipation. Despite Ollie's drunken interruption, the sweet moments she and Rob had shared in the library had cleared away the debris of jealousy and uncertainty. Norah had expected him to begin a serious courtship. But in the days that followed the Denmore party, Rob failed even to send her a message, let alone put in an appearance. Norah became so overheated with anxiety, she could hardly sit still. The occasion of his birthday, she figured, would calm her down and put their relationship back to rights.

With Guy's help, Norah painted the sketch she had made aboard the *Orion* the day of the *Rajah*'s sighting. The view looked down the length of the brig. It showed the stunsails spread wide, the livestock crates lined up at the break of the deck, and the galley spewing smoke. Norah had decided the small watercolor would be her birthday gift to Rob. For hours she worked over it with love and care. But two days before the tenth of August, Rob sent a note to the dowager countess expressing regrets. He would be unable to accept the invitation to dinner. A bouquet of stephanotis, tuberoses, and camellias accompanied the message.

Norah passed his birthday night in crushed silence.

Following dinner and a desultory game of whist, Guy took Norah aside. He was sensitive to faces, and Norah knew hers was open for reading.

"I have an errand in the City tomorrow," he said. "If you have Captain Mackenzie's address, you and Alice can accompany me, and you can deliver your painting."

Norah spent a restless and tearful night agonizing over Guy's offer. She was reluctant to pester Rob, and yet she felt compelled to see him. Once and for all, she had to force him to make clear his intentions. By daybreak Norah had decided to accept Guy's invitation. She had also come to some dramatic conclusions about herself and the reasons for Rob's inattention.

As Mavis fastened her into a cool morning dress of rose and white striped silk, Norah reviewed her latest theory. Rob was bored by her need for stability, her compulsion to be planted in one spot like a tulip bulb. He was a man of action who thrived on challenge and change of scenery. Admittedly, their natures were different, perhaps incompatible, but there was no reason why one could not change one's nature. Surely, Norah thought, the pleasure she took sitting in a dreary bookshop writing numbers on cards was nothing more than a bad habit. If Amanda could cavort around India, relishing the heat, the tedium, and the strange native customs, she could become equally intrepid. Instead of transforming Rob, Norah decided, she would transform herself.

She dismissed the little pangs of distress she felt at the prospect of giving up her placid existence in Boston. That old Norah, she told herself, was utterly tiresome. If she wanted Rob, she would have to become a woman with a nature as peripatetic as his own.

As soon as Mavis left the room, Norah adjusted the string on her pantalets so that a fringe of lace peeked daringly from beneath her skirt. She tilted back the crown of her straw bonnet and tossed a rose-colored scarf rakishly over one shoulder. Once she had pulled on her silk net gloves and picked up her tiny white silk parasol, Norah decided she looked naughty and quite delectable.

Not a half hour later, however, as the carriage rattled

through the jumble of traffic on Gray's Inn Road, she sank into perspiring apprehension. "He might be annoyed, having us call unexpectedly," she fretted. "He might not even want my painting."

"Of course he'll want it!" Alice exclaimed.

Guy smiled. "From my observations, I think he'll want it very much."

Norah said, "If he's not home, we shall leave it with the landlady."

"No, Norah," Guy said. "If he's out, we'll leave a card and call back another time."

The carriage passed into a courtyard and stopped before a sturdy wooden structure of three stories fronted with flower-bedecked galleries. The neatly swept walk and the shiny windows, no small feat in grimy London, attested to the proprietor's care.

Guy helped Alice and Norah out of the carriage. Norah clutched her package, her pulse throbbing. Guy's intentions were kind, but it was wrong for her to come to Rob's rooms like a supplicant to a shrine. Perhaps she had misunderstood his attentions all along. She quickly reminded herself that his kisses had been genuine, not to mention the ardent response of his body whenever he held her. Anyway, she told herself as they stepped up to the doorway, it was too late for second thoughts.

A small, tidy woman, her cheeks sunken in a toothless mouth, answered their knock. When Guy presented himself, she bobbed a curtsy and scurried up the stairs, leaving the trio standing in a dim but spotless hallway that smelled of soap and polish.

"I wish we'd never come," Norah moaned. "We're sure to be bothering him."

"He deserves to be bothered," Alice said. "He missed his own party."

The landlady appeared at the top of the stairs. "Captain Mackenzie will see you, m'lord," she said as she descended.

Rob stepped onto the landing, shrugging his powerful shoulders into a frock coat. He looked down, smiling faintly. "To what do I owe this pleasure?"

His waistcoat hung open, and his neckcloth was loosely

tied. They had inconvenienced him, Norah thought with dismay. She touched the brim of her bonnet to be sure it was fashionably askew and felt Guy push her toward the stairs.

"Go along," he murmured.

Norah mounted the stairs with eyes cast down, unwilling to look up and meet Rob's gaze.

They entered his small sitting room. The furnishings were sparse, but every surface shone, and the white muslin curtains crossed over the open windows had been scrubbed to a brilliant white. A pot of freshly gathered blossoms brightened the plain wooden mantel. The fringed cloth on the round table had been pushed aside to accommodate Rob's papers and ink, further evidence to Norah that they had interrupted his work.

No sooner had they seated themselves on horsehair and flowered chintz and exchanged pleasantries than Guy rose again, announcing that he and Alice must be off to make a call in the neighborhood. He promised to return for Norah in a half hour.

As the sound of their footsteps faded down the stairs, silence descended on the room. Rob turned away from the door to face Norah, his expression expectant, as if waiting for her to explain why she had come. She frantically tried to think of something clever to say, something that would reveal her new flamboyance, but she could only stare at Rob with dumb embarrassment.

At last he spoke. "Forgive me for not attending your party."

"We were all disappointed," Norah replied much too quickly. She endured a moment of silence, then added, "The flowers you sent were lovely."

"Norah—"

"I have a birthday gift for you." She stood up and handed him her package. "That's . . . that's why I came, to deliver it to you."

Rob took the bundle, tied with red satin ribbon. He opened it slowly while Norah watched, miserable with apprehension. When he had folded back the last of the paper and held the little painting in his hands, a flood of nerves overcame her, driving her to inane chatter.

"I sketched it the day we chased the *Rajah*. Guy helped me

with the watercolors—I never was much good at painting—and he framed it for me."

Rob placed the painting carefully on the mantel beside the mug of flowers. Standing back, he studied it. "Thank you, Norah. I shall always cherish it."

Before she could sigh with relief and hope, he turned to her. His face was solemn, and a cold dread gripped Norah's heart.

"We must end our association," he said softly. "I can't marry you. I can't be your lover."

Norah stared at him, too stunned even to blink.

"What happened between us is my fault," Rob went on. "I took advantage of your tender feelings and allowed myself too many liberties. I led you to expect more than I can possibly give. My behavior has been unforgivable."

Norah's heart sped up, sending blood pounding in her head like thunder. "You've done nothing I didn't want you to do," she said faintly.

"It's finished between us."

She had not yet put into motion the vague strategy she'd mapped out. She hadn't yet shown him her new carefree view of life, her rootless and spontaneous nature. She was losing him and she couldn't bear it. In a heartbeat, diffidence and pride vanished. "You said you loved me!"

The shock and sorrow that overlaid her words continued to hang in the room long after the sound faded. Rob showed no reaction. He stood in iron silence, watching her, and in his rejection, Norah felt the last remnants of her womanly honor fall to shreds.

Finally he spoke. "Men profess such things when they hold a woman. It's despicable of us, I know, but it happens."

Tears swam in Norah's eyes. "Then . . . then you don't . . . don't want me? At all?"

Rob crossed to the window, his hands clasped tight behind his back. "You don't want my sort of life, Norah. I'll spend months traveling. I'd never be home."

"I would go with you! I would go anywhere with you. I don't care about Boston or Miss Peabody. I only want to be with you!"

Rob turned and looked at her, an expression on his face that Norah was too dismayed to read clearly.

"I . . ." She blinked hard. "I love you."

He turned away. "Forget me, Norah."

"How can I?" she whispered. "We made love like husband and wife."

Rob came to her and took her gloved hands in his. His thumbs played with the little bows at her wrists. "Before you know it, you'll be back with Miss Peabody and the Burnhams," he said. "Remember last May? You were reluctant to give up that life even for a few months in London. You belong there in Boston, sweetheart, and you know it."

There was a husky tenderness to his tone and a darkness in his eyes that belied the finality of his words. But Norah was too shattered to sense any ambivalence in his declaration.

Rob reached out to straighten her bonnet and tuck a strand of hair under the crown. He touched her as one would touch a disappointed child, and Norah knew then the full extent of her humiliation. She had begged and he had declined. She looked away from him and tried to arrange her face in an expression of dignity. Her lashes were heavy with unshed tears and her heart was mortally wounded, but she would not cry. Never again would she allow a man to hurt her so. Never again would she allow herself to love.

The carriage pulled up before the lodging house. Rob placed Norah's parasol in her hand and accompanied her down the stairs. Numbly she mounted the carriage. Numbly she heard Rob speak to Guy and joke with Alice. Then the carriage was driving off. Rob lifted his hand in farewell. Norah clutched her parasol to her heart. She would never see him again. For a long, horrible moment, she wondered how she could endure the rest of her life.

Lord Denmore and Amanda had departed for Brightsgate a few days after the countess's assembly in honor of their marriage. Not until a week later did the Berkeley Square household leave to join them. The ride to the Hertfordshire estate couldn't have been more unpleasant. After leaving London under a threatening sky, the carriage was soon pounded by a cold, teeming rain. Patches of roadway had been washed away, subjecting the passengers to a continual jouncing over loose stones. On one occasion they were forced to stand in the rain while the horses strained to pull the carriage out of the mud. For the entire four-hour journey, the oilskin shades were lowered, shutting out the passing countryside, obliging Norah to immerse herself in her own gloomy thoughts.

They would remain at Brightsgate for months—dreary months, Norah expected—with nothing to do but walk through meadows by day and, in the evening, sit by the fire doing handwork and making polite conversation with Amanda. At least in London there were diverting sights and amusements. But now the opera and galleries, the elegant shops and the peculiar little exhibitions, not to mention the fine houses and the splendid parks, were behind them. The Denmore town house had been shut up and the staff moved to the country.

Lady Denmore dozed, waking now and then with a snort, only to sleep again. Guy and Alice spoke softly to each other with the absorption of lovers. Two days ago a packet of letters had been dispatched to Boston. Norah, Lady Denmore, Alice, Guy, and Lord Denmore had all written in favor of Guy and Alice's marriage. At India Docks, Guy found a ship bound for Boston and entrusted the letters to the captain with a few pieces of silver to ensure their prompt delivery. The westward voyage might take five or six weeks, followed by another three or four to return to London. Not until the second week of October, at the earliest, would the Burnhams' answer reach Brightsgate.

Alice's perfect happiness was marred only by the fear that her parents would refuse Guy's bid for her hand. More distressing yet was Guy's expressed reluctance to act against the Burnhams' decision. He said that no honorable man would go against the wishes of his beloved's parents, especially if they were blood relations.

Norah felt impatient and out of sorts for other reasons, but the thought of Guy sacrificing Alice to his conscience only added to her frustration. She told herself it was too early to lecture and threaten, but in her heart Norah knew the Burnhams would not permit the match. If Guy allowed Alice to be sent back to Boston a brokenhearted maiden, Norah would leave him with a substantial piece of her mind.

Norah pulled her shawl around her and closed her eyes. Regardless of the answer, in a few months her own English sojourn would end. If the Burnhams rejected Guy's suit, Alice would return to Boston. If, by some chance, Alice and Guy married, they would no longer need Norah. In fact, she thought drowsily, Alice hardly needed her now. Between Mavis's assistance in the bedchamber and Guy's assumption of Alice's other waking moments, Norah's responsibility for Alice had dwindled to nothing.

The old countess's snort woke her with a start. The carriage had stopped moving. The door flew open, and servants carrying umbrellas hurried toward them through the rain. Norah's sleepy eyes took in the vine-covered facade of a stone house, wide stone steps, and a heavy door that stood invitingly open. Under dripping umbrellas, the passengers made their way from the coach to the door of the manor. Norah, drowsy and disoriented, stumbled along behind the others, trying to rub the sleep from her eyes and clear her head.

They entered a large square hall, paneled in oak from ceiling to tiled floor. Around the walls hung a stately procession of portraits of gentlemen in wigs and ladies in stiff brocades. At the far end of the hall near a broad open staircase were mounted two impressive stags' heads. No sooner had the company stopped to warm themselves before the blazing logs in the fireplace than Amanda hurried down the hall, extending her hands in greeting.

Dressed in a high-necked gray wool dress, her richly colored hair simply arranged, she looked more like the modest wife of a country squire than a London libertine. After kissing each member of the party on the cheek and welcoming all of them to Brightsgate, Amanda apologized for the weather and assured them that the following day could only be better. Then they removed bonnets, hats, shawls, and cloaks and trooped into a sitting room where a fire and candles blazed, lifting the gloom.

"Denmore has gone out with the bailiff to see about some estate matters," Amanda said as she made sure everyone was settled. "Guy, do tuck this blanket about Alice's knees. Philip," she said, addressing the footman, "a glass of negus for everyone." She turned to the old countess. "Grandmama, are you sure you're quite comfortable?"

Lady Denmore stiffened. *Grandmama?* Norah couldn't imagine the old countess being addressed with such familiarity by a woman whom she regarded with lingering suspicion. Norah waited for an outburst.

Instead, Lady Denmore let the remark pass and responded with a grumble. "I see you've quickly taken to the role of lady of the manor, my dear Amanda. Don't forget I still have some life in me yet."

"I've no doubt of that, Grandmama," Lady Amanda said with a laugh. "I shall gladly pass the mantle back to you if you wish it."

They chatted in a desultory manner until Alice, glowing in the warmth of Amanda's display of kind concern, could no longer contain herself and burst out with the happy news of her engagement. Exclamations followed, along with enough kisses to make Norah feel ill.

"I've always longed for a sister," Amanda said. "Now I shall have one. A much younger sister, to be sure," she added with a smile, "but a sister, nonetheless."

"The way is not yet completely clear, Amanda," Guy cautioned. "Alice's parents have yet to give their blessing."

Amanda scoffed. "A person could spend a lifetime awaiting approval," she said with a humorous glance at the old countess. "In matters of the heart, one does what is necessary and hopes for approval later. I pray you will keep that advice in mind," she admonished gently.

Norah turned to look at the fire and sipped her hot, sweet drink. She was contemplating the possibility that Amanda could be an ally in the matter of Alice's marriage when the young countess spoke again.

"Norah, I suppose you saw Captain Mackenzie before you left London?"

Norah snapped to attention. "Yes, my lady—Amanda."

Her eyes briefly met Guy's, and they both glanced away. After leaving Rob, the journey from Gray's Inn Road back to Berkeley Square had been an embarrassment to both of them. Norah's numbness had faded into despair, and she had been unable to contain her tears. Her misery had stunned Alice and Guy. Later Alice had tried to coax an explanation from Norah: Had Rob not liked the painting? He's a beast to have made you cry! But Norah's wall of melancholy had been unassailable, and she had refused to speak of him since.

Now she looked into Amanda's smiling face and heard the young countess say, "He is off in Ireland for a few weeks selecting linens for the cargo to Boston, but when he returns, I shall insist he come for a visit. We would all enjoy his company, don't you agree?"

"Oh, we would indeed!" Alice exclaimed.

Norah curved her hands around her glass and squeezed with a furious pressure, as if to break it.

Blessedly, a great stamping and grumbling from the hallway announced the arrival of Lord Denmore. His large head and square muscularity appeared in the doorway, commanding everyone's attention. He took in the company, his face brightening only when he found his wife.

"Charles, our guests have arrived." Amanda crossed to him and offered her cheek for a kiss.

"So I see!" The earl beamed at them all. "Grandmother!" he shouted. "The tenants are asking for you. Mrs. Marner's daughter's got a new boy for you to see!"

Woken from a brief nap by her grandson's booming voice, the old countess snapped at him, "No need to raise the dead, Charles, unless you think I'm already among them."

"Perhaps you'd like a rest upstairs, Grandmama," Amanda offered.

"If I choose to take a rest in my own house, I'll do so without your suggestion," the old countess answered irritably. "I trust you've been to call on the tenants, Amanda. You must tend to your responsibilities."

Lord Denmore glanced proudly at his wife. "She's called on them, Grandmother. Charmed the hay right out of their hair."

"Hay indeed," Lady Denmore scolded, leaning on her staff and hauling herself to her feet. "I won't stand for such condescension. Our tenants are Englishmen, Charles, not your uncivilized Indians or your equally uncivilized troopers." She motioned to Philip, the footman, and took his arm. Halfway out the door, she turned to Amanda. "I'm hungry. You serve dinner at a decent hour, I hope?"

Amanda looked amused. "Six o'clock, Grandmama."

* * *

The dining room was surprisingly simple for so grand a house. Portraits hung on the paneled walls, but aside from the dining table, the chairs, and an oaken sideboard, the room was free of furnishings and decoration. The meal was sumptuous. Silver platters of salmon, cutlets, French beans, pigeon pie, roast chicken, and mashed potatoes crowded the table. Champagne, served in honor of Guy and Alice, raised Norah's spirits considerably. To her surprise, Lord Denmore enjoyed not only consuming his food and drink but discussing recipes as well. When Norah praised the salmon, he launched into a discussion of the relative merits of grilling and baking, coming down on the side of grilling in oil with bay leaf, parsley, and scallions, and of course a generous dollop of butter and a sprinkling of capers.

Norah thought of Rob and his Chinese vegetables and felt a sudden sinking sensation. But she reached for her champagne, took a hearty gulp, and told Lord Denmore she'd never known a man to take much interest in his food, except that it be tasty and plentiful.

Amanda laughed. "My husband makes a pest of himself in the kitchen. He maintains that outside of the Indians themselves, no one but he can fix a decent curry."

"It's the truth!" his lordship barked, wiping his ginger-colored mustache with his napkin. "I shall fix a chicken curry for you one night, Miss Paige, and you shall see."

"In the autumn," Guy added, smiling at Norah, "you shall dine on stewed pheasant and cabbage . . ."

". . . seasoned with mace and sherry!" Lord Denmore finished triumphantly. "There's nothing finer than freshly shot pheasant eaten at this very board on a crisp October night with a glass or two of mountain Malaga. How does that sound, Miss Paige?"

Norah smiled and agreed it sounded most appealing. She felt warmed not only by the champagne but by the hearty familial atmosphere. Glancing at Alice, flushed with wine and happiness, she felt a moment of envy. It was an odd family in many ways—the awkward, artistic Guy and his blustering brother, the earl; the crotchety dowager countess and the elegant, somewhat infamous new one—but their informality and good humor made them likable. Norah glanced at Amanda, picking delicately through the bones on her plate. Jealousy died hard, but Rob was right. She did have a good heart.

Norah's spell of thoughtfulness was interrupted by another bark from the earl.

"You look to be a sturdy young woman, Miss Paige!" Norah glanced up to find Lord Denmore's eyes on her once again. "You're not a milkmaid beauty like Alice here, but neither are you one of those anemic wraiths who decorate London drawing rooms these days. Do you walk?"

"Walk?" Norah asked, puzzled.

"Walk!" he bellowed. "Hike! March! Outdoors."

Alice broke in. "Oh, Cousin Charles, Norah is one of America's most ardent walkers. She marched me about the deck of our ship for two hours each day, and in London she quite scandalized Great-Aunt Isabel by forever escaping into the streets by herself."

"Disgraceful!" the old countess muttered, while Amanda touched her mouth with her napkin to hide her amusement.

"Excellent!" cried the earl. "Then tomorrow you shall be my walking companion. I rise before dawn, eat a decent breakfast, and am out in the meadows by six o'clock. Can you manage that?"

"I shall look forward to it," Norah said with a smile that rose to the occasion. Perhaps the next few months wouldn't be so bad after all.

Amanda caught her eye. "You're a blessing to me, Norah. Now I can lie abed in the morning like a proper countess."

Chapter Sixteen

BRIGHTSGATE HALL WAS a square block of a house, as solid and unpretentious as its lord. Made of brick and stone and covered with ivy, it sat on rising ground among a semicircle of great oaks facing a lawn that ran down to a small wooded valley. Meticulously kept paths, gardens, and hedges softened the landscape and delighted the eye. On fine days, Norah passed a few hours each morning seated on a bench on the front lawn, sketching while the sun warmed her back. She thought it no wonder the English were so proficient in drawing; they had exquisite country to render.

At Brightsgate, Norah found a measure of contentment. The serenity of the place relieved the intense emotions of the past weeks. If she wished to be alone, she was not disturbed; if she sought company, there was plenty to be had.

Nearly every morning she walked out with Lord Denmore. They hiked over wet grass, invigorated by the crisp air and spectacular vistas. Their destination was a ruined abbey that lay in a small valley on the Denmore property. Each time she came upon it amid the green hills and dales, Norah was struck by the beauty and mystery of the place, especially in the rising mist of morning when the stones glistened with dew. She occasionally packed a small lunch of cheese and ginger cakes and passed the placid afternoon at the ruin, sketching and thinking.

As best she could, Norah kept her thoughts away from Rob. The scars on her heart were fresh and tender; even a cursory examination might prompt a new rupture. On some future day she would ponder the heedless summer months of her twentieth year and draw some lessons from the perplexing and disastrous affair. But for the time being, when she lapsed into melancholy, Norah reminded herself that a person became what she dwelt upon. Turning into a dreary and brokenhearted wretch would serve no purpose at all.

So she kept herself busy. When she wasn't off on her own, Norah accompanied Guy and Alice on their daily three-mile walk down a country road to the village of Exton. Or she joined Lord Denmore in his herb garden, where he harvested marjoram, tarragon, and savory for his favorite dishes. With Amanda and Alice, she listened to the old countess's stories of the Denmore ancestors, which caused great hilarity among all four of them.

Norah was warming to the young countess, who seemed to have an endless reserve of kindness and good humor. One afternoon Norah discovered Amanda in the orchard. She was dressed in old clothes and sturdy shoes and was climbing an apple tree, nimble as a mouse. The embarrassed countess explained that she had grown up on a farm and had spent many happy hours in trees. She found her husband's orchards too tempting to resist. Besides, she said, the summer apples would make a delicious pie. Norah laughed at Amanda's humble pleasure and realized that her jealousy and mistrust were fading.

"I'm told you joined the tiger hunts in India," Norah said, taking the basket of apples from the countess's hand.

Amanda stepped carefully from the tree to the ladder that leaned against the trunk. She looked elegant, even in faded calico and a battered straw bonnet. "Did Denmore tell you that? I suppose he also told you that when he first laid eyes on me, I was perched on the back of an elephant. Sir Anthony, my late husband, was very much alive at the time, but that didn't stop Charles. He informed me that very day he intended to make me his wife, and *voilà*! Here I am!"

Norah smiled. "Do you love India as much as Lord Denmore does?"

"Oh, yes," Amanda said, reclaiming her basket. "The heat is beastly and the society petty, but the temples upcountry are fantastic, and the wildlife and scenery are extraordinary. Of course the servants spoil one dreadfully."

"My father traveled to India," Norah said, surprised that she should so casually mention him. "My mother said his stories about princes and wild animals were nonsense."

Amanda laughed. "Your mother was wrong. There is no shortage of princes and wild beasts. Of that I can assure you."

They continued to the house in silence, but when they reached the door, Amanda paused. "Perhaps one day you would allow me to accompany you on a sketching trip. Or you might care to join me on a brisk gallop across the meadows."

Norah's warm feelings flowed with remarkable ease. "I would like that," she said.

"I hope we shall spend many hours together and become friends," Amanda said. "From all I've heard from Captain Mackenzie, I feel I know you rather well."

Norah flushed. She was determined not to breach the careful barriers she had erected around her memories of Rob. "I prefer not to speak of him," she said.

A hint of surprise passed over Amanda's face, but she smoothly covered it with a torrent of chatter. By the time they reached the kitchen, she had moved on to a discussion of country social life.

"You must think we are duller than a hundred posts here at Brightsgate after the excitement of London. But Tuesday week we've been invited to Oak Park for a dinner ball. I've heard they're exhaustingly gay affairs that keep the guests dancing until four o'clock in the morning." She gave Norah a weary smile. "Even the smallest dinner in this neighborhood requires full ball dress, and as the new countess, I must be presentable. Tomorrow I'll go down to Exton and purchase some tulle. My necklines are hopelessly daring. I hope, dear Norah, that you will advise me."

The estate at Oak Park, thirteen miles to the west of Exton, was larger and more formal than Brightsgate. Vast grounds extended from a winding, heavily wooded avenue that approached the house over a range of hills. Inside the manor, fine carvings, rich fabric, and priceless ornaments bespoke wealth lavishly displayed.

"There are more than two dozen guests in attendance," Norah said excitedly to Alice as they prepared for dinner. "And a retinue of servants for each. The Oak Park footmen wear red plush breeches and blue coats with silver buttons, and some of them have powdered heads. Oh, Alice, it's ever so elegant."

Alice, attired in her dressing gown, reclined on a chaise longue covered with slippery buff satin. "Wouldn't the Sprague girls be sick with envy?"

"The Spragues!" Norah exclaimed with a hoot of laughter. "What about their mother? She would turn absolutely green."

"Be still, miss," Mavis admonished. "I'm getting your buttons mixed up."

Norah stopped wriggling long enough for Mavis to finish fastening her into her gown. It was one of Norah's favorites, a violet *chiné* silk with a low square neckline and ribbon knots down the front.

"There'll be dancing till four in the morning, Alice," Norah said once she was fastened. "Amanda says these weekends are completely exhausting."

Alice smiled. "It's wonderful to see you so happy, Norah."

Happy? Norah felt a sudden twinge. Of course she was happy. At least she was trying to be happy. She certainly behaved as if she were happy.

But when she stepped before the mirror so Mavis could fuss with her hair, Norah glanced at her reflection. Lately she hardly dared look at herself. She felt if she looked too closely, she might discover something that should best remain hidden; she might glimpse her heart and find the emptiness there.

The lavish, high-ceilinged Oak Park dining room resounded with laughing voices, the clatter of silverware, the chug of pouring wine. Norah sat at the long, well-laden table beside a young army captain named Malcolm Hardy, who was proving to be an utter bore.

"Hand-reared pheasants, Miss Paige," Captain Hardy said. "Hand-reared pheasants are replacing partridges as the principal game bird."

Norah pretended interest as she spooned up her hare soup and eyed the next course, broiled cod in oyster sauce. "You're a keen shot, Captain Hardy?"

Hardy turned on Norah the full force of his solemn blue-eyed stare. His pudgy face was softly handsome, his thick chestnut hair gleamed in the candlelight, and he had wonderfully broad shoulders. But his agreeable appearance was spoiled by his lack of wit or charm.

"I don't mean to boast, Miss Paige," Captain Hardy said, "but in one day last week I bagged twenty-five brace of grouse, six hares, and five rabbits." He watched her expectantly, awaiting her praise.

"Oh, my," Norah said, thinking sadly of Brightsgate's beautiful pheasants, running in and out of cover. It seemed a shame to shoot them.

"We drive the game to the guns now," Hardy went on. "Makes for bigger bags than walking up with dogs."

"Indeed?" Norah stifled a yawn. Hardy eyed her so intently, she felt she was being devoured.

"A foreign idea, driving game," Hardy said. "Don't usually care for foreign ideas myself. This time I think they're on to something."

Norah smiled vaguely and tried to think of a response. But before she could get her bearings, Hardy launched into a detailed report of that day's kill, how many cock pheasants he had shot and how many hens. He recounted which gentleman shot on the west side of the dingle and which had shot on the east, whose cock pheasant had fallen tail up and whose had fallen tail down, until Norah felt buried beneath the weight of hundreds of dead birds.

"Do you enjoy other activities, Captain Hardy?" Norah asked, trying to nudge the conversation in another direction.

"Besides shooting?" Hardy furrowed his brow in what appeared to be painful thought.

"Music?" Norah suggested hopefully. "Or politics? I'm particularly interested in the state of the financial markets. In London there's great discussion about the impending panic."

Hardy's expression went blank. "Financial markets?"

Norah proceeded to explain what she knew about the current state of economic affairs, more to amuse herself than to enlighten him. When she finished, Hardy sat in silence, his expression unreadable. "Miss Paige," he said at last, his voice soft with amazement, "you're an exceptionally clever young lady."

Norah felt a flush creep up her throat to her cheeks. "Oh, no," she said, hoping Hardy didn't think she'd been showing off. "I'm only—"

"But you are," Hardy insisted. His own cheeks had reddened, and his blue eyes overflowed with admiration. "Far more clever than I."

Good heavens, Norah thought to herself. Most gentlemen would not tolerate being lectured to by a woman. Captain Hardy apparently liked it. "I'm no more clever than any other girl," Norah said firmly. "And as for you, why, you are ever so knowledgeable about . . . about, well, shooting. And military matters."

Hardy's gaze grew even more ardent. "With your permission, I'd like to call on you at Brightsgate."

Norah stared at him in consternation. Without realizing it, without wanting to at all, she'd dazzled this tedious man. "Call on me? But Brightsgate is hours away! And Lord Denmore is very strict. You see, he feels it's his duty to protect—"

"Miss Paige," Hardy said with a smile. "I have Lord Denmore's fullest confidence. He's been shooting with my father since they were boys. And Brightsgate Hall is a mere two hours from my father's estates."

Norah said no more. She sat quietly through the pudding and fruit while Captain Hardy recounted hunting expeditions gotten up over the years by his father and Lord Denmore. When the ladies were excused, Norah fled to Amanda's side. The young countess listened sympathetically as Norah recounted her struggle through dinner and Hardy's intention of calling at Brightsgate.

"What a shame he turned out to be a bore," Amanda said as they moved toward the drawing room for coffee. "He's got such marvelous shoulders. And bags of money, I hear." She twined her arm with Norah's and sighed. "I'm afraid, my dear, he's smitten with you."

Norah groaned. "Oh, Amanda, what am I to do?"

When the dancing began, Norah looked frantically for Guy or Lord Denmore, but before she could locate a welcome partner, Captain Hardy appeared at her side. He gathered her into his arms for a polka, staring doggedly at her face as they flew about the polished floor. Guy rescued her for the quadrille, and the local vicar, who stood only to her shoulder, engaged her for the schottische. Once that dance was concluded, Captain Hardy again laid hold of her and insisted on taking her to a quiet corner to talk about his regiment and prospects for promotion.

As she listened to him, Norah thought how sad it was that such a handsome man should be so devoid of sparkle and wit. To her relief, Lord Denmore, sent by Amanda, came after her for a waltz.

"You have captured the man's heart, Miss Paige," Denmore said with a teasing smile. "And you could do worse. He's the younger son of a marquess. He has inherited his mother's lands in his own right and would make a fine husband. If you gave him encouragement, he'd speak for you this very night."

Norah stared over Lord Denmore's shoulder at Hardy, who watched her intently, ready to pounce the moment she was once again free. "Oh, Lord Denmore," she said glumly. "He's the dullest man I've ever met."

Relief from Captain Hardy came only when the ball concluded near dawn.

At noon Norah rose wearily, dreading their next encounter. As she expected, he gazed at her through breakfast, and then he astonished her by joining the riding party organized for the ladies and those gentlemen who chose not to shoot.

"Really, Captain Hardy," Norah implored him, as he tenderly helped her onto the back of an Oak Park mare. "I feel wicked taking you away from the shoot."

Hardy regarded her solemnly. "My dear Miss Paige, the grouse will keep, but you, I'm afraid, will not last the season."

Distracted by that peculiar remark, Norah urged her horse forward and suddenly found herself on the ground. She was hanging by one stirrup, her habit halfway up her leg, and the mare looking back at her in surprise.

"Miss Paige!" Captain Hardy cried, rushing to her side.

"I'm perfectly fine!" Norah said through clenched teeth as

he disengaged her ankle from the stirrup. Hardy tried to take her into his arms and comfort her, but Norah gave him a firm push and got to her feet under her own power.

After her mishap, Hardy insisted on mounting no more than a gentle trot. As a result, they lagged well behind the others and were obliged to deepen their acquaintance.

Later in the day, but none too soon for Norah, she and Hardy said their good-byes and the Denmores set off for Brightsgate.

Norah was grateful to return to her comfortable routines, hiking, riding, sketching, and reading. But she couldn't seem to recapture the contentment she'd felt before the visit to Oak Park. As the days passed, Norah felt increasingly glum. She knew it was only a matter of time before Captain Hardy would come calling, and she had neither the stamina nor the interest to endure his suit. Yet she didn't have the heart to be rude to him. As dull a man as he was, Hardy had been kind to her at Oak Park, and he seemed genuinely interested in hearing about life in Boston. It was obvious that he was thoroughly infatuated. The prospect of hurting him gave Norah no joy.

She mulled over her predicament one rainy afternoon in the small sitting room that adjoined her and Alice's bedroom. How, she wondered, staring into the low fire, did a person refuse a suitor without giving offense? She recalled Rob's words that day in his London rooms and felt again the pain and embarrassment of his rejection. Never, she thought angrily, would she so humiliate a man as Rob had humiliated her. Never would she be so cruel.

"Miss Norah."

Norah jumped at the sound of the footman's voice. "Oh, Philip, you startled me! What is it?"

"It's Mr. Burnham, miss, come down from London."

"Mr. Burnham?" Norah asked in dismay. "Ollie Burnham?"

"Yes, miss. Her ladyship wishes to see you in the sitting room."

Dear heaven, Norah thought. Wasn't that just what she needed. Ollie Burnham. After he'd come upon her and Rob in the library, Norah had no interest in seeing Ollie again. But what was she to do? Lock herself away? Refuse to see him? Offend the Denmores and create a scene? Reluctantly Norah descended the stairs and entered the cozy, fire-warmed sitting room.

"Look who has come to entertain us," said a smiling Amanda.

Ollie, looking sheepish, stood up to greet Norah. He appeared uncharacteristically pale and humble in simple dark wool.

"Luncheon will be served in a half hour," Amanda said. "Do entertain our guest, Norah, while I round up the rest of our brood."

Once they were alone and seated, Ollie studied his smooth, folded hands and said, "I hope you've forgiven me for my appalling behavior."

Norah gave him a grim look. "You seem to require forgiving at every turn, Ollie."

He glanced up. The firelight made his eyes sparkle, and his hair blazed gold. "It's the drink, Norah. I don't mean to say the things I do, but somehow when I drink, it all comes out."

"Then perhaps you should stop drinking," Norah said sharply.

"I have," Ollie said, his face a picture of earnest resolve. "I've taken the pledge."

Norah eyed him skeptically. "Have you?" Ollie dropped his eyes and Norah shook her head resignedly. "Very well. I guess we've both done things we might not be proud of."

Ollie gave her a grateful smile. "I'll behave myself, I promise."

For the first several days of his visit, Ollie did just that. He was a delight, gossiping shamelessly, teasing and flirting. He flattered the old countess and bantered with the young one. At charades, he made a fool of himself for the enjoyment of his audience. Everyone seemed to appreciate his antics, and even Lord Denmore, who had earlier expressed nothing but contempt for the useless young man, seemed to excuse his foppish ways.

Norah rode with Ollie every afternoon. At first she'd been wary of going off with him alone, but he proved to be so diverting that she forgot her qualms and even stopped worrying about Captain Hardy. On one excursion, as they drew up at the ruined abbey, Norah recounted her equestrian disgrace at Oak Park. She even confessed to the story of Captain Hardy's efforts to win her heart.

"A marquess's son!" Ollie exclaimed. "Why, Norah, I congratulate you. You must write a detailed account to my mother. She'll faint dead away."

The afternoon sun was warm, and beads of sweat shone along Ollie's bright hairline. Aside from those few damp curls, he was, as usual, spruced and shined to perfection. He leaped from the back of his bay hunter and helped Norah dismount. She felt the pleasant exhaustion that came from vigorous exercise. Her legs wavered unsteadily. Laughing, she said, "I feel the same as when I stepped off the *Orion* in Liverpool."

Ollie pulled Norah's arm through his. As they walked into the silent abbey courtyard, he said, "I don't know about your seamanship, but your horsemanship has certainly improved." He guided her to a warm, flat stone in the shade of a ruined wall. "I'm sure even your Captain Hardy would be impressed with your graceful riding today."

Norah removed her hat and veil, letting her hair blow in the breeze. She thought of Captain Hardy's ardor and her own empty response. "In a way I feel so sorry for him," she said.

Ollie glanced at her and sighed. "Ah, the torments of love. How we men suffer."

"And what do you know of such things?" Norah retorted with a smile. "Let me guess. Daphne Sprague?"

Ollie stared out over the sunny fields, bright with flowers. His solemn expression piqued Norah's curiosity. "Why, Ollie," she teased, "who is she?"

He turned and looked at her with soulful eyes. "It's you, Norah."

Norah drew in her breath, uncertain whether to laugh or scold. Surely, after all her warnings, he was not going to begin this round of nonsense again! Before she could respond, Ollie smiled mirthlessly and said, "If you haven't noticed how I feel about you, you're not as clever as I thought."

"Ollie," Norah said in a voice full of warning.

"I want you to be my wife, Norah."

Norah felt her face grow hot. Suddenly Ollie had become

tiresome and her temper dangerously fragile. "You know that's impossible," she said coldly.

"Impossible? I think not. I suspect my parents sent you to London as much for my sake as for Alice's."

"What on earth are you talking about?" Norah said impatiently. "I came as a chaperon to Alice; our trip has nothing to do with you."

Ollie swept a hand over his golden curls and watched her with pale, unsmiling eyes. "They would be delighted if we married. You can't deny that."

"Perhaps they might, but—"

"Father gives me a comfortable allowance," Ollie went on. "Should I marry someone acceptable, he will settle a substantial sum on me. We can travel to the Continent, back to America, anywhere you wish. It would be an easy life, Norah."

Ollie's relentless stare and his determined pursuit of the ridiculous subject of marriage made Norah uneasy. They were far from Brightsgate Hall, but surely she had nothing to fear from Ollie. She was thankful that he hadn't been drinking.

"I'm sorry, Ollie, but I don't love you," Norah said, choosing blunt words over polite equivocation. "And I doubt you really love me. You're more interested in placating your parents and continuing your allowance than you are in taking a wife."

"Norah! That's unfair—"

"Ollie, please," Norah said, rising from her seat. She had become truly exasperated. "Don't spoil a pleasant afternoon with foolish talk. I don't want you for a husband and that's that."

Ollie's face twisted into a bitter scowl. "Mackenzie won't marry you," he said. "If you're waiting for his proposal, you might as well forget it."

So there it was. His rivalry with Rob. Norah fixed her mouth in a stern line and fastened on her hat. She was anxious to return to the house. "My feelings toward you have nothing to do with him."

Ollie stared at her, grim-faced. "Good God, Norah. I'm offering you a good life with all the advantages wealth can bring. Any woman would jump at such a proposal. And you, a girl with nothing, a girl who is . . ." He paused, a muscle working in his jaw. "I know what Mackenzie did to you."

In an instant Norah's temper snapped. She stamped her foot hard, furious words leaped from her tongue. "How dare you!" she cried. "You are rude and vulgar and revoltingly uncouth, Ollie Burnham. I won't have you speculating on my relationship with any man. It is none of your affair, and I *simply will not have it*! Do you understand?"

Ollie looked calmly back at her as if he hadn't heard a word of her diatribe. His odd demeanor and set expression made Norah increasingly uncomfortable. Turning, she hurried off toward the horses.

Ollie came after her. "Don't run from me, Norah," he said, seizing her wrist. "Mackenzie's not the only man who knows how to please a woman."

A cold, uncertain fear replaced Norah's earlier heat of temper. She struggled to free herself. "Ollie, stop it!" she cried.

He dragged her to the stone seat and pulled her into his arms. Frightened and lost for breath, Norah fought hard. Yet even as she battled to free herself from Ollie's grasp, she could not quite believe he would truly force her.

"Stop!" she screamed.

He ignored her command. Grasping her face in his hands, Ollie clamped his mouth hard on her own, and Norah's sudden fear turned to rage. He forced her lips apart. He savaged her mouth. She twisted and writhed against him in disgust, striking at his head.

"Don't fight me, Norah," Ollie panted. He pawed at her bodice. "Stop fighting and I won't hurt you."

With her free hand, Norah clawed his face, digging her nails deep into his skin.

Ollie yelped and pulled back. "Bitch!"

Norah saw beads of blood spring to his cheek. She jumped to her feet and ran for the horses. Grasping the reins of her mount, she turned to Ollie and wiped her hand across her mouth as if to destroy all traces of him. "You want to bully me into accepting you?" she screamed. "Never in a thousand years would I ever consider it!"

She mounted from a stone slab, throwing her leg across the saddle like a man. With a smart kick to the mare's sides, she was off, pounding across the meadow toward Brightsgate Hall.

Ollie departed for London the next day. Norah, shaken and furious, remained in her room until his departure. When she emerged from her isolation, the Denmores showered her with curious glances, but not one of them asked for an explanation.

Not more than an hour after Ollie's departure, a note arrived from Captain Hardy, asking to call three days hence. Norah stared at the letter in dismay. "Oh, Amanda," she said, "what shall I do?"

The countess gave her a sympathetic pat. "I'm afraid there's nothing to do but receive him."

Norah lay in bed that night and wondered how she could bear Captain Hardy's eager gaze, his ponderous conversation. She had barely recovered from Ollie, and now she had to manage yet another suitor. Longingly, she thought of Boston, of Miss Peabody's shop, of the peaceful rhythms of her former life.

Amanda presided over tea in the sunny downstairs drawing room. Despite her efforts, and those of Guy and Alice, to steer conversation in an interesting direction, Captain Hardy droned on about his lands and the upcoming harvest, encouraged by the dowager countess, who prodded him with questions about crops and swamp drainage. Throughout the ordeal, Guy studied his hands, Alice ate nearly a dozen sandwiches, and Amanda hid numerous yawns behind her teacup. Norah wished Lord Denmore were there, as he enjoyed such talk, but his lordship had departed that morning for London. Norah forced herself to appear interested, since Hardy focused his attention on her.

After tea, he invited Norah to walk in the garden. They strolled the path at a snail's pace while Norah, her mood fluctuating from sympathy for Hardy's hopeless infatuation to irritation at his tedious manner, tried to respond to his observations with some measure of liveliness.

Suddenly Hardy came to a halt. "Miss Paige, are you promised to another man?"

Norah had been dreading the question. "No, Captain Hardy," she said with a sigh. "I'm promised to no one."

His blue eyes gleamed with ardor, and before Norah could react, he grasped her hand and pressed it to his lips. "Miss Paige, do me the honor of considering me," he pleaded. "I'm not as clever as you, and I may bore you with my talk, but I—"

"Captain Hardy," Norah interrupted, gently extracting her hand, "you flatter me with your attention, but you must not kiss me and you must not speak ill of yourself."

He backed away, flustered, his soft cheeks crimson. "I only meant to say that . . . that when I marry, I shall sell my commission and settle on my land. I can provide handsomely for a wife." He gulped hard. "And for our children."

Norah lowered her eyes and fought down the scream of impatience that gathered in her throat. "Please, Captain Hardy, you're embarrassing me."

"Forgive me. I meant only—"

"Please." Norah wanted to grab the shoulders that Amanda thought so marvelous and shake Captain Hardy into silence. *Tell him,* she thought fiercely. Tell him you don't love him and you'll never marry him.

But when Norah spoke, she was gentle. "You're very kind, Captain Hardy, but I'm not prepared to marry anyone. I think it would be best if you left me now."

He stared at his boots in a flushed and wretched silence. "As you wish, Miss Paige," he said, his voice frail with emotion. "But I shall not give you up."

He gave her one last, desperate look, turned on his heel, and strode down the path, his footsteps crunching on the gravel.

When he had disappeared from view, Norah sank onto a garden seat. She didn't feel relieved to be rid of him; she felt shaken and strangely moved. Captain Hardy, poor man, was a bumbler and a bore, but he was decent and honest, and he thought he loved her. For her, he would sacrifice his commission and give up a life he loved.

Warm tears filled Norah's eyes. How sad, she thought, that such a selfless gesture should come from the wrong man.

Chapter Seventeen

ROB FELT PLEASANTLY satisfied after a hearty dinner and mildly drunk on brandy. He leaned back in the deep leather chair that faced a low fire and drew on his cigar. Twice in as many weeks, Lord Denmore had come down to London on council business and invited Rob to dine at his club, the Oriental on St. James's Street. To his surprise, Rob felt at home among the club members, all men who had spent time in the Indies. He found himself listening with great interest to their discussion of the opium trade, and although an American sea captain was something of a curiosity to the lords of the empire, the gentlemen seemed equally eager to hear his views on the subject.

British merchants, Rob learned, were rapidly entering a trade that until recently had been carefully controlled by the East India Company. Rob figured an increasing number of enterprising Americans would also make their fortunes carrying Patna opium from Calcutta to Lintin and even smuggling it up the China coast. Rob said as much to Lord Denmore, who puffed contentedly on his after-dinner cigar in the chair beside him.

"And do you count yourself among those enterprising Yankees, Captain?" Lord Denmore asked.

Rob was silent. Indeed he had thought of it, as he'd thought of many things during the past weeks. He'd spent hours considering what he wanted in life and then acknowledging what he must settle for. His exercise in self-examination had plunged him into a persistent, irritating malaise.

"No doubt you could make a fortune," Denmore went on. "But what price are you willing to pay? Your life?"

Rob shrugged. "I'm no stranger to dangerous waters. I managed to survive in a sluggish vessel. With a fast little clipper, I could outrun any rig the pirates put to sea."

Rob didn't look at Denmore, but he sensed the man's disapproval and vaguely wondered why he should care.

"And what of your partnership with Oliver Burnham?" his lordship asked.

Rob shifted uncomfortably. Once Burnham heard about the reduced orders for the spring season, he'd probably rescind his partnership offer. No papers had been signed and no money had changed hands; in fact, Rob hadn't even agreed to the arrangement. A man like him didn't belong in European capitals or Boston drawing rooms. The dangerous life of a smuggler was familiar, it suited his temperament, and it made time pass.

"I'm not sure the life of a traveling merchant is for me, Colonel," Rob said.

The beat of impatient fingers sounded on the arm of Denmore's chair. "You need a wife, Captain. Take my word for it, committing yourself to a woman you love can make a new man of you."

Rob tensed. "Marriage doesn't suit every man," he said and wished heartily for another topic of conversation.

Denmore continued as if Rob hadn't spoken. "I've become well acquainted with Miss Paige over the past few weeks, and so have some of the young bloods in the neighborhood. She's had one proposal already, and more are bound to follow before she leaves us in December."

Thoughts of Norah with another man added the throb of anger to Rob's wretched state of mind. He nervously rubbed his palm on his trouser leg and managed a barely civil response. "My compliments to her."

"Is that all you have to say, sir?" Denmore's booming voice sounded irritatingly amused.

"And what do you expect me to say?" Rob snapped back.

"Damnation, Captain! Don't play coy with me. Amanda tells me you have an interest in the girl. Blast your pride or your secrets, or whatever is keeping you from your business, and go after her. She's got beauty and spirit and a brain that's more than up to the mark. Maybe she can't ride worth a damn and can't tinkle the pianoforte like my cousin Alice but I guarantee she'd make you devilishly happy."

Rob felt a familiar hollow yearning settle into the pit of his stomach. "Thank you for your interest, Colonel," he said coldly. "I prefer not to discuss Miss Paige."

"That fool Burnham is following her around."

Rob's efforts to appear unmoved suddenly failed him. He grasped the arms of his chair and turned to face Denmore. "Ollie's been with her?"

Denmore eyed Rob narrowly. He took a long sip of brandy before speaking. "My cousin was our guest this past week, and he'll no doubt be back. As a matter of fact, my wife tells me that Ollie and Miss Paige had something of a misunderstanding. When they returned from riding a few days ago, they were barely speaking, and Burnham bore marks of battle on his cheek. Miss Paige didn't come out of her room until he departed."

"She rode with him *alone*?" Blood pounded in Rob's head, sobering him to the point of panic. "You didn't send a groom with them? Good God, man! You allowed her to go out unchaperoned?"

Denmore stroked his mustache. "Burnham may be a fool, but he's not dangerous."

Rob ground out his cigar. "In the future, Colonel, I would advise providing a groom when Miss Paige rides out by herself or with a male companion."

Denmore chuckled. "Perhaps, Captain, you would care to visit us yourself and offer further instructions on how I should operate my household."

Rob flushed. "I meant no impertinence, but I don't like the idea of Norah riding alone or with some bloody fool who . . ." He gestured wildly and muttered a curse. "That flaming idiot Burnham makes me madder than fire."

"So I see," Denmore said dryly. "But I'm sincere in my in-

vitation. My wife was most emphatic that you accept. Come
down Friday week and spend a few days."

Rob opened his mouth to make an excuse, but Denmore interrupted him. "Take pity on me, Captain. Amanda will never
forgive me if I allow you to decline."

After several more moments of badgering, Rob agreed.
Thoughts of Norah quickly crowded his mind. He wondered if
she had recovered from the hurt he had inflicted on her. He
worried about her suitors, her disagreement with Ollie. The
more he thought, the more agitated he became, until he was no
longer paying attention to his companion's conversation. With
apologies, Rob excused himself. Forgoing a cab, he set off on
foot in the cool night air across the City toward his lodging.

"I'd be the last person in the world to discourage you from
attending the ball, Norah," Amanda said, "but I know for certain that Captain Hardy will be there."

Norah looked up from her embroidery and made a face.
"Say no more. I'd rather stay home with the boys."

They sat in Amanda's small yellow and white sitting room.
The young countess worked at her embroidery frame as sunlight poured over her glistening silks. "You're a dear to take
such an interest in Richard and Ned," she said. "They adore
you."

The arrival of Ned and Richard Downing, ages seven and
eight, had rescued Norah from a shaky melancholy, the aftermath of her episodes with Ollie and Captain Hardy. The
russet-haired, freckle-faced boys had spent the summer with
Miss Templeman, their governess, in a château near Paris, visiting their father's sister. Since they'd come to Brightsgate,
the boys seemed to exhaust their mother, and she frequently
exclaimed at Norah's endurance.

Norah loved entertaining the children. Her enthusiasm for
adult social occasions had faded to nothing, and she lived in
dread of another embarrassing encounter with Captain Hardy.
When an invitation arrived for a weekend at Belvoir, a
good four hours away, she was grateful for Amanda's considerate
suggestion that she remain behind.

Alice was at first distressed about Norah missing the ball.
But Norah assured her that she much preferred running in the

maze or sprawling on the floor of her sitting room, where the boys were reenacting the Battle of Waterloo, to any ballroom in all of Hertfordshire.

"We'll be away until Sunday," Amanda instructed. "If you grow tired of the boys, for heaven's sake send them away. I'm afraid Templeman has become rather spoiled by your interest in my sons. You've given her too much of a rest."

Norah was relieved when everyone set off after Friday luncheon. The roof of the carriage was piled high with trunks and bandboxes that held finery for two days' entertainment. Mavis and Philip, along with the two maids and a coachman, accompanied the party in another carriage. Norah assured Amanda she could manage just fine for two days with only Mr. Wiggins, a footman, and a housemaid to wait on her.

Before the dowager countess mounted the carriage, she pulled Norah aside. "Just because you're alone for a day or two doesn't mean you should forget about your appearance. Those boys are running you ragged. Take my advice and have a good long rest this afternoon."

"Grandmama!" Amanda called impatiently. "Albert, do help her ladyship to the carriage."

As soon as the carriage rounded the circular drive and disappeared through the oaks that lined the roadway, Norah asked Mrs. Bishop, the cook, to pack a picnic of cold chicken, fresh bread, and berries. She gathered up the boys and saw them mounted on their fat ponies, and they all set off across the fields toward the small artificial lake Lord Denmore's father had constructed on the property. The sun was hazy, the breeze hot. It was a perfect day for water games. Norah lay peacefully on the fragrant grass, listening to the shrieks of Ned and Richard as they exhausted themselves in the lake.

She roused herself to wade into the water. Skirts hiked to her knees, Norah watched the boys frolic, delighting in their quick young bodies, which leaped and flashed through the water as swiftly as minnows.

Clouds gathered and the air grew denser. Norah set out the picnic, and the boys dug in hungrily. As berry juice dripped down their chins, they chattered about India, interrupting each other to tell Norah stories of the country of their birth. With an eye on the heavens and another on the boys' excited but weary faces, Norah insisted they head for home. The storm broke when they were barely under way. Violet clouds fled before heavy black ones that seemed to swallow up the light. Huge streaks of lightning split the sky. Crashing thunder rolled over the meadow like artillery fire.

"If you're brave, I'll see that you stay up an extra hour to-night," Norah shouted through the tumult.

Their spines thus stiffened, Richard and Ned made no complaint as the wind and rain lashed their backs.

When they arrived back at Brightsgate, soggy and cold, Norah ordered hot water for baths and turned Richard and Ned over to Templeman. In her own steaming tub, she scrubbed herself from hair to toes with lemon soap. Afterward, in her sitting room, she rubbed herself dry before a fire that warmed her body and cast a ruddy glow over the oak-paneled room.

Norah fastened herself into a frogged Chinese-style dressing gown of dark blue brocade and lit the candles. The storm had brought an early nightfall and, with it, the feeling of a snug winter evening. Norah settled down on the sofa, feeling marvelously relaxed. Two whole days of near-solitude lay before her. Tonight she planned to curl up in bed with one of Miss Sedgwick's novels.

But first she had to keep her promise to Richard and Ned. They bounded into the sitting room, wrapped in nightshirts and robes, followed by Albert with a tray of supper and cups of chocolate. After their meal, Norah joined the boys on the floor with their soldiers while thunder and wind rattled the windowpanes.

Norah looked up when Wiggins appeared at the door. "Yes, Wiggins?"

"Captain Mackenzie has arrived, miss," the butler announced. "Will you be coming down?"

Norah stared at Wiggins in disbelief. "Captain Mackenzie!" she cried, struggling to her feet. "What is he doing here? Oh, Wiggins, I can't possibly receive him. Are you certain it's he? Didn't you tell him everyone is gone?"

The butler watched her impassively. "When his lordship returned from London, he said the captain would be arriving at some undetermined time in the future. The west bedchamber has been prepared for him. If you wish, I can tell him you are indisposed and send him directly up to his room."

"Oh, dear. Oh, Wiggins, what am I to do?"

Norah knew she was perfectly capable of receiving Rob, and she didn't want to tell a lie in front of Ned and Richard. But why was he here, and why hadn't she been warned?

"What's Captain Mackenzie's regiment?" Ned said excitedly. "Do you think he likes to play soldiers?"

"He's a sea captain, Ned," Norah said, thinking frantically. Drat! There was nothing to be done. "I'll receive him here. And, Wiggins, if he hasn't dined, send up supper."

"Very good, miss."

Norah turned to rush to her bedroom. The hem of her dressing gown caught Wellington's left flank, knocking over soldiers, horses, and cannon. The boys shrieked in dismay.

"Oh, forgive me, Ned!" Norah cried. "Richard, look how clumsy I am." But she didn't stop to help the fallen troops. Rob could be on the staircase this very minute, and she was completely unprepared. She would have to be civil and calm and gracious and composed and . . . Dear heaven, how did she look? Norah slammed the bedroom door and plopped herself down before the mirror. Her hair was still damp, but it framed her face in pretty waves. Her dressing gown was presentable, but certainly not proper to receive a man. It would have to do, since there was no time to dress. She knew she should send the boys off to bed, but she didn't want to be left alone with Rob. Oh, why, why, of all times did he arrive tonight? And why hadn't she been warned?

Norah started to pinch her cheeks, then realized they were already too bright. She closed her eyes and said a little prayer for strength, then forced herself to remember how Rob had hurt her. For a moment she allowed her mind to curl around satisfying thoughts of revenge. In her tableau, Rob professed his love and begged to be restored to her good favor, but she cruelly rebuffed him and watched pain dim the light in his eyes.

Norah took a slow, deep breath, filling herself with courage and indignation. She rose and opened the bedroom door.

Rob was crouched on the floor, helping Richard and Ned line up the soldiers she had knocked down. As he glanced at her over Ned's russet head, his stony expression made it plain he had not come to plead or beg. With a sinking heart, Norah knew she would have no revenge, not this night, not ever. Her knees began to quiver.

"Welcome to Brightsgate," she said faintly.

Rob stood up. "Hello, Norah."

His sullen tone and impatient eyes wrung her heart. Norah knew then it wasn't revenge she wanted, but something much sweeter.

The boys watched in wide-eyed silence, their soldiers momentarily forgotten. Rob glanced at the children. "Amanda's boys?"

Norah nodded. "Richard and Ned Downing. Boys, say good evening to Captain Mackenzie."

Rob shook hands with each of them and offered a tight smile. "It seems your parents played a bit of a joke, inviting me down here and then going off for the weekend." He glanced back at Norah. "I'll leave first thing in the morning."

Norah cringed. Dear Lord, had the Denmores lured Rob down here for her benefit? Oh, how could Amanda, of all people, have thought up such a ruse, and how could she have imagined its success? Norah dared not look at Rob. With thundering heart, she turned to the boys and plunged into words. "No more battles tonight." She stooped to pick up a stray soldier that lay at her feet. "It's way past your bedtime, and Templeman will be cross with all of us if you don't get to sleep."

At that moment the footman arrived bearing a tray. "Here's Albert. He'll see you to your room." Norah kissed the boys lightly on the hair and sent them on their way.

The room fell quiet. Norah stole a peek at Rob, but before she could open her mouth to make some apology, to explain that she'd had nothing to do with Amanda's trick, he spun on his heel and tramped off to the fireplace. He propped one foot against the fender, rested an elbow on the mantel, and stared into the fire, silent and withdrawn.

Norah busied herself with the supper tray, wincing each time she thought of Amanda's foolishness. Her miserable thoughts tumbled over all the clues the Denmores had left— their cheerful warnings about Captain Hardy, the meaningful glances exchanged, the old countess's parting words. She glanced at Rob, a great, black-clad figure brooding in silence. Surely he thought she was part of the plot. Oh, how could she bear this new humiliation?

Norah smoothed the front of her dressing gown and touched her hair. "Your supper is ready," she said, forcing a cheerful tone.

Rob's chin dropped between the sharply starched points of his shirt collar. "I don't want it," he said.

Norah clasped her hands and wished he would at least look at her. She couldn't bear his accusing silence. "Mrs. Bishop makes lovely chicken." She moved cautiously toward the fireplace, stepping onto the white tiger skin that served as a hearthrug. Lord Denmore told her he'd shot it the day he met Amanda.

Rob turned to her abruptly. "Did you know I was coming?"

Norah shook her head. "No one told me. You have a right to be angry. It was wrong of them—"

"Why did you stay behind?"

"I . . . There's a young captain who—"

"Never mind!"

"I refused him."

"I don't want to know!"

Rob crossed his arms, jamming his fists under his armpits, and stared furiously at the fire. Light gleamed on his raven hair, tousled by his nervous hand. Norah studied the proud outline of his nose, the stubborn jaw, and felt suddenly annoyed at his sulk. Of course she regretted the inconvenience and embarrassment his visit was causing them both, but she would not take the blame for Amanda's actions.

"You needn't be rude," she said irritably. "It's not my fault you were brought down here."

"Isn't it?" He gave her a hard look. "You and Amanda cooked this up, for what purpose God only knows. What do you want from me, Norah?"

"What do *I* want from *you*?" Norah's embarrassment was buried by a sudden impulsive anger. "Why, nothing, Captain Mackenzie. Nothing at all. Why should I want anything from a man who cares nothing for me, when there are plenty of gentlemen who . . . who would sacrifice a great deal for my happiness?"

Rob's flint-hard eyes narrowed dangerously. The corners of his mouth pulled downward with an ominous quiver. "Then take your suitor and be damned," he said softly. His eyes shone with a strange liquid light. "I don't care what happens to you any longer, Norah. Just leave me in peace."

He turned abruptly, strode across the room and out the door.

Norah watched him go, feeling stunned. Well! So much for him, she thought, trying to muster some satisfaction. He deserved a good takedown, after what he'd put her through. She'd salvaged a bit of pride and wounded him as well. Wasn't that what she wanted?

The log in the fireplace burst, sending out a shower of sparks. Norah knelt by the fire, watching the sparkling wood, and tried not to think of Rob's anguished face. What had she said that hurt him so deeply? Good heavens, had those been tears in his steadfast eyes? Norah sucked at her lower lip and stifled the urge to run after him.

The door opened. Norah dared not turn around. In the silence she waited, her emotions still, her breathing imperceptible. She wondered if her heart was beating at all. Then the door closed, the fire snapped, and she heard the tread of boots on the thick carpet. Rob crouched beside her, one knee on the hearthrug. For a moment he said nothing. When he spoke, his voice was so low Norah could barely hear it.

"I thought I could forget you."

Norah covered her face with her hands and drew in a long, fortifying breath.

"I love you," he said, his voice a husky whisper. "I miss you. I worry about you every day."

Norah dropped her hands to her lap. "Then why did you lie to me? You were very cruel, you know."

Rob touched her hair so gently she barely felt his hand. "I didn't know what else to do."

Norah looked up at him. The firelight cast shadows on the rough planes of his cheeks and lit his dark and anguished eyes. As Norah watched him, it came to her that now and forever, Rob needed her. He needed her to keep him from drifting off to a life he no longer wanted. He needed her to be his anchor for a lifetime.

Norah rose to her knees and reached for him, and as she did, her wide silk sleeves feel back, exposing her slender arms. Rob bent down and trailed his lips from the inside of her wrist to the sensitive little hollow of her elbow. He nipped gently at tender skin, then touched her with his tongue.

"Oh, Rob." Norah burrowed her fingers into his coarse hair. The sweetness of his kiss left her limp and aching. She caressed his bent neck and brushed her lips against its rough skin. He was mumbling something, some agony she couldn't hear; then he gripped her waist and pressed his face to her breasts. Norah held him close. His emotion left her dizzy with tenderness. She murmured his name and rubbed his broad back, and suddenly he shook with a great breath or perhaps a sob, and tears stung her eyes.

"My dearest," Norah whispered. "It's all right. Oh, my love, it's all right now."

Rob lifted his face, but before she could glimpse his expression, his arms went about her and he pulled her into a breath-crushing embrace. He kissed her hard, desperately, incinerating those few stubborn embers of reason and doubt, leaving her depleted of all but the hot urge to possess him.

Rob dragged her arms from his neck. "We can't do this."

She kept him for a moment, running her fingers over his cheeks, his damp eyelids. Then with a faint smile, she sat back on the hearthrug and let him go. Rob stood up, trembling, and stumbled to the window. Stars peeked through the clouds. The moon flashed in and out, trying to regain its dominance of the sky. Rob dropped his head and swore softly. Why hadn't he walked out of this room and out of her life? Didn't he yet understand that bitterness and heartache were the only emotions that would save him? If he loved Norah tonight, he would promise her his life. If he took her now, it would be forever.

"Rob."

He turned. Norah stood before him, her dressing gown gone. Candlelight flickered on the translucent shift, caressing her full, pink-tipped breasts.

Rob's throat contracted with a hard swallow. "Dear God."

In one graceful motion, Norah pulled off the shift. Fine

linen drifted to the floor. Rob stared at her shy inviting smile, her body fired to a rosy gold, and felt nearly numb for wanting her. Candlelight made her hair penny-bright; the curls between her thighs sparkled like a handful of jewels. She looked so tantalizing, so painfully beautiful, he almost forgot to breathe.

She moved into his arms, offering him the gift he wanted above all else, and Rob knew in that moment he could fight no longer. He would live the lie; he would deny anything to have her.

"We belong together," he whispered. "For always."

She was light in his arms as he carried her to the bedroom. The moon illuminated the bed in a silver glow. Rob peeled off his clothes and went to her. She reached up, her lovely body bare to his gaze, her smoky eyes welcoming his love, and he felt humble and desperate and very relieved.

His kisses were tender, his hands relentless. Norah's breath trembled with silent delight.

"Tell me you love me," he whispered.

She told him what he wished to hear, again and again, until his mouth covered hers, and she was melting under his heated caresses. She clung to him, biting at his lips, crying out with frantic pleasure. All her pent-up yearnings, her long-denied passion, throbbed for relief. At last he moved between her thighs and eased into her. Powerful, debilitating sensations surged and contracted in glorious waves. Slowly and deliberately, he moved in her until his own vigorous excitement rose, his rhythm built, and her body was deadened to all but the sweet fury of his thrusts and her own swelling response. Just when she thought she could bear it no longer, when she thought she would surely die from it, he drove deep and held, and a blinding, quivering rush burst from the very core of her, sending silent sparkles of light floating in a dreamy void.

Then she was drifting in a drowsy languor, twined about him, held tight by strong arms. She heard in the distance, "My beautiful angel. My beautiful wild girl."

Chapter Eighteen

NORAH WOKE IN the dark and found Rob gone. A crack of light showed beneath the door leading to the sitting room. Norah slipped out of bed, shivering in the cool night air, and pulled on a robe. Opening the door, she blinked into the dim light and focused her eyes on the odd sight before her. Rob had pulled the table close to a cheerful fire. He sat there, stark naked, finishing off Mrs. Bishop's chicken. He looked magnificent in his undress, his burly shoulders hunched over his meal, his muscled legs spread comfortably wide. He took a long swallow of Lord Denmore's finest Malaga and hummed a little tune. Norah couldn't suppress a giggle.

Rob looked up and grinned. "Why are you awake, you wanton woman?"

Norah ran to him. She threw her arms over his shoulders and rubbed his bristly chest. "You look funny."

Rob turned his head so she could kiss his mouth. "Is that any way to speak to your lover?" He wiped his fingers on his napkin and tugged at the tie on her wrapper, which promptly fell to the floor. "I prefer you not dress for dinner, my dear," he said, and pulled her onto his muscular thigh. He playfully kissed her lips, her throat. He nuzzled her breasts.

"Ouch!" Norah protested. "Your whiskers hurt."

Rob muttered something against her skin, and then his fingers crept around her ribs, where they danced and teased in an agony of tickling.

"Rob! *Stop* it!" Norah squirmed to get away, but he held her fast. *"Don't!"* Laughing and breathless, she wriggled on his lap until she realized she was provoking him in a most pleasurable way. Her laughter quieted to quick shallow breaths. When his hand closed over her breast, Norah sat very still. He played with her gently, nipping at her neck, tantalizing her with his mouth, until her subtle need grew palpable and immediate. She ran her hands over his shoulders and through his hair.

"Rob?"

"Hmm?"

"Shall . . . shall we go back to bed?"

"No, love. I like it here by the fire."

"Here? In the chair?"

Rob laughed and teased her with his lips. "Don't be impatient, sweetheart."

His warm mouth took her. His tongue roamed over taut flesh, wooing her until she was afire. She held him close, flushed with desire, her every sense entranced. His fingers lay gently on her waist. They moved leisurely over her hips. She waited, quivering with expectation, while he caressed her thighs. She shifted impatiently on his lap, trying to show him what to do. He delayed with soft kisses, with enticing nips and licks.

"Please," she whispered.

"Please what?" he whispered back.

"You know," she panted.

"Show me, Norah. Show me what you want."

She wouldn't have done it if she hadn't felt such a rampant need, but she took his hand and showed him.

"Ah," he said. His searching fingers made her shimmer and throb. Norah bit her lips with pleasure.

Rob drew her down on the hearthrug. Norah clung to his neck as he ranged over her. She stroked his face, its dark planes defined by firelight and shadows. "I love you."

Rob smiled. "Yes, I think you do."

He took her with all his quiet power, with hoarse words sweet against her throat. Norah felt him all through her, the familiar thrust of heat, the glorious surge of passion, and her blood ran hot. She forced herself to lie still, to hold back, to absorb the feeling of it all.

Rob slipped his hands beneath her hips. "Raise your knees," he whispered, and when she did, he drew in a sharp breath. "That's it, sweetheart. Oh, yes. Ah, Norah, you're beautiful."

He moved in her warm, smooth depths, and all her being centered down on him. When Rob drew back, Norah followed, desperate to keep him. She grasped him, moaning softly against his mouth. Her need gathered and tightened, pulsing and driving, leaving her mind blank with pleasure. His body moved more purposefully, and Norah felt his wildness, his sweet, tempestuous lust. Heat flared red behind her closed eyelids. "Rob," she gasped. *"Rob!"*

He drove deep, taking her beyond pleasure to someplace lost in space and time, to some unknown hour of their own creation. Norah hovered there for a blissful eternity, and then she felt his triumph, heard his joy, and with a rapturous cry she shattered in his arms.

She opened her eyes to find a pillow beneath her head. A quilt covered her from her shoulders to her toes. Rob was stoking the fire to a roaring blaze. His stubborn hair and the dark whiskers sprouting on his jaw made him a most appealing ruffian.

He looked at her. "How are you feeling, sweetheart?"

Norah smiled and snuggled happily in her quilt. Beneath her, the tiger pelt made a cozy nest. "Wonderful."

"It's one o'clock. Time you went to bed."

"I want to stay with you."

Rob stretched out beside her and rubbed her chin with his knuckles. "Close your eyes and sleep, my love. I'll be here."

Norah lifted the quilt. "Lie under here with me."

Obliging, Rob slid close beside her. He drew her into his arms and sifted her hair through his fingers. "Go back to sleep," he murmured and lightly kissed her lips.

Norah lay against his chest, inhaling his damp heat and the faint scent of bay rum. She wanted this night to go on forever. Only when she held Rob intimately could she be sure he was truly hers; only when he gave himself over to passion was he safe from harm.

Her hands moved stealthily over him, memorizing the hard lines of his body. She caressed his torso and felt the pulse that jumped beneath solid muscle. She stroked his hips, strong and narrow as a tree, and his taut, sculpted thighs. Her fingers closed over the male part of him, hard as hickory, and she thought how easy it was to capture a man's soul. Surely their joyous understanding would bind him to her for all time.

Rob tipped up her chin. He looked down with hot, searching eyes. "What are you doing to me, Norah? You make me feel as if I could go on forever."

He kissed her, and Norah felt a heart-rush of joy that he should need her so. But when he drew back, his eyes seemed haunted, and Norah felt the old, sick ache of doubt. So many troubles lay buried in those eyes, she thought. Perhaps the past that had formed him could never be erased. Perhaps she would always capture him only to lose him again. Norah touched his dark bristly cheek and felt an ominous shiver. There were answers she might never know. If only Rob could understand that his happiness would always be her sweetest pleasure. If only he could see that she would mend him with her love.

She stroked his hair and said, "What are your secrets?"

Rob looked startled. "Secrets?"

"Why do you . . . Oh, Rob, why do you look at me that way? As if you were sorry?"

He stared at her, his face ashen. "What are you talking about?"

"Is it something from your past? You can tell me."

Rob glanced away. Norah saw a muscle jump in his jaw. When he looked back at her, his face had gone stern and strange. He spoke softly. "You know I love you, Norah."

She smiled reassuringly and ruffled her hair. "Of course I know it."

His anxious eyes searched her face. "Nothing will ever hurt you. I promise you that."

"But why do you—"

He kissed her fiercely. Norah wanted to ask him more, but Rob's mouth was too demanding, his body too heavy on her own. His hands began their delicious stroking, and Norah forgot her questions; she felt only the quick familiar leap of fire, the dewy warmth of wanting him. Rob pressed her down on her back and took her quickly with a blind, helpless hunger, a frenzy she couldn't seem to satisfy, and then he took her again.

Through the dark, silent hours of early morning, they spoke few words. The secrets of Rob's heart remained hidden, but Norah learned the secrets of his body. And of her own.

Rob took her with hands and mouth; he made her sob with passion. Norah lost herself, found herself, yearned and reached, and still he demanded more. Again and again she achieved ecstasy, but no amount of her pleasure was enough for him. Their bodies merged and tangled until Norah no longer knew which breath was his, which limb was hers, and how their heartbeats could not be one.

During a quiet interlude, she held him close, inhaling the dreamy fragrance of his hair, and wondered at the torment that drove him. But when she tried to soothe him, Rob grew impatient.

"If you want me to stop, I will."

Norah knew she should tell him to stop. They had gone beyond exhaustion; it was madness. She knew she couldn't take him again. But then his lips moved against her, sensations blossomed, and she discovered that she had still more to give.

At the faint light of dawn, Norah found herself back in bed. Rob bent over her, looking haggard in the gray light of morning. "Forgive me, love. If I possessed a shred of decency, I'd be ashamed of myself."

"Don't leave me," Norah murmured drowsily, twining her fingers with his. "Don't leave me alone."

He kissed her forehead. "You've had enough of me for a while, sweetheart," he said wearily. "Besides, I have to put in an appearance in my own bed. The servants will wonder."

But he lay with her until she slept.

Sunlight filled the room. It spilled over the figured carpet and shattered against the mirror. Norah stretched, feeling languid, liquid, wonderfully well used. Throwing back the covers, she looked down at herself. There were a few whisker burns and a nibble or two, but for having been the object of such frantic masculine ardor, her body appeared remarkably unchanged. She bathed and dressed singing.

In the dining room Albert held the serving dish covers while she heaped her plate with eggs and biscuits and potatoes.

"Captain Mackenzie will see you in the garden, miss," the footman said. "Miss Templeman has taken Master Ned and Master Richard on an outing to Exton."

"Thank you, Albert," Norah said politely, as if she were the same proper girl she'd been yesterday.

The more Norah ate, the hungrier she became. She consumed two helpings of everything on the sideboard. After a final sip of coffee, she touched her napkin to her lips and pushed back her chair. She hurried down the hall, stopping only to check her appearance once again in the mirror. Every part of her, from her hair to her eyes to her dazzling smile, shone with a bright, happy light. Her dress of delicate green muslin, embroidered with green and white flowers, was modestly cut, but the fabric was sheer. She had left off her stays to a most tantalizing effect.

Norah stepped outside into a brilliant windless morning. The song of birds and the scent of flowers dampened by yesterday's rain made the air deliciously sweet. Norah paused to take in the maze of hedges and shrubs, flower beds and fountains. The landscape was achingly beautiful. She set off down the gravel walkway to an intersection of paths and turned the corner. Rob stood with his foot on a garden bench. His forearm rested on his bent knee, and his fingers played negligently with a rose. Watching him, Norah felt a keen possessive joy. He was her lover, her own.

Rob turned and saw her, and his face broke into a smile. Norah ran into his open arms. He held her in a long, crushing hug.

"What were you thinking of?" Norah asked.

He kissed the top of her head and squeezed her tighter still. "What could I be thinking of besides you? You're the loveliest woman in the world, madam, and without doubt the most accomplished seductress in all of Hertfordshire."

Norah laughed, feeling daring and gay. "Perhaps in all of England."

Rob held her away from him and glanced over her with wistful affection. The skin under his eyes was dark with fatigue. A spot of blood crusted a razor nick on his chin. He looked as if he'd spent the night struggling through a hurricane rather than doing loving battle with her.

Norah studied his closely. "You look tired."

Rob tweaked her bosom. "Your fault, my sweet."

In his eyes Norah saw a hint of last night's disturbing wariness, and she felt a stir of disquiet. "Rob, are you all right?"

He laughed, a tired, husky laugh that didn't quite ring true. "Of course I'm all right. What man wouldn't be in fine spirits on such a morning when he's about to propose marriage to the woman he loves?"

"Oh, Rob." Norah leaned hard against him, dizzy with relief. There was no need to worry.

"Don't I get a kiss?" he asked playfully.

Norah smiled up at him, and his mouth quickly covered her own. In his arms Norah felt his fierce strength; in his kiss, all his tender longing. The sun beat down, insects hummed, and still he held her. *Husband.* She would give him her life. Wherever he went, she would follow. With Rob, every moment would be new and full and happy. Her heart beat joyfully, unmarred by thought or doubt.

Rob released her and cupped her chin. "Do you accept?"

"Yes. Oh, *yes!*"

He touched the rose blossom to her nose. Norah laughed and sniffed its sweet perfume. "I shouldn't be so eager," she said. "It's proper for a lady to refuse the first proposal."

Rob caught her fingers and brought them to his lips. "That would be a foolish waste of time. We must marry soon, so we'll have some time together before I'm off to India."

Norah's head jerked up. "But I'm going with you!"

Rob's expression changed. In the space of an instant what had been open and loving became remote and guarded. Last night's wariness spread from his eyes to his mouth. Even his body drew back, suddenly stiff and distant. Norah realized with a cruel shock that he planned to leave her behind.

"No, sweetheart. It's impossible."

"But why?" She threw herself at him, clutching at his coat.

"Your place is in Boston."

"Boston!" Norah couldn't believe what she was hearing. Rob would part from her after what they'd shared? He would leave her for more than a year? "My place is with you! I will not be separated from you. I won't stay home."

Rob sighed. "Listen, Norah. It's a dangerous five-month voyage."

"I don't care!"

"Damn it, Norah. Calcutta is like living in hell. The heat, the stench, the—"

"Amanda loves it!"

"Amanda's different."

"She's not!" Shock and frustration boiled over into sudden fury. Norah would not permit her stamina to be called into question, especially when measured against that of Amanda Jessup Downing Massingham, Countess of Denmore. "I can do anything she can! I can sail to India. I can go on tiger hunts. I can be charming at teas and balls. I can entertain your . . . your business acquaintances. . . ." Her voice caught and she swallowed hard.

Rob reached out to pull her close. "Norah. Sweetheart. We'll have a long honeymoon. It's nearly a month before I go. Stay here with Alice till December and then go back to the Burnhams."

Norah pulled away. "I'm going with you, Rob. I won't be sent off to Boston like a . . . an unwanted parcel. I spent my girlhood waiting for my father to come home. I refuse to do that with you."

Rob rubbed his palms together nervously. He looked at Norah's cheeks, bright with vexation, her lips plump from his kisses. On her neck he saw marks of his passion and felt a heady rush of tenderness. He would labor for a lifetime to keep her safe and happy and unafraid. He would give her his body, his heart, his entire fortune. But taking her to Calcutta would be madness, a constant reminder of Jody and more than his conscience could possibly bear.

"I'll come back to you, Norah. I love you too much to leave you for long."

"A year isn't long? And after that there will be the next voyage or travel to Europe or whatever it is that will take you away. There I'll be in Boston. Alone."

"I'll come back to you."

"I'll come back to you," Norah mimicked bitterly. "Oh, I've heard those words before. From my father."

Rob groaned in exasperation. His exhausted nerves were grating like ill-fitting gears. "I'm not like Jody, Norah. Believe me, I understand how you feel, but I'm not like him."

She stared at him, bewildered, and Rob wondered what he had said that brought on such a look.

"Jody?" Norah said in a very small voice. "My father? You knew my father?"

Rob felt the blood rush to his head. What had he said? *Jody* . . . Sweet Christ. He stared at Norah, her eyes anxious and disbelieving. For an instant he balanced on the edge of the truth, wondering if he could somehow deny what she was asking. But if he lied now, she would never believe another word he said.

Rob looked away from her. He was finished. Ruined. Last night he'd held springtime in his arms, young and ripe and artless. Never again would he know such happiness. "Yes, I knew him."

Norah sat down on the garden bench and folded her hands. "And you didn't tell me?" Her voice was barely audible.

Rob stared at the ground. The sounds of the garden were deafening, or maybe it was the roaring in his own brain.

"Tell me the truth," she said. "Tell me everything."

Rob told her. Empty of emotion, dead to hope, he told her how Jody had found him at the dock wall in Liverpool. He told her how Jody had taught him to read and figure, how Jody had fueled his ambition and had given him his dreams. From Jody, Rob had learned of seamanship, of sailors' lives, of all the practical wisdom of human nature. Together they had sailed up the China coast and to all the wild shores of the Indies.

As he spoke of the past, Rob registered every detail of the present: the sound of the gravel beneath his boots as he paced, Norah's green dress, the white-painted garden bench, Norah's hair shining golden brown in the sun.

Then he told her about the opium, and her rosy skin turned pale. He watched her eyes fill with shock, then anger, then pure hatred.

"Opium," she breathed, uttering her first sound since he'd begun his confession. "Your filthy opium."

Rob ran a finger over his upper lip. The air was cool, but he was sweating hard.

Norah's blue-gray eyes, chilly as a winter sea, didn't leave his face. "He died of it, then, the opium."

Rob had gone beyond feeling. "He's not dead, Norah."

Her eyes closed. She reached out to steady herself on the bench, and for a moment Rob thought she would faint.

"Not dead," Norah repeated softly. "You're saying my father is not dead, and you let me believe . . ." She bit her pale lips. "Why did Mr. Burnham tell me he'd drowned?"

Rob met her cold gaze and spoke very quietly. "We were in Calcutta. He was due to ship out on a brigantine for New York—not Burnham's ship—and I was going off to Lintin to the opium station. Jody had been on the pipe for two years. He got worse. He . . . he stole from his mates, Norah. No one could trust him."

Her eyes brimmed with tears, and her chin trembled. Rob watched helplessly as the shock cut deeper.

"Jody disappeared and missed his ship. I found him, dragged him out of his filthy den, and we had a row. I was furious at what he was doing to himself. We came to blows. It was the end between us. I was . . . crazy. Crazy with . . ." Rob paused, his throat full of hard emotions. "God, Norah, Jody meant everything to me. I was angry, disgusted, hurt. I spread the word he was dead. I figured in short order it would be the truth. Somehow the news got back to Burnham. I didn't know you then. I'd all but forgotten you existed. I had no idea of the grief it would bring—"

Norah jumped to her feet and flew at him. Rob was quick to grab her wrists before she struck.

"You kept him from me!"

She had turned into a wild thing. Rob wrestled with her to subdue her flailing arms and legs. He held her tight as she sobbed with rage. "Norah! Stop it, now!"

She crumpled against him, weeping, her body trembling and heaving. Rob's blood was pumping again, and it made him dizzy. "He's not the man you remember, Norah. It's better you think him dead."

As quickly as it had come, Norah's feverish outburst seemed to pass. She rested limply against him, gulping air. "Let me go."

Rob released her. Norah stepped away, then turned and faced him. From nowhere, the blow came. Her palm struck flat against his cheek with surprising force. Rob twisted his head and let the sting flow through him.

"You . . . *you killed my father!*"

Rob moved numbly away. All he could think of was getting back to sea, to the breezes that blew away a man's past and centered him in the present. He longed for the crises and boredom of shipboard routines. That was his life—long, solitary passages with nothing to distract his mind and heart.

Norah came toward him, her face pale and bitter, her filmy green dress stirring as she walked. "Take me to India. Take me to find my father!"

A terrible vision rose up before Rob's eyes: Norah on his ship for five months, staring at him with fury and hatred.

"I can't."

Her face crumpled. A fist came up to rub her trembling mouth. "You owe me that much!"

"No."

"You're despicable!" she cried through choking sobs. "I wish to God I'd never laid eyes on you."

Rob turned on his heel. Pebbles slipped under his boots; he couldn't seem to keep his footing. Then he realized he was running. The garden path blurred before his eyes. Hedges closed in on him, the fountain became a thundering waterfall, bees and butterflies swooped threateningly. When he reached the house, he was panting. Rob raced to his room, taking the stairs two at a time, and threw his belongings into his bag. When he pushed past the bewildered footman and set off on the dusty road to Exton, he knew the memories of Brightsgate Hall would keep him in hell for a lifetime.

Chapter Nineteen

"MIGHTY STRANGE BEHAVIOR," Lord Denmore said at dinner the next day. "After I spent weeks encouraging him to come down here, he didn't even have the courtesy to stay around to greet his hosts. And it's a pretty ways up here from London, not just an afternoon's jaunt."

When the Denmores and Alice returned from Belvoir, they talked of nothing but Rob's visit. Norah was besieged with questions. When had he arrived? Why had he left so hastily? Had he thought Amanda's little joke amusing? Norah tried her best to behave as if everything had proceeded normally, but her composure rapidly deteriorated. She cast a beseeching look at Amanda, who alone among the group seemed to sense her distress, and the young countess gracefully shifted the conversation to the previous evening's entertainment.

Old Lady Denmore, however, apparently dissatisfied with Norah's vague responses, persisted. "Wiggins said Captain Mackenzie left quite abruptly. He didn't even wait for the carriage to be readied, he *walked* to Exton. And then you, my dear, didn't come out of your room for the rest of the day. Now, I hope you haven't spoiled your chances for a perfectly good match."

Norah's fork crashed to her plate.

"Grandmama," Amanda said reprovingly, "I think we've examined Norah enough."

Alice turned to Norah with an expression of sudden alarm. "Norah, are you . . ." Belatedly she seemed to sense a crisis. "I mean, Aunt Isabel, it can hardly be Norah's fault if Rob was called away."

The table fell silent. Norah's hands trembled as she retrieved her fork. She bit her quivering lips and looked around at the company, who stared at her with varying expressions of surprise and concern.

Amanda said gently, "My dear child."

Norah, her emotions at their breaking point, could bear no more. With a gasp of apology, she pushed back her chair and ran from the dining room. Without stopping to fetch her bonnet, she dashed out of the house. She fled through the fields, pushing herself with great strides up and down hills, trying to exhaust the sobs that grabbed at her throat. Only when she heard shouts did Norah realize Richard and Ned were tumbling after her. She stopped long enough to gather them into a hard, wriggling hug. Thank heaven for their dear freckled faces, she thought. The boys would keep her company; their bright chatter would divert her thoughts. If she allowed herself to contemplate one more time how Rob had torn her heart to shreds, how he had kept her beloved papa from her for all these years and then had given him back in the form of a monster, she feared she would lose her mind.

At the abbey ruins, Norah rested only for a moment so Richard and Ned could jump off the crumbling walls. Then she retraced her steps, the boys clamoring after her, rolling and frolicking like puppies through the tall grass and wildflowers. Back at Brightsgate, Norah left the children in the yard and stumbled up the stairs to her room. She felt thankful that the family was resting and she would have to answer no questions. Exhausted from her exertion, Norah collapsed on the bed beside the sleeping Alice.

When she awoke it was dark, the room empty. Norah felt sticky with perspiration, and her face burned from the sun. She washed herself, put on a dressing gown, and sat down on the window seat. She stared out at the black night, not daring to think of the future. Tomorrow, she told herself. Tomorrow I'll make my plans.

A light tapping sounded on the door, and Amanda put her

head in. "I need someone to hold my embroidery thread. Denmore is with the boys, and Guy has taken Alice out to the studio. Will you come?"

In a daze, Norah wandered into the hall. Falling asleep in daylight and waking in the dark had left her in a twilight world. She felt she was sleepwalking. It was a feeling not much different from her mental state since yesterday morning when happiness became falsehood, love vanished from her heart, and the solid ground she had walked on for the past eight years crumbled into sand.

Amanda's sitting room blazed with candlelight. The countess patted the cushion beside her on the sofa. "Come, Norah. I do need company tonight."

A small fire kept the chill off the air. Norah stared at the flames and tried to blot from memory a tiger skin hearthrug and the warmth on her limbs as Rob led her through their supple dance of passion. It seemed a lifetime ago, that night of love with a stranger. When she thought of him now, her heart lay in her chest, cold as a stone.

Amanda sighed contentedly. "It's so pleasant to sit quietly in one's own room after a weekend of socializing." She picked up her hoop and handed Norah the hanks of thread with which she was embroidering a horse cloth for Lord Denmore. "It was just as well you didn't accompany us to Belvoir, Norah. Captain Hardy barely left me alone for a moment, inquiring about you. He was dreadfully unhappy that you weren't there. His face fell quite to the floor."

"How sad for him," Norah responded softly. A great tear splashed on her hand. She touched her face and found it wet. After laying down the embroidery thread, Norah fumbled in her sleeve for her handkerchief and wiped her cheeks.

The countess was not one to ignore such a display. After a moment's silence, she spoke gently. "Tell me what happened, my dear. I'm rather good at listening."

Norah sat very still, trying to master her emotions well enough to speak. When she finally opened her mouth, her voice was so low Amanda had to lean toward her to hear.

"He told me my papa is alive," Norah said, and immediately thought, How odd, how unreal, to be saying those words. Once she got started, it became easier to talk. She told

Amanda about her papa, how she'd thought him dead, how dearly she'd loved him. She spoke of the opium and Rob's cruel deception. She made no mention of their night of wild passion, the proposal of marriage, the love that had died in an instant of flaming pain. As she spoke, Norah basked in Amanda's quiet sympathy. Not once did the countess interrupt, nor did she take her eyes from her work.

"I asked him to take me to India to find Papa," Norah concluded bitterly. "He refused. He's the most contemptible man in the world."

Amanda looked up, the color drained from her face. "He loves you, Norah."

"Loves me!" Norah cried. "He never could love me and play such a callous, lying trick. I despise him!"

Amanda glanced down at her embroidery. Her hands were still. "Rob," she said, as if to herself. "How he must be suffering."

"He!" Norah's sunburned face was scorched with indignation. "How *he* must be suffering! It is I who was wronged, not Rob Mackenzie!"

Amanda laid a gentling hand on Norah's arm. "I'm sure he did what he thought best, however misguided," she said firmly. "I'm not denying that holding back the truth was wrong, but I know he would never intentionally hurt you."

Norah's throat ached with grief and rage. Of course Amanda would defend her former lover, she thought. Even Alice would probably take Rob's part. Oh, she had never felt so utterly alone!

"But you have every reason to be angry," Amanda continued. "You want to go to India, and of course you must. You shall accompany Denmore and me when we return to our post in December. We'll have you in Calcutta by April. It will be ever so pleasant having you as a companion on the voyage, and once we arrive, Denmore will do everything in his power to locate your father. I'll speak to him this very evening. Perhaps he can write some letters now to put things in motion."

As the countess spoke, a vague plan stirred in Norah's mind. She grasped it, molding it into shape, and suddenly it became so real to her, so heavy with possibility, that Norah felt a palpable sense of excitement. The dreadful, numbing malaise seemed to fade. She felt herself ease miraculously back to her senses. The dawn of purpose showed Norah exactly what she must do. December was months away. Papa was sick, perhaps dying. She had no time to waste. Yes, she would go to India, but not with Amanda and Lord Denmore. She would sail in October aboard the *Orion*.

"Thank you, Amanda," Norah said, her voice suddenly firm, her thoughts moving quickly. "You are very kind."

George Crawford swung his leg up onto the table, setting it rocking. "Sorry," he mumbled around his pipe stem. He reached out to steady the table, and Rob bent once more over his calculations.

"We'll be carrying two hundred chests of the best Turkish. At three hundred dollars a picul . . . a hundred catties to a picul . . ." Rob scribbled quickly. "We'll be carrying thirty-nine thousand nine hundred dollars' worth of opium, George." Rob sat back and gave a low whistle. "A bargain. This stuff will bring seven hundred dollars a picul in Batavia to Canton's five. But, Christ, man, if we ran it up the coast ourselves, we'd double the profit." He threw down his pencil and tilted his chair against the wall. "What do you think, George? Feel like an adventure?"

Crawford removed his pipe from his mouth and took a draft of ale. He wiped his mouth with his hand. "Ain't your opium, Captain, nor your thirty-nine thousand, neither. Burnham said—"

The front legs of Rob's chair banged to the floor. "I don't give a fish's tit what Burnham said! I'll buy the stinking stuff myself. Then you and I'll round up a crew and set off north."

Crawford pulled on his pipe, his brown face wrinkled in thought. "I thought you were going civilized, Captain. Traveling partner for Burnham. Europe and all that. I half expected you'd be hitched up with Jody's girl by now. You seemed pretty fond of her last I saw."

Rob replied with a raw laugh. "Three months of that life's been enough to last me a lifetime. Stiff collars, dirty cities, shuffling papers in coaches, strange hotel rooms. Damn it, George, I'm going to buy a clipper and run opium again. My own operation, not Burnham's. I want you to join me."

Crawford's brow furrowed deeper. "Don't try to bring back the past, Captain," he said softly. "You and me and Jody, we're gone. We're not the same men, none of us."

"The past!" Rob jumped to his feet so suddenly his chair crashed to the floor. "Christ Almighty, this has got nothing to do with the past or with Jody. I've been in this business before, and I want it again. If you want no part of it, just say so. But don't start preaching at me."

Crawford's eyes narrowed. "Sorry, Captain. Didn't realize I was preaching."

Rob paced the shabby room he had taken on the second floor of the Crow's Nest Tavern. It was a dismal place with a bed, a table, and a few chairs. It suited his frame of mind.

"You're wound tighter'n a miser's pocket watch, Captain," Crawford said. "Looks to me like you need a woman."

Rob leaned his shoulders against the wall and glared at the mate. "If I need a woman, mister," he said sarcastically, "I think I can manage by myself."

"Your face ain't as pretty as it used to be, neither. You're too old for brawling."

Rob touched his sore jaw. His left eye was ringed with black, his lower lip was swollen, and his knuckles were a mangled mess. For an hour of crashing fists, grunted curses, and shattering furniture, he'd enjoyed the once-familiar exhilaration of a tavern brawl. But the next day, lying in agony from a few well-placed kicks in the ribs, he'd wondered at his sanity.

"A small misunderstanding," Rob explained. "A bunch of grog-happy Frenchmen. Can't recall what started it." He attempted a smile, but Crawford didn't seem amused.

"What's bothering you, boy? You look like hell, your temper's hot, and you're talking wild as a loose bowline."

Rob righted his chair and sat down. Keeping his gaze well away from the mate's, he toyed with his pencil and tried to figure out how to unburden himself to someone like Crawford. The one person he had confided in, the one person to whom he had revealed a fraction of his dreams and fears, was gone.

Rob stared doggedly at the floor and said nothing.

He'd come to Liverpool three weeks ago. Once his cargo was safely stored in the warehouse, he'd had little to do but wait for the *Orion* to arrive from Boston. He'd paced the streets, hating the city, despising himself. The very thought of opium disgusted him. Rob would gladly have set a match to every chest in the warehouse if such an act could have erased the misery it had brought to Jody and Norah and him. But it was too late for moralisms.

To ease the pain, Rob had drunk himself into oblivion, trying to blot out the image of a green muslin dress, of stricken blue-gray eyes. But his body couldn't forget a night blurred with ecstasy, a night of liquid fire that he would have sold his soul to live through again. He'd been untiring that night, and so had she. Never again would he touch a woman without thinking of Norah.

"While you're feeling low," Crawford said, "here's a bit more bad news." He drew from his jacket pocket a long white envelope and laid it on the table. On it was Oliver Burnham's handwriting and Alice's name.

Rob stared at the envelope. "What is it?"

"Burnham's not pleased with you, Captain. Not pleased at all. His daughter's got it into her head to marry. The old man won't hear of it. He's on his way to London to fetch her and his son and Jody's girl. He's going to take the lot of them back to Boston."

Rob swore. He grabbed the envelope and threw it down. "My fault, is it? Does he think I made the arrangements myself?"

"There's more, Captain. You cut orders for the spring season."

"Christ! Doesn't he know there's a panic brewing?"

Crawford shrugged. "And he don't like your pestering him about remittances. He thinks you've been high-handed about things. He wants to do business as he's always done it. If you can't go along, he don't want you as part of the firm."

Rob jumped to his feet, swearing. "Then let him keep his goddam partnership! I've been here for months, talking to bankers and agents and manufacturers, while Burnham's sat on his backside in Boston counting his money. Dear God, give me back the China coast where a man's not beholden to anything but his own wits."

Crawford puffed on his pipe and said nothing. His silence

and his appraising glances made Rob uncomfortable. At last the mate spoke. "When something bothers a man," Crawford said, "he either faces it or runs away. The sea is full of us that's run. You can become one of us, Captain, like Jody and me. But I figure it ain't worth it. You got nothing to lose, because you ain't got nothing." The mate stood and stretched. "I guess I'll be getting back to my bunk." His hand dropped onto Rob's shoulder. "You told her, didn't you, told her about Jody? That's what's eating at you?"

Rob nodded mutely, his chest tight as a fist.

"Can't help you with that, boy," Crawford said. "Only a miracle would bring Jody back. Better you'd left him dead."

Crawford grasped Rob's shoulder. It was a brief, comforting gesture, one without precedent for the taciturn mate. The door opened and closed, and Rob was alone with his thoughts. He sat quietly for a moment; then with one ferocious sweep of his arm, he cleared the table, sending papers, pens, ink, and ledgers crashing to the floor.

Autumn arrived in Hertfordshire in a blaze of warm afternoons and brilliant colors. Each day Norah mounted her chestnut mare and pounded across the fields, carried along like wings of the wind, wearing herself to exhaustion. She kept to her seat with perfect ease. Even that old cavalry officer, Lord Denmore, complimented her on her equestrian skills.

Norah had changed during the past weeks, and, oh, how proud she was of her new outlook. She thought back with scorn upon the compliant young woman of last summer, the spineless girl who had allowed herself to be used and bruised, who'd wept and vacillated like the insipid heroine of a bad novel. These days she faced life with a grim new confidence. Everything she undertook, from teaching herself to ride to expressing her disgust with shooting parties, she carried off with quite admirable brass.

Courage, Norah decided on one of her morning rides, went beyond the bravery of soldiers. It was a simple act of defying convention and taking one's life in hand. She thought of Alice's valiant battle for self-reliance and Guy's daring portrait of the woman he loved. She admired old Lady Denmore's outspokenness, although it often stung, and Amanda's brash as-cent from farm girl to countess. And of course, there was Lord Denmore's determination to possess the defamed Amanda Downing. Such examples gave Norah the grit and drive to accomplish the formidable tasks that lay before her.

At the stables, Norah reined in her mare and slipped from the saddle before the groom could assist her.

"There's company in the sitting room, miss," he said. "Miss Alice wants you to come immediately."

"Thank you, Stephens." Norah tossed the reins to him and hurried up the walk.

Amanda and Lord Denmore had gone off on a month's holiday to Scotland after taking the boys to school. Norah would not see them again until Calcutta. And just as well, she thought. If they were at home when she took flight, Lord Denmore would surely put the hounds on her trail.

In the hallway, Norah cast off her hat and glanced in the mirror. She was sweaty and dusty, hardly presentable for visitors. A bath and a change would certainly be in order. She started for the stairs, but halted at the sound of a familiar voice from the sitting room, a voice she surely must have been imagining. Norah wiped a damp strand of hair from her forehead and stepped into the sitting room.

"Jan!"

Janner rose to greet her, grinning shyly as he pushed back the white hair hanging over his bright blue eyes. To Norah, the young sailor in his checked shirt and loose trousers was nothing less than a gift of Providence. With his arrival, a major complication in her plan was neatly swept aside.

"Whatever brings you here?" she cried. "You don't know how pleased I am to see you."

Then Norah saw Alice's sad, still face, and her joy faded. Norah glanced at Guy, standing at the fireplace, a letter crumpled in his hand. She sank down on the sofa with a sigh. "Oh, Lord," she said. "Mr. Burnham."

"He forbids our marriage," Guy said, his long face pale with distress. "He's coming to take you and Alice and Ollie back to Boston."

Norah's first urge was to laugh; she wouldn't be here another week, let alone when Mr. Burnham reached Liverpool. But then she glimpsed tears standing in Alice's eyes, and her mood changed to anger. So the Burnhams would interfere with their daughter's happiness, she thought. She glanced at Guy and her heart sank. At Alice's parents' intransigence, Guy's courage had faltered. She'd feared as much.

The clock ticked away the silence. Janner shifted uncomfortably and tugged at the slip tie of his black silk neckerchief. Norah turned to the young sailor. "When does the *Orion* sail, Jan?" she asked.

"Close to the tenth of October, I'd say."

"I see. Guy, when does Mr. Burnham say he's arriving?"

Guy unfolded the paper and stared at it. "He's unable to leave Boston until October first."

"Good. He won't arrive here for another three weeks at the earliest. By then you two will be married."

"Married!" Guy exclaimed, his voice raised with frustration. "Didn't you hear me? He expressly forbids our marriage."

"And you accept that?" Norah snapped. "You're a grown man, Guy, and Alice is of age. If you two plan to forgo your future together simply because Alice's father forbids you to marry, then I say you're both fools and don't deserve each other."

The drooping Alice suddenly came to life. She straightened her shoulders and tucked her handkerchief into her pale blue sleeve. "Norah is right, Guy. I've reached the age of majority. If I wish to marry, there is no reason I can't."

Guy's face flushed. "We'll marry after I speak to your father. Once I prove to him that I can be a good husband to you, he'll give his consent."

Norah laughed rudely. Oh, the man's stainless honor! She was in no mood lately to suffer fools, and Guy was proving himself to be a rather large one. "You can prove you're a good husband by *becoming* a husband," she informed him. "Mr. Burnham is determined that dear, afflicted Alice live at home in serene spinsterhood until she dies of a broken heart or of boredom, whichever comes first. He won't listen to you, Guy, nor will he consider what will happen to Alice when he and his wife are gone—"

"Norah!" Guy interrupted. "You are being unpardonably insulting—"

"Who will care for Alice then?" Norah continued, raising her voice to drown out Guy's. "Ollie? Oh, that would be fine! A dependable man like Ollie! The Burnhams don't think of Alice's future, but only of themselves. When it comes to their daughter, they are selfish, Guy, and if you think you can defy Oliver Burnham when you meet him face to face, you are mistaken."

Guy stared at Norah, his face gone gray. "That speech was quite unnecessary, Norah. You show shockingly little gratitude to the Burnhams for their kindness to you. But aside from that, I know what's best for Alice and me. Defying her parents is not in our best interests."

Norah held Guy in her stubborn gaze and demanded, "What do you have to say, Alice?"

Alice's head had remained bowed during the exchange. She sighed and raised it. "Norah is right, Guy. We must marry now without their blessing. I don't know if even I will be able to withstand my father's arguments once he gets here."

Guy remained silent. Norah rose and motioned to Jan. "Jan and I will walk in the garden," she said. "We'll join you again later."

Janner silently followed her down the cool, dim hallway, past the Denmore portraits to the door. When they stepped into the garden filled with sunshine, Norah took no notice of the view, but grasped Jan's arm and hurried him down the path to a secluded arbor.

"Jan," she said eagerly, pulling him onto the seat beside her, "I desperately need your help."

Guy traveled to Exton village the next day to speak to the clergyman and arrange for his wedding. Lady Denmore, insulted at the Burnhams' lack of faith in her grandson, enthusiastically supported the elopement. With Norah's and Mavis's assistance, the old countess rummaged in the attic until she found her own veil and an old-fashioned gown of shimmering white. Two village seamstresses remade it in a size and style suited to the bride's figure and taste.

Norah was loath to spoil Alice's bridal happiness by disappearing without warning. Once the wedding arrangements were complete, she swore Alice to secrecy and explained that she would soon be on her way to Liverpool to board the *Orion* for its voyage to Calcutta. Alice sat in horrified silence, listening to the outrageously dangerous plan Norah had concocted.

"Jan will help me get aboard," Norah said. "Once we're out to sea, there's no way Rob can send me back. I have to find my father. You must understand that."

Alice's face was pale. "But Liverpool is a dreadful place! For you to be there alone is out of the question. Oh, Norah, perhaps Guy or Ollie could escort you."

Norah pressed her lips together impatiently. Lately her temper had been constantly frayed; maintaining it even before her dear Alice had not been easy. "Ollie and Guy mustn't find out," she said firmly. "That's the point. If they know what I'm doing, they'll stop me, and that would spoil everything. I must make my escape with no one knowing, and you must keep my secret until after the date of sailing. I know it will be difficult for you, Alice. They will be begging you to reveal my whereabouts. But you must tell them only that I am gone and that I am perfectly safe. Not a word more. Do you understand?"

"But what if something happens to you?" Alice cried. "I could never forgive myself."

"Nothing will happen," Norah said, adding unkindly, "If you don't agree to be silent, Alice, *I'll* never forgive you. Never."

Alice's eyes filled with tears. "Oh, Norah," she whispered, "how can you say such a thing!"

Norah despised her own cruelty. She hated hurting Alice at the happiest time of her life. But it couldn't be helped. Firm measures were necessary to ensure the success of her plan. She took Alice's face in her hands and said more gently, "Please, my dear, say you agree."

"Of course I agree, but, Norah—"

"Hush, now." Norah pulled Alice into a tight embrace. She smoothed the shiny black curls and kissed Alice's cheek. "Think of your wedding day, your wonderful life with Guy. And, oh, Alice, do be happy!"

Guy and Alice were married before the low altar of Exton's quaint stone chapel. Norah and Ollie stood up for the bride and groom. Aside from the wedding party and the parson, only Lady Denmore and Mavis were present.

That night, after a festive dinner, Ollie, who had been hastily summoned from London and who seemed as uneasy in Norah's company as he was with Alice's marriage, departed for a friend's estate in nearby Shilton. Alice went off to her husband's bedchamber.

Norah lay awake for hours. She worried about Alice, about her innocence, about the shock of a man's passion suddenly thrust upon a girl. She worried about leaving Brightsgate, about hurting the Burnhams, the Denmores, and everyone who had offered her kindness. She worried about her own future. Tomorrow she would be on her own. Tomorrow she would begin a journey that would lead her across the world and back in time, back to her papa.

Thoughts of Jody brought on an avalanche of memories and a torrent of tears. Through the long, lonely night, Norah wept for her papa and mama and for all the heartache that had touched her poor doomed family.

The bridal pair didn't appear until noon the next day. Norah was in her room preparing for her departure when a tap on the door sent her flying across the room. Alice stood in the hallway. She wore peach muslin and a radiant smile. Guy lounged against the wall beside her. He grinned at Norah.

"Alice wants to visit. I told her I'd let her out of my sight for no more than a half hour." He touched Alice's cheek, and she flushed crimson. Guy strolled down the hall, whistling.

Norah pulled Alice inside and slammed the door. "Alice!"

"Oh, Norah!" Alice threw herself into Norah's arms and burst into tears.

"Are you all right?" Norah demanded as she hugged Alice close. "Was Guy kind to you?"

Alice giggled through a sob. "Of course I'm all right! And Guy is wonderful. Norah, he . . ." She stopped herself. "Oh, but I mustn't tell. I really mustn't. You don't mind, Norah, do you?"

Norah disengaged herself from Alice's embrace and smiled with teary happiness. "Of course I don't mind. All I want to know is if you're happy."

Alice beamed through her tears and patted her curls, which looked roguishly disordered. "I feel I'm the happiest woman in the world."

Norah felt a swift, bitter pang. Hadn't she felt the same way one glorious August morning?

"Norah," Alice said, "I must talk to you."

"Of course," Norah said, surprised at Alice's peremptory tone. She led Alice to the window seat, and they sat down, fingers entwined.

"I've been thinking about Rob," Alice said.

Norah made a sound of disgust. "About Rob? On your wedding night?"

Alice flushed at Norah's sarcasm. "I've been thinking about him and you ever since we returned from Belvoir to find you so upset. I'm very fond of him, you know. I hoped you two would marry."

"Show me some mercy, Alice," Norah said impatiently. "I have no interest in marrying anyone, especially a man whose character leaves so much to be desired."

Alice continued undaunted. "Rob loves you. He's wanted you ever since our crossing on the *Orion*. That was plain enough for the lowliest crewman to see, not to mention me, even though I'm blind. Now that you've told me about your father, it's obvious Rob thought you'd be better off not knowing the sad truth. I think he's actually quite noble."

"Noble!" Norah cried. "May God spare me such nobility!" Would this round of pity for Rob among the women of the Denmore household never cease? Had Amanda and Alice no understanding of treachery? Would they mouth such forgiving platitudes faced with their own husbands' deceptions?

Alice's mouth curled in an infuriating smile, and she gave Norah's fingers a loving squeeze. "I'll miss you dreadfully, Norah, but I'm glad you're running off with Rob. You'll love him again. You'll forgive him one day. I know you will."

Norah scowled. "You're speaking as a happy new bride. There's more to a man that *that* side of things, Alice. I shall never forgive Rob Mackenzie. He's my enemy now. All I want from him is a passage to Calcutta. Nothing more."

Chapter Twenty

ON THE EVE of her departure, the second night after Alice's wedding, Norah packed her box. In it she placed a few under-things, stockings, a warm nightdress, and two of her plainest dresses—a Merrimack print and a rust-colored silk. For her traveling costume, she settled on a dark blue cotton, which she figured would be dignified and unobtrusive, and a bonnet of Tuscan straw. Into a carpetbag she stuffed books, writing paper, and the jewelry box containing her papa's silver ring and Mama's few pieces of jewelry.

From beneath a pile of linen drawers, Norah drew a bulging handkerchief. Miss Peabody had given her a generous gift before she left Boston, a token of her gratitude for Norah's hours of work. That gift and the small allowances Norah had husbanded over the years gave her more than enough money to pay for both the journey to Liverpool and her expenses in Calcutta until the Denmores arrived.

The next morning Norah rose well before dawn. She slipped quietly out of the house into the cool darkness. The sky was tinted by sparkling stars. A gentle rustle of leaves relieved the stillness. Norah trod carefully as she set off down the dark road to Exton, fearful she might fall and spill her belongings. She told herself she was beginning a grand adventure, but her spirits were shaken by the dark, the cold breeze that chilled her bones, and a vague nausea, no doubt due to hunger and excitement. She looked back toward Brightsgate, but the mansion had already disappeared behind the trees. Norah squared her shoulders and faced Exton; this was no time for second thoughts.

In Exton she met the mail coach to Liverpool. The few people abroad at that hour paid her no mind. The coach driver barely glanced at her. After a night in Worcester, Norah reached her destination late the following afternoon.

Liverpool was wrapped in patches of mist that made Norah shiver with cold and apprehension. It was a dreadful city under the best of circumstances, but to a lone traveler facing a dangerous and uncertain adventure, Liverpool seemed doubly oppressive. Norah could find nothing in the bleak streets and grimy buildings that offered a bit of cheer.

She found her way to the inn where she and Alice and Rob had stopped in July. Once settled, she summoned the porter's boy, who was willing to earn a few pence by running an errand to the waterfront. When the boy returned, he carried a bundle. Norah unwrapped a pair of men's trousers, a shirt, a cap, and a jacket. Tucked inside the jacket pocket she found a map and a message: "We sail with the morning tide on Wednesday the twelfth. Meet me at midnight Tuesday at the Crow's Nest." It was signed with Jan's initials.

Norah read the note with satisfaction. So far the plan had worked beautifully.

A sudden spell of dizziness forced her to sit down on the bed. It annoyed her to be coming down ill at such an inopportune time. Just one more day, she told herself. Tomorrow night she would be safe in her cabin on the *Orion*, where she could rest for five solitary months.

Norah passed the following day reading in her room. Her illness tempered her desire for food, but by nightfall she knew she needed to eat to keep up her strength. She decided she'd best have a nap as well, for it would be well after midnight before she was settled on the *Orion*.

Norah sent the porter's boy to fetch a loaf of bread and some cheese. When she finished her meal, she lay down on the bed and closed her eyes.

* * *

She awoke in the dark, frightened, not knowing where she was. Then she remembered: she was in Liverpool; tonight was her rendezvous with Jan.

Norah struggled upright, and nausea struck with full force. Her body felt clammy, and her mouth was stale from the cheese. She lay back with a groan, feeling disoriented and homesick. Brightsgate and her final tearful embrace with Alice seemed long ago and terribly precious. She thought of the laughter around the Denmore's dining table, the warm autumn sun on her back as she sketched at the abbey ruin. She thought of her little chestnut mare, and tears stung her eyes.

Don't be a child, Norah told herself sternly. This was no time for sentiment. She'd made her plans and she would see them through.

Sniffing, she lit the lamp. The clock read ten-fifteen. She had no time to waste.

Norah brushed her teeth, washed her face, and got into Jan's clothes. The trousers hung down over her shoes. Norah rolled up the cuffs and did the same to the sleeves of his shirt and jacket. She studied the map one more time before gathering up her box and carpetbag. Quietly she crept down the back stairs and into the darkened yard.

The inn was situated in a respectable neighborhood, but at this time of night, the street was spooky and deserted. A steady drizzle of rain made the pavement shine in the lamplight. Glancing about nervously, Norah hurried down the street in the direction of the docks. Under each pool of light she shrank a bit, feeling a strange sensation, as if someone were watching her. She passed a closed carriage standing by the curb, its coachman dozing on his box. If it had been a public coach, she might have tested her disguise and hired it. Instead, she scurried past without a second glance.

Norah had gone several yards beyond the coach when she heard footsteps behind her. Gooseflesh rose on her skin. She tightened her grip on her box and carpetbag and sped up. The footsteps quickened. Norah's gooseflesh turned to shivers. She glanced over her shoulder and saw a man, a large fellow by the looks of him, not more than ten yards behind her.

"You, boy!" he called out, pointing directly at her.

Panic clutched at Norah's throat. She broke into a run. Her

heart thudded in her chest, her carpetbag bumped against her legs. The man's footsteps pounded behind her, gaining fast. Dear Lord, Norah thought frantically, help me!

The man laid hold of her arm and yanked so hard that Norah dropped her box. In unthinking terror, she flung her carpetbag at him and opened her mouth to scream. Before she could utter a sound, he clamped a hand hard across her mouth and nose, cutting off all breath. He dragged her, then shoved her hard against a damp brick wall. His hand slipped from her nose and covered only her mouth. Norah took deep, desperate breaths, inhaling the stench of the alley and the foul odor of sweat and spirits coming from her attacker. He pressed his thumb firmly against her windpipe.

"You make a sound and 'twill be yer last."

Norah leaned hard against the wall, her eyes wide, her body frozen with fear. The man's hand left her mouth and throat, and he pulled off her cap. He laughed. "He was right, the guv'ner. Said you didn't have much hair." He reached inside Norah's jacket and clamped his hand over her breast. She shrank back, her head swimming with terror.

"Ah, don't worry, dearie. The gen'l'man what wants you said we was to treat you like a lady. But then, 'ow's he to know, eh?" He took his hand from her breast and pinched her cheek.

The sound of her abductor's voice awakened Norah from her initial numbness. Her mind began to race with silent pleas and prayers that quickly formed into words. "You're making a mistake," she whispered urgently. "I'm not the girl you want. Please release me. I'll give you money—"

She felt cloth against her mouth. Her abductor's fingers dug into her cheeks, forcing her jaw open. In a fury of panic, Norah struggled and kicked. He stuffed the cloth into her mouth and quickly bound her eyes with another cloth, then picked her up like a sack of meal and tossed her over his shoulder. She hung upside down, dizzy with horror, beyond fear, screaming into her gag.

My box, my bag, she thought desperately. My dresses, my money, Papa's ring . . . She began to sob, the sound muffled and hopeless. Save for the inevitable final ravishment, her life was ended. Norah clung to thoughts of her possessions, strewn about on a dark Liverpool street, as if clinging to life it-self. In a swirl of nausea and despair, her mind went blessedly blank.

Norah woke to find herself upright in the corner of a car-riage seat. The vehicle careened through the night, jouncing her against the plush interior. Immediately she remembered all that had happened. Dear Lord, how would she ever extri-cate herself from this living nightmare? Surely she was in-volved in a case of mistaken identity. She had to do something. But what? Norah thought of those agonizing sec-onds with no air in her lungs and decided she couldn't risk an-gering her captor. Feigning unconsciousness, she tried to clear her head well enough to assess her situation.

She was free of her gag, but her eyes were still covered. Al-ice often said she could sense the size of a room, the number of people in it, and whether they were standing or sitting. But try as she might, Norah could discover nothing about her envi-ronment except that the plush seat was threadbare and the in-terior smelled of stale tobacco and unwashed men.

The carriage swung around a corner. Norah, unable to maintain her balance, fell against someone beside her. She reached out to steady herself and touched fine, soft fabric. Her hand slipped over an arm. She was seated beside a man clad in an expensive coat. His scent differed markedly from the as-sailant's. A gentleman. In the alley, her captor had mentioned a gentleman. Without thinking, she spoke.

"Won't you help me, sir? I believe I was taken by mistake—"

"Quiet!" It was the voice of the kidnapper. The gentleman remained silent.

Norah's heart pounded. The gentleman was her only chance. He had to acknowledge this terrible mistake. Norah tried again, beseeching. "Please. I can explain why I was dressed like a boy."

"Shut up!" Again it was the voice of her abductor.

Norah bit her lip. The coarse man spoke, but with more kindness. "Don't fret now, little girl. You won't be harmed."

Not be harmed! After he nearly strangled her in the alley? Made brave by the gentleman's presence, Norah retorted,

"You threatened to kill me! You almost suffocated me in that alley, not to mention taking liberties with my person."

The gentleman beside her stirred, and Norah heard a thwack of something like a riding crop. A grunt of surprise came from her kidnapper. She was right! The gentleman was in charge. She would continue to play on his sympathies.

"How can I believe you won't harm me when already you've been so cruel?" Her voice rose plaintively.

"Mother o' God, she talks too much," her assailant grumbled. "Better shut her up, guv'ner, before she talks you out of this."

The gentleman's arm went around Norah's shoulders and held her firmly against his chest. Something pressed against her lips.

"Drink up, girlie," the abductor said.

Norah struggled. A strong hand forced her head back. A bitter liquid assaulted her tongue, the same bitter liquid Rob had given her when he set her shoulder. Norah tried to spit it out, but the draft went down, catching in her throat. She coughed and gasped. They forced her to drink more. Norah's mind grew fuzzy. "Please," she sobbed, terrified of losing consciousness once more.

Gentle hands wiped at her wet cheeks. Her head lolled against soft superfine. She was vaguely aware of the coach stopping, of being dragged out into fresh air. Her blindfold was removed, but she couldn't focus her eyes. Her legs refused to work. When she felt herself lifted into strong arms, Norah sagged against the stinking body of her captor and gave herself up to her fate.

Norah opened her eyes to a room that was tiny and dimly lit by candles. She lay on a lumpy mattress, free of her blindfold, a bitter taste in her mouth. She felt ill and groggy. Sounds of laughter and stomping feet drifted up from below. A fiddle cried in the distance.

"He said no drink."

The words came from a thin man who sat at the rickety table playing cards with the man who'd attacked her. The gentleman was nowhere to be seen. Through half-closed lids, Norah observed her abductor toss down a glass of amber liquid. He had a round face with flat features and a vacant cast to his eyes.

"Don't matter," her abductor said. "Any man thinks I can't watch over a girl when I've had a few nips don't know Jamie Fensen."

"And what if he don't give us our due?" the tall man snapped back. "What then, Fensen?"

"Lordy, quit worryin', Magee. You see a fine gen'l'man and you're all in a dither like a bleedin' schoolgirl. I suppose you hoped he'd take a bleedin' shine to ye."

Fensen opened his mouth, and a long burp issued forth. Norah closed her eyes in disgust. She wished she knew what time it was. The *Orion* would sail shortly after dawn.

Norah looked around the bleak, smoke-filled room. She was surprised to see her box and carpetbag on the floor near the door, along with her cap and jacket.

Her movement caught Fensen's attention. "Ho, the girl's awake." He rose and came to stand over her. Norah averted her face from the man's stupid leering gaze and fought the urge to be sick. "A pretty one, don't you think, Magee?"

Fensen reached down to grasp the front of Norah's shirt. Magee was on him like a lion. "Lord A'mighty, Fensen, you're dumber than I thought. He won't pay us a bleedin' cent if we harm her. He already's fit in knots 'cause you touched her before."

"Ah, it's nothin' much I want," Fensen complained. "Just a squeeze and a bit of a look."

Magee had thinning fair hair and eyes that drooped at the corners. His smile revealed the blackened stubs of front teeth. "Sorry to detain you, miss," he said to Norah, "but there ain't much we can do till the captain agrees to our demands."

"Captain? What captain?" Norah asked weakly. "What demands?"

"Why, the master of the *Orion*. We're holdin' you fer ransom."

Ransom! For the second time that night, Norah felt she was suffocating. Someone had known of her plan and hoped to get money from Rob by holding her! But who? And for what reason? She thought of Jan and dismissed the possibility out of hand. He was totally trustworthy. Who else knew of her flight but Alice? But Alice was miles away, safe at Brightsgate. And who was the gentleman—the guv'ner, as her assailant had called him?

Norah's mind moved into action. Her captors were stupid and careless. If she kept them talking, she might learn something. Norah pushed herself into a sitting position. "How much ransom?" she asked.

Magee scratched his head. "Think 'twas about a thousand pounds, weren't it, Fensen?"

The other man agreed, grinning. "Come to think of it, 'twas 'bout a thousand."

A thousand pounds! Norah gulped hard. Would she be worth a thousand pounds to Rob? And how could she repay him such a sum? She couldn't bear the thought of being indebted to him, but worse, what if he chose to ignore the demand and sail for India, leaving her to the mercy of these men?

"We're tellin' the captain if he wants to see you alive, he's got to pay fer ye," Fensen cackled. "If 'twere me, I'd cough up a pretty penny for a sweet thing like you."

Norah gasped. "If he wants to see me *alive*?"

"Shut up, Fensen," Magee said. "Y'ain't s'posed to frighten her. Now, miss, we ain't going to kill you. The captain's bound to come through with the money."

Desperation made Norah bolder. "Is the gentleman the one who wants the money?" She thought her mention of their benefactor would anger them. Instead, the two men laughed. They laughed so hard, they had to sit down. Encouraged, Norah continued. "Where am I?"

"Spar and Anchor," Fensen said and got a stern frown from his mate.

"Do you know the Crow's Nest?"

Both men nodded. Fensen jerked his head toward the window. "Two doors down."

"Who is the gentleman?" Norah persisted. "I must know."

Fensen laughed. "Ye'll know soon enough, lovey."

"Can't you keep that trap shut?" Magee shouted. "She ain't to know about him and you know it. Now no more talk or I'll have to gag the both of you."

The men returned to their game, grumbling, and Norah lay

back on the bed. Her fear was now mingled with frustration. Her plan was ruined. If Rob rescued her, he would be furious about the thousand pounds and he'd send her right back to the Denmores. In no time at all she'd be on her way to Boston with Mr. Burnham. There would be no hope of ever reaching Calcutta.

But Rob would never pay her ransom. He had walked away from her papa when he was in need. He'd falsely taken her love. Rob Mackenzie was not a man to be entrusted with one's heart, let alone one's life. The more Norah thought, the more truly desperate her situation seemed to be. If she didn't appear at the appointed place, Jan would figure she'd changed her mind and he'd sail with the ship. Then what would become of her? No one knew where she was! No one! Would she be kept in this room to be used by seamen to fill her captors' pockets?

A wave of sickness lifted Norah's stomach. The room was unbearably stuffy with tobacco smoke and the smell of spirits and sweat. Norah gasped for breath. Moaning in misery, she pressed her face into her hands.

A knock on the door brought her head up with a start.

"Who comes?" Magee called out.

"Delivering a bottle, mates," the voice responded.

Fensen almost knocked over his chair in his eagerness to reach the door. He swung it open, and there, with a bottle under his arm and a plate of steaming mussels in his hands, stood Jan.

Norah opened her mouth and closed it again, thankful she hadn't shouted his name.

"The gentleman sent this up," Jan said, giving Norah an uninterested glance.

Norah's brain swam with relief. She stared hard at Jan, trying to figure out what he was up to.

"And who are you, lad?" Magee asked, assessing Jan with interest. Jan's fair hair dipped over his brow. In the dim light he looked young and delicately handsome.

"Janner, sir."

"And what's yer country?"

"America, sir." Jan set the plate and bottle on the table.

"What's yer ship?" Magee continued, while Fensen pulled eagerly at the bottle.

"No ship, sir, just a friend of your employer." He gave Norah a sideways frown as if to indicate to Fensen and Magee that she not be informed of the gentleman's identity.

"Aye, but you're a pretty one," Magee said with a leer. "Sure you don't want a spell at sea with me, Janner my lad? The *Conquest* sails in a fortnight for Canton."

Jan blushed crimson. He backed toward the door. "I'd best be going along. He's got more errands for me to run."

"Wait, Janner. Stop and have a drink with us." Magee snatched the bottle from Fensen and splashed some of the whiskey into a glass.

Jan shook his head. "He doesn't like me to linger."

Magee grumbled his displeasure, and Jan seemed to hesitate. "I'll come back in a bit," Jan said. "Perhaps within the hour." He glanced at Norah again, and she thought she saw a message in his eyes.

"Good lad!" bellowed Magee. "You'll help pass the time until we finish up our business here."

When Jan departed, Norah was as much in the dark as she'd been before his appearance, but she saw a glimmer of hope. And in her predicament, a glimmer equaled the radiance of the sun.

"Mighty peculiar feller, that gent," Fensen said as he poured more liquor into his glass. "Seems to like pretty boys and girls dressed as boys." He drained his glass and smacked his lips. "Cognac! The guv'ner has taste, mate, good taste."

"You wouldn't know cognac from horse's piss," Magee retorted. He frowned at his glass. "Tastes a mite strange to me. And it don't make sense, him telling us not to drink and then sending up a bleedin' bottle." But Magee shrugged, drank up, and returned to the card game.

Norah waited and watched, wondering what would happen next. It took only a short time for her to find out. Fensen was the first to begin yawning and stretching.

"Christ, it's a long night," he muttered. "When in hell's he going to bust in here?"

"Shut up, Fensen. Yer babbling again," Magee mumbled, and then he, too, seemed to reel in his seat. In a few moments both men had their heads on the table and were snoring like bullfrogs.

At first Norah dared not get up. She feared the men would awaken and punish her if she tried to creep out. But she couldn't forgo her one opportunity for escape. Just as she swung her feet tentatively to the floor, the door opened and Jan stepped in. His face was drawn with fright. He jerked his head, indicating she should follow him. When Norah motioned toward her box and carpetbag, Jan shook his head. Snatching up her cap, he grabbed her arm and pulled her out the door.

They crept down dark greasy stairs that echoed with the raucous laughter and banging mugs from the taproom below. The tavern sounds pounded in Norah's exhausted, half-drugged brain. Overlaying the racket in her mind was the fear that at any moment Fensen would come roaring out of the room and crash down the stairs after her.

At the foot of the stairs, Jan grasped her wrist and pulled her past the taproom to the outside door. They stumbled into the dark night, running and slipping on damp cobblestones, their footsteps echoing down the empty street. The earlier drizzle had turned to a steady rain that soaked through Norah's shirt. Shivering and gasping, she followed Jan until he turned a corner and stopped. Jan leaned heavily against a warehouse door, then slid down to sit on the ground, unmindful of the mud and garbage. Norah collapsed beside him. She was trembling from head to foot. Her legs were so weak from shock and running they could no longer hold her. She huddled close to Jan. She could feel him trembling as hard as she. Aside from the sound of the rain that beat steadily on the warehouse eaves, the night was quiet.

"What's the time?" Norah whispered.

"Close to three," Jan said. "By four the captain will be aboard, and the pilot by six."

They said no more for the next several minutes. Once Norah felt more collected, she asked, "How did you find me, Jan? Is it true they held me for ransom?"

He shook his head. "A gentleman hired the two men to snatch you. He wanted you to believe you were being held for ransom. It was a lie."

Jan rested his head against the wooden door. Norah couldn't see his face, but in his weary, unsteady voice she heard his distress. Jan had saved her life. She would thank him later with words. For now she fumbled for his hand and squeezed it.

"The gent wanted you to be held until the *Orion* sailed," Jan said. "I heard the story from a man he tried to recruit. The fellow said he'd have nothing to do with kidnapping a lady."

"Does Captain Mackenzie know about this?"

"No."

Norah's muddled mind tried to piece it all together. She was supposed to think Rob would pay her ransom. But why, if it wasn't true?

"Who is the gentleman?" she asked.

"I don't know. When you didn't appear at the Crow's Nest, I stopped at some other taverns. At the Spar and Anchor I heard the story about the gent hiring two roughnecks to kidnap a girl."

A fresh wave of nausea surged in Norah's belly. She hadn't eaten since her bread and cheese supper, but the thought of food sickened her. A soft moan came from her throat.

Jan sat up quickly. "Are you unwell, Norah?"

"I'm fine," she answered wearily, "considering my evening."

"Come, then. We have no time to waste."

Once more they set off through the night. At the dock gate, Norah pulled her cap low and crossed her arms over her damp, clinging shirt. Jan identified them as *Orion* crewmen, and they entered the vast fortress that was Prince's Dock.

The *Orion*'s gangplank was down. There was no activity on deck. Jan said the watch officer was most likely asleep under the bulwark. The custom-house man, who was kept on board to prevent smuggling, retired drunk every evening by nine. Willie would be awaiting Norah in the main cabin.

"Willie knows about me?" Norah asked in alarm.

"I had to tell him," Jan said. "Once I learned where you were being held, I didn't know how to save you. I ran back here, and Willie prepared the drink that put those men to sleep." In the dim light cast by ship's lanterns, Jan's face was sharp with worry, his eyes ringed with fatigue. "I would have gone to the captain only as a last resort."

Norah could have kissed Jan with gratitude. The chances he

had taken for her sake left her feeling woefully inadequate. "Thank you, Jan. You were ever so brave."

"I hope I'm as brave when the captain finds out what I've done. He's been in a powerful bad temper."

"He'll never find out, I promise."

Jan's sigh was full of resignation. "He'll find out. Captain Mackenzie seems to know everything."

Chapter Twenty-One

THE CABIN WAS bare, stripped of its carpet and fine furnishings. Along the bulkhead where Norah's sleep sofa once stood, packing cases were stacked up to the beams. The velvet-covered window seat, however, was clear and inviting. Norah—wet, dirty, and exhausted—gratefully collapsed there and promptly fell asleep.

She woke to shouts and pounding feet, the familiar commotion of a ship getting under way. Her body ached from sleeping in the confined space, and her damp clothing had left her chilled. But her ordeal was over. She was on her way to India. Norah shifted to a more comfortable position, and her stomach pitched. Drat! She needed a decent meal and a change of clothing. Maybe then she would feel better.

A tap on the door sent her scurrying into the corner of the window seat where the packing crates hid her from view. The door opened.

"Missy."

Norah peered around the cases and saw Willie limping through the door with a plate of ship biscuit and an apple. He looked at her sternly through a lock of lank black hair.

"Missy bad. Missy very, very bad, come on ship. Captain be angry. Every day captain angry. Captain find you, he more angry."

Norah crept from her hiding place. She was delighted to see

Willie, but his reception was hardly cordial. "The devil take the captain," she said irritably. "I need water for washing."

Willie pursed his mouth in disapproval and left the plate on the window seat. Not fifteen minutes later he was back with a bucket of water, a block of soap, and a basin. Norah gratefully washed herself and climbed back into her gamy clothes. With her fingers she tried to make some order of her tangled hair. Her scanty toilette completed, she managed to choke down two pieces of biscuit and the apple. Then she lay back on the window seat and cursed her unsteady stomach.

Three times a day the nervous Willie delivered meager meals. Each morning began with such nausea that Norah could barely lift her head. When she told Willie she was seasick, he brought her a sugar cube with a drop of essence of peppermint. That, along with salt beef and sea biscuit, helped to settle her distress.

Norah heard Rob moving about next door. At first his proximity inspired only angry memories, but as the days passed Norah found his presence oddly comforting. To occupy herself, she kept track of Rob's comings and goings. He seemed to be standing a regular watch and spent a good deal of time on deck.

Boring day followed boring day. In calm weather, Norah slept for hours. When the sea grew rough, she was tossed from the narrow window seat to the floor. After a few tumbles, she decided to sleep on the hard planks, wrapped in her blanket. With nothing to read and no writing implements, Norah was forced to stare out the stern window at the wake of the ship and think. She recited every poem she knew, quoted Shakespeare to herself at length, and retold her favorites of Mr. Scott's Waverley novels. In her mind she wrote a long letter to Alice in which she gave an abbreviated account of her stay in Liverpool and her successful rendezvous with the *Orion*.

As Norah's mind wandered, reality mingled with possibility. Thoughts of her papa, which had brought her nothing but anguish during the past weeks, began to take on a more cheerful aspect. She envisioned taking him back to Boston where he would find renewed health and contentment in her care. His opium addiction, she decided, had started as a trick perpetrated by Rob or some wily Chinese. Papa would never have voluntarily forsaken his loved ones for the dream world of the opium pipe. Certainly he had been lured into the vile dens against his will.

Norah washed out her linen underclothing every other day. How simple life must be for a man, she thought, wearing the same old clothes day after day, no need to think about things like corsets and petticoats and monthly courses. . . . Norah's thoughts stopped dead. Her monthlies! Dear God, she hadn't had one since August, and now . . . Of course, it was the upheaval of running away. It couldn't be anything else. Then she thought of her recent nausea, the tenderness of her breasts, and she dropped her head onto her arms. She was carrying a child! Rob's child.

The more Norah thought about her situation, the more hopeless it seemed. If she had a baby in her, how would she search for Papa? How would she hide the fact from Rob? Could she possibly remain in this cabin for months and creep off the ship unnoticed once they reached Calcutta, a pregnant woman in men's clothing? Impossible!

She began to rationalize. Surely there could be some other explanation for what ailed her. Her illness could have been brought on by any number of things—the laudanum or the putrid air of Liverpool or rancid cheese. If only she could be sure.

Then she remembered the medical book in Rob's cabin, *The Planter's and Mariner's Medical Companion.*

Norah was on her way to the door before she stopped to consider her strategy. It was just after five bells: half past ten in the morning. Rob stayed on deck until eight bells when he came down to get his sextant for the noon readings. Yes, this was a safe time for an expedition.

Norah opened her door. The main cabin was empty. She scurried the few yards to Rob's cabin and slipped inside. She took the key to his bookcase from the desk drawer. Fumbling in her haste, she dropped the key and it clanked to the floor. With a roll of the ship, the key slid under the desk, forcing Norah to her knees to retrieve it. Finally, with the medical book in hand, she perched on the chair and flipped the pages to "Pregnancy." She skimmed over the description: darkened nipples, nausea, tender breasts . . . Dear God! She had every sign.

Heavy footsteps sounded on the companionway. Norah slammed the book shut and ran to the door. Too late! The latch clicked, the door opened, and Rob stood before her. He looked at her with an astonished expression that Norah would have found comical if she hadn't been so utterly frightened. She stared back at him as if entranced. This can't really be happening, she thought. No, no, it was one of her dreams.

Then Rob's expression changed from astonishment to outrage. He took a step toward her. "What in hell are *you* doing here?" he shouted. "Who brought you aboard?"

He was terrible to behold. His voice was loud with fury, his eyes bitterly narrowed. He advanced menacingly, and Norah backed away, clutching the book to her chest. She stumbled against the chair and sank into it, speechless with fear.

"Answer me!" Anger blazed on Rob's face. He looked ravaged and worn. His left eye was bruised, and his lower lip discolored as if he'd been in a fight.

"N-no one," Norah said. She struggled to get her bearings, to sound reasonably assured. Aside from a few words to Willie, she'd spoken to no one since she'd boarded five days ago.

"You're lying." Rob dragged her roughly to her feet. Pulling the book from her arms, he heaved it against the partition, where it struck with a loud smack. His gaze swept over her. "Who gave you those clothes?" He yanked at the open collar of Jan's shirt. "Janner!" He bared his teeth. "That goddam little fool."

Rob pushed her back into the chair and turned toward the door. Norah jumped to her feet. "Where are you going?" she cried.

He surveyed her with disgust. "To give Janner a punishment he'll long remember."

"No!"

"I'll deal with you later," Rob snapped, pointing a threatening finger at her. "In the meantime I forbid you to leave this cabin." He flung open the door and stormed out.

"Rob! You can't!" Norah pursued him through the main cabin, clutching at his arms, trying to pull him away from the companionway. "It wasn't Jan's fault! It was mine. I forced him to do it! Oh, Rob!" Suddenly Norah was sobbing, terrified of what he would do to the brave young man who had risked his life for her sake. "Please don't hurt him!"

Rob swung around and grasped Norah's shoulders so hard she winced. "Listen to me," he said, his voice so low and tight it crackled as he spoke. "You don't run this ship. I give the orders, and everyone aboard obeys, including you. What I do with my crew is none of your affair. Janner not only broke the law by bringing you aboard, he violated my command. He deserves a flogging, and he's going to get one. You're going to stay below until it's over, and then I'll decide about your fate."

"Don't you dare," Norah hissed. "Don't you dare strike him. He saved my life."

But Rob wasn't listening. He turned on his heel and took the companionway steps two at a time. With a cry, Norah went after him, grabbing and pulling at him, hitting him with her fists, hanging on to him. He brushed her off as if she were no more than a pesky fly. The painful brightness of the deck after days in the dim cabin forced Norah to shade her eyes, freeing Rob of her clutches. Frantically she tried to adjust her vision to find him again, to locate Jan, to beg someone for help.

Rob was shouting orders to have Jan stripped and tied. He paced the deck, snapping a thick, ugly rope. Crewmen stared at Norah in bewildered silence as they tied the young sailor's wrists to the shrouds.

Norah looked at Jan's slender back, so young, so unmarked, so vulnerable. She began to scream. "Don't tie him!" she shrieked at the second mate. "How can you!"

She lunged at Rob. He sidestepped her and bellowed to the mate, "Remove her, Mr. Crawford. And see that she stays below."

Norah threw herself at the mate, fists swinging. Crawford took her from behind in a fierce bear hug, pinning her arms to her sides. "Come along, my girl," he said. "Ain't nothing you can do."

Norah fell limp. "Don't let him do it, Mr. Crawford!" she sobbed. "Not to Jan! It wasn't his fault!"

Crawford dragged her screaming and sobbing toward the companionway. Jan glanced over his shoulder and acknowledged her defense of him with a brave smile. Warm tears flowed down Norah's cheeks. What had she done to this boy who had so willingly risked himself to help her? How could she live with herself for making him suffer?

Norah struggled one last time in Mr. Crawford's iron grip before falling against him with exhaustion. With her last ounce of strength, she flung parting words at the man who had been her lover, who was the father of the child growing in her, and who now prowled the deck, waiting to flay the back of a boy who had wanted only to please.

"I'll hate you forever, Rob Mackenzie!" Norah shouted. "Do you hear me? I hate you more than anything in this world!"

When they reached the main cabin, Mr. Crawford released her and began pacing. His small muscular body was hunched tight. His weathered face looked strained and closed. At the sound of the rope striking its mark, he jumped to his feet and darted up the companionway, swearing. Norah tried to follow, but Willie tugged at her arm.

"No, Missy. You no see. Very bad you see." Willie stared up the companionway steps, bewilderment and disappointment in his eyes.

Norah collapsed on the steps, trembling with rage and fear. She covered her ears so as to blot out Jan's cries, but her hands were not dense enough to block the sound of rope striking flesh. A dozen times it struck. At each blow Norah saw in her mind Rob's face twisted with satisfaction. Then all was silent. Norah lifted her head in time to see Rob's boots pounding down the steps toward her. She rolled out of his path just before he trampled her.

"Christ Almighty! Can't you stay out of my way?" He dragged Norah to her feet. "How am I supposed to be free of you? Will you answer me that? How in hell am I ever to be free of you!"

His eyes were wild. His temple throbbed. With his blood-shot eye and his day's growth of beard, Rob looked to be exactly what he was: a remnant of the docks, an unprincipled ruffian, who lied, who seduced women, who took pleasure in beating well-meaning young sailors.

Norah turned her head away. To think she could have loved

such a creature! "Let me go, you hateful man!" she cried, pulling herself from his grasp.

The door to Rob's cabin slammed shut, shaking the very timbers of the brig. Willie ran up the steps to the deck with his box of potions, prepared to tend to Jan's back. Norah dragged herself after him. She had to see Jan and offer some feeble comfort for his suffering on her behalf.

At the top of the steps she saw the second mate cutting Jan down. Norah looked at his back and blinked. He hadn't a mark on him. The rope lay on the deck where Rob had dropped it. Mr. Crawford was barking orders for the men to return to work. Norah leaned against the hatchway, staring in disbelief. Jan stooped and picked up his shirt. Glimpsing Norah, he attempted a smile.

"Go below," Crawford told Norah irritably. "We've had enough excitement on deck today, what with the captain making a bloody fool of himself. He beat the life out of the deck and took to the boats and masts like they was Satan himself." He turned away, and Norah heard him mutter, "You've caused him enough trouble. I expect you'll cause him more."

Norah descended the companionway in a daze. She didn't return to her cabin, that prison of boredom and darkness, but sat at the table in the main cabin listening to the sounds of normal activity returning on deck. He hadn't touched Jan. Norah closed her eyes and offered a brief prayer of thanks. A wave of sickness washed over her, and her forehead damped with sweat. She gripped the edge of the table. The baby. *His* baby. Tears gathered in her eyes. Her lips began to tremble. What in the world would become of her? What could she do? Norah had never felt so alone, so defeated, so utterly at a loss.

"Come in here, Norah."

Rob stood at his cabin door. His face looked more weary than angry, and his voice was free of its earlier bitterness. Norah rose and strode by him into his cabin. He closed the door behind her and went to stand by his desk. Swallowing her nausea, Norah met his eyes unflinchingly. He mustn't know. Not yet. Perhaps not ever.

Rob's stare brought to her attention her manner of dress, her disheveled hair. Oh, what did it matter? What did anything matter any longer? Norah blinked hard, forbidding herself to show emotion.

"You look ridiculous," Rob muttered.

"I suppose you think I'm grateful you didn't beat Jan," Norah retorted coldly, "but I'm not. You don't deserve my gratitude for anything."

Rob turned his back on her and addressed the stern window. "I'm not taking you to India. I'm not taking you a day farther than I have to. We're stopping at Gibraltar, and I'm putting you on a vessel bound for London or Boston, whichever I find first."

"I won't go back!" Norah cried. "I'm going to Calcutta, and if you don't take me, I'll find another captain who will!"

Rob went on as if she hadn't spoken. "Once I find a ship, I'll give the captain clear warning that you need a firm hand, that you're not accustomed to obeying orders."

"I won't go!"

Rob turned and looked at her. Norah's legs were stubbornly spread. Folds of white cotton and dark twill draped her from neck to the bare toes that peeked from beneath dragging cuffs. He could see no trace of the eager, pliant body beneath the ill-fitting sailor's togs, but his mind saw everything and remembered too much.

Never mind that, Rob thought. It was finished between them. "You'll go where I tell you."

"I won't!" Norah cried. Her cheeks burned indignantly bright. Beneath her tangled golden brown hair, her blue-gray eyes gleamed cold as a new knife. "You owe me my father! I *demand* that you take me to India."

Rob's rage had eased, and his mind was clearing, but his restored reason brought him no peace. Instead, he was tormented by questions too terrible to contemplate. How had Norah come to be on his ship? How had she gotten from Brightsgate to Liverpool to Prince's Dock? She'd said Jan saved her life. Sweet Christ, had she been in some mortal danger?

"I don't want you on this voyage, Norah, and that's final."

But of course he wanted her, his muddled mind told him. Where else could she be safe, other than with him?

"I'm very sorry to hear that, Captain Mackenzie," Norah

said. "Because although you may want to be rid of me, and I find myself most indifferent to you, I am carrying a child, which happens to be yours. It would be rather awkward for me to return to the Denmores or the Burnhams in my condition, and even more awkward should I announce the identity of the father."

A whirling roar started up in Rob's head. He steadied himself against the desk and fought the urge to reach for her. Terror, confusion, joy, all struggled in his chest. *A child.* Quickly he checked himself. It was a ruse. She was using the promise of a child to arouse his sympathy and get her way.

"I don't believe you," he said.

"Don't believe . . ." Norah gasped. "You . . . you abominable man!" She was sobbing. "You're not only a liar, you're cruel and unfeeling and—"

"Norah!"

She ran from the cabin, slamming the door behind her. Rob waited. A second slam, of her door. Rob sank into his chair, stunned beyond feeling. *A child.* Now what was he to do?

A knock on the door interrupted his thoughts. George Crawford stepped into the cabin. "You'll be taking the noon observation, Captain, or shall I?"

Rob wearily pulled himself to his feet. "I'll take care of it." He opened the wooden case that held his sextant, aware of the mate's silent assessment of him.

"What will you do with the girl?"

Rob glanced at Crawford. For all his inscrutability, the mate could not hide the concern that lurked in his squinting eyes.

"I was going to set a course to Gibraltar and put her on a ship to Boston or London."

The mate frowned. "Was?"

"She's carrying a child, George. My child." Rob ran his hands over his face. Saying it aloud was more of a shock than he'd anticipated. "Now I don't know what to do."

The two men stood in silence. Crawford shifted his feet and cleared his throat. "You'd best marry her, then."

Rob cast a desperate look at his old friend. "How does a man go about marrying a woman who loathes him?"

"She'll get over it, Captain. She always was fond of you, and no woman wants a child without a husband."

Rob scratched his head. "Norah's as stubborn as a snarled gantline. She'd have a baby on her own just to spite me."

Crawford's face took on a ruddy hue beneath the brown. "Go in there and tell her she's got no choice in the matter. A man lets a woman get away, a woman he wants . . . well, he'll regret it, sure as he's born."

Rob stared in surprise. He'd never heard Crawford utter such impassioned words, nor had he seen him so agitated. Had Crawford once longed for a woman? Had that crusty old salt felt passion and love?

"Why, George," he said, "do you speak from experience?"

Crawford's eyes shifted. He moved toward the door. "I'll take the altitudes," he muttered. "You see to your woman."

Chapter Twenty-Two

ROB WALKED INTO Norah's cabin without knocking. Something was blooming inside him, a fragile hope he dared not consider too closely. Norah sat on the window seat, half hidden behind a stack of packing cases, brushing tears from her cheeks. Rob glanced around the cabin. How had she managed to live in any comfort, sleeping on that narrow space, breathing the stale air belowdecks? Rob frowned. He would soon change all that.

Norah fixed him with an angry stare. "What do you want?"

"We'll be married."

"Never!"

"Norah, you're having a child."

"So you believe me!" she cried, her lips trembling. "Are you certain it's yours?"

Rob ignored her taunt. "How are you going to explain a child without a husband?"

"The baby will be born in India. I can return to America a respectable widow. Perhaps my husband drowned at sea like my father." She glared at him. "You're clever at making up stories of that sort."

"Assuming that story is believed," Rob said impassively, "then what?"

"I'll . . . I'll go away somewhere and forget you ever existed."

Rob gave a short laugh. "You've thought it all out. Except for one thing, Norah. My child won't suffer a hole in his life where a father should be. He'll carry my name and he'll know I care about him."

Norah continued to stare at him stubbornly. "You can't force me to marry you. I'll go where I want and take the baby with me."

"I'll forbid it."

With a start, Norah realized that Rob could indeed forbid it. He could take her baby away from her, just as Mr. Norton had taken Mrs. Norton's children after the Lord Melbourne affair. The thought of Rob's power over her left Norah frightened and confused. It also made her feel a good deal sicker. Norah drew up her knees and leaned her forehead against them, fighting her nausea. "Leave me alone," she moaned.

"Marry me and I'll take you to Calcutta. Refuse me and I'll put you off in Gibraltar."

Norah wiped her sweating forehead and thought how happy she would be if she could lie down in a proper bed and have someone look after her.

"I want your answer, Norah," Rob said. "If we're putting in at Gibraltar, I have to change course immediately. What will it be, Calcutta or Gibraltar?"

Norah lay down on the narrow window seat and tried to curl into a ball. The rocking of the vessel was compounding her misery. Tears rolled from her eyes and into her hair. "I won't marry you," she cried. "I hate you."

"Very well." Rob crossed to the door and opened it. "I'll have you in Gibraltar in three days."

Norah pushed herself up on her elbow. "Wait!"

Rob paused.

"Damn you, Rob Mackenzie! Damn you to hell! All right, I'll marry you! But I'll never love you. And you'll never touch me again!" Sobbing, Norah fell back on the window seat.

Rob allowed himself a smile of triumph. He went to Norah and bent over her miserable form. "If you renege on your promise," he said touching her tangled hair, "I'll send you back from Madeira or Cape Town."

Norah pressed her face into wet velvet, her shoulders shaking. Her body felt clammy, her mind and spirits defeated. She hadn't an ounce of fight left in her. When Rob lifted her into his arms, she didn't resist. He carried her to his cabin and placed her on his bunk. She lay still as he sponged her face with cool water. He brought a basin for her sickness. She heard Willie drag in the hip bath. Then Rob's hands were at her shirtfront. Norah's eyes snapped open. "Don't you dare!"

He removed his hand and smiled at her. "As soon as you're feeling better, you're to take a bath. Those clothes have to be laundered. Your hair needs a good washing. I'll help you if you wish."

Norah turned her face to the wall.

"Go to sleep now, sweetheart. When you wake up, I want you to bathe, eat a good dinner, and go on deck for some air. No baby can grow in a mother who doesn't rest and doesn't eat."

"Don't tell me what to do," Norah said, her eyes clenched tight.

Rob's hand rested on her forehead. "If you don't take care of yourself, I'll have to do it for you." She heard him open the cabin door. Before leaving, he said cheerfully, "Cape Town is quite nice in December. We'll have our wedding there."

Rob stepped out on deck and marveled at the beauty of the day. The sun shone on sail and water, on scrubbed planking and polished brass. A good six-knot clip stretched and filled every inch of canvas. Rob leaned on the rail and stared across the quarterdeck through the shrouds and ratlines at the blue-green water that churned away toward the horizon. For the first time in months he felt a measure of contentment.

He took a deep, satisfying breath of salty air and surveyed the familiar scene on deck. Jan sat amidships splicing a shroud. The lad was surely aware of his captain's presence, but he kept his eyes carefully averted. Rob would speak to the young sailor later when he was prepared to learn exactly what had transpired in Liverpool.

Crawford passed his line of vision and Rob called to him. Crawford turned.

"I need a place to sleep, mate," Rob said. "Mind if I share your quarters?"

Crawford squinted, then offered Rob a rare, brown-stained

smile. "My pleasure to have the company. You getting married?"

Rob grinned. "Cape Town. To a most reluctant bride."

Crawford joined him at the rail. "That's mighty fine, Captain. Mighty fine."

They stood side by side, manfully silent, and listened to the waves slap against the hull. At last, Crawford spoke. "Jody would sure be pleased. He was awful fond of his girl."

Rob felt a vague uneasiness. He preferred to think of Norah as simply Norah, not as Jody's girl. In fact, he preferred not to think of Jody at all. "He never mentioned her to me," he said abruptly. "I stopped at his house once when I was a boy and never went back. I all but forgot he had a girl."

The mate freshened his chaw and worked it silently. "Some things about Jody I could never figure out."

Rob frowned at the horizon. The conversation was making him uncomfortable. He wished Crawford would leave off his newfound garrulousness.

"His wife and little girl had a hold on him, and he didn't like it," Crawford went on. "Kept away from 'em as if he was scared. Jody only felt comfortable being free. Leastways that's what I think." Eight bells sounded. Crawford tugged at his cap and moved off.

Later, as Rob stood shaving before the glass in Crawford's small, plain cabin, he thought of the mate's words and wondered about Jody's failure as a husband and father. He'd had a beautiful wife and a daughter who adored him, and yet they weren't enough for him. What was the compulsion that kept a man from settling down? What of himself, who'd been molded by Jody, who'd absorbed his lessons, whose aim in life had been to follow his example?

Rob wiped the streaks of soap from his chin and stared at his reflection. The eyes that looked back at him held traces of fear. A baby, he thought. A wife. What would become of them all?

Norah—rested, bathed, and wrapped in one of Willie's sarongs—joined Rob and Mr. Crawford for dinner. She could manage to get down only a few sips of tea and a bite of biscuit. After a few moments the smell of the fried pork and onions the men were eating forced her to excuse herself and flee to Rob's cabin.

Rob watched her go. He knew illness was normal for pregnant women, but he didn't like it one bit. Illness of any sort bothered him, but depriving a mother of the ability to eat, and a baby to grow, seemed a particularly cruel trick of nature.

On deck during the early twilight Rob pretended to be busy, but he spent most of the time staring up at the poop where Norah sat, clad in Willie's sarong and one of his own shirts. From Jan she'd borrowed a black tarpaulin hat with a long flapping ribbon that made her look like a forlorn little sailor. The sight of her sadness brought to Rob a frustrating feeling of helplessness. He barely mastered the impulse to race up the steps and seize her in his arms. Not yet, he told himself. He would win her back slowly. After their wedding he would move back to his cabin, *their* cabin, and be welcomed as a husband. For now he would keep his distance, watch, and wait.

Before Norah went to bed, Rob oiled the squeaking hinge on the cabin door so he could look in on her during the night without waking her. Once Norah was asleep, Rob settled into the second bunk in the mate's cabin, opened *The Mariner's and Planter's Medical Companion*, and by the dim lamplight began to read about pregnancy.

Once he'd absorbed the doctor's advice about the importance of warm baths, unrestricted clothing, and cheerful thoughts, Rob turned to the section on childbirth, which he read with mounting dismay. In the midst of a particularly gruesome recounting of possible complications, he put down the book and calculated. The baby should be born in late May. Amanda would be in Calcutta by that time, thank God. He'd turn Norah over to her and sail north. Just as well to leave this birthing ordeal to the ladies.

Suddenly the comfortable belowdecks thump and slosh of the sea was shattered by screams. Norah's screams. Rob's heart climbed so high in his throat it almost choked him. He leaped off his bunk and raced down the passageway, colliding with the white-faced second mate. When Rob threw open the door to Norah's cabin, the screams had stopped. Norah was sitting up in bed, her hands to her head. Rob couldn't see her face in the dark, but when his arms went around her, he could feel her trembling. She clung to him, gasping, with surprising strength.

"It's all right, Mr. Giles," Rob said to the second officer. "A bad dream, I'd say."

Giles closed the door behind him. Rob sat down on the edge of the bunk and rubbed Norah's back. Her body felt warm and damp beneath the cotton nightshirt she wore. She held him fast, taking breaths in great hungry gulps. Rob buried his face in her sweet-smelling hair. "Tell me, my love. What was it?"

Norah eased her hold on his neck, and Rob laid her back on the pillow. Her hand, limp and trembling, unintentionally brushed his chest and then fell into his lap. Rob jumped at the unexpected intimate caress. Only then did he realize he was naked. Norah snatched her hand away with an embarrassed gasp.

Rob smiled and smoothed her hair. "What was your dream, sweetheart?"

"Nothing." Her voice trembled with unshed tears.

"I'll stay here until you tell me."

Norah wiped at her eyes. "I . . . I dreamed I couldn't breathe, that I was trying to scream and I couldn't, and . . ."

"And what?"

"That was all," she whispered. "Then you were here."

Rob sat in the darkness, caressing her hair and cheeks. "What happened in Liverpool, Norah?"

Norah turned away. "I'm very tired. I wish you would go."

"I want you to tell me."

"Go away." Her voice took on a hostile edge. She rolled away from him onto her side and buried her head in the pillow.

Rob stayed with her until her shoulders stopped shaking and her breathing steadied. Then he returned to his cabin, dressed, and hurried on deck. All was silent, save for the languid creaking of timbers, the soft thunder of waves against the hull. Jan stood watch in the bows. He stared out at the black night, his pale hair lit by the lantern affixed under the foretop.

"Janner."

The young man turned. "Captain?"

"I want to talk to you in the cabin."

Jan followed Rob aft and down the companionway. He

stood awkwardly in the cabin, worrying his cap in his hands. Rob motioned for him to sit. "Care for a brandy?"

Jan's eyes widened. "Yes, sir. Thank you, sir."

"Water?"

Jan shook his head. Rob half filled two tumblers and set the bottle on the table between them. He seated himself beneath the swinging lamp, threw a leg up on the table, and began to speak. "You deserved a flogging, Janner. Bringing a stowaway aboard ship is serious business. You knew that, I suppose, when you agreed to help Norah."

Jan nodded. "Yes, sir. I knew it."

"In all my years at sea I've never struck a crewman in anger. Flogging is a despicable practice best left in the Dark Ages. I'd sooner place an insubordinate man in irons until he can be delivered to the proper authorities. This morning I was angry at more than just finding a stowaway on my ship."

Jan stared at the table. "I know that, sir.'"

Rob tried not to smile. "What do you know, Janner?"

The young sailor squirmed uncomfortably. "I know that you're fond of Norah and that you quarreled, sir. She told me about her father. . . ." His voice trailed off in embarrassment.

Rob rubbed his chin. "Do you have a sweetheart?"

Jan shook his head, his eyes now fixed on the cabin wall.

"You'll find out one day that a man can make rather a fool of himself when something interferes with his happiness with a woman."

Jan met Rob's eyes for the first time that evening. "Yes, sir."

"Drink up, Janner."

Jan took a huge gulp, gasping as the force of the brew claimed his insides.

"Not much of a drinking man, are you?" Rob asked.

Jan shook his head, swallowing and choking. "Just ale," he managed to say.

"Take it slower, then."

They sat quietly. Rob sipped at his drink and watched Jan twist and turn his glass, staring at it distrustfully. Finally Rob decided it was time to get to the point. "I want to know what happened in Liverpool."

Jan looked uneasy.

"No matter what you tell me, I won't be angry. I suspect the worst, and I expect to hear it."

Once he got started, Jan seemed eager to relate the tale. Rob listened calmly, as the dangerous plan unfolded. He managed to stem the fear that gripped him until things got under way in Liverpool. Then he could no longer maintain his silence. "Why the devil didn't you go to the inn and fetch her yourself?" he burst out. "My God, man, allowing her to find her way alone to the Crow's Nest at night was madness."

Jan flushed. "I didn't think of it, sir. I would have fetched her if she'd asked, but she said to give her a map. She's . . . she was so sure of herself, so determined. It was her plan; she was giving the orders. I told her from the first that it was crazy, but she was . . . She got angry and said if I wouldn't help her she'd do it herself."

Rob told himself to be calm; he couldn't blame Jan for Norah's headstrong ways. But by the time the sailor finished his story, Rob's insides were churning with impotent rage and he had to struggle to maintain his composure.

"How long was she alone with those men?"

"About four hours, sir."

"Did they . . ." Rob passed his hand over his face. "Do you think they harmed her?"

Jan watched him sympathetically. "I don't think so, sir. She was frightened, but not . . . She didn't act as if they'd done that, sir. The gentleman in charge said she was not to be hurt."

"Did you see him? The man in charge?"

Jan shook his head. "He was an American, a fancy one. That's all I heard."

Rob frowned. "No description?"

"No, sir."

An icy sheet of perspiration covered Rob's body, brought on by pounding fear of what might have happened. He reminded himself that Norah was safe. Safe with him, healthy and unhurt. Rob got to his feet. "Well, Janner, I guess I owe you my thanks. You acted bravely and cleverly, although you should have told me about this business before it got started."

"I couldn't betray her, sir."

Rob glanced at Jan's earnest, sober face. It hadn't been necessary to ply him with drink to get to the truth. "You're a brave man, Janner." Rob extended his hand.

Jan grasped it, grinning.

"You'd best return to your watch before Mr. Crawford comes down here after you."

"Thank you, sir," Jan said. "For the brandy, I mean." Before he mounted the companionway, the young sailor turned. "I'm glad she's with us again, sir."

Rob stood thoughtfully in the middle of the cabin. "So am I, Janner," he said. "So am I."

Chapter Twenty-Three

WHEN NORAH PLANNED her flight from Brightsgate, and during her first days aboard the *Orion*, she hadn't considered the meaning of her father's abrupt resurrection. She'd preferred to dwell on plans for his rescue rather than the reasons for his downfall. But gradually she came to face the probable truth that Papa hadn't been tricked into his addiction by Rob or by anyone else. A strong and confident man like Jody Paige couldn't have been duped in a card game, let alone into taking up a filthy habit like opium. For some reason, he had willingly abandoned her for a devil drug. Acknowledging his betrayal filled Norah with a bleak, numbing sorrow.

Limp and spiritless, she dragged herself through each day. She sat in the saltwater baths that Rob insisted upon, and forced down food while he stood over her. She walked around the deck under his eye and joined him for long, silent games of chess. Occasionally she woke at night to find him sitting by her bunk. At Madeira, he loaded a goat and forced her to drink cup after cup of milk, as if she were a child.

Norah rarely spoke to Rob, but she didn't object to his presence. He came and went freely from her cabin. When he walked in on her while she was bathing, she didn't bother to cover herself. If he'd decided to make love to her, she would have lain impassively beneath him and let him have his way. With his child inside her, a child that meant only illness and entrapment, her body seemed to belong more to Rob than to her. He might as well have been living her life for her.

One afternoon while Norah was reading in her cabin, Rob interrupted her. "You don't have to drag around in Jan's clothes forever, Norah. I'm carrying twenty cases of millinery goods. Let's see what we can find for you to sew on."

The idea immediately intrigued her. She was tired of stumbling over the legs of Jan's trousers, and completing a task, however small, never failed to lift her from a spell of melancholy. Norah followed Rob into her old cabin and watched him pry open the packing cases.

The muslins were fine and soft and beautifully embroidered. Norah selected a clear blue, a pale rose, and a print with a sprig motif of muted reds and browns. For bedgowns and undergarments, she chose sturdy flannel and the sheerest French linen. There were packets of pins and needles, threads, scissors, measuring tape, ribbons, stays, and silver busks, all destined for the deprived English ladies of Calcutta. Norah carried her booty back to her cabin and spread it out on the bunk. For the first time in weeks she felt a stirring of real interest.

Norah attacked her sewing with a vengeance. She structured the day around her task, cutting fabric when the light in the cabin was best and when she wouldn't interfere with Willie's table setting. Instead of sleeping the afternoon away in her cabin, she sat under the awning on deck, basting and stitching. She wished for her spectacles, but she managed without them. And she found that her proficiency with needle and thread had not diminished since her days as star pupil in Mrs. Burnham's charity sewing school.

By the time the *Orion* dropped anchor in Table Bay, Norah's sickness had abated, her despondency had eased, and she possessed a small wardrobe that was simple and undeniably presentable.

Three days after their arrival she and Rob were married by a Scots minister in St. Andrew's Church, Cape Town. Norah took her vows in a gown of oyster white satin trimmed with blond lace. A veil of embroidered net fell over her shoulders, and she wore matching gloves. She would have been married in Jan's seaman's clothes, for all she cared about the ceremony, but Rob had insisted on a proper wedding gown. He'd gone so far as to select the fabric and supervise the design. The issue of the wedding gown had caused Norah to lose her temper on more than one occasion. Rob had only laughed and said he was glad to see a spark of spirit in her again.

And so Norah kept her part of the bargain that would take her to Calcutta. She stood before the Presbyterian altar in her fine gown, wilting in the December heat, her shaggy hair pinned up beneath her veil, her cheeks an overheated pink, and promised before God to cherish and obey Rob Mackenzie for as long as they both should live.

Obedience. Submission. Norah thought of Frances Wright's brave principles and stumbled over her words. Then the minister pronounced them man and wife, and Norah was sealed in marriage to a man she didn't trust, a man she could never love, a man who would order her life as if she had no free will.

Rob had made arrangements for a wedding feast at the White Swan Tavern. He invited the *Orion*'s crew and a group of Cape Town merchants of his acquaintance. He'd noticed some familiar ships riding at anchor in Table Bay, a customary stopping place for India-bound ships, and extended invitations to their several captains and mates as well. At the tavern, wine flowed alongside plates of fresh fish, strange fruits, and baked delicacies. The noise level grew with each bottle of wine until Norah's head pounded from the raucous good time. Rob kept her firmly at his side, except when he permitted a gentleman to dance with her. He claimed not to dance himself, a deficiency that Norah had once found intriguing, but now thought was an absurd affectation.

During the festivities, Norah looked out over the motley company of sun-blackened sailors, merchants merry with wine, and some rather garishly dressed women and thought of Mrs. Burnham's hopes for this very occasion. Thank heaven the poor woman had been spared this spectacle. Even dear, loyal Jan was flushed with spirits and loudly joined the other sailors in songs and toasts and exaggerated stories. Norah was not so much miserable as bored; her wedding feast had turned into a release of ship-bound energy. She was thoroughly relieved when Rob decided it was time to leave.

They returned to the white stucco house overlooking Table Bay, lent for Norah's use by an acquaintance of Rob's. Rob left her with strict instructions to rest. Norah bathed and changed out of her wedding finery, making herself comfortable in a dressing gown of shimmering coffee-brown silk. After dismissing the maid, she threw open the casement window and leaned out into the breeze. The sky was a stainless blue, the sea a sparkling azure. An herb garden sent up a heavenly scent that mingled with the bowls of red and white roses that Rob had brought to fill the room.

As Norah studied the view and breathed in the fragrant air, she discovered she felt surprisingly mellow. Perhaps it was being free of the ship for a few days or having had a proper bath or having put the wedding festivities behind her, but Norah was suffused with a feeling of good health and well-being. The baby inside her, more than three months old now, was treating its mother with greater kindness than it had during their first several weeks together. Norah found herself thinking about the little life with more affection than she had in the past. After all, she reasoned, it wasn't the baby's fault that its mother had suddenly left off being a proper Boston girl and succumbed to the passions of a virile seaman.

Thoughts of the baby's conception reminded Norah of what lay ahead. Rob had made no demands on her during the voyage, but he would no doubt claim his marital rights. When he did, Norah would remind him of her words when she'd capitulated to his coercion. She'd agreed to marry him only to go to Calcutta. She would never love him, nor would he ever touch her again.

It was after sunset when Rob knocked on the door. Norah opened it, prepared to get right down to the business of marital rights. But at the sight before her, that issue fled from her mind. Rob stood in the doorway laden with books. Perched precariously on top of the pile was a bottle of wine.

"Books!" she cried. "Oh, Rob!"

"Take the bottle before it falls."

Norah grabbed the wine bottle and set it on the table beside a blazing candelabrum. Rob spilled the books onto the sofa, and Norah fell on the volumes, exclaiming, "How did you know what I liked? Oh, look! Miss Sedgwick!"

On the *Orion*, she'd read and reread Rob's dry accounts of voyages and natural history, and she had gone through Mr. Cooper's *Red Rover* three times. Now she had a veritable library at her disposal. "Oh! A new edition of Davenport's *Life of Ali Pasha*. And here's *Corinne*, the very same volume we have at the bookstore."

"There's more on the *Orion*," Rob said. "I figured I'd only bring enough to keep a bride occupied on her wedding night."

Norah ignored the tease in his voice. "But this is marvelous! Where did you ever find them?"

"Remember the stout fellow with the mustache you danced with?"

Norah nodded. "The cotton broker."

"His wife died last year. He was willing to strike a bargain."

The room fell silent, save for the sound of rustling pages.

"Does your husband get a kiss for his trouble?"

Norah glanced up. The cowlick on Rob's newly shorn hair stood at attention. Little gold lights, a reflection of the room's blaze of candles, flickered in his brown eyes. For a moment she saw a dear familiar face. Then she blushed and looked away. Good heavens, was she thinking of him that way again?

"There's not much point," she said feebly.

Rob took her hands and drew her to her feet. "Not much point in showing a little gratitude?" He tucked a strand of hair behind her ear.

"I don't mean I'm not grateful. I . . . Thank you. I know I'll enjoy the books."

The faint fragrance of his shaving soap brought back disturbing memories. Norah pulled away, her heart beating much too fast. She thought how fine Rob had looked at the wedding, his hair neatly clipped and brushed, his dark eyes laughing and exhilarated. Norah felt a momentary pang that everything between them was ruined. If he weren't so false-hearted, she might believe he truly loved her.

Rob said, "We're married, sweetheart."

"I find that no cause for celebration."

"At least drink a glass with me."

The wine was sweet. Norah licked it off her lips and drank some more. She hadn't had an appetite at the reception, but now she felt empty. Rob filled her glass again.

"You were a beautiful bride. I even saw some mist in old Crawford's eyes."

Norah tried to give an offhand laugh, but the sound caught in her throat. Rob had shed his coat and loosened his neckcloth. When he folded his arms, muscles shifted beneath the taut fabric of his shirt. The planes of his brown face seemed leaner than ever and more rugged. Norah pulled her gaze away, realizing it wasn't his insistence she needed to worry about, but her own weakness. Was there no limit to her appetite for this man? Didn't she realize he was the enemy of her heart?

Rob drew her close. He rested his cheek against hers.

"Don't," Norah begged. The scent of bay rum and the fragrance of roses, the ripe-sweet wine and the vital power of his arms, all soaked her senses and threatened her resolve. "Please don't."

Rob sought her mouth. As he always did, he nipped at her, teasing her, until she made a little sound of impatience. His tongue touched her wine-stained lips, and the old yearning hit her with full force.

"No!"

Norah pulled away, appalled at the treachery of her emotions. Was there nothing this man could do to turn her heart from him? She hugged herself, struggling to subdue the internal clash of will and desire. "I can't. Never again. Not after what you did. Oh, why did you force me to marry you?"

Rob made no move to touch her. "I married you because I love you, Norah," he said patiently. "I also married you to give our child a name and to save you from scandal. I even thought our marriage might make you want me again." He lightly touched her hair. "I was wrong not to tell you about Jody, and I'll take the blame. But it's been months, Norah. Every moment since you agreed to this marriage, I've tried to make amends for hurting you."

Norah bowed her head. "You've been very kind."

"Kind!" He took her head in his hands, forcing her to look into his face. There was a sharply etched set to his lips that he always got when he was angry, and his eyes snapped with frustration. "I'm not acting out of kindness, Norah. We're husband and wife. We're going to have a child. I'll do anything to make you happy, but my patience isn't endless, and I'm not going to spend my life pleading for your forgiveness. I've waited weeks for this moment. I want to be with you again, to hold you, to love you as a man loves a woman. If you need more time, I'll give it to you—my God, I'll wait until after the baby, if necessary. But I need something from you, Norah—a kiss, a smile, a gesture of affection. Something besides your . . . gratitude!"

Norah fought the flow of emotions that dragged her toward him. She had to regain her balance, her perspective. She tried to revive the fierce anger she'd felt in the Brightsgate garden, an anger sparked by Rob's disloyalty to her father and to her. But instead of anger, she found herself confronting the indisputable fact that Jody's was the true deception, not Rob's. Her papa had abandoned her; Rob had been only the messenger.

Suddenly Norah felt defenseless against the searching hope in Rob's eyes. He was begging for a response, and every fiber in Norah's body longed to yield. But then she glimpsed her past, and in an instant she felt herself fill up with the old terrible grief of a child weeping for an absent father. Her mother's anguished face blurred into Norah's own future. Just as Jody had left Annie, Rob would leave her behind, cold and alone. No, it would never do. Norah knew her love could no more anchor Rob than her mother's love could anchor her father. The excruciating sorrow of Jody's betrayal washed over her anew, drowning all possibility of happiness with her new husband. To save her own sanity and that of her child, Norah knew she mustn't love Rob at all.

"I'm sorry," she said softly. "I can give you nothing in return. Nothing."

Rob swore. He drained his wineglass, all the while staring at Norah with hard, haunted eyes. He slammed the glass on the table. "All right, my *wife*. I'll take you to Calcutta. I'll find what's left of Jody. Then you can go back to Boston and get yourself another man to bring up my child. I hope to God I never set foot in that city again." He strode to the door and threw it open. When he turned to Norah, his face was black and bitter. "I'll come for you tomorrow afternoon. We'll sail on the evening tide."

The door slammed shut. Norah stood staring at it. A sense

of loneliness crept over her, widening and deepening until she couldn't move for the ache in her chest. Suddenly she wanted to leap for the door and call Rob back. She wanted to beg his forgiveness. She wanted him to hold her close, to fill her vast emptiness. But he was gone. It was too late. And all her good sense told her it was just as well.

By the New Year they had left the squalls and running seas of the Cape for the fierce heat of the Indian Ocean. The rigging, stretched by the hot weather, needed frequent resetting. Rob stripped to his trousers and joined the crew. When he wasn't aloft, he worked on deck, performing the most mundane tasks. He repaired the leaky companionway top and fashioned new grates for the after hatches. He caulked the poop deck and repaired the winch.

One afternoon Crawford wryly asked if he'd care to paint the boats and knock the rust from the anchors.

Rob wasn't amused. He wiped the sweat from his eyes and squinted at the mate. "Bring up the stump topgallant masts from between decks so I can prepare them for going aloft."

Crawford shook his head in disgust. "Might as well pay off the crew and run this brig yourself, Captain."

Rob worked as hard as he did to keep his mind off Norah. She was growing before his eyes. The slender girl he'd loved was now ripe and womanly; everything about her was round and full. Rob stared at the swell of her belly, her plump breasts straining at the fabric of her bodice, and felt a greed, an endless desire that shamed him. Looking at her, he could almost feel her round softness, her secret places. He told himself it was the heat. He warned himself if he wasn't careful, he'd do something he'd regret.

To divert himself, Rob thought of his future, smuggling opium up the China coast. He dreamed of a swift little clipper, its decks scrubbed spotless, its ropes coiled, everything in place. He manned it with lean young Chinese under Crawford's charge. He armed it with pikes and pistols and a small traversing cannon. In his mind, Rob fought off pirates, matching his wits and his ship against the coast's most vicious adversaries. By God, he'd welcome them. When the wind died, it would be close combat, their heavy swords against his cutlass. Thoughts of the slaughter sent life surging through him, fierce as his long-denied lust.

Often Rob climbed into the rigging and soothed his fevered brain with an hour of solitude. He stared off at the blazing horizon and fell into a timeless state, contemplating nothing. But thoughts slipped into the blankness, his most private and painful thoughts of Norah, and he knew he needed to reconcile himself to losing her.

Despite all that she had given him—his parents, herself, and now a child—Rob knew he could never fit Norah into the pattern of his life. He'd been fooling himself even to consider it. Norah would be lost and unhappy in Calcutta while he plied his smuggler's trade. Burnham didn't want him in the firm, so her world was closed to him. Hadn't he always known he could offer a woman nothing beyond a few hours of love? Norah had been a delightful episode. Now it was finished. He would give her her freedom and again take up his outlaw life.

One afternoon when Rob crawled off the bowsprit after replacing a bobstay, he encountered Norah on the foredeck. The freckles on her nose had darkened, and a sheen of sweat covered her face. She had torn the sleeves from her dresses, leaving her brown arms bare to his gaze. In this climate, bonnets and parasols did little to protect a woman.

Rob passed an arm across his face to wipe away the sweat. "What can I do for you, Norah?"

She smiled hopefully. "Could we play chess?"

"I'm busy at the moment."

Norah's face fell. "Later?"

"Maybe."

He was ignoring her; it was easier that way. His urge to hurt her was unkind, but when she looked sad and lonely, he told himself it was for the best. The more Norah hated him, the less painful it would be to leave her.

"My cabin is so hot I can't stand it," Norah said, following him back to the mainmast. "I wish I could sleep on deck."

"You can nap in your deck chair in the afternoons. I don't want you on deck at night."

"But you sleep there."

"That's different."

"I . . . I could sleep beside you." Norah bit her lip. "I don't mean . . . Just to sleep."

Her full cheeks and brown skin made her appear robust. But looking closer, Rob saw circles under her eyes. He felt a sudden chill of alarm. "Are you ill?"

Norah shook her head. "Only hot and tired."

Her eyes revealed her loneliness, her need to be held and loved. Rob glanced away. "I'm sorry, Norah. The answer is no."

The next day the meager breeze died altogether, leaving the sails limp in the torturous heat. The sun continued to beat down mercilessly, and the *Orion* drifted in the exasperating calm. Norah ran with sweat. Sleep was impossible. She glanced aloft. The light canvas of an upper sail flapped lazily against the mast, then wilted. Norah wished she might command the errant wind to return, but the sails continued to hang straight down.

At dinner Rob said to Crawford, "Let's hope we don't lose our breeze in the Sunda Strait. The Malays will have us easy as a grouse on a lawn in hunting season."

Norah stared at him. "Pirates?" She well knew the story of the Salem ship, *Friendship*, attacked and captured off Kuala Batu, its entire crew taken prisoner.

"I'm only joking," Rob said hastily and pushed away his plate. "You'd best sleep on deck tonight, Norah. There's not a breath of air below."

Rob fixed a bed for her under the spanker shroud and one for himself beside her. The spot was secluded enough for Norah to wear only her shift. Still, even under the dark, moonless sky, she felt exposed and uncomfortable until Rob lay down next to her.

Norah stared at his dark shape as he settled himself. The barriers she had erected against him might have been made of gauze, so great was her longing. She needed a husband to fill her with strength and kindness; she needed a friend. The creature inside her was growing inexorably. She wished she had someone to talk to, someone who understood.

"Rob?"

He lay on his back and grunted.

"I can feel the baby moving."

Rob made no answer.

"Dr. Morley's book says it's the quickening. If I hadn't read that book, I would have been terribly frightened."

"That's good, Norah," Rob said indulgently and turned on his side. "Now get some sleep."

Norah stared hungrily at his back. Passion had once driven him to madness in her arms. Now he barely acknowledged her. But who could blame him for turning away from a woman damp with sweat, bloated with child, and dragging with loneliness? A woman who had rebuffed him on his wedding night?

Norah strained to hear Rob's breathing, but he was perfectly still. If only he would turn over and take her in his arms. With one of his fierce hugs, he could squeeze the misery right out of her. But he would never touch her again. It was her own doing. She had made her decision in Cape Town; now she had to abide by it. A little sound of despair squeaked in her throat.

Rob rolled toward her and raised himself up on his elbow. "What is it, Norah?"

She pressed her lips together, determined not to add blubbering to all her other unattractive traits.

Rob touched her cheek, wiping away tears. "Why are you crying?"

Norah could no longer hold back her labored sobs. "I'm . . . I'm so *lonesome*."

Rob's fingers rustled through her hair and down the nape of her neck where he kneaded gently. "Ah, sweetheart, it's hard being with child and no woman to talk to."

Norah inched her way toward him until she lay against his hot chest. She longed for him to hold her, to love her. Before she could check her words, she was begging. "I don't need a woman as much as I need you."

Rob's hands stopped their massage. His body stiffened, as if prepared to draw away. Norah curled her fingers around his neck, slick with sweat, and held on tight. "Please don't let me go."

The sea lapped gently at the hull of the ship. A mournful song drifted back from the bow. Rob seemed to relax. His arms gently enfolded her. When Norah raised her head, his mouth was there, warm and comforting. Norah clung to him, fitting her fingers into the ridge of his spine, kissing him desperately. When she heard his sounds of pleasure, when she tasted his tongue, something took hold of her, a desire beyond her control. Her hand slipped down over his hips, strong and tight beneath the fabric of his trousers, and gripped his muscular thigh.

"Norah," he muttered. "My God . . ."

Her fingers moved upward and closed over the hard heat of him.

"Jesus, don't!"

He dragged her hand away and pulled her up into a sitting position. "What do you want from me?" he whispered fiercely. "You turn me away on our wedding night, claiming you have nothing to give, and now you come on like the devil's own child! I can't adjust myself to your whims, Norah. We're finished, don't you remember?"

Tears and sweat ran down Norah's neck and onto her breast. "I'm . . . I'm sorry."

She felt naked and humiliated and thoroughly ashamed. But before she could pull away from him, Rob's arms surrounded her and he pressed her hard against his chest. "Oh, sweetheart, it's not your fault. Strange things happen to women in your condition." He eased her back down on the mat. "Now try to rest."

Chapter Twenty-Four

"KUKUI NUT OIL," Willie said. "You rub." He waved his hands over his belly and thighs. "Feel very good."

Norah took the bottle from the steward's hands and gave him a smile. "Thank you, Willie. What would I do without you?"

Willie was proving to be the very friend Norah needed as she approached her sixth month of pregnancy. He supervised her with nagging concern. He saw that she ate plenty of sweet potatoes, which he claimed were especially nourishing during the final months before a baby's birth, and he gave her a special herbal tea, which supposedly guaranteed that the child's body would have all its necessary parts. He even sat on the floor and demonstrated the lateral movements Norah should practice while bathing.

"Make belly strong," Willie said. "Baby come out very fast."

At first his willingness to share his wisdom on the most minute details of the birth process had embarrassed Norah. But when she learned that men of the Sandwich Islands assisted their wives in childbirth and viewed the whole business as quite normal, she decided that if Willie felt no qualms about discussing the ordeal, it needn't bother her.

One morning while Norah sipped lukewarm coffee in the main cabin, Willie said, "You sew holoku."

"A what?" Norah asked.

He described a loose robe with a low, open neck and full sleeves. Norah drew a design to his specifications, and after one full day of work she had a finished garment. The holoku was unfitted from yoke to hem and marvelously comfortable. After studying her reflection in the mirror, Norah decided that besides being roomy, the bright muslin flowing over her figure was quite pretty. Norah also found that her hair had grown long enough to pin up in back. She was too brown and plump to be attractive, but the loose garment and her new hair arrangement made her look healthy and graceful.

When Rob gave her a wan smile and said, "You're devilishly pretty in that getup," Norah glowed with happiness for the first time in months.

After weeks of broiling on the limitless sea, they finally reached the coast of Sumatra. The island's vivid green was brightened with clumps of red kinas and tamarind trees. Groves of palms fringed the shore, and the air, laden with the scent of cinnamon and orange and clove buds, was magical. Sumatra's fragrant breezes mounted to Norah's head like wine.

Darkness fell swiftly in the tropical latitude. During the haunting dusk, the very air turned pink. Sounds took on a strange, peaceful clarity. On one such evening, as Norah stood on deck, Rob approached her. It was the first time he'd sought out her company since the disastrous night she'd tried to seduce him.

"We'll be navigating some dangerous waters in the next few days," he said. "I doubt we'll run into trouble as long as the weather holds, but at the first sign of an unfriendly prau I want you below."

Already they had glimpsed the sleek native vessels with their sharp bows and single sail. The *Orion* had landed briefly at the Malay village of Labunan for water, fowl, and canoes full of exotic fruits. The Labunan natives had been friendly enough, but Rob warned that the danger would come later as they made their way through the strait. The passage was rife with shoals and reefs and treacherous currents. Pirate craft lurked in the island coves, ready to dart out upon unsuspecting vessels and strip them of their cargoes.

"The opium in our hold would keep these fellows happy for

a long time to come," Rob said as he stared out at the heavily wooded shore.

Norah felt a visceral disgust whenever she thought of the hated drug. Thank heaven this was Rob's last voyage with that cargo. "At least you won't be trading in opium when you're in Europe," she said.

Rob glanced at her. "In fact," he said, "I won't be trading in Europe at all."

Norah looked at him in surprise. "You won't?"

"Crawford delivered a letter to me in Liverpool," Rob said. "Burnham and I are finished."

Norah felt a pulse leap in her throat. "Finished?"

"I've been dismissed."

Norah's face went hot, even as the blood froze in her veins. "Because you cut the spring orders? Because . . . But he couldn't dismiss you. You did the right thing! Oh, Rob, he couldn't dismiss you. He *couldn't*!"

Rob shrugged. "Well, he did. I guess I was also too abrupt with my demands for remittances."

Norah tightly gripped the rail. So that was that. She'd known all along the partnership hadn't been settled. But somehow she'd assumed it would come to pass. Now Rob would not return to Boston. There would be no chance for them. Not ever.

"It's for the best," Rob said. "I've been too long at sea and too long in command of other men to begin taking orders from Burnham."

Norah stared dumbly into the falling twilight. She'd imagined him in Europe, traveling, to be sure, and restless, as always, but somehow safer, well away from the temptations and dangers of his old life out east. "So you'll remain in the Indies?"

"There's nothing for me back in America."

Norah's throat thickened. Nothing for him in America. Nothing but a wife and child. "I suppose not," she said.

In the darkness Rob's profile was barely visible, but Norah sensed his weariness. He began to speak, slowly, deliberately, his voice burdened with regret. "For a time after I met you, I thought I could fashion myself into a Boston merchant. I was fooling myself. I don't belong in Boston. I don't belong with

Burnham. As for you . . ." Norah heard a tremor. Rob paused. The silence was fraught with pain. "Our lives don't fit, Norah. You know it as well as I. I'm the sort of man who's better off alone."

Norah's heart had shrunk to a tight little knot. She thought of the naive and hopeful girl who had once thought to transform him, and wondered at her stupidity. If only she'd heeded her mother's words, the warning she'd heard from the time she was a small girl: "If you love a man who loves the sea, Norah, your life will be nothing but misery."

Norah blinked back her tears. "All alone," she said softly. "It sounds so sad."

Rob laughed, but the sound was forced. "Don't worry about me. It's you who will have to return to the wagging tongues of Boston. Burnham will know what to do about the divorce—desertion should be sufficient grounds—and there will be plenty of funds for you and the baby. But you'll face some rough seas. The ladies of Boston will be merciless when it comes to the woman Rob Mackenzie ruined."

"You didn't ruin me," Norah said faintly. "And I don't give a fig for scandal. They can gossip all they want."

Rob laid a hand on hers. It was a sweet gesture and all too brief. "I hope Miss Peabody is so open-minded. I'd hate to see you lose your situation in the shop."

He left her to go below. Norah remained at the rail in the cool tropical evening and felt grief seep into the bedrock of her soul. She loved him. There was no denying it. Returning to Boston would not end her love; it would only add to her misery. But there was nothing to be done. Rob was right, their lives didn't fit.

Dawn found Rob dozing at the rail. A cry from aloft jerked him fully awake.

"Malays! To starboard!"

Rob peered into the morning mist. He saw nothing. He rushed to the brig's waist where weapons were stored for an emergency. "Serve out those cutlasses, mister," he shouted to Crawford. "Get your men to their stations and wait for orders. Mr. Giles! Call your watch on deck."

Giles took off for the forecastle, shouting, "All hands!"

"Wind's dropped, Captain," Crawford said. "We're reeling four knots."

Rob tightened his grip on his pistol and ran forward. In the mist he could see the outlines of three praus. The steersmen had gone to their oars, and the praus were gaining. Fear rushed through him, making his heart pound, his mind focus in defensive preparation. No doubt there were half a dozen more vessels somewhere in the murky dawn.

"Cursed wind," Rob muttered. "Willie!" The steward appeared at his captain's side. "See that the missy stays in her cabin. Lock her in if necessary, and don't leave her."

"Aye, Captain."

"And, Willie"—Rob looked hard at his faithful friend—"you know where the pistol is. Use it if you have to."

Willie nodded and disappeared below.

They played with the praus for a good hour. The *Orion*'s men hung in the rigging and along the rail, firing when the Malay boats came within pistol range and cursing when they drifted away. Rob paced his brig, foredeck to stern, swearing at the fog and praying for a fresh breeze. In this soupy air, a prau could sneak up on the *Orion* unseen. Pirates would be swarming over the bulwarks before the men could reload and scramble from the rigging back down to the decks.

Jan stood at the taffrail, pistol at the ready. "Ever shoot a man, Janner?" Rob asked.

Jan shook his head, his face as white as the gathering mist.

Rob grasped Jan's shoulder. "How's your swordsmanship, then?"

Jan managed a feeble smile. "I can butcher a pig."

Rob laughed. "Stick by me if we have a tussle. And keep an eye on our wake. I wouldn't put it past those crafty little buggers to come up on us from behind."

By the end of the morning watch, the praus continued to drift out of range, waiting and watching. Rob didn't understand their hesitation. The Malays weren't fools; they'd make their move before the fog burned off and the wind came up.

As the *Orion* made her way slowly through the treacherous channel, Giles heaved the chip log over the side to measure the depth of the water. He called out the depth, and Rob shouted commands to the steersman at the helm. Rob stared at the mist as if his vision could burn through the thickness and see what threats lay in wait. Suddenly he felt a movement of air, a quickening dampness against his face, and he knew his prayers had been answered. The mainsail stirred and fattened.

Someone shouted, "By God, we've got our wind!"

A cheer went up from the rigging. Rob ran abaft. Something was bound to happen. They couldn't get away this easily.

"Looks like we'll outrun them devils, Captain," said the freckled Denny at the helm.

"Captain!" shrieked Janner from the taffrail.

"All hands aft!" Rob bawled.

The prau had shot beneath the stern. Before Janner even cried out, the Malays had grappled the taffrail. By the time Rob reached the rail, a dozen wet half-naked pirates were lunging onto the afterdeck. He fired, and one attacker fell. Rob charged, cutlass raised. "Damn you, Janner, fire!"

He heard a report and then another as the crew tumbled aft. One of his men screamed. Rob's cutlass clashed with the short, heavy sword wielded by an agile brown figure. Rob slashed and the pirate fell. Another took his place and met the same fate.

"Put up your guns," Rob hollered, fearing that his men would kill half their mates, firing at such close range. "Sabers!"

The melee lasted only moments. Three wounded Malays scrambled back over the taffrail to their boat. Rob figured the worst was over. Then he heard, *"Captain!"*

Janner was backed up against the rail, his cutlass at his feet. The wavy double-edged blade of a kris descended. Rob threw himself forward and met the kris with his blade. The Malay's sword went flying. Rob thrust, but the pirate leaped over the rail into the water below.

Rob heard Janner shout again. Before he could turn, he felt a blow and his sword arm went numb. His saber clattered to the deck. He stared at it in surprise and saw blood spatter on the blade. Someone swore, and the *Orion* seemed to shoot forward. Rob staggered and glimpsed the shore, a pale line of sand against dense green. The fog was lifting; the breeze felt fresh and strong against his face. A shout came from the sea, and the last of the pirates leaped over the rail. Rob wavered on his feet.

"Captain, my God!"

Rob tried to focus his eyes, but all the figures on deck seemed to blur one into another. He took a step forward and felt himself falling. Someone grabbed him and screamed for Crawford. Rob felt no pain, but he couldn't open his eyes. He fell into a swirling darkness.

At the first shot, Norah sat bolt upright in bed. More shots came at long intervals. Then came cries, the pounding of feet, the report of more pistols. Screams. The blood froze in her veins. She leaped from her bed and ran to the door. Willie pushed her back into the cabin.

"Captain say you stay inside."

Norah pressed her fists to her cheeks. Her knees shook so hard she had to sit down. "Willie," she said beseechingly. "Oh, Willie."

Willie stood as still as a statue, listening.

The fighting seemed to last an eternity. Fear grasped Norah's throat with strong fingers and held tight. She licked her lips and waited. Then feet thudded on the companionway.

"Willie!" Mr. Denny's freckled face was ghastly pale. "The medicine box! Mr. Crawford needs it right away."

He glanced at Norah, his eyes wide with horror. The expression on his face told Norah the worst. She groped toward Willie, clutching his arm, and felt her emotions freeze, as if to defend her against the unspeakable anguish that would follow.

"Oh, my God," she moaned.

"He's alive, missus. But he's cut bad."

"You stay, missy!" Willie pushed Norah back into her cabin and slammed the door.

Norah pulled off her nightdress and dropped her holoku over her head. Without putting on her shoes, she ran out of the cabin. The afterdeck was crowded with men and slick with blood. The smell of it made her gag. A lifeless form lay sprawled on the deck, unattended. Her eyes focused on the men huddled over another figure. A booted leg protruded from the group. Norah's hands flew to her cheeks and she screamed, a soundless scream that rang inside her head and chest. She ran toward him, slipping on the puddled blood. Someone grabbed her arms.

"Norah! Wait! Don't go there."

She turned on Jan and fought him, silently, viciously, until he released her. She pushed her way through the cluster of men to Mr. Crawford. He knelt by Rob, twisting a cloth around his arm. Someone had torn Rob's shirt off. Blood matted his chest and soaked his trousers. His face was pale and still, his eyes closed. A sick dread rose from Norah's insides and clogged her throat. Dear God, she prayed, give me strength to bear this burden. She knelt by his head and took it in her lap. His blood covered her hands and soaked through her gown.

A sailor held the tourniquet while Mr. Crawford probed the wound, a gaping slice to the bone that laid Rob's arm open from shoulder to elbow.

"Hold it tight!" the mate commanded, but the sailor was shaking with fright, and he appeared ready to faint. Norah pushed him away and took the cloth in her hands.

"Take her away," a man muttered.

"I'm staying!"

Mr. Crawford glanced up at Norah. His face was dark and closed, his eyes like steel. He returned to his work. "Can you stand this, missus? 'Tis a bloody mess."

"He's my husband," Norah said numbly. "I must stay with him."

Crawford didn't look away from his business. "Let her be, then. Where's Giles?"

"Here, sir."

"You're in command, mister. Get this brig to Batavia."

"Aye, sir." Giles began shouting orders, and the men moved off to their posts.

Norah's eyes traveled from Rob's wound to his face, relaxed in an expression past caring.

"Don't die," she whispered. She looked at his sprawled body, broad and firm as a mast, soaked with his life's blood. "Don't die."

Norah tightened and loosened the tourniquet so Mr. Crawford could see where the blood spurted. Willie held pads of linen inside the wound to mop up the blood. Each time more blood spurted out Norah wondered that Rob had any left.

They worked for what seemed like hours. Mr. Crawford finished sewing the arteries and worked deep in the wound to bring tissue together. When it was over, he sank back on his haunches and wiped an arm wearily across his forehead. "That's all we can do, missus. Now we pray."

"We must wash him," Norah said. "We must wash away the blood."

"The men will do that." Crawford got to his feet and pulled Norah up, holding her steady. "We'll wash the deck and him as well. And we've got a dead sailor to think about." He nodded toward another limp form, twisted grotesquely.

Norah looked away. "Will you bring the captain to his cabin?"

Crawford nodded and nudged her gently toward the companionway. "Go along now, girl. He won't be asking for you right away."

As Mr. Crawford intoned the service for the dead sailor, the wind they had needed in the strait playfully rattled the sails. It danced about the rigging, unmindful of the tragedy its absence had brought upon the ship. Norah stood dry-eyed, staring straight ahead. She dared not look at the shrouded form that lay on the board waiting to slide into the depths.

The men consigned the body to the sea with a splash. The subdued crewmen murmured the benediction and replaced their caps. They glanced at Norah and shuffled their feet. A few men spoke to her in hushed tones. Mr. Crawford took her arm and led her back down the companionway.

Rob grew feverish. He groaned and tossed. Sweat soaked his sheets. Norah and Willie took turns sponging his face and body. Mr. Crawford held him down while they forced broth between his lips.

"He'll bust those stitches if he don't stay still," the mate said.

So they tied him down with straps. Norah sat with him far into the night. She wiped his face, which ran with sweat. She listened to his moans. When he opened his eyes, they were full of wildness, and when he spoke, he made no sense.

Willie entered the cabin with a tea tray. He placed some leaves in the bottom of a cup, poured water, and dropped in a clean hot stone. He covered the cup to let it steep. "Sacred herb," he said. "Captain drink five times one day. He get well."

Norah knew Mr. Crawford scorned Willie's herbal remedies, but Rob's condition was desperate; she had no time to worry about the mate's opinions. During Crawford's absence from the cabin, Norah forced the tea down Rob's throat.

Night blended into day and again into night. To Norah, nothing mattered outside the small cabin. She felt as if her life were hanging in the balance as delicately as Rob's. If he lived, she would survive; if he died, her own future would be pointless.

The *Orion* made port in Batavia. A Dutch surgeon came aboard and examined the wound. It exuded a pasty yellow-green mess. The surgeon conferred quietly with Mr. Crawford, then told Norah she needed to rest.

Crawford came into the cabin early the next morning, waking Norah from a fitful doze. "Get some sleep, missus. You've got to think of your own self and that baby you're carrying. Take my cabin. I'll stay with the captain."

Norah shook her head. "I belong here."

"He'd want you to rest, missus."

"Captain Mackenzie is in no condition to give me orders, Mr. Crawford," Norah answered curtly, "and I won't take them from you."

The mate shrugged and unwrapped Rob's arm.

"How is it?" Norah demanded. Her nerves felt near to shattering.

Mr. Crawford shook his head. "It don't look good to me, missus. I'm afraid for the arm."

"What do you mean?" Norah cried out, barely mastering her panic.

"The surgeon said if it starts to turn, it had best come off."

Norah sobbed and gasped at the same time. *"No!"*

Mr. Crawford gave her a hard look, and suddenly Norah saw his exhaustion. The lines in his weathered face were etched deeper than ever, and his eyes glittered with grief.

"Oh, Mr. Crawford," she said softly.

For the first time since she'd met him, Norah felt a stir of affection for this gruff and distant man without whose doctoring Rob surely would have died. Hysterics would achieve nothing. She had to compose herself and trust him. That's what Rob would want her to do.

"Would . . . would taking his arm save him?"

"He'll have more of a chance without it, if it's done in time, before the poison spreads. But it still don't mean he'll survive, missus."

So that's how it would be, Norah thought. All those wasted days fighting her love for Rob, worrying that she could never be happy with an absent husband, blaming him for what Papa had done of his own free will.

"It must be done," Norah said. "You must summon the surgeon again, Mr. Crawford." She was weeping silently.

The mate laid a hand on her shoulder. "We'll see how it looks tomorrow."

Norah nodded. "Please," she whispered. "I must be alone."

After Crawford left, Norah pulled her chair close to Rob and emptied her heart. She spoke the words he'd once wanted to hear; she made promises she'd once been too frightened to keep. The wedding vows she'd thought to be lies now came easily to her lips. Norah didn't care any longer that their lives wouldn't be perfect. What did it matter if she was forced to bear lonely times? Had she really believed that sharing a portion of Rob's life would be worse than sharing nothing at all?

"Missy!" Willie was shaking her awake.

Norah blinked. The lamplight hurt her eyes. Exhaustion lay heavily on her body. She looked quickly at Rob, jolted by the fear that grabbed her whenever she had not been faithfully watching him. He appeared unchanged. Sweat ran down his face. The shallow breathing continued. He moaned with every shiver.

"Missy hold lamp!"

Norah obeyed. She watched Willie grind some leaves in a medicine pounder made from porous coral. He added salt and juice of a deep red color.

"What is it?" she asked, dazed with fatigue.

"Popolo. Heal wound. Very good."

"Oh, Willie, Mr. Crawford won't want you to touch the captain's arm. He says his ways are best."

"Mr. Crawford ways kill captain," Willie said grimly. "Mr. Crawford say arm . . ." Willie made a sharp noise in his throat and drew his finger sharply across his arm. "Cut off! Captain with one arm no good. Can't hold baby. Can't hold wife."

He bent over Rob, pulling down the covers to reveal the bandage soaked with sweat and suppuration. Norah knew she should stop him or risk Mr. Crawford's wrath, but instinct told her to trust the steward. The herbal brews had done no harm; perhaps the paste would do some good. In the end, Norah felt too weak and befuddled to object.

Willie nodded toward the basin. "Get hot water."

Norah soaked clean cloths in steaming water, and Willie laid them on the wound. They worked silently, Willie giving directions and Norah obeying. The wound looked so terrible that Norah didn't believe anything would help. She held the lamp high as Willie applied his paste and laid hot cloths over the whole mess. Norah's eyelids drooped and snapped open again. She wavered on her feet.

When they finished, Norah staggered to her chair. She sat gratefully, closed her eyes, and tumbled into sleep.

When she woke, she was lying under a blanket on a woven mat. She'd slept so hard, it took her a moment to realize where she was. Then she remembered Rob and jolted awake. The thrashing and moaning had stopped; she couldn't hear his rasping breath. For a terrible moment Norah thought he was dead. Stumbling to the bunk, she found him resting quietly. His face looked almost peaceful. Norah crouched down beside him and stroked his cool, clammy forehead. She nuzzled his bearded cheek and found his lips.

"Thank God," she whispered between kisses. "Thank God."

Rob's hand moved beneath hers. Norah's heart almost stopped. His eyes opened and he looked at her.

"Norah."

At the sound of his voice, the decades Norah had aged during the last torturous days fell away. The hellish crisis had passed; the future was restored. Rob was hers, to love with passion, to cherish with tenderness. Somehow they would build a life together.

Norah kissed Rob's parched lips and told him so.

* * *

Mr. Crawford wasn't pleased to hear about Willie's medical treatment, but his relief kept him from growling more than few curses. "Captain's tough as old strap leather," he said. "Probably would've healed himself without that heathen witchcraft."

The next day the *Orion* left Batavia. Rob drank some broth and ate a biscuit before falling asleep again. Norah watched his face, monitoring every flicker of an eyelid, every grimace and sigh, waiting for him to waken and acknowledge her.

At last he seemed to be rested enough to stay awake more than a few moments. He looked at her and said, "Where are we?"

Norah let her fingers play over his palm. "We've left Batavia. Mr. Crawford got a good price for the ice and cheeses. . . ." She was stopped by a flood of emotion. Pressing her lips together, she stared silently at Rob's hand, fighting to swallow the lump that swelled in her throat.

His fingers tightened around her own. Norah looked at his weary smile and whispered, "I'm so happy you're well."

Rob closed his eyes. "Get some rest," he murmured. "You look damned tired."

The next day he insisted on sitting up. When Norah fussed over him, he sent her out of the cabin and called for Crawford.

The mate scrutinized him good-naturedly. "I hear you're meaner than an old bear."

"I'm making a will, George. I'll have it drawn up properly in Calcutta, but I want you to know the provisions now."

Crawford grinned and rubbed his chin. "A bit late for a will, Captain. Looks like you'll pull through just fine."

"Well, I'm going to die in a few months. After the baby is born."

Crawford's smile faded. "What the hell are you talking about?"

Rob pushed back the covers and maneuvered his feet to the floor. He felt as if quicklime were eating away at his arm. His head seemed to be floating around, light as a veil.

As he expected, Crawford started nagging. "What d'you think you're doing? You ain't gettin' up, Captain, and them's orders."

Rob pushed himself to his feet. "Stow it, mister." The cabin swayed, and he grabbed an overhead beam.

"You fall and I'll haul you up just once," Crawford said. "After that you can lay there, far as I'm concerned. We spent a good deal of sweat tending you. The least you can do is heal proper."

Rob set off across the cabin on wobbly legs, gripping the beam with one hand as a fire seared his other arm. "I'm obliged, George. You saved my life, for what it's worth."

"It's worth a damn sight to that wife of yours."

Rob grimaced and licked his dry lips. "Where in hell is that blasted Willie? I want some food."

Rob rummaged on his desk until he found a clean piece of paper. He began to scrawl as he talked. "I'm asking you to see that my wife and baby get safely back to Boston. I'll take enough money from my account to buy a little schooner. The rest will go to Norah. If she doesn't survive the voyage, the child inherits it all. Under no circumstances is Norah or the child to learn of my whereabouts. Ever. By the time the *Orion* sails for Boston, she'll think I'm dead."

"Blamed fool," Crawford muttered. "You'll never get away with it, Captain."

"Jody did."

"You planning to take up the pipe, too?"

Rob ignored the gibe and stared out the stern window at the gray wave-tossed sea.

"Don't you think," Crawford said after a pause, "that girl's had enough of this sort of trouble?"

Rob's gaze swung back to the mate's. "We're not suited, Norah and I. A week ago she knew it. Now, just because I nearly slipped my cable, she's getting notions about sticking with me. My sort of life will only bring her heartache. Making her a widow is the kindest thing I can do. She can return to Boston a respectable woman and forget about me."

"Just like she forgot about Jody," Crawford said and shook his head. "You're whistling up the wind, Captain. Better you sling your hammock and go ashore with that girl."

Rob sighed. "It would never work, George. Never."

Chapter Twenty-Five

IN CALCUTTA, ROB settled himself and Norah in a hotel in a quiet section of the city. "There's no need to take a house," he said, "since you'll be moving in with Amanda in a few months."

Norah didn't care one way or another. She felt as if her brain had been crippled by Calcutta's soaking heat, the putrid smells, the sights of misery and squalor. What on earth, she wondered, was she doing in this tropical hell? The Denmores' affection for the city was beyond her comprehension. The fact that her own papa had actually chosen this netherworld over a sane and cozy life in Boston left her heartsick.

At least their suite of rooms was comfortable. Vivid carpets and potted ferns made a handsome effect, the tatties kept out the burning sun, and punkah wallahs pulled great fans of plaited reeds that stirred the air into a faint breeze.

They ate three times a day in the hotel dining room. Norah was dismayed the first night when Rob summoned an army of bearers with a snap of his fingers. The waiters bowed obsequiously at his officious commands.

"Surely you needn't be so rude," Norah said, flushing with embarrassment.

Rob seemed greatly amused by her reprimand. "You're in British India, Norah. The English would be most displeased if their subjects forgot their unworthiness."

Rob engaged a quiet dark-eyed Indian woman named Rosina, who spoke a bit of English. Rosina wore gold bangles and saris of sheer cotton embroidered with colored silk. She pampered Norah with massages and baths and cleverly tamed her hair, rebellious in the humid climate. A new wardrobe of cool, broad-waisted muslins further shored up Norah's spirits. But nothing could cushion the shock of her reflection in the mirror. Norah hardly recognized herself; she looked like a ship about to be launched. She despaired of ever returning to normal and saw no hope that Rob would ever again find her desirable.

He had grown stronger in the weeks since his injury. His arm still pained him and he carried it stiffly, but the hotel's sumptuous meals were filling out the muscular frame that had sadly diminished during his recovery. To Norah, Rob had never looked more handsome.

She saw little of him. He slept in a small bedroom off their sitting room. Each morning after a dawn ride on the Esplanade, he disappeared for the day to do business. Norah had his complete attention only in the evenings when they strolled on the maidan and viewed all of European Calcutta.

The only other person Norah saw with any frequency was Jan, who was helping Rob assemble the *Orion*'s Boston-bound cargo. Poor Jan had suffered wretchedly for his dismal performance during the pirate attack. He blamed himself for his captain's injury and was only now beginning to display any signs of cheerfulness.

It was to Jan that Norah brought up the subject of her father. After months considering the meaning of Jody's disappearance, she dreaded the prospect of finding him. He had not wanted her all those years ago; by now he had probably forgotten her. And Norah knew that men enslaved to opium could not be cured. The drug became their master, more important than family and livelihood, more important than their own lives. The strain of finding her beloved papa in a wretched condition would surely be more than she could bear.

Jan didn't want to discuss the matter. "Captain Mackenzie says you're not to worry yourself so close to your time."

"But surely you can tell me if Rob has made inquiries."

"He has," Jan said with a stubborn frown. "But I won't tell you anything more."

When she mentioned Jody to Rob, he claimed to have heard nothing. "I doubt we'll find him, Norah. Perhaps it's just as well."

Rob also made inquiries about Lord Denmore. Amanda and her husband were expected within the month. Once Norah was settled with the Denmores, Rob would take the *Orion* around to Lintin Island with six hundred chests of Patna opium.

Norah kept her disapproval to herself. She hated the opium and worried about the dangers Rob would face going through the Straits of Malacca. But she knew scoldings would only drive him farther away from her. His close call with death had taught her a lesson about the precious and precarious nature of life, about fighting for love and having faith in one's future. Somehow she had to show Rob the way to happiness. Somehow she had to convince him that he could set down roots and form ties, that he could belong to someone other than himself.

But until she regained her slender shape and held a robust infant in her arms, Norah would postpone her assault on his heart. When Rob returned from Lintin, the baby would be two months old, a perfect age to win over an uncertain papa.

One night when the baby was feeling rambunctious and sleep eluded her, Norah heard Rob moving about in the sitting room that separated their bedchambers. Her door opened and he came in, holding a branch of candles.

"Norah?"

She raised herself up on one elbow. "I'm awake."

He set the candles on the table, pushed aside the netting, and sat down on the bed. His face looked worn and worried. He smelled of the outdoors and a good amount of whiskey. Rob drank hard only when something upset him, and Norah felt a jolt of alarm.

"What is it?" She spoke softly so as not to waken Rosina.

"The *Thistle* is off Sands Head. The Denmores will be here tomorrow."

He took her hand and twined their fingers. From the expression on his face she could see that the long-awaited arrival of the Denmores' ship and his own departure were causing Rob some distress. Norah felt a stir of satisfaction. She gave his hand a squeeze. "Now you can sail off to China and not worry about me."

He smiled wanly. "Can I?"

"The doctor says the baby is healthy. And Amanda is experienced in these matters. There's nothing to worry about, Rob. When you come back, we'll all be bouncing and healthy."

"Oh, sweetheart." To Norah's astonishment, Rob pulled her into his arms, crushing her against his hot chest. The muscles of his arms and back were tense, and Norah could feel him shaking. She clasped him tight. He hadn't touched her since the humiliating night on the *Orion*'s deck. It felt wonderful to hold him close.

"I love you," he murmured against her neck. "Remember that."

His words filled Norah with a hazy delight. Before she could respond, he drew back to look at her, his eyes glittering with emotion. Norah could do no more than sit in dumb-founded happiness.

"Your hair's so pretty." He pulled off her cap and ran his fingers through the silky waves. "Bright as sunshine. That's what I thought the first time I saw you. You have sunshine in your hair."

Norah laughed softly. "But see how long it's become. It's time you gave me another haircut."

Rob didn't smile. Instead, his gaze drifted off, and Norah saw his throat working.

"Rob?" She laid her hand on his cheek. She hadn't seen such emotion in his face since the night at Brightsgate when she'd mentioned her other suitors.

He pulled her close again and pressed his face against her hair. Norah lay quietly against him, listening to the punkah squeaking rhythmically above their heads. She felt a sleepy contentment in his arms, a dull kind of longing.

He eased away from her and spoke very softly. "I'll leave day after tomorrow. I'm going to miss you." He ran his fingers over her face as if to memorize her features.

"Do you want to feel the baby?" Norah asked. "He's very active tonight."

Rob looked doubtful. Norah took his hand and held it on her belly. "Do you feel it?"

His throat contracted with a hard swallow. He stared at his hand resting on the round thumping place where his baby kicked. "Does it hurt?"

Norah smiled. "Oh, no, but it keeps me awake."

Rob's hand, warm through her nightdress, moved gently. His eyes took on a strange dark glow. He bent over to kiss the mound and rested his cheek there for a moment. Then he straightened and took Norah in his arms, covering her face with chaste but loving kisses. "When the baby is being born," he whispered against her lips, "think of me. And be brave."

Amanda's lovely face was grim with annoyance. "You, my dear, stand in need of a proper birching. I don't suppose you considered the turmoil you left behind when you ran off to Liverpool."

Norah, deliriously happy after Rob's tenderness the previous night, only wanted to laugh. She formed a suitably repentant expression, then flashed a smile at Rob.

He looked exhausted and gloomy. "It's over and done with now, Amanda," he said.

Amanda glared at him. "That's all very well for you to say. But you didn't have to endure the anguish of waiting and worrying and imagining what might have befallen this heedless girl in a place like Liverpool. Denmore and I were in Scotland and so were spared the ordeal. But her ladyship was quite beside herself, and Alice was hysterical. Thank heaven for Guy's cool head."

"I wrote you from Madeira," Rob said.

"Oh, I received your letter. After several weeks." Amanda sank down on a wicker settee, one of three on the wide cool veranda of the Denmores' home. She looked superb in blue silk, frogged and laced and molded to her figure. "*Mon dieu!* This heat is too much." She touched a handkerchief to her damp forehead and glanced from Norah to Rob. "I'm afraid, my dears, there's a good deal more to the story than Norah's simply running away." Amanda patted the settee beside her. "Come sit by me, *chérie*. My, but you look lovely. Not many women carry a child so prettily."

She gave Rob a sideways glance, and Norah saw him flush.

"I know all about your ordeal in Liverpool," Amanda continued. "My, my, what an adventure. Worthy of the worst sort of novel. I suppose you realized that the villain of the piece was none other than Ollie Burnham."

"Ollie!" Norah breathed. "*He* was the gentleman?"

"Rob suspected as much," Amanda said. "If he hadn't suggested in his letter that we investigate, Ollie might have carried the secret to the grave."

"But why would he do such a thing?"

"After you were found missing, it didn't take Guy long to extract the truth from Alice. Guy then appealed to Ollie, who was less than an hour away in Shilton. Ollie galloped off into the night to rescue you. Since Alice told him where you'd be staying, your little escapade could have been stopped quite easily. But then Ollie put into motion a more complicated scheme. He decided that to win you for himself he had to put Rob in a bad light once and for all. So he hired these"— Amanda paused and shuddered—"*ruffians* to snatch you and make believe you were being ransomed—Rob, of course, being the man to furnish the money.

"If all went according to Ollie's plan, Rob would have sailed off to India none the wiser, leaving you to think he held you in such low esteem he would not even post a thousand pounds to save your life. Thereupon Ollie would burst into the room and mount a rescue. He would be your hero, while the cold-hearted Captain Mackenzie would be shown up as a scoundrel."

Amanda gave Rob a stern glance and added, "If my arithmetic is correct, Captain, my little Brightsgate matchmaking scheme worked far beyond my expectations. I'd intended a bit of courting, but it seems you dishonored my household and betrayed my trust. Of course you never were a man to respect convention."

Norah smiled at Rob's discomfort. "Enough of that, Amanda," he said gruffly. "Now tell us how you extracted this confession from Ollie."

"I must give my husband credit for that. I neglected to inquire about the particulars of Charles's method of interrogation, but suffice it to say that voices were raised and I overheard the word 'prison' mentioned more than once. Ollie is not a man of great courage, so the discussion did not continue for long."

"Does Mr. Burnham know about Ollie?" Norah asked. "He must be furious!"

"Ah, the *formidable* Mr. Burnham," Amanda said with a laugh. "Guy was the first object of his wrath. Mr. Burnham quite overplayed the outraged father. He behaved as if Guy had most brutally ravished his helpless daughter. He went so far as to demand that Alice be removed from her husband's bedchamber. But the dowager countess came down on him quickly enough, and in a few days the man was quite docile. When Alice announced she was happily enceinte, Mr. Burnham transformed himself again, this time into a jolly grandpapa."

"Alice with a baby!" Norah burst into delighted laughter. "How wonderful!" She caught Rob's eye and beamed.

"As for Ollie," Amanda went on, her eyes twinkling, "his father boiled over into a froth of rage, vowing that his son's days of idleness were finished. Ollie was placed on notice that he would be settled with a position and a wife by the New Year. Before we knew it, Ollie had taken up quite rigorous duties at the London offices of Crafts and Sprague, and Mr. Burnham announced the engagement of Oliver Thornton Burnham the Third to Miss Daphne Grace Sprague."

"Daphne!" Norah gave a whoop of laughter. "Oh, no. How terrible!"

"I'd say they deserve each other," Rob muttered.

"In one area, Mr. Burnham has unfortunately not come around to see reason," Amanda said with a meaningful glance at Rob. "Like so many in the City, he is quite blind to the financial crisis that's brewing for all to see. He's quite put out with you, Rob."

Rob shrugged. "I know that."

"Denmore has friends in the Exchequer who agree that a most serious crisis exists. Perhaps you'll be proved right in time."

The bearer brought in a tray of lemonade. "Good heavens, I'm parched," Amanda cried brightly. She turned a smile on Norah. "I demand a toast to our newest little *maman*."

* * *

Rob was determined that nothing would disturb Norah or arouse her suspicions. When he bade her good-bye, he freely poured out his heart. He blurted out promises and assurances he knew would never be fulfilled. Even after he had nothing left to say, he blundered on in misery and confusion, and ended up kissing Norah so ardently that she finally pushed him away.

"You'll squash the baby," she said, laughing. She took his head in her hands and pulled him down to kiss his forehead. "Hurry back, my dearest love," she whispered. "Next time I see you, you'll have a fine son. Rosina says it's sure to be a boy from the way he's lying."

Rob descended the steps of the Denmores' veranda, blinking away the final image of Norah's glistening eyelashes, her sunlit hair, the breeze-tossed apricot gown that caressed her well-ripened figure. Against his better judgment, he turned for one last look. Norah stood in a radiant sunbeam, shielding her eyes with one hand and blowing him a kiss with the other.

As the *Orion* crossed the Bay of Bengal and entered the Andaman Sea, Rob's thoughts of Norah brought on a deep and bitter sadness. He told himself that his disappearance was for the best. Norah would return to Boston and get on with her life without him. In a few weeks she would be lavishing her love and attention on the baby, and memories of him would fade into the background. But the realization that she would eventually adjust to widowhood brought Rob no comfort. Indeed, such thoughts aggravated his already fragile temper, causing Crawford to warn him he'd have a mutiny on his hands if he didn't curb his tongue.

Rob channeled his frustration into twice-daily stick fighting sessions with an agile young lascar he'd added to the crew. Morning and evening the afterdeck rang with the grunting of men and the clacking of sticks as he and the Indian sailor fought with sawed-off spars. Rob's weakened right arm needed strengthening if he ever again hoped to wield a saber or climb a rope. The fighting was agony for him, and he took the worst of it from the smaller man, but he welcomed the sweat and pain. It kept his mind from forming images of Norah, who at that very moment might be bringing their child into the world.

At Lintin, Rob sold his cargo and took as his profit five thousand finely milled silver dollars. The *Orion* sailed up the Pearl River to Canton, where Rob hoped to transact for a slim-masted opium clipper.

At the Whampoa anchorage, he found the *Rajah* riding at anchor. He passed a bleary, brandy-soaked evening with Elias Marsh.

"You can probably have the *Nile* for three thousand," said the English skipper. "She belonged to a Spaniard who argued with his partners and left China."

Rob grunted. He was having a hard time keeping his mind on business.

Marsh tugged at his whiskers and eyed Rob curiously. "Thought you'd decided to settle down, Captain. Counting-house too stuffy for you, or did that pretty wife of yours make you cross?"

Rob poured another tumbler of brandy, wishing the drink could wash Norah's image from his mind. Her time had come and passed. She intruded on his thoughts without mercy. "How do you know about my wife?" he grumbled.

"Oh, word gets around," Marsh said easily. "I hear you're most likely a papa by now."

Rob's eyes began to burn. He stared hard at his glass. "I need a dozen heavy guns and a crew, Marsh, not your prying questions."

Marsh laughed. "No need for heavy guns, Captain. Putting a pistol to your head will do quite nicely."

Rob poured a long slug of fiery liquid down his throat and slammed the glass on the table. "What in hell is that supposed to mean?"

Marsh ignored the question. "You might meet your friend Jody Paige up the coast. I understand he's on a lorcha headed for Ningpo."

Rob felt a jolt. He got unsteadily to his feet, his head pounding, despair settling deep in his bones. Dear God, he thought, would Jody never cease to haunt him?

"Obliged for the brandy, Marsh," he said. "Sorry I can't linger. If I'm going to negotiate for a ship tomorrow, I'd better dry out my brain."

"Captain."

Rob focused his eyes. Marsh was regarding him soberly. "I've got a wife back in Somerset," the Englishman said. "I wanted her once, but can't for the life of me remember why. Now I can't stay far enough away from her and her whining brats. But I'll tell you something, Mackenzie. If I had a woman as pretty as the creature I saw on your deck last July, I'd think more than twice before I armed an opium clipper and headed off into oblivion, leaving word that I was dead."

Rob stumbled toward the door. "Go to the devil, Marsh."

The hot wind blew in heavy gusts, churning the water and setting the *Orion*'s timbers to creaking. Streaks of lightning dazzled the night sky. Rob leaned on the rail, thinking of Norah and of Marsh's words. A tide of longing surged through him, bringing with it the warm swell of desire, the familiar melting in his chest. She burned like a fever in his veins, mounting to a consuming fire and then fading again to a low warmth, but never entirely quenched. How long would it take to forget her, or at least to ease the pain of loving her?

"Evenin', Captain."

Rob turned to see Crawford approaching. He glared at the mate, even though the night was too dark for Crawford to read his face. "I hear you've been talking to Marsh. I never took you for a gossip, George."

"I thought he could talk some sense to you. You sure as hell won't listen to me."

Rob reached for his throbbing temples. "All I ask is for you to take her back to Boston where she belongs. She'll get over me in time."

"I ain't going to do it, Captain."

Rob reared back and fixed the mate with a furious stare. "I'm giving you an order, mister."

"There's no way in hell I'm going to tell her you're dead."

"Goddammit, George—"

"It ain't my way to interfere, but your life will be a misery without that girl. Hell's fire, Captain, you think you've got a squall in your gizzard and can't settle down, but all you got is a case of being afraid to try."

Crawford's vehemence took Rob by surprise. But in the moment it took for him to digest the mate's words, a slow anger began to burn in his gut. So Crawford thought he was afraid. It wasn't fear that drove him, but rather the hopeless feeling that he had nothing to offer Norah—no place, no position, no prospect of stability. He could never give her the sort of life she wanted.

"What do you know about settling down, an old seaman like you?" Rob asked bitterly. "Not a damned thing."

Crawford stuck his pipe in his mouth, sucked on it for a few moments, and pulled it out again. "That's where you're wrong, Captain. That's where you're wrong. I don't suppose you knew that before she became Jody's wife, Annie Paige was my sweetheart."

Rob dragged his brandy-dulled senses to attention. "Your sweetheart? Jody's wife?"

A flash of heat lightning illuminated Crawford's face, set dead ahead, staring off in the distance. "No point in relating the details," he said. "Let's just say I lost out. I would have quit this life in a minute if she'd have had me. But you know how Jody was, loaded with charm. Annie was crazy for him. All she wanted was for him to quit the sea and stay home with her and the little girl. Well, he talked a fair amount about quitting, but never could bring himself to do it. I heard Annie was run down and killed by a runaway wagon, but it was Jody who killed her, sure as you're born. Killed her by breaking her heart. And he knew it, too."

Crawford took a few more drags on his pipe. Rob waited, stunned and cold sober.

"When he heard Annie was dead, Jody came to me and said, 'She'd have been better off with you, George.' That was the only time we mentioned her, Jody and me. And then he went off and took up the opium pipe. That's why he did it, Captain, because he couldn't stand thinking of what happened to her, and how he was to blame."

Rob leaned heavily on the rail, his mind forming an image of a small, curvy red-haired woman and the way she'd looked at her husband. The vision was replaced by a memory of

Norah, her cool hands on his cheeks, saying, "Hurry back, my dearest love. . . ."

"Don't know if there's a lesson there for you, Captain," Crawford went on. "But I seen how you're drinking these past weeks and fighting and talking crazy. Seems to me it won't be long before you wade into a crew of pirates and let them finish you off. It don't make sense, seeing how you've got a wife with spark enough to set fire to any man, a wife who looks at you with eyes that don't see even half your faults. Now you've got a baby and still you're willing to throw it all away."

Rob's shock at Crawford's revelation gave way to a sudden and cutting guilt. He had never thought of Jody as a man torn between the sea and his family. He would have scorned that side of Jody, the side that would forsake the hard, lonely life of the seaman for the sweet and simple pleasures of his family. Hadn't Rob spent his young manhood silently gloating that Jody hadn't succumbed to his wife's demands that he quit the sea?

It was almost as if he and Annie Paige had been in a battle for her husband's soul; Rob had won, and Jody and Annie were destroyed. Suddenly Rob was oppressed by that woman's despair. "George? Do you think . . ." His voice drifted off, and he tried again. "Do you think he stayed at sea because of me?"

Crawford chuckled in the darkness. "Don't take credit for Jody's actions, Captain. He done what he done without your help. You just worry about his girl and her baby. If you want to make something up to Annie and Jody, do it by going back to your wife."

Rob ran his hands over his face. He felt a dead weariness, but it lay on him gently, almost like relief. "I've got no place to take her, George. I'm finished with Burnham, and Calcutta's hell for women and babies."

"It don't matter where you take her, Captain. Just go to her. The rest will fall into place." Crawford tapped his pipe on the rail and tucked it into his pocket. "Guess I'll turn in. If we're heading back to Calcutta, I'd best be up early, rounding up the crew."

"George."

Crawford stopped.

"Marsh says Jody's on a lorcha to Ningpo. I want to go after him."

Crawford scratched his head. "Ningpo's a fair piece, Captain, nearly to Shanghai. That's a month's voyage in dangerous waters."

Rob grinned. "My sword arm is working again. What do you say, George? Don't you think it's time Jody saw his little girl again?"

Chapter Twenty-Six

NORAH SAT ON the long veranda of the Denmores' bunga-
low, staring at the dense foliage and flagrant colors of the back
garden. Light faded from the evening sky. Insects chirped.
From the servants' quarters came the smell of woodsmoke
and the murmur of voices. It was a melancholy time of day.
Amanda had gone off to a boating party on the Hooghly River.
She encouraged Norah to partake of social occasions, but
Norah had sampled the interminable conversation parties and
the sneering gossip that passed for entertainment in Calcutta.
She concluded that she was ill-suited to Anglo-Indian society.

Norah wanted nothing so much as to leave this place. The
rains had arrived in June, settling the dust and bringing a
breath of freshness. But along with sheets of water and crashing thunder came sticky dampness that rusted stays and pins
and spotted gowns so they disintegrated at the touch. A body
could hardly take a breath without being drenched with heated
sweat. Norah longed for the crisp New England fall. She wondered under what circumstances she would next find herself in
Boston. She might be a married woman or a divorced one; the
third possibility she dared not consider.

September was drawing to a close, and still there was no
word from Rob. He had been expected at Sands Head in early
August. Jan, left behind to tend to the *Orion*'s Boston-bound
cargo, called at the bungalow each afternoon. For a while he

had offered optimistic reasons for the *Orion*'s delay; now he simply looked anxious.

During the day Norah kept an iron grip on her fears, but at night she was plagued by insidious dreams that left her pillow wet with tears. She knew that before long she might have to face a terrible dilemma: whether to wait for a man who might never return or to arrange for passage home.

The bearer rustled softly across the veranda's marble floor carrying a platter of pineapple and diced mango. He set the plate on the table along with a bowl of nuts dipped in honey and sugar. Norah crunched a nut between her teeth and rested her sugar-coated finger on the rosy lips of the baby in her arms. She smiled when he opened his mouth, grasped her finger, and sucked hard.

Matthew Joseph Mackenzie possessed his grandpapas' names and his mama's looks. Fair curls peeked from beneath his ruffled cap, and golden lashes ringed his blue-gray eyes. To Norah, her baby was a wonder of perfection. She never tired of admiring him. At times, however, she wished he'd inherited Rob's thick black hair and vigorous nature. Surely, a father would prefer a son who resembled him. But then Matthew would swing his tiny fists and burst into a sly, plump-cheeked smile, and Norah would laugh aloud, knowing she couldn't bear for him to be other than his own special self.

The baby smacked his lips in his sleep, and Norah cuddled him close. "Your papa will love you very much," she murmured against his cheek. "If only he would come. . . ."

Despite her brave efforts, Norah's heart was slowly splintering. Every day she bargained with God, promising that Rob could find his son wanting, that he could send them both away, in exchange for an end to this terrible uncertainty.

"Mem."

Norah glanced up. Rosina stood in the dusk, the faint light of the garden lanterns illuminating her pale sari.

"The sahib, mem," Rosina said softly. "He come."

Norah stared. Denmore was not due back from Barrackpore until next week. "Lord Denmore?"

Rosina shook her head. "The captain, mem."

"The captain?" Norah asked dumbly. She stood up and Rosina took the baby from her arms.

Rosina smiled and gathered Matthew close. "He's come home, mem."

Norah raced down the hallway, lit with candles in their girandoles. Rob looked dark and massive in the soft glow. A broad smile broke across his face. Norah stopped for a breathless, unbelieving second. "Rob," she whispered, suddenly weak.

With a cry of joy, she threw herself into his open arms. He caught her up, swinging her high. Norah pressed her lips against his prickly neck, hugging him desperately. Her knot of terror began to unravel faster and faster until she was dizzy with relief. She gasped and sobbed against him.

Rob laughed. "What sort of a welcome is this? When I left, I was given only smiles. Now I return to tears."

He tried to disengage her arms, but Norah held tight. She couldn't get enough of his salt-air smell, the particular flavor of his skin, the feel of his shoulders and back. He rocked her gently until the tears subsided.

Norah pulled away. "I'm so happy," she whispered. "I thought you'd never come."

Rob tilted her chin with his fingers, and Norah looked into his dear dark eyes, alive with happiness and longing.

"How about a proper kiss for your husband?"

Their lips touched with a slow, gentle pressure. Norah's fingers crept up his shirtfront and around his collar, savoring every proof of his solid presence. Rob's lips parted, teasing her with feigned passivity, and Norah laughed softly against his mouth before accepting his impudent invitation. No sooner had she tasted him than she felt his passion flare. His arms tightened impatiently, crushing the breath from her, and his own mouth demanded the satisfaction his body craved. Norah responded, promising all she had to give, every ounce of love she's saved and cherished these past long months.

When Rob released her, the smile was gone. "Norah—"

She pressed her fingers to his lips. "You must see our baby. We have a boy."

Rob dropped his gaze. For a perplexing moment Norah thought he was disappointed. Then he looked at her. "I found Jody, sweetheart. I brought him back to Calcutta. He's aboard the *Orion*. He's ill, and he wants to see you."

"No!"

The shock of his words snatched away their perfect moment of reunion. Dark emotions from the past rolled over Norah, bringing feelings that were too deep and too complex to master. She tried to push them away, to focus on the man who faced her.

"I . . . I can't see him!"

Rob gathered her close, soothing her. "It's all right, Norah, I promise you. Come, sweetheart, I'll be with you. I'll stay beside you."

Currents of love and loss and unforgiven pain churned in a heart already exhausted by worry and longing. "Where's Matthew?" Norah cried.

Then Rosina was beside her, placing the baby in her arms. Norah held him close. He was the one precious person she could count on never to leave her alone.

Rob and Rosina took Norah to her room. In a daze of unreality, Norah prepared to meet the father who had spurned her, the man she had loved above all others until Rob so abruptly turned her life around. Norah no longer understood what she felt for Jody, love or hate, and she knew she would not know her own feelings until she saw him.

The sound of low, delighted laughter jarred Norah's thoughts. "He looks like you, sweetheart."

Norah glanced up from Rosina's ministrations to find Rob leaning against the doorframe. He stared with bemusement at the baby cradled in his arms. Matthew waved his fists and emitted a happy coo. As quickly as it had come upon her, Norah's apprehension melted away. Rob was making his son's acquaintance. Nothing could spoil the joyful moment of their meeting.

And as she watched the father and the son, it suddenly came to her that Rob's smile was different, or perhaps it was his face. He had lost the hard-edged set of his mouth, and the strain around his eyes had softened. Even his body seemed to move with newfound ease. Rob looked up and met her gaze, and Norah saw a countenance no longer harshly touched by time and trouble, but an unguarded smile and dark eyes brimming with happiness.

Norah felt something magical pass between them, a poignant promise for the future, a lifetime of contentment for her small family.

"Oh, Rob," she said softly, "I'm so happy you're home!"

The tonga driver raced through the damp night air, splashing over muddy streets toward the wharf. Norah held tight to Rob's hand as he told her of finding Jody's lorcha off Foochow. The craft had been running opium north and was carrying silver. It had been looted, stripped, and partly burned by pirates. Its crew had been left to die of their gruesome wounds. Jody was one of the few to survive.

"I figure he was in a stupor when the attack came, hiding out in some secret corner below. The opium saved him. But he went through days of withdrawal and thirst. He went nearly mad in the sun. When we found him, he was incoherent." Rob put his arm around Norah and drew her close. "He's had a bad time, and his heart is weak. If it hadn't been for the prospect of seeing you, he'd have given up long ago."

Norah made no response. The father she'd loved had long been dead. Now she had to contend with his sick and ruined shadow. Norah clutched the battered silver ring Jody had given her the last night she saw him. She wished he had simply died, sparing her this final misconceived confrontation.

Mr. Crawford waited in the *Orion*'s main cabin. "I've got him in my quarters, missus."

Norah thanked the mate. Her courage was growing apace of her determination to conclude the painful reunion. She untied her bonnet and handed it to the solemn Willie. To Rob she said, "I'll see him alone."

The mate's small cabin smelled of illness. A guttering lamp left the room in shadows. Norah waited as her eyes grew accustomed to the dimness. Then she made her way toward the figure lying on the bunk. As she drew near, Jody lifted his hand. Norah took it, a frail set of bones. The handsome vital man she'd known was gone, replaced by a wraith with sunken cheeks, a gray matted beard, and a body that seemed fragile as a feather beneath the blanket.

Yet it was him. Oh, yes, she knew it was her papa.

Norah's chin began to tremble. She felt the hot sting of

tears. There was no need for fear or anger or even forgiveness. Her father was with her at last. He had kept his promise.

Norah knelt by the bunk. "Oh, Papa. Papa, do you know me?"

He turned his head and studied her with burning eyes. His tangled beard moved as he tried to smile. "Norah," he said, his voice straining. "Such a . . . a pretty thing. Always was."

"Papa, I have your ring." Norah opened her fist and showed him. "You told me if I kept it I'd see you again."

He touched her cheek, her hair. His eyes seemed focused on distant memories. Norah wondered if he heard a word she said. "I thought you were dead, Papa. If I'd known, I would have come for you long ago. You don't know how I missed you, how lonely I was."

His brow fell into a frown. "Burnham. He was good to you?"

"Oh, yes, Papa. The Burnhams were very good to me."

" 'Twas better for you there." He closed his eyes briefly as a grimace of pain crossed his face. "Better without me."

"No, Papa."

"Yes, child. Better for you."

Norah leaned toward him and rested her cheek against his wasted one. Tears slid down her cheeks, silent and unnoticed. "I wanted *you*."

Jody's trembling fingers slipped over her hair. "Your mama . . . your mama . . ." A sound came from his throat, a soft wail of sorrow. Norah clutched his hand in both of hers and gulped down sobs. "She didn't die because of you, Papa, I swear it. She would have waited forever for you to come home. She loved you so."

Jody's chest heaved as he struggled to regain his composure. Norah kissed his grizzled cheek.

"Your baby," he said faintly. "Tell me."

"Oh, yes, Papa. Rob and I have a boy. A wonderful happy boy."

Jody's eyes shone with tears. "Rob. Thank God he found you. Thank God he'll take care of you. . . ." He groaned softly, his face contorted. "Kiss me and go. Let me rest."

Norah touched her lips to his. "I love you, Papa. I love you very much."

Jody struggled to speak, his eyes closed. "I always loved you, girl. You never left my mind."

Norah was shaking with a strange mixture of euphoria and despair when she returned to the main cabin. "He's resting," she said and sat down beneath the lamp. She looked at Rob's and Mr. Crawford's anxious faces and smiled. "I'm happy. Oh, I'm so very happy to see him."

The night wore on. Jody lay still, his breathing labored. Norah fell asleep in Rob's cabin and woke to full, leaking breasts.

"Matthew needs me," she told Rob urgently. "I shouldn't have left him."

Rob took one look at Norah's spotted gown and raced off into the night. He returned with Rosina, who placed the baby in her arms.

After his feeding, Norah took Matthew to see his grandfather. The baby burped and blinked and promptly feel asleep. Jody touched the child's silky head. His eyes glistened; his lips moved, but he didn't speak.

Then Jody seemed to give up. He lay back, clutching the blanket edge, oblivious of Rob and Norah and his old rival, Crawford. His breathing grew rough. His eyes appeared neither open nor closed. Rob drew Norah into his arms and pressed his lips to her hair. No one spoke.

Norah rested against Rob and watched her childhood slip away forever. She grieved silently, without despair. Her husband's arms surrounded her, her son slept in a milky stupor, her papa had found his peace. How fortunate they all were, she thought, how truly blessed.

Rob hugged her and whispered, "He's gone, Norah."

Norah had no words. She looked at Rob and touched his cheeks. She wiped away his tears.

At the quiet dawn, Mr. Crawford brought by a sloop. They sailed out beyond Sands Head. The sea was calm, but banks of clouds foretold another day of rain. Rob read the words over Jody's shrouded form, and Mr. Crawford slipped him over the side. It was a true seaman's burial. Norah dropped a crimson blossom after him.

"Good-bye, Papa."

* * *

Amanda supervised Norah's bath. Then Rosina gave her a vigorous massage and put her to bed.

"Poor thing," Amanda said, pulling the tatties closed. "It's been a hard few months, giving birth to a baby and worrying about a missing husband. And now this business with your father. What you need is a good long sleep." She gave Norah a meaningful glance. "Undisturbed."

"I wouldn't mind being disturbed," Norah said with a drowsy smile, as she nestled down in bed.

Amanda gave her a reproving look. "I'll not have a selfish man looking to satisfy his needs on a little *maman* who hasn't had a proper sleep in weeks. I've given your husband specific instructions to leave you alone."

"Yes, Amanda," Norah murmured as the door closed.

She woke with a start, sensing someone's presence in the room. Daylight peeked through the cracks in the tatties. Outside she heard the constant drumbeat of rain. Norah blinked her eyes clear and saw Rob sitting in a chair beside the little half-moon table, watching her. He wore his shirt untucked from his trousers and loosened at the throat. One bare foot was slung carelessly over a small leather stool.

"Rob!"

He touched his finger to his lips and grinned. "If Amanda finds me, she'll toss me out with the sweepers."

"Oh, Rob!" Norah scooted out of bed and ran across the stone floor into his arms. His face was freshly shaved, and his hair, still damp from a scrubbing, stood on end in a coarse ruffle. Norah nestled against him as he stroked her own sleep-tossed locks.

"Amanda's afraid you'll take me to bed," Norah said.

Rob laughed softly. "Now, what would give her an idea like that?" He nuzzled Norah's cheek. "I only wanted to look in on you and apologize for causing you so much worry. When we left Calcutta, I didn't know we'd be going after Jody. The trip up the coast added another two months to the voyage."

"I'm glad you found him. I didn't think I wanted to see him again. But now I feel so peaceful. . . ." Her voice drifted off. "Rob?"

He drew back and looked at her. "What is it?"

"I . . . I can't bear the thought of you going off again." The words spilled out in a tremulous rush.

Norah expected a shifting of his eyes, a grim tightening of the jaw. Instead, Rob drew her head down on his shoulder and kissed her lips. "I don't know about our future, Norah. God knows where we'll end up or what I'll do. But whatever it is, we'll be together. If I learned one thing these past months, it's that I'm not cut out to be the lone wayfarer I imagined myself to be. Crawford says that without you, I'd probably end up like Jody. I don't doubt he's right."

The words he spoke and the certainty in his voice poured over Norah like a balm. "Say it again," she demanded.

Rob smiled. "I won't leave you, Norah, not ever."

That promise, more precious to her than the vows he'd sworn in the Cape Town church, resonated in Norah's heart, affirming a constancy she'd never dared believe in. She twined her fingers with his. "Is that a promise?"

Rob brushed his lips against her temple. "A promise."

Norah wriggled out of his arms. "I have something for you."

Ollie had retrieved Norah's lost possessions in Liverpool and passed them on to Amanda. Norah opened the little wooden box and took out her father's silver ring.

"Do you recognize this?" she asked, holding it in her open palm.

Rob rubbed a hand over his face. "It's Jody's."

"Now it's yours."

"Norah . . ."

"Please wear it, Rob. He gave it to me as a promise he'd return one day. If you wear it, I'll know we'll always be together."

Rob smiled. "I would be honored, madam."

Norah took his large square hand in her own and worked the ring onto his finger.

"I suppose this means I'm chained to you forever," Rob teased.

"It means I love you." Norah again settled herself on Rob's lap and slipped her hand inside his shirt. She caressed his rough, hot chest and kissed the warm skin of his throat. She pressed her forehead against his shoulder and said shyly, "Come lie down with me."

Rob tightened his arms. "I'm overdue at the customs house. Damn it all—"

"Hurry, then," Norah said. "And you'd better see Jan while you're out. He's wringing his hands over the cargo. Every day you were gone he complained to me."

Rob stood up, tucked in his shirt, and pulled Norah into his arms. "Get some rest, sweetheart. I plan to keep you awake most of the night."

His kiss lingered and deepened, and he swore mightily when he left her.

Norah had finished feeding Matthew. He lay squirming and chortling on the bed while Rosina brushed Norah's hair. She'd bathed for the second time that day, and Rosina had rubbed sweet oil into her every pore. Her limbs were as soft as butter; even her toes had been massaged. Her blue silk wrapper caressed her skin with sensual whispers. As the brush slipped rhythmically through her hair, Norah felt a drowsy happiness.

Suddenly the door opened and Rob burst in, soaked with rain, his trouser legs caked with mud. The expression on his sun-browned face made Norah whirl from the mirror.

"Rob! What is it?"

She saw a letter crumpled in his hand, and her heart spun with alarm. *Alice! Oh, dear God!* Norah jumped to her feet.

"It's Burnham. He . . . he wants me back in Boston."

Norah laid a hand on her pounding heart. Boston!

Rosina gathered Matthew into her arms and slipped out the door. Norah pulled Rob to a chair. "Tell me."

"The panic." His voice caught with excitement. "Just as they predicted, merchants can't meet their obligations, banks are suspending specie payments, firms are failing. Burnham says the spring was the worst season in memory."

He fumbled with the letter, opened it, and began to read: " 'I'm turning to you to see that our credit remains unsullied, that all obligations are met at any price, even at a loss. I want you to get our finances snug and prepare to recommence business when prospects justify. Because of your foresight, our warehouse stocks are low. I have faith that with your help the firm will emerge from this difficult time stronger than ever.' "

Norah felt the blood thumping in her head. Boston! Her own dearest hope!

"There's more," Rob said. "The Burnhams are moving to England to be near Alice. He says the past year's turmoil has made him lose his taste for the game. He has decided to settle in London and take over the traveling partnership." Rob paused. "Norah, he wants me to run the entire Boston operation and eventually buy him out."

Their eyes locked. Norah read in Rob's his glaring doubt. *You will do it!* she cried silently. *You must!*

Norah watched his jaw working as he struggled to master his apprehensions. She dared not push him, but, oh, how he would come to savor the challenge. Rob Mackenzie would be a superb Boston merchant—clever, unorthodox, flouting conventional thinking, defying the tradition-bound ways.

"Burnham is offering to sell us the house."

Norah gasped. "The Summer Street house?" It was too much to hope for—her entire life returned to her with two beloved additions, her husband and her son.

Rob fell back into the depths of his chair, watching her. A smile tipped the corner of his mouth. "It would make you happy, wouldn't it, to live in that house, to be surrounded by all that's familiar?"

Norah crouched beside him, resting her hands on his mud-spattered knees. "I would be happy. We'd both be happy. And Matthew . . . oh, we'll give him a wonderful life."

Rob got to his feet and paced across the room. When he turned, his eyes, tender and pensive, told Norah his answer even before he spoke. "We'll do it. We'll sail immediately for Boston and take Burnham up on his offer. But I'll need your help, Norah. Your help and your patience. And your advice."

"Yes, oh, yes." Norah's heart filled with pride and love and all the promises of their future. "You won't be sorry. I swear it. Oh, Rob, I'll see that you're happy."

Rob came to her and drew her into his arms. "If you want to make me happy, you'll help me off with these wet clothes."

Norah rested her palms on his chest and lifted her face. "Kiss me first."

Rob obliged her. He held her close, his mud-streaked trousers soiling her gown, his mouth hot and hungry on hers. As Norah sighed against him, Rob fumbled with the tie of her wrapper. Silk whispered to the floor, laying her skin bare to the moist evening air and the touch of his hand.

If you enjoyed
Sea of Dreams,
you'll look forward to
Elizabeth DeLancey's newest
romantic and unforgettable novel
The Defiant Bride,
coming soon from Diamond Books.

Turn the page for
a preview of
The Defiant Bride.

May 1858

ANNA MASSIE SET her fists on her hips, tapped her toes, and swayed to the lively strains of a jig. The fiddler's tune sang to her west-country heart, stirring up memories of village fairs, of tables laden with apples and sweet cakes, of horse auctions and tales told over pints of porter. It brought back thoughts of green fields and fuchsia hedges, of drifting mists and the sharp tang of burning peat. More than twelve years and an ocean of heartache separated Anna's girlhood in Kerry from the deck of the *Mary Drew*, bound for America. But time and distance meant nothing when hearing a familiar tune.

Suddenly she felt a gentle shove from behind. "Go to it, girl," urged a masculine voice. "You'll be a pretty picture. Give the lads a show."

The lure of the fiddle was too strong for caution. Caught up in the moment, Anna moved toward the fiddler. There was nothing wrong in a bit of a dance, she thought. She was a woman alone with a face and form that made men stare, but what harm could come to a strong girl on a stout ship packed with emigrants? Let any man step out of line and she'd knock today clear out of him. Oh, yes, she would.

The fiddler gave Anna a wink of encouragement, and she was beside him, hands on hips, torso erect, pounding the deck with her worn leather boots. The crowd of men pressed closer. Sun-browned faces, crammed beneath rough cloth caps, creased into smiles. Coarse hands clapped and feet stomped amid shouts of approval. Sunlight poured down from a blazing blue sky, and Anna's feet skipped and hopped and beat out their rhythm.

"You're a cure for sore eyes, you are," a man called.

Anna's brow grew damp and her breath short, but she kept up the rhythm as the *Mary Drew* surged and dipped with the roll of the sea.

"Mother o' God, did I ever see the likes of you in all me life!"

Anna raised her skirts above her ankles. Her legs, free of their long woolen stockings, flashed bare beneath her red flannel underskirt. The men cheered louder. Anna tilted her head back and laughed. Pins slipped from her hair, and her thick red-brown curls spilled into the breeze. The music carried away the troubles of her twenty-four years, and for the moment there were no thoughts for poor dead souls and times best forgotten, for faithless husbands and dead dreams. Anna recalled her mam and her da, the handsomest couple in the valley, dancing on the long line, while she and her little brothers watched with pride. And then she thought of her new home, America, where bellies were full and there were no masters. America, where a woman could keep herself with no need of a husband. Oh, it was worth a dance.

Anna swayed and hummed and stamped her boots until she could dance no more. With one last flourish of her skirts, with a final skip of her feet, she dropped a curtsy to the fiddler and pushed her way through the crowd of smiling emigrants.

"Give us another, love."

"Faith, you're a fine, shapely one."

A brawny, red-haired youth in a battered cloth cap seized her arm. "I think I'm in love. Marry me and spare me what I'm thinking."

Anna gave him a good-natured shove. "You'd be better off with a bit of sense. I think God forgot to put the brains in you."

She disengaged her arm from the young man and made her way across the deck, over cordage and crates, around shallow tubs of potatoes, through mobs of children who rushed and shrieked. A group of men bent over a three-card trick, another man doodled on a tin whistle and gave her a wink. Humming to herself, Anna picked her way around clothing spread to dry on the deck boards and beneath shirts and petticoats that hung from the mainstay.

A cluster of boys huddled at the chicken coop teasing the hens that would be served in the first-class dining saloon. The cook ran out of the galley brandishing a spoon. "Git," he shouted at the children, "or I'll have you in the pot!" The boys fled and Anna laughed.

She turned to continue on her way and promptly bumped into a figure that gave off a musty, unwashed odor.

"In a hurry, Irish gal?" A thin, chinless face leered down at her. Yellow hair stuck out from beneath the seaman's cap, and a growth of whiskers sprouted on his receding jaw.

Anna drew back, feeling her cheeks flush. "I've nothing to say to you."

Since the start of the voyage, she had ignored the sailor's stupid gaze, his obscene mutterings as she passed. Now she stepped to one side to go around him. But the man moved with her, matching her step for step. Anna turned to find another avenue of escape, only to encounter three more men, one behind and another to each side of her. They moved closer, eyeing her with slack, insolent smiles. Anna's cheeks grew hotter. She turned back to the first man. "Let me pass!"

"There now," the sailor drawled. "Ain't you on yer high horse." A long dirty finger scratched at his pale-stubbled neck. "Figure you'll be needing a bit of companionship before we reach New York. The name's Tom Spinner, at yer service." He touched his filthy cap. "This here's Fallows and Cockburn." He nudged the hawk-nosed companion to his right. "And Nosy Gibbs."

The men shuffled their feet. Anna glimpsed their wet grins and fixed her eyes straight ahead. "I'm needing no companionship," she said curtly, "so let me pass."

The men made no move to step aside. "We'll let you pass, all right," Spinner said. With his dingy red sleeve, he wiped a bright drop from the end his nose. "Just wanted to make yer acquaintance. Anna," he added with a purposeful leer.

A hand fumbled low on Anna's belly. She jerked back only to bump into a second man, who gave her a hard pinch on her behind. She yelped and thrashed out with her arm, striking at

the hand. The sailors drew away in mock fear. Anna stood
with fists clenched, panting with fury.

"Oh, there's fire in that one," Spinner chortled.

"And you're the one to put it out, Tom," said the hawk-
nosed Gibbs. "A handful, she is, a fine handful."

Anna backed away, her head ringing with curses. "You
touch me again," she warned softly, "and there'll be the taste
of blood on your teeth." She turned and plunged back toward
the crowd of emigrants.

When she reached the dim sloping space behind the cow
shed, Anna sank onto a coil of rope, her body trembling with
rage and self-reproach. Oh, hadn't she just brought this on
herself, she thought? For a few careless moments, she'd forgotten her life's cruel lessons—that she was a woman alone
and that trouble followed wherever she went. From now on,
there would be no more frolics, Anna told herself sternly. No
foolish enjoyments would imperil her future. She was going
to America to start a new life.

Anna rubbed her neck, easing herself from the tense grip of
anger. She reached back to pin up her tumbled curls and
glanced around her hideaway. The first day at sea she had
staked out the shady nook for herself. It smelled like a barn-
yard and the tarry ropes stained her dress, but it was a comfort
having her own place. Here, she could think and work in
peace, away from the noise and crush of people on deck.

Reaching into a small opening in the bulwark, Anna drew
out a white bundle. She laid the bundle on her lap, wiped her
hands on her skirt, and unfolded the cloth. Within lay a steel
hook, a ball of white cotton thread, and a half dozen pieces of
white cotton crochet. Anna set the finished pieces on her
knees, inspecting the pinwheels, the flowers, the perfect little
leaves. Her stitches were uniform and compact, without any
flaws.

Anna picked up her hook and thread and bent over her
work, humming softly. She worked a rose motif, tightening
the foundation cord to assure the curve of the blossom. As her
hook moved swiftly through the stitches, the encounter with
Spinner and his mates faded. Anna imagined herself in New
York, in a shop of her own with a small group of girls, creating
lace for the fine ladies of the city.

A timid voice interrupted her thoughts. "Will you be wanting a drink, then?"

Anna glanced up. A dark-haired boy stood before her, holding a dipper of water. His pointed face was small and pale, and his eyes shone with admiration. He gave her a shy, appealing smile and extended the dipper.

Anna couldn't help but smile back. "Would that be for me, now?"

The boy's porcelain cheeks bloomed crimson. "I thought you'd be wanting a sip after your dancing."

"Bless you," Anna said, taking the dipper from his hand. "I'm parched, that's for sure."

Mercy, she thought, here's a gallant little lad, a pleasant change from the usual lot of men. She had glimpsed the boy among the others shouting and climbing about the deck and teasing the chickens. Anna glanced over his bony frame. Beneath his box jacket and crisp shirt, the boy looked thin as a spoke. Her own brother, Sean, gone these twelve years, had been about the size and color of this one, probably not a day over ten.

Anna lifted the dipper to her lips and filled her mouth. The water had been none too fresh when they'd started out, and in the days since it had turned warm and brackish, only palatable mixed with peppermint or boiled with tea. But to please the boy, Anna drank deeply, as if it was as cool and sweet as Kerry spring water.

When she handed back the dipper, the boy made no move to leave. He shuffled his boots and stared at her as if trying to think of some way to prolong his stay. Anna patted the deck beside her and the boy sat down, his cheeks aflame with pleasure.

"So who are you?" Anna asked.

He lifted his eyes to hers. His brows were charcoal strokes upon his pale brow. His thatch of black hair, surely enough for three heads, was badly in need of a brush. "Rory," he said. "Rory Flynn."

"Rory, is it?" Anna leaned her back against the bulkhead, crossed her ankles, and laced her fingers together in her lap. "A fine, noble name. The last high king of Ireland was Rory O'Conor."

Rory Flynn's eyes brightened and his reserve abruptly fell away. "I know of Rory O'Conor. My gran told me the tales of the high kings of Tara and the great chiefs. And she told me of Grainne de Mhaille, the warrior queen. None in her court could do a finer dance than you."

Anna laughed, which brought a deeper flush to Rory's flawless cheeks. "Why, that's a pretty compliment," she said. "And your gran, is she traveling with you to America?"

Rory shook his head. "My gran's dead. I'm with my da." His small face burst into a proud smile. "He's a prize-fighter. He's taking me to New York. I never saw him before he came to Kilkenny to fetch me."

Anna glanced down at the crochet work in her lap and fingered it absently. She'd heard the emigrants speak of Stephen Flynn. They'd buzzed excitedly when the sailors reported his presence aboard the *Mary Drew*. Stephen Flynn of Kilkenny, Stephen Flynn of the 'Forty-eight rising, Stephen Flynn, the prizefighter.

"So he's your da," she said, no more than being polite.

"He's the champion of America." Rory's voice was hushed with reverence.

"Well, then. Aren't you in luck."

"He says he won't be fighting again. He says he's too old and sore." Rory's eyes dimmed wistfully. "But I know my da's not old. He's stronger than any man. I wish I could see him fight, just once."

"It's just as well he's quitting," Anna said, thinking that the boy's father was probably as much a legend to him as were Cormac MacArt and Finn MacCool—hardly a mortal man at all. "It's a brutal business, fighting. You wouldn't want your da to be hurt, now, would you?"

Rory regarded Anna with disbelief. "He wouldn't be hurt."

Anna rolled a strand of crochet cotton between her fingers and studied Rory more closely. She'd heard that the man and the boy were traveling with no woman. Did Flynn see to his son as a mother would, making sure his hair was combed, his stockings pulled up, his ears kept clean? Except for his rumpled hair and the smudges picked up on the forward deck, Rory Flynn did look well cared for.

"Would you like to see his book?"

Before Anna could respond, Rory pulled from his pocket a wrinkled sheaf of cheap paper and thrust it at her. Anna took the book and smoothed it flat on her lap. A solemn, wide-browed man wearing a stiff collar and dark bow stock stared from beneath the words, *The Life and Battles of Stephen Flynn, the Emerald Flame*. A banner beneath the portrait read, *Champion of America!*

Rory leaned close to Anna, his thin shoulder brushing her arm. "That's my da," he said proudly.

Anna leafed politely through the pages, dense with accounts of championship contests and crude drawings of Flynn's opponents—muscular, bare-chested men dressed in fighting drawers, their fists raised high. Headings slashed across pages. "Flynn Brought to New York!" "The Flame Burns Coughlin in New Orleans!" "Prolonged and Desperate Contest in California!"

Anna browsed through the text with distaste. "Poole caught a smacking cut on the cheek which brought him to the ground . . ." "Platt down on his knees, up again, knocked down by Flynn . . ." "A terrible right-hand blow on McClusky's ribs, which were dreadfully swollen from Flynn's repeated hittings . . ."

Anna closed the book and handed it back to Rory. He tucked it tenderly into his pocket and said, "You'd like him."

"I'd like him, would I?" To herself, Anna thought, isn't that just what I need, another one with a brain as hard as his fists? She picked up her crochet work.

Rory said, "He'd like you."

Anna sighed. How well she knew Flynn's sort, men who strutted and swaggered and gave a girl smiles powerful enough to crush stone. They begged like children to have their way, and when they'd had their fill, they hurried off to their crude and noisy mates. The thought annoyed her, and she spoke sharply. "You leave your da to himself, Rory Flynn. He won't be pleased to know you're bothering the emigrants. Now, go along and let me do my work."

Anna didn't look at Rory's face, but she knew her words had stung. After a hurt silence, she dropped her crochet work into her lap and thought, what was the harm in befriending the lad? It was a comfort to chat with him, and he did remind her of her own brother, Sean.

"All right, then," she said. "You can visit me, but don't be dragging your da up here. I've no wish to meet with him."

Rory scrambled to his feet, grinning. "Next time I'll bring you an orange. We have lots of oranges in the cabin."

"And don't be getting yourself in trouble taking oranges," Anna scolded. But her mouth watered at the thought of the sweet fruit. In her box of provisions she had nothing but oatmeal and eggs and a small slab of salt pork. The ship stores provided a bit more, but nothing as tasty as an orange.

"I'll be back!" Rory cried, and with a slipping of boots, he spun off around the cow shed and disappeared.

The sun moved down the sky. The bell at the foremast rang eight times. Four o'clock. The emigrant women would already be standing in line with their pans and kettles as they waited for a turn at the grates. The grills closed at seven, and more than once Anna had arrived too late. If she wanted to cook her supper, she had best get going.

Anna wrapped her crochet work and tucked it into the bulkhead. She glanced around the nook for her head shawl, but it was nowhere to be seen. It must have slipped off while she was dancing.

She emerged from her little shelter into the confusion of the deck. A group of women worked around the large wooden cases lined with brick, which served as the emigrants' stoves. Anna hurried toward the hatch that led below. As she passed the foremast a voice sang out, "Anna! Oh, Aannaa!"

Spinner stood at the galley, one shoulder braced casually against the door frame, his hands behind him. Anna started away, anxious to be gone, but Spinner's hand darted out before she'd taken two steps. Her head shawl dangled from his tar-stained fingers. He grinned at her. "It fell off while you were doing yer Irish dance."

Anna paused. The shawl wasn't so precious, but the thought of Spinner possessing it disgusted her. Anna held out her hand. "I'll thank you to give it to me, then." She kept her voice flat, her tone deliberate.

Spinner laughed. "And what'll you give in return, pretty girl?"

Anna stared doggedly into his small, pale eyes and made no response. Spinner's tongue dampened his thin lips. "I seen you dance. I bet you can do it just as good laying down."

Anna curled her hands into fists to keep them from trembling. "Give me my shawl or I'll report you to the mate."

"Mr. Kincaid don't much care for emigrants, especially you Irish ones. And he thinks you're showing yerself off. Asking for it, he says. Whatever happens to you, Mr. Kincaid'd say you deserved it."

Two sailors lounged against the rail, smirking and nudging each other. Anna turned abruptly from Spinner. "Keep the shawl," she said over her shoulder. "I'll not touch what you've soiled with your filthy hands."

Spinner flung the shawl to the deck. It lay there, a sad dark rag on the bleached deck boards. "Pick it up, girl," he said. "It's yourn, and I've no need of it."

Anna hesitated, then bent to retrieve the cloth. As soon as she reached out, Spinner was beside her, his fingers clamped on her wrist. "You'll be needing me, Irish girl. Real soon, you'll be wanting me to do you favors." He spoke quickly, in a low voice. "You might be getting hungry, or be needing an extra ration of water to wash that pretty face o' yourn, or you just might need some company back of the cow shed where you hide yerself."

"Never!" Anna hissed. "I'd never ask you for a thing!" She tried to pull away, but he held her wrist fast, his rough fingers tight as a vise.

"Don't be so sure, beauty. We drawed straws for you the first day out, me and my mates. I got the long straw. You're mine whether you want me or not. I have three weeks of you, and one's near gone. I don't want to waste more time."

Anna's body turned hot with revulsion, her throat tightened with rage. She yanked her arm away with such force that Spinner's ragged nails dragged across her forearm, leaving a trail of scratches. "I'll spit on you before I give you the time of day!" she cried. "Don't think I can't take care of myself and anyone who gets in my way." Snatching up her shawl, Anna scrambled to her feet and hurried past a group of gaping women to the hatch.

Anna climbed down the ladder into the steerage deck. The humid tunnel was lit only through the open hatchway, and the air stank of slop jars and sickness. She groped her way down the aisle, stumbling against emigrants' chests and boxes toward the women's quarters and the bunk she shared with a widow and her two daughters. Oh, the curse of being a woman, she thought. Defenseless, to blame for every man's lustful thoughts. She'd heard of outrages against women on emigrant vessels, but they occurred on slow sailing ships. Twenty-five pounds of her precious resources had gone to purchase passage on a steamer with a reputation for safety and speed—not one with a crew that played a lottery with her as the prize.

Anna sat down on the straw mattress of her bunk and tried to calm her thumping heart. Surely Spinner and his mates could not harm her in the midst of so many people, she told herself. At night, she lay with three other women, and on deck she was never more than a few feet away from another human being. Captain Blodgett, who had spoken to the emigrants on deck the first day out, seemed a decent man. He would never permit his passengers to be abused.

Anna reached for her supply chest. Like all of the emigrants, she locked her provision box with a padlock. But as she fumbled for it, she found the lock hanging loose. For a moment, she thought she'd forgotten to secure her box, but with sudden alarm she knew she wouldn't have been so careless.

Anna sank to her knees and flung back the top of the small chest. The sight inside made her cry out. Her fresh eggs were smashed, her hard-cooked ones were broken and squashed. Bags of oatmeal and tea had been torn open and mixed with the salt in which she had carefully packed the eggs. And her supply of salt pork was gone.

Anna dug frantically through the mess. Egg shells scratched her skin, yolks and whites covered her fingers and stuck to clumps of meal. There was nothing to save!

A shiver of panic raced through her. No food! Nothing but meager ship stores—moldy biscuits, a bit of flour and tea.

Suddenly she was back in Kerry, scratching among the thistles while the stench of the potato blight filled her nostrils and the little ones chewed on grass and wailed.

Stop! Anna commanded herself. You'll not starve.

She sat back on her heels and stared at her hands, filled with lumps of ruined oatmeal and tea. It was Spinner's doing. He had spoiled her food so she would turn to him, so he could use her as he chose. A sick feeling rose in her stomach. Guilty memories, long buried, seeped into her mind. Memories of a shop's storeroom, sacks of corn against her back, the smell of molasses, a man's groping hands. Anna bowed her head and drew in a quick sobbing breath. She had traded her body for food. She'd only wanted to save her family.

Tears slid down her cheeks and across lips clenched tight against sobs. It would not happen again, she told herself fiercely. Not on this ship. Not in New York. Never again would she be obligated to a man for her survival.